D1476731

Also by Lisa K. Stephenson

Late Bloomer
Covenant: The Sister Series Compilation
Borderline
Green Trees

The Yellow Brownstone

LISA K. STEPHENSON

The Yellow Brownstone

ISBN:

978-1-798-97705-7

Printed in the U.S.A.

First Paperback Edition

For my late Grandmother
Jocelyn H. Abney

Part I

1989

Irving was kicking up rocks, simultaneously gripping the straps of his backpack in fear that it would fall to the ground, or worse, be taken again. The sneakers squeezing his toes was nothing new, and the unfit pants which stopped inches away from his ankles were all reasons he found himself alone. Bullied on campus and a loner off, he made good with his path, meticulously avoiding the pits where he was known to have spent many evenings with his face in the ground.

Too young to understand the depths of his misfortune, Irving was learning to find solace in the thought of simply being alive, as many times he found himself unconscious standing amidst the white gates. Sunday morning churchgoers his parents were, their routine perfunctory—breakfast, shoes, tie, shirt causing mild suffocation, a brush to his roots, oil to his face, and off they went.

Their one-bedroom apartment just off the Grand Concourse in The Bronx, New York became home to his action figures, his father, his mother, and himself. With just a twin bed in the living room overlooking the bustling streets and angry patrons, he was a second grader fueled by the world's dysfunction and taking pleasure in eavesdropping on his belligerent neighbors—their youngest his nemesis. Never speaking to his parents or administrators about the issues plaguing him within the school walls, he was living vicariously through the G.I. Joe action figure he carried around with him—the action figure resilient and strong. Irving decided to no longer dilly-dally with the thought of defending himself, he remained inside even on the warm days like the ones soon approaching.

A pariah he became, socially awkward and afraid to face the challenges set before him while dealing with the challenges at home; his clothes unclean, his shoes two sizes too small and the ringworm to the rear of his head expanding—causing him to bald. As troubling as they were, the cockroaches had become another form of entertainment as he wondered at night how many would awaken him from his slumber. Counting, one, two, three, four—and those pesky ones that would fall from the ceilings onto his mattress, his eyes red from being kept up at night itching his bites through his pajamas—but it was good because he was alive and that was more than he could have asked for.

Injured by his mother two years prior at the tender age of five; a sprained arm that was treated at home since his parents had no health insurance, through the pain, then and the chronic discomfort up to now, he continued to smile. Administrators questioning him daily, but Irving now knew better after the kind woman came to their home years ago informing his mother that he would be taken from her—his mother furious, causing him to experience his first unconscious state, remembering vividly that day, Irving vowed to never anger Mama again.

Speaking to the action figure just at the edge of his bed, he imagined the broken television set playing cartoons that he would see in passing on his way to school playing through his neighbors' curtains—he was amused.

"Boy!" she called; her voice startling him. Had he lost track of the time again? he wondered. Michelle Dudley, age forty-seven, gave birth to her son seven years ago, at a time when she thought her ability to bear children was no more—then a surprise came. But Irving was no miracle in her eyes, only a mouth to feed on her impoverished income. His father was Marvin Houston, the janitor for the building they resided in; Michelle knew had her son's father been kind enough to assist her in raising him, they would, in fact, have a roof over their head, and surprisingly enough, he was kind.

But his apparent kindness did not stop the abuse; weekly, her right cheek and bottom lip met the back of his right hand as Irving wept from his cradle

"Shut that damn boy up!" he would scream. Michelle began resenting her son; her punishments were always a direct result of his decorum, "he is not a miracle baby at all," she would think as she allowed him to remain soiled in his pampers, unchanged for days, sometimes weeks at a time. Irving's father started keeping the company of another woman, growing weary of the constant crying and unwanted source of responsibility, but as time pressed on he began to show more interest.

"That little one," he thought. "My own flesh and blood." Irving was resembling his father day-by-day as Marvin had grown accustomed to fatherhood once Irving turned five and could prove himself useful by fetching beers, changing the television channel in their bedroom, and lifting the grocery bags because his father simply chose not to. This infuriated Michelle as she watched her son struggle to carry the milk cartons, eggs, and water.

But he remained persistent and never complained, no matter how heavy the bag, she remembered his soft voice telling her, "I got it, Mama," all before inching his way up the stairs, grabbing a hold of the passage railings or stepping in the urine found in the elevators, struggling to keep the bags off of the ground. Irving was strong-willed, his father taught him this much with the use of sheer neglect. The public housing projects were filled with disheveled men and women who would mean Irving harm, but although Marvin did not coddle his son, he swore to protect him from the dangers of the world, even if that danger was him. Marvin found himself depressed, feeling hopeless even as Irving continued to grow and the weight of aiding him in his day-today was proving itself to be far less burdensome.

Marvin spent many nights away from home, fearful that he would return inebriated and want to inflict harm on his only son. Because of that he would simply spend his time elsewhere. But while this protected their son, it began to create a wedge between his parents, a wedge his mother would continue to blame on Irving—wanting him gone for good. As she struggled with finding new ways to keep her boyfriend home and her child outdoors, Michelle decided to get creative, encouraging Irving to play outside and introducing her son to the men in the neighborhood, forcing him to interact, hanging out late at night. By age seven, Irving found himself dreading the outdoors, afraid of having to run from the stray bullets, forced to sneak into the bodegas and steal snacks for the older gentlemen who told him he was swift on his feet.

Irving did it, against his better judgment, his own conscience consuming him as he knew right from wrong but felt it had become too late to reason.

"Boy!" his mother called again, snapping him out of his daydream. As Irving tossed his G.I. Joe aside, he made his way to the kitchen only a few feet from his bed. Standing by the kitchen threshold he watched as his mother removed a spoon from a pot in the sink filled with filthy water to share his dinner—boxed macaroni and cheese with a boiled hotdog she was going to slice before placing it on a plastic plate she would serve on the floor before him.

"After you eat this dinner, you going to go outside and play; understand?" She coughed, leaving her mouth uncovered. But Irving did not understand, he had school in the morning and the sun was beginning to set. As he took a seat on the cold floor, sitting Indian style, he watched as the spiders climbed up and down their webs, the ones they created just under the bottom cupboards. But Irving remained unbothered, having grown accustomed to sharing his home, toys and his body with the creatures from the beyond, as he would refer to them. Irving did not have an appetite, stretching his body across the floor as his mother stood in the kitchen cleaning the dishes, he took his silver fork, poking it into a piece of his hotdog as he tried feeding it to the cluster of spiders.

Turning, his mother kicking him.

"Boy, that is my good fork, what the fuck are you doing?" she shouted landing another kick to his ribs. Irving cried, the fork and his food falling to the floor as he squealed, lying in the fetal position.

"If I feed them they won't bite me," he sobbed, his hands placed firmly in front his face. Michelle could not bring herself to face him; she turned, resuming the dishes.

"Pick up my damn fork and finish your dinner so you can go outside," she snapped.

Once Irving finished his meal he was instructed into his room to get dressed; feeling tired now, all he wanted was a bath and sleep. But Michelle insisted.

"Get them jeans on and go on outside, your father coming home in a minute." Irving struggled to keep up as the sun had now gone down and outside was pitch black, street lights beginning to shine. He thought he had gotten acclimated to this, as Michelle would instruct him to leave at least three nights a week, the nights his dad would come home. Michelle was always looking for new ways to please Marvin, to keep him happy and satisfied so he would want to spend more time at home, but nothing she had done so far was enough to keep him for more than three days a week.

As the keys turned in the lock, Michelle made her way into the kitchen, grabbing a plate from the oven that had been wrapped in aluminum foil and placing it on the dining room table accompanied by a fork and knife. Chicken, rice, and beans with collard greens all sat nicely atop the kitchen table, steaming. Marvin made his way inside wearing a navy-blue Janitorial jumpsuit; his nametag hanging from the left pocket as Irving scurried past him.

Pointing, he said to Michelle, "Where the hell that boy going this time of the night?"

"The boy is fine, eat your dinner, baby," she instructed. Marvin did as he was told; removing his shoes he took a seat at the head of the table to indulge in his meal. Placing a tall glass of lemonade in front of him, Michelle took a seat, beginning her interrogation,

"Where do you sleep when you're not here, Marvin?" Fearful she may upset him, Michelle prepared herself for the worst—a slap, a punch, a kick, but she was willing to risk it all, just for the chance to learn how she could fix what had been broken. Marvin's absence causing her to question her own sanity; years upon years of deception, disappearances, and an uneasy feeling that she may in fact not be the only woman in his life.

"Woman, where I lay my head is not your business, the rent is paid, that boy is taken care of, and the lights are on, that's all that matters. Why you have to give me a hard time? Have I not done enough?" Michelle hung her head in shame as Irving now made his way down to the playground where he struggled to get onto the swing set to rock himself slowly as the group of men standing just outside his building kept a steady eye on him whilst completing their transactions. Another young boy joined him.

The swings creaked so loudly that Irving thought he would fall, his feet unable to reach the playground swing mat underneath him.

"What's your name?" the young boy turning to Irving asked.

"Irving, yours?" he replied, extending his hand.

"Kevin," he said, smiling as he returned the gesture— something about the cool breeze blowing that night and the lights shining just above their heads created a comfortable atmosphere. Irving and Kevin communicated with one another as though they had been friends for years,

"I'm from Baltimore," he informed Irving, who was telling Kevin about the school he was attending and how the children there were terribly mean and he found himself now dreading the thought of having to return in the morning, praying he did not oversleep because Mama did not like that. The bruises on his stomach began to hurt as he wondered to himself if this was something he would endure forever,

"Do you get hit?" he asked Kevin sadly,

"Not by my mommy, but my dad from time to time," he answered, swinging his legs. Just then his father bellowed from the fifth-floor window.

"Kevin, get on up here." His voice echoing through the project sector; the group of men stared at him. Quickly, Kevin propped himself up from the swing,

"I will see you tomorrow, right?" he asked Irving, swinging his arms and rocking his body in excitement.

"Sure," Irving replied hesitantly. Kevin stepped lightly towards him and gave Irving a kiss on the lips. Marvin, standing by the window overlooking the city streets caught only a short glimpse of this from their eleventh-floor apartment and was not sure what he had seen. The alcohol seeping through his veins slightly impaired his vision as he made his way downstairs, infuriated. Moving ferociously past a bewildered Michelle, Marvin pushed her as he slipped his feet into his shoes, pulling up his jumpsuit, her voice in his ear like the buzzing of a fly, he swatted her away.

"Baby, what's wrong, why are you so mad, let's finish, let me finish," she repeated, begging him as she tugged on his jumpsuit.

"Let me go!" he screamed, heading downstairs, a naked Michelle staying behind scurrying to find her clothes. Once downstairs both Kevin and Marvin made eye contact once Kevin neared the steel doors to head inside.

"You fucking pansy ass nigga, did you just kiss my son?" he screamed, pointing his finger at Kevin, infuriated.

The young man stepped back, eyes wide and darting back and forth. The light from the street lamp shone down on him as the men standing in front of the building looked on. As Irving made his way over to his father in hopes that he could speak to him, a stocky man came barging out of the doors shouting obscenities.

"Step away from my fucking son before I knock you the fuck out!" he shouted, pointing his finger at Marvin. It was all happening so fast and with Irving now standing to witness his father prepare to participate in a street fight he did not know how to react. Both Kevin and Irving looked on as their fathers stood before them fighting. The angry man shoved Marvin in his chest and Marvin then lowered his body to tackle him, both men falling onto the concrete, punching one another as Irving and Kevin continuing to watch and the men from the front of the building now decided it best to intervene. It was a catastrophe as everyone began shouting over one another.

With the police sirens blaring loudly, the men groaning as they continue to throw fists, Kevin disappeared, running towards the forest across the street, Irving shouting his name, but he did not turn around; he continued on running as though he was happy to have gotten away. The angry man realizing his son had gone, and with the police officer racing toward him had little to no time to process the fact that his son just ran away. The officers beat both men with batons—the strange men from in front of the building scattered, one police officer shouting as they prepared themselves to place handcuffs on both the old man and Marvin.

Michelle barged her way through the slate doors, shouting to her boyfriend as the police officers escorted them to the back of the squad car, placing their hands firmly atop their heads and forcing them inside. Irving continued standing as the street lights began to flicker, watching his father be taken away as he turned to face his mother who greeted him with a slap across the face. Irving fell to the ground.

As Marvin witnessed this, he shouted from the backseat, his voice indistinct, "Bitch, don't you dare touch him!" Marvin screamed, hysterical now as the officers threatened to beat him if he were not quiet—the car pulled away, Irving resisting the urge to stand and run.

"This is your entire fault!" Michelle cried. It felt all too familiar, Irving was always blamed for daddy leaving, his mother never taking into account that perhaps Marvin simply did not love her; she would not hear of such blasphemy.

That night Michelle prayed long and hard, wishing the good

Lord would fix her relationship and that Marvin would make an honest woman of her, although she prayed, cried, and spoke in tongues, she was losing faith in that part of her life. Together for almost eight years, she was beginning to question whether or not she could continue on this way, feeling unloved, unhappy, and resentful of her own flesh and blood. And then it dawned on her, while watching Irving fast asleep tucked neatly into the bed under the wool blankets, she wanted to know the truth. As she rummaged through Marvin's things: uniform, laundry, and casual clothing, she came across an address where the name should appear on the inside of his lunch bag.

1748 Allenwood Drive
Bronx, NY 10463

Michelle stopped breathing, then dressed quickly, turning down the lights and turning the lock behind her, she headed to her 1982 Silver Toyota Camry lift back where she drove until finding her way to the front of a house, the kitchen lights on as the children and a strange woman all sat watching what appeared to be *The Cosby Show*. They seemed cheerful, oblivious to what could possibly have taken place a few hours earlier.

Reclining her seat, Michelle continued watching them from the inside of her car. The house stood alone, the roof white and the lower half brick on the outside with large windows and a screen door to the right. The multi-family home brought her tears as she continued to peep through the uncovered windows. One hour and seven minutes later she had had enough watching; as different parts of their home illuminated indicating their whereabouts she stepped swiftly from the car. Covering her upper body with her light cardigan, her ankles cold, exposed from the short khaki pants she wore and the light V-neck shirt providing her chest no protection from the cool breeze.

Stepping past the little white fence, she continued listening to the children playing inside, the cackling of two young girls as she made her way up the concrete steps, opening the screen door and exposing the front door where she knocked two times using the ball of her fists. Michelle did not know what to expect, knocking again, this time louder, more aggressive. A younger woman opened the door, one hand stretched along the doorframe and the other firmly gripping the handle behind her.

"May I help you?" The lady appeared to be in her mid-thirties, dark-skinned complexion, her hair in small twists, her face long and her eyes chunky—she was not the most beautiful woman.

"Again, who are you and what do you want?" she repeated, this time angrily.

Michelle froze before saying, "My name is Michelle Dudley and I was wondering how do you know my son's father, Marvin? I found your address in the lunch box he takes to work and I just need to know." Smiling nervously, anxious now as she was burning, fearful that at any moment she would pass out. The woman was staring at her with a blank look on her face, unreadable.

"Son?" she whispered, cracking her back. Her ankle length pink cotton nightgown an indication she was readying herself for bed. It was late, after ten, and yet Michelle would not bring herself to sleep without knowing the truth.

"Yes, my son, he is seven."

The woman continued to stand before her, her eyes welling. "A son?" she asked again.

Michelle, now growing irritated, "Yes, dammit, I have a seven-year-old son, who are you and how do you know his father?" she screamed. The stranger immediately placed her hand on Michelle's shoulder.

"Please, my children are preparing for bed and they do not need this, but I am going to ask as politely as I can, do not ever return to my house," spoke the woman, retracting her arm as she fought back the tears.

"Okay, but I just need to know who you are!" shouted Michelle, placing the tip of her foot into the door frame to stop the door from closing, her left hand extended, pushing the door open.

Just then the woman replied, "I am Nyema, his wife of

fifteen years and the mother to his two daughters. You will never come back here again," she said forcefully; Michelle removing her foot, Nyema slamming the door in front of her. Michelle remained stationed for what felt like over ten minutes before the sound of sirens came blaring from the around the corner, she only assumed that Nyema called the police.

Racing into her car and starting the engine, she wept as she drove home, telling herself it was not so and that Marvin merely only had a mistress, in which case she could win him back, fix what had been broken. Never did she suspect a wife. But there was nothing more for her to do as she made her way inside the building; opening the front door she took a long whiff of her home; the 650 square foot apartment, taking a few small steps to her son's bed where she watched him sleep peacefully. Irving appeared as though he had been fighting with the sheets; cockroaches crawled alongside him. Michelle stood now, a witness. But she was unfazed. There was nothing left for her now as she removed her shoes, opening the window just above his head and stepping out onto the ledge, thrusting herself from the eleven-story window. Her body was lying dead on the concrete when a young woman and her boyfriend appeared, screaming.

Irving remained in a deep slumber as the winds blew the curtains just above him.

2

The next day Irving awoke to the voices of men and women shouting in his home, everyone speaking in an uncomfortable chatter as he sat upright, wiping his eyes, his pajamas causing him to itch. A shocked Irving nervously began playing with his G.I. Joe action figure as CPS, EMT and the NYPD all made their way inside to witness the young man. A tall woman stood hovering over him,

"Do you remember me?" she asked with a pleasant smile on her face, holding in her hands a clipboard, pen, and legal pad as Irving began scratching the rear of his head, dandruff flakes falling onto his skin and the bed. She looked familiar to Irving; he knew seeing the tall lady meant trouble for him when Mama came home. Shaking his head no, Irving lied.

The tall woman asked Irving if she could see the back of his head. Irving complied, as she turned her body to look, she noticed he was suffering from traction alopecia and ringworm now formed in other areas creating a pattern of bald spots. Taking a deep breath, the tall lady motioned over to her superior, a short and stocky man.

Introducing himself to Irving, "Hey kiddo, I know all these

people here are scaring you but you're going to go somewhere safe now, alright?" Just then Marvin ran inside, bypassing the caution ropes as the officer and EMT specialists all stared at him with disdain.

"That poor kid," one woman whispered,

"They should be ashamed of themselves," said another as they all continued to rummage through the apartment, some standing in the hallway because everyone could not fit inside. Marvin made his way to Irving seated on the edge of the bed, a first for the young boy to see. He was not accustomed to his father coming close to him, touching him, or even sitting near him. He looked him up and down, bewildered now.

"This is my son, I don't know what happened to his mother, I was away last night," Marvin stuttered to the woman and the man standing just above him.

"I think it may be best if we take this conversation outside," voiced the tall woman, motioning for them to head into the hallway, but Marvin would hear of no such thing.

"No, I'm not leaving my son again," he advised them, crossing his arms. Marvin smelled putrid after spending the night in jail and returning home in his janitor's uniform.

"Sir, we do not want to have to get the authorities involved, we are asking nicely that you please come with us," said the stocky old man, finding it wise to intrude. Marvin deciding to stand, making his way past the officers who snapped photos of their home and into the hallway as Irving remained stationed, watching as the people around him smiled, offered him water, food, and made light conversation, but he was in no mood to converse with strangers.

Outside in the hallway, the tall woman could not help but feel queasy as the malodorous scent of urine came rushing to her nostrils. Trying not to face Marvin, she immediately turned away, leaving the older gentleman to carry on their conversation.

"Sir, can you tell us your relation to the woman who jumped from the window?" The tall woman standing behind him.

"First of all, no, who the hell are you people?" Marvin

snapped.

"Sir, my apologies, my name is Reggie Helms and this is Rose Appleton, we are from child protective services. We want to get some insight on what was taking place here. Her death was ruled a suicide, but neglect will come into play considering the boy's condition," Reggie concluded.

Marvin stood now with his feet apart, arms folded. "Condition?" he questioned.

Rose interrupted. "Yes, he has ringworm dispersed in the back of his head," she said, using her hands for demonstration.

"See, that's the problem with you White motherfuckers, wanna come around here and try to tell us how to raise our damn kids! My son is healthy, he got food, he got clothes, and he had a mother! Now I don't know what the hell you people need or what ya'll are doing here, but everybody needs to get the fuck on out my apartment so I can continue to raise my son!" Marvin shouted. Marvin grew nervous, his hands remained folded as to show no indication of fear, but deep down he was indeed worried. "Well?" he questioned as Rose and Reggie continued standing adjacent to him.

"Were you aware that your son has bite marks all along his legs and a bruised stomach? We are going to request to have a computerized axial tomography scan completed and I can assure you, if the results are what I think they are, we can have you arrested," Rose advised calmly. Just then a man was heard shouting from the end of the hallway exiting the elevators.

"Hey!" the old stocky man screamed, making his way towards them, neighbors continuing to eavesdrop. "My son is missing and I need to file one of them report things," he continued. Reggie turned to face Rose, motioning to her that he would assist the man approaching them. Rose and Marvin continuing their conversation,

"If there are things happening with my son that I don't know about then I have to fix it," his tone melancholy.

"Sir, if you reside here I find it hard to believe that you could have missed this abuse," she replied.

"I don't live here, I mean, I come and go, but this is not my primary residence," Marvin mumbled, the admission tearing him apart because he would now have to come face to face with his wife, disclosing his affair. He unfolded his arms. "I live with my wife and children," he continued. Rose gripped her clipboard as she began putting the pieces together. Realizing this to be a custom practice in the African American communities, she decided it best to return inside where she stood facing Irving as he lay on his side, facing the window, playing with his G.I. Joe action figure enacting a battle scene.

Irving turned slowly, facing Rose, the Caucasian woman standing at 6'2 with loafers, a blazer, beige pants stretching just above her navel and a polka-dotted shirt tucked away in her pants. A redhead, Rose had strong features favoring her father with a muscular build despite her sedentary lifestyle. Although kind, her appearance was intimidating to even the toughest of men. Irving had no reaction, he wondered why he was not at school, why his mother had not beaten him out of his sleep and why his home was filled with strangers. But he was not the talkative type, an observer he was, waiting patiently for his father to emerge. However, Marvin remained in the hallway with Reggie and his new foe that was revealed to be named Carl Robinson. The old man was in his late fifties, short and bald. Mr. Robinson was in no mood to play nice, his son was missing and he had not received any updates on his whereabouts.

Both Marvin and Carl insisted on listening keenly to Reggie outline the nature of their visit, their next course of action for each of their boys and how the police will look to handle the suicide of the young boy's mother. This was all too much for Marvin to accept, he knew now that it was inevitable, Irving would have to come home with him, raised amongst his daughters and his darling wife, Nyema. Rose looked perturbed as she took Irving by the hand instructing him to gather his things and change into a new set of clothes. Irving, reluctant to comply, did so eventually after finally coming to the realization he would not be going to school today. Rose followed, diligently taking notes on his routine for preparation.

"Is Mama mad at me?" his soft voice whimpered. Rose knelt to face him, through her pants she could feel the dirt on the floor, making her uncomfortable.

Holding his hand, she replied, "No, but my name is Rose and I am going to try and take you somewhere safe now, is that alright with you?" she asked softly.

"Okay," Irving replied, gripping his G.I. Joe even tighter now—afraid. Irving paced around the room as the officers took a stand out in the hall, his father and Carl looking on as Irving removed a pair of ripped, stained jeans from his dilapidated cubby and a shirt that he had been wearing since the age of five. The shirt stopped inches above his navel and the jeans a pair of high-waters, staring down at the Skechers he was going to put on—cringing as he prepared his feet for the pain he was to endure. Marvin now allowed a tear to fall.

"What the fuck, man?" said Carl to Marvin, turning to face him, one hand now covering his mouth as he looked away in disgust. "This is not how we treat our young black men!" he shouted.

"Before you go tryna tell me how to raise my son, why don't you focus on finding your own," Marvin snapped, Carl gripping him by the throat as the present officers struggled to pry them apart.

"Let him go now!" one officer yelled at Carl, who complied, as he feared having to spend another night in jail. Making his way down the hall towards the elevators, Carl realized he should, in fact, be out looking for his son, so that is what he decided to do. Heading back down to his apartment, Carl located his grey hooded Champion sweater, instructing his girlfriend who reported their son missing and their four-year-old daughter to remain inside; Carl now embarking on a journey through the forest across the street, shouting his son's name in anguish.

As they climbed in the back of the 1984 blue Nissan Altima, Rose contemplating whether or not she would stop and get clothes for little Irving before heading to the office. But quickly she decided against this, as Reggie stayed back advising Marvin on where they would be headed, Marvin returned to the inside of the apartment, taking a look around, finally noticing the broken television set in front of his son's bed, the dead cockroaches on top and under his bed, along with the tiny bedbugs scattered along the mattress cushion. Marvin did not grieve Michelle; he simply could not bring himself to mourn.

As he stood, taking a look out of the window just above his son's mattress, he wondered why Michelle would dive head-first just above their sleeping child, the image causing him to quiver. Marvin showered, finding a bar of soap nearest the medicine cabinet, moments later dressing as quickly as he could, grabbing the keys to the Camry and making his way down to 125th street—OCFS.

With an investigation now in full-effect, Marvin feared the thought of losing his only son forever, but he had no one else to blame as he drove recklessly along the highway, pondering his actions, regret filling both his heart and mind. Arriving at the office after stepping briskly past security and successfully making his way through the metal detectors, Marvin raced to the elevators heading up to the ninth floor. The light hooded sweater he wore along with his denim blue jeans and sneakers were all indications that he was the neglectful parent in question as the men and women around him all dressed in business suits and ties.

Upstairs Rose spoke softly, handing Irving a cup of water and sitting adjacent to him in the small room, a camcorder facing him. Rose decided it best that his clothes go unchanged, giving them a stronger case. Watching through the two-way mirror, Marvin stood in his favorite stance, arms folded, feet apart, his eyes straight forward as he watched his son. Seeing him closely in the light for what felt like the first time, it was then he realized the damage he had done. Irving had scratches along his face, his nails unclipped—chipping, no haircut, and multiple bald spots.

Marvin listened closely, standing alongside Reggie, who also had a clipboard in his hand, examining closely. Their voices seemed mechanized,

"Irving, how old are you?"

Irving feared being honest, afraid of upsetting his mother, or worse, his father, as the bright lights from the ceiling continued to shine on him, the air conditioner pumping on high behind him and the camcorder light shining brightly in his eyes.

"Where is my Mama?" he asked, innocently.

Marvin was filling with rage. "My son needs to be taken home with me, now!" he screamed as he pointed to the two-way mirror, but Reggie remained unmoved. A fervent Rose turned to face the mirror as she pondered whether or not she should disclose the news, she decided against it—momentarily.

"Irving, your mother asked us to look after you for a few hours and once you answer these questions I will give her a call, okay?" Rose felt terrible for lying, but she knew he was simply terrified and needed to establish a sense of trust if he were ever going to talk to her transparently. "Would you like some cookies?" Irving smiled, nodding profusely; turning to the two-way mirror, Rose smiled. Reggie on the other side received her gesture and made his way to the lounge where he retrieved three chocolate chip cookies, placing them on a plate to serve Irving.

"Great, those are some freshly baked cookies, good, right?" Rose asked smiling as Irving chewed aggressively. It was as though he had not eaten in days.

"Now, Irving. How old are you?"

"I am seven," he responded as he chewed, scooting his way up in the belted seat, swinging his legs as he took a sip of the water provided to him.

"Would you like some juice?"

"No, too much sugar, that's unhealthy," he replied. Rose's eyes widening, Marvin looking on began to knit his brows as the two continued to converse.

"Irving, can you tell me about your Mama, has Mama ever hit you?"

Finishing his snack Irving sat upright, placing his hands under her thighs as he rocked side to side—a dark-skinned boy with a slender physique, hazel brown eyes and skin as smooth as silk. No longer timid, Irving asked, "Where am I?" avoiding the question asked of him.

"You are in an office," replied Rose, folding her hands atop the silver table; the room resembling closely that of an interrogation room in a police station.

"Oh, my Mama is dead, isn't she?" Rose, unsure of how to answer, decided it best to now tell the truth, nodding her head in agreeance.

"She is, but, that's why I am here, to ensure that you are taken care of and that we find you a wonderful home to grow up in," she said softly.

Irving, now growing impatient, replied, "You should not take a child from their natural habitat. I have toys and I need to get home to them," A bewildered Rose arose from her seat.

"Irving can you excuse me for a quick second?" she rhetorically asked as she raced through the doors to the neighboring room, standing alongside Reggie and Marvin who were both in complete shock,

"Um, is this kid some kind of a prodigy?"

"What the hell does that mean?" Marvin snarled, believing he had heard an insult. Rose, rolling her eyes, awaited a response from Reggie who also remained puzzled as he massaged his mustache.

"Rose, why don't you bring Irving down to our playroom, and Mr. Houston, why don't you and I have a talk," instructed Reggie. Rose quickly obliged.

Marvin struggled to make his way into the conversation room as Rose called it, he was reluctant to speak with the people who were trying to take his son away, but after what felt like hours he was finally prepared to talk in hopes that this would end and he could finally head on home with his child.

"Mr. Houston." Reggie turned the pages found inside of a manila envelope he'd asked Rose to fetch, she now sat to the rear of them, watching him closely.

"I apologize for my informality earlier on, but please

consider this a formal interview between you and I in relation to your son Irving Houston. According to our documents, Irving is seven years old and has remained in the custody of both you and a Ms. Michelle Dudley. Is that correct?"

Marvin sat upright, his eyes growing weary, "Yes and no," he responded, the camcorder buzzing.

"Please explain further," Reggie instructed.

"I made a mistake a few years back, um, met Michelle at a bar one night when I left my wife and daughters home. We had just had our second daughter and with a toddler and a newborn it was just too much, so, I needed a break. Went out, met Michelle, the rest is history," he said as he fidgeted.

"Was she supposed to be a one-night stand?"

"Something like that, then she told me she was pregnant and I never told her about my wife or my daughters. I was angry, told her to kill it, but then she decided to keep the baby anyway. When I heard it was a boy, I couldn't bring myself to abandon him, um, so I made my way between houses from time to time and it worked. Things were smooth for years, I never tried with Irving, she seemed to have things under control and plus, I was wiped out from my daughters, they require a lot more attention, tenderness from their father," Marvin replied as he was growing nervous, fearing he was saying too much. "Look, I just want to make things right, take my son to my home, raise him with our family and just have things go back to normal," he pleaded.

"I'm afraid it's not that black and white, Mr. Houston," Rose interrupted. "This young man is malnourished, shows signs of physical abuse, currently suffering from emotional and mental abuse, neglect, and has blisters on his body and bacteria growing on his head. This is a very serious case and even if you do manage to get him from our care you will be heavily monitored, and hearing that you have two additional children we can open a case to have you investigated on their behalf as well. Mr. Houston, I don't believe you truly understand the seriousness of all of this, you could potentially lose all of your children," Rose emphasized.

Unfazed, Marvin turned to face Reggie, asking, "Why is this bitch talking to me?" creating an uproar in the room as they all begin speaking simultaneously.

"Mr. Houston I am going to have to ask you to please watch your language," commented Reggie.

Minutes turned to hours and Marvin grew impatient, convinced now that both Reggie and Rose were not willing to give him the benefit of the doubt, he was pegged as an abusive parent and there was simply nothing he could do to change that stigma. Feeling hopeless, Marvin decided it best to remain quiet, with their family dynamics now less than ideal, Marvin remained deep in thought.

3

S tanding next to his father whilst Rose and Reggie looked on, Irving—afraid to take his hand—wanted nothing but to return home. He was growing uncomfortable and fidgeting; this made Marvin happy as the CPS representatives did not want to aid in his discomfort and granted his father temporary guardianship until their home visit the next morning. Elated almost, but frightened as he dreaded the thought of going home to face his wife, having to now explain the child he kept a secret for years. Marvin prided himself on being a good man but fell short time and time again, and although he missed Sundays with his wife and daughters, he was sure to attend Sunday service with Michelle and Irving, a tradition upheld due to his guilty conscience.

The double life he lived weighing on him day by day, causing him to lose focus on the things that mattered, often times forgetting birthdays, anniversaries, and mixing up the likes and dislikes of both women. But it was over now, he was ready to change and raise his son the best way he knew how. Having been raised without a father and spending years in and out of a foster home after his mother left him on the church step as an infant, Marvin knew the horrors, and despite the fact that Irving was unplanned he by no means going to allow him to be raised by a system designed to tear apart the black family. On the ride home he repented profusely for his sins, praying to God, placing his hands together to plead for forgiveness as he turned the last corner onto his street.

Irving sat quietly in the back seat, reluctant to move because every step he took caused his feet to hurt. But Marvin remained oblivious to this, completely engrossed in the fact that his wife was going to be devastated. He had broken his vows often, however, he loved his wife, the feelings he had for her remained unchanged as he dreaded going to apartment IIA for the past eight years. Marvin prayed for an opening, a release, he even contemplated lying to Nyema but figured that would not have gone over well. Twenty-four hours since his last appearance, she had grown accustomed to what she was led to believe were simply long hours at work. Years of hassling with his supervisor for his silence in exchange for free labor and partial visits to his paramour, Marvin was tired and oftentimes found himself taking his frustrations out on Michelle, the woman he blamed for his misery.

Irving took in the scenery as he pondered his whereabouts, confused on why he was not yet home, a place he so longed to be as he watched the clouds slowly passing them. He squirmed in the backseat, trying to find a position to lessen his pain, licking his chapped lips, scratching his face and leaving a new mark from his chipped nails. Marvin, watching him through the rear-view, turned to face him.

Look what I've done, he thought. Furious now, punching the passenger seat headrest, Irving curled into the fetal position—afraid, closing his eyes. Stopping immediately, Marvin felt empathetic, comprehending the nature of his fear, but his feeling was far greater as his mind began preparing for the worse possible outcome—losing his wife and children to whom he had come to love more than life itself. Marvin instructed Irving to climb out of the backseat, Irving dreading the thought to stand on his two feet as he lifted the door handle to make his way onto the sidewalk. The sun was beginning to set as Marvin then slapped himself on the head, thinking he had not yet fed Irving who by now could have been starving.

"You hungry?" he asked, turning to face him, stepping lightly to grab his hand before making their way across the street.

A receptionist, Nyema Houston worked for an art gallery in Manhattan, six years today; she was elated and decided to celebrate. An avid lover of the African-American culture, she found herself investing heavily in her craft, their upstairs den filled with canvases, paint brushes, markers, pencils, and completed portraits of her family members. The breeze from the outside gracing her skin felt like a small piece of heaven—if she had known the feeling to compare; she would say that was it. Marvin listened as she sang loudly near the open window, realizing that she was most likely working on her art.

Gliding her brush aggressively atop the blank canvas with the use of a dingy yellow to express her rage and deep levels of jealousy, she wondered as she sat, "Am I not good enough? Beautiful enough? What happened to my marriage? When did things go wrong?" The questions consumed her, causing her to feel faint as the fumes made their way into her nostrils, her migraine now increasing and her palms sweating, her body the harbinger just as the door slammed on the first floor.

The multi-family dwelling contained a finished basement which the couple rented for supplemental income to a dear friend: Bordon Hughes. Residing in a middle-class neighborhood, both Nyema and Marvin learned to never live above their means. Their children shared a bedroom, Nyema utilizing the den for her art and the master bedroom only a few feet away from the bedroom their children shared. Marvin knew it would not be easy. Making his way inside, stomping into the kitchen where he rinsed his hands, advising Irving to remove his shoes and take a seat along the wooden dining table. Irving struggled to remove his shoes and allowed himself to let out a shrieking cry. His size thirteen feet forcing their way from the size eleven sneaker did more than just hurt, it caused his feet to bleed; toes throbbing, the blood dried up from the open wound found on his heel where he had multiple untreated gashes.

As Marvin knelt to inspect his son's injury, Irving watched him, worried he might cause his foot to sting, the anticipation is what he feared as he retracted his legs each time Marvin made an attempt to touch him. Witnessing the marks on his feet, Marvin removed a paper towel, took a seat on the floor sitting Indian style and patted Irving's feet. Irving screeching in pain as he sobbed uncontrollably, the bruises had no doubt gotten worse, bringing Marvin to believe that a visit to the hospital would perhaps be needed. Nyema made her way downstairs, watching in horror as her husband continued his bidding,

"Why?" she cried, her arms folded. "Was it not enough that I had to find out the way that I did, but you bring this child into my home?" she continued as she sobbed. Marvin remained quiet, unsure of what to say as he was smart enough to know that his words would simply cause more harm than good. Advised against speaking, he continued to listen; hearing the growling of Irving's stomach, he rose from the ground to retrieve the bread, peanut butter, and jelly from the refrigerator. Nyema immediately intervened, snatching the jar from his hands and slamming it to the floor.

"You answer me Goddamit! Why would you do this to us, Marvin?" she screamed. Marvin took a deep breath as he proceeded to remove the table cloth from the counter, rinsing it to clean the mess she created. Nyema could not face Irving, her back to him as he sat, petrified by the belligerent woman; the innocent look on his face causing Marvin to proceed with haste. Standing, he continued fixing the sandwich, retrieving another jar of jelly from the pantry. Nyema stood with her hand over her mouth, embarrassed by her decorum and feeling rather disrespected, she wept before taking her leave—the gown flowing swiftly behind her.

Marvin cut the crusts from the whole wheat bread he was preparing to serve, then handed Irving the plate.

"Eat up, you're going to need your strength," he told him as he proceeded to pour him a glass of milk. Slamming the refrigerator door shut, he assisted Irving with turning his knees under the table, wondering why he had not simply known to do that. But deciding to ponder this no further after making his way up the stairs, grabbing hold of the wooden handrail, shaking now. Nyema had decided it best to lock herself away in their master bedroom without turning the lock. Entering inside, Marvin fell to his knees before her as he watched his wife wallowing in her tears sitting along the edge of the bed. Marvin wept, pleading for forgiveness, eradicating his hubris as the thought of losing his wife and children was enough to make him contemplate ending his life.

"I made a mistake, Nye, I swear I did," he begged.

Nyema—afraid to look her husband in the eye—believed he was lying. "You have a son, you made a son with another woman before making one with me, Marvin," she cried. Their conversation intense, the room filled with anguish—Irving downstairs swinging his feet at the kitchen table, enjoying his meal and taking in the décor. Nyema could not stop crying, she felt robbed and weakened by her sadness. She could feel nothing else but devastation, an emotional wreck now, she listened as Marvin outlined every detail of the affair; the woman, their son, where and how they met, even the one bedroom apartment he was paying the rent for, his visits there when he would say he was working overtime and all else that could have been explained. Marvin knew it was time to confess, a burden released from his shoulders as his wife became violent, smacking him, punching him, and threatening to take his life had he not left her alone.

Irving, still downstairs, stepped lightly into the living room, thrusting himself atop of the cushioned brown sofa, something he had never seen before.

"This is so soft," he thought, smiling after weeping momentarily from walking on his feet. Due to his extensive bruising, Irving had trained himself to walk on the toes of his feet, allowing his heels to rarely, almost never, touch the ground. He would run fast, his small feet pattering along the house, this would upset Mama, but the faster he ran the less time he had to endure the pain. Just then the door to the basement flung open, an older gentleman making his way out carrying a black suitcase and a tub of paint. The man stood 6'4 in height, had a huge stomach, a long grey beard, a bald head, and a medium toned complexion. Irving peeped out from behind the sofa pillows.

"Aye you bwoy," the man uttered, his voice groggy as though he had smoked an entire pack of cigarettes—the Jamaican accent not making him easy to comprehend. Irving continued to watch him as he struggled, just then the stranger called to him again.

"Aye! I said come here," he yelled. But Irving refused to move, he was not allowed to speak to strangers and his feet were hurting too bad, he needed at least another couple of minutes before he could walk again. Shaking his head no, Irving found himself face to face with the tall man hovering down over him.

"You don't speak?" he asked as he tried to speak America Standard English, his dialect gone. A timid Irving nodded his head yes.

"My name is Bordon, what is your name?"

"Irving," he whispered, his hands now atop the sofa cushion, his body twisted and his shirt rising to his chest.

"Ah, wah kind ah shirt dat yah wear?" the man asked, peeking down on him, a disgusted look on his face. "Yuh look like dem lickle bawty bwoy. Whey yuh modda and yuh fahda?" he continued, setting the suitcase and the paint down steadily. Irving shrugged; he honestly could not understand what he was being asked. Realizing this, Bordon repeated himself, rather this time in what he believed to be Standard English. "I said where your parents are?"

"Daddy went upstairs and Mommy left me," Irving,

speaking just above a whisper. Bordon was confused.

"What do you mean? Where she went?" Bordon standing with his hands on his hips.

"Through my window," Irving replied, his head down, sad. Bordon was unsure of what he was hearing from the young boy and decided to question him no more. Bordon left the living room and made his way back down the basement, Irving, alone again, continued to swing his feet as his eyes began to get low.

Upstairs there was silence. Nyema and Marvin speaking all that needed to be said and with nothing left, Nyema feared to ask another question, she simply could not bring herself to as the truth begun to stab into her like a thousand knives. Marvin crawled his way along the carpeted floor to rest his head on her lap—hesitant at first, Nyema allowed it, caressing him.

"I cannot take that boy into my home," she cried out loud, her thoughts becoming words.

"He is my son, Nyema, he will live here and we will get through this, we have to," Marvin pleaded, squeezing her legs passionately, closing his eyes. Nyema allowing more tears to fall, wondering if Marvin ever loved her at all or if he was simply swallowing his pride so that he would not have to raise his son alone.

"I cannot love that boy!" she screamed, pushing him away. "How can you even expect that of me? What on earth is the reason that I am to take on that additional responsibility, is it so you can go about cheating again? I cannot do it, Marvin, and I will not do it. You have made a fool of me and now you are wishing to do this once again?" she cried.

Marvin wished his migraine would cease and caught himself before he could allow his temper to rise and get the best of him. "I will give you time. Where are the girls?" he questioned, getting to his feet.

"With my mother for the weekend, I told you they were going to be gone. The mere fact that you did not even remember that and wanted to bring this child around our daughters is simply irresponsible, Marvin!" she screamed. "How could you have forgotten? The girls do not know this boy, I do not know this boy, and yet you were okay with bringing him around our daughters?" her eyes widened.

Marvin, now agitated, shouted, "He is my son! He will be raised with my children and we will love him so help me God." Pointing his finger at her face, Nyema flinched, fearful that he would hit her. She had never seen this side of him. Arising now, a silent Nyema simply making her way down to the kitchen where she wept while preparing dinner. Irving was fast asleep on the couch, curled into the fetal position. Nyema did not bother to look for him, removing the flat metal dish used to serve him, she placed it quietly into the garbage.

Rose turned the key to her Yonkers apartment and made her way over to the bar where she poured herself a glass of wine, kicking off her shoes and taking a seat on the leather sofa. As she reached for the case files she had for the evening, she found herself intrigued by her newest intake: Irving. She thought of his demeanor, how unafraid he was when she was speaking to him and while gathering his things to head downtown. Inside the car he was quiet, taking in the scenery as she drove. A strange feeling came over her as she pondered the possibility of having him in her care, she would be interested in seeing his day-to-day development—something about him, after all, was intriguing to her.

Setting her wine down on the coffee table centered in her living room, Rose arose and decided to head across town, back into the office. The time now 7:35 p.m., which meant the building was closed for cleaning and everyone had gone home. As she drove slowly fearing the police pulling her over and earning herself a DUI, Rose was meticulous, using cognitive dissonance to convince herself it was only a sip. The cool breeze flowing freely through her hair, thirty-five minutes later her Air Force blue 1984 Nissan Altima pulling into a designated parking spot just off the sidewalk nearest the parking lot exit. Rose, wearing her clothes from earlier that morning, swiped her access badge and stepped inside the building. Unsure of what she specifically needed or wanted, she made her way upstairs and into the storage room where she spotted the video, the one she had recorded of Irving earlier that day.

Sliding the cassette into the VCR at the rear of the office, Rose replayed the video, listening keenly to their conversation— her arms folded,

"Hello Irving, I am back," shutting the door behind her, although she was out of view, she could hear herself speaking perfectly fine. Irving said nothing. "I apologize that we have to keep moving you, are you okay?" she asked as she pulled her chair closer to the table, staring Irving in the eyes. He was distracted, mentally he did not seem to be there, looking around the room, swinging his legs, and not necessarily interested in any form of conversation. Rose remembered feeling defeated.

"Irving, I need to ask you a few questions about Mommy and Daddy, if that is okay?" she continued. Their eyes locked.

"Um, okay," his head held down.

"Irving, I know you are upset about your mother passing away, but—" Rose said before Irving interrupted her.

"I am not upset," he mentioned softly, knitting his brows, at first Rose thought she had heard him incorrectly.

"Irving, are you not upset that your mother died?" she questioned.

"No." He resumed swinging his legs.

"But you asked for your mother earlier today, you wanted to be with her, no?"

"I just wanted to be sure, but I am not sad. I just want my toy." Rose was bemused, wondering, *Did he understand the concept of death? Was he simply in denial? Was this a child so traumatized that he perhaps felt a sense of relief?* Scribbling these questions on her notepad now, she was beginning to feel apprehensive.

"Why don't you tell me what it's like at home?" she asked as she concluded her writing.

"Home?" Irving questioned.

"Yes, how are Mom and Dad? Have they ever hurt you?"

"Mama says children must be disciplined when they misbehave—the Bible says so. I misbehave and Mama will get mad." Just then he got to his feet, walking around the room bearing the excruciating pain he was feeling, his hands rubbing against the walls as he hummed what sounded like a church hymnal.

"That sounds like a beautiful song," observed Rose as she watched him pace, growing emotional. She could not bring herself to look at him draped in clothing that was all too small. She wondered if his feet hurt, but he appeared to be ignoring the pain, ignoring her, a tactic she knew all too well.

"Irving, why don't you come back over and have a seat so we can finish our conversation?" said Rose. But Irving did not comply; rather, he continued, sliding his hands across the wall, taking a seat in the corner of the room on the floor.

Rose grew worried and she continued by asking, "Irving, what's wrong?"

"You do not have my permission to record me," he whispered, lying on the ground now, using his fingers as legs, racing them up and down the cold floors.

Rose turned immediately to face the camcorder she had completely forgotten was there, immersed in their conversation. Unsure of how to proceed next, Rose took a look at the double-sided mirrors—watching the video playback, Rose recollected this moment.

"I do apologize Irving; I indeed should have asked your permission. May I record you?" she requested pleasantly.

"No, that is voyeurism and Mama says those people are insane and not well." Rose did not know how to respond, and so she did not, she simply whispered to herself the word *voyeurism* over and again as she scribbled the word in her notes. Rose wondered how and why a seven-year-old would have such a word in their vocabulary.

"Irving, where did you learn that word?" Focused on the recording, Rose was startled by a man wearing a janitor uniform standing on the threshold of the room, he had come to change the bags in the trash cans, his cleaning cart out in the hallway. "Oh my!" she yelled, her hand to her chest.

"Did I scare you?"

"Yes, but-but please carry on," she said, motioning for him to continue.

"I apologize, I will be out of your hair in no time." The African-American gentleman appeared to be in his mid-twenties. Rose immediately returned to the video, where she pressed the rewind button firmly. *Where did you learn that word?* her voice repeated.

"My Samuel," he advised. Rising from the ground, sitting up now, his body turning to face her, a smile streaked across his face. The video then stopped, a black screen in front of her. Rose continued standing as she ponders the meaning of his response. *His Samuel,* she thought.

Returning home, Rose could not sleep after she showered, washed her hair and listened as her home phone rang. Answering it, "Yes, how may I help you?"

"Rose, it's me, Marley. What are you doing?" Rose settled into her couch, her right hand holding a glass of red wine and her left hand holding the telephone. She was in no mood to converse with Marley, her sister-in-law.

"I am getting ready to watch a great movie," Rose lied, placing extra emphasis on *movie* in hopes that Marley would hear how busy she was and end their call, however that tactic did not work.

"So, Ryan and I are having a party next weekend—spur of the moment type of thing—and although we were hoping to make it a couples only engagement, we would still love for you to come. What do you say?" Rose could tell she was smiling, Marley was always smiling, always perky and full of life, easily the nicest person she had ever met, but Rose decided a long time ago that it was best to take Marley in small doses considering she did not consider herself to be quite as sociable.

"Oh, wow, I appreciate the invite, but I may have to pass. I just got this case and I know these next few weeks are going to be pretty relentless," she stated, praying that her response was enough to get her out of their endeavors.

"Listen, Ryan and I barely get to spend time with you anymore. Ever since you got this job and you've been dealing with the divorce settlement, you don't seem to want to hang out at all. Can we at least have dinner?" she insisted, her voice melancholy. The last thing Rose wanted was to be reminded of was her soon-to-be ex-husband.

"Look, we can do dinner, but Marley, I am truly busy, I just have a lot going on right now." Her tone harsh, massaging her temples after placing the wineglass on the coffee table atop a coaster.

"I understand, just know that Ryan and I love you, okay?" she said before hanging up. Rose was beginning to feel a surge of emotions, from anger to complete disappointment. Marley just could not relate to the issues that were plaguing her and why she needed to invest her time into work—she was feeling depressed.

4

Sunday Morning

A s the morning came Rose found herself standing in front of the Houston house banging on their front door at 10 a.m. Her car parked on the opposite side of the street, she stood, banging again, this time more ferociously. She heard no one, which was beginning to worry her until a man made his appearance from the back of the home.

"May I help you?" Bordon asked, wearing a wife beater in the chilly weather and a pair of sweat pants with sneakers.

"I am sorry, but yes, I am looking for the Houston family and a young boy named Irving," she said softly. Lifting his head in suspicion, Bordon replied, "Who are you?"

"My name is Rose Appleton and I am from Child Protective Services. Mr. Houston knew I would be dropping by today." Growing impatient, "Do you happen to know where they are?"

"I knew something had to be wrong with dat bwoy, but, um, no, dey not here. I think they went to the doctor with him."

A confused Rose found some parts of his response incomprehensible, using the context clues to determine what he had told her.

"Yes, thank you," she said, waving him goodbye and stepping swiftly to her vehicle.

As Rose took off, Bordon went back inside, stepping up the wooden stairs to peek his head into the hallway, announcing, "It looks like she gone." Marvin and Nyema were sitting in the kitchen at the dining room table.

"Bordon, I appreciate you fella. Many thanks," Marvin said, tilting his head, his back to him.

"Not ah problem," Bordon told him, taking his leave.

The couple sat in the kitchen by the table for what felt like hours, Nyema had not spoken a word since serving dinner the night before.

"We need to talk if we are going to move past this. I need to know, Nyema, how long should I wait; a month, maybe two, before you decide to have a conversation with me again?" Marvin asked politely, but Nyema remained quiet, she had no desire to speak to him. Knowing this now, Marvin decided to advise Nyema of the changes their family was going to undergo.

"Well, I was thinking, since we now have Irving, you can possibly clear out the den and we can turn that into his bedroom," Marvin suggested, standing to clear the table. Turning on the water, he began to clean the dishes. Nyema could not believe her ears, squeezing her eyes shut tightly she allowed a small tear to flow freely down her cheeks. The day dragged, their home dismal, Irving slept the day away as Marvin would periodically check on him in their daughters' bedroom.

After a long, restless night, Nyema had awakened by 5 a.m. to sit in the den amongst her art where she lingered on the thoughts of her future. She was no longer feeling like herself, internalizing her emotions, afraid to speak, not sure of what to say, she simply could not find the words. This did not worry Marvin, although he did not know whether or not she would come around, he convinced himself that things were going to work out fine. This was Marvin, a realist but also a man who knew that admitting his wrongs and making amends meant moving past the pain and finding peace again—in this case, it was only a matter of time.

Although Marvin was a heavy sleeper, he too found himself feeling restless, deep in thought as he wondered how to incorporate Irving into their lives. *How were the girls going to react? Nyema, will she ever forgive me?* Questions plagued his mind as he turned to find that he had been sleeping alone, his confidence shaken.

Working as a janitor for the Bloomfield Housing projects for the past seventeen years, Marvin was no stranger to early mornings and late nights; deciding to rest a bit longer, he arose out of bed by 7 a.m. to the sweet smell of eggs and bacon sizzling and the sound of a car approaching, parking in front of their home. Nyema was in the kitchen preparing a meal for her children—her mother returning them home to fetch their school supplies and have breakfast. As she concluded preparing breakfast and listened for the car engine to shut off, Nyema removed her apron and made her way to the front door where her children, Asha and Amara, both came running towards her, giving her the biggest hug they could muster.

Standing inside, the girls spoke with glee, excited they had returned home as Nyema instructed the girls to head to their room, forgetting the sleeping child who now resided there, she panicked when she remembered.

"Girls, wait!" she shouted, her mother standing inside and closing the door behind her, seemed bewildered.

"Nyema, is everything okay?"

"Girls, um, why don't you both start working on your breakfast while I grab your things? Okay?" Nyema spoke nervously as she took a deep breath, watching her daughters' make their way back downstairs just before reaching the top. "Mom, can you watch them?" she asked, turning to face her mother as her daughters made their way past her. Thankfully, the girls were dressed in their uniforms and ready for school.

Nyema stomped her way up the stairs, thrusting her bedroom door open to find Marvin dressing for work.

"I need to go into the children's bedroom, they need their book bags for school," she demanded. Marvin was stunned, he was happy she was speaking, yet he was not ready to oblige.

"Go into the room Nyema, he is a child, he will not do you any harm," Marvin stated, completely oblivious to the fact that his wife was still grieving.

"No, I cannot look at that boy. Please go and get the supplies so I can take the girls to school," she pleaded.

"Irving will have to be taken too, now you've had a day to gather your thoughts, but we will get past this. Nyema, I have to go to work and he needs clothes, materials, and to be taken to school." Calmly, Marvin adding his nametag to his uniform. "Also, will you please clear the den by evening? Now that the girls are home we will have to get Irving settled inside. Plus, I have a strong feeling the CPS lady gonna be coming back, maybe today, maybe tomorrow…" he continued, paying her no never mind, never making eye contact as he paced, preparing himself for a day's work.

Nyema entertained the idea of leaving, taking her children to reside with her mother, leaving Marvin and his prized possession. But despite his actions, Nyema could not bring herself to do such a thing, a life without her husband felt almost unimaginable. But she was feeling drained as she continued to withhold her emotions, slowly reaching a breaking point. Hatred consumed her as she turned away and entered her daughters' room after turning the doorknob unhurriedly.

Entering inside she could not locate Irving and wondered where he had gone. The room was occupied by two twin beds, the walls a light pink with sky-inspired borders. There was a little cubby in the corner for the books the children read and a wardrobe for their clothing. Her motherly instincts caused her to feel concerned as she made her way in between the girls' beds where the nightstand was located, kneeling, she found Irving lying on the floor underneath the bed closest the window, reading a book he had found. The thumb from his left hand in his mouth and his right arm bent under his head—he appeared to be comfortable. Their eyes locked, taking a deep breath, Nyema arose, grabbing the book bags before running back through the door; her eyes filled with tears as she stood momentarily sobbing before regaining her composure and making her way downstairs.

At the bottom of the steps she waited, wiping her eyes with the apron she had on, Nyema found the strength to face them, turning as she forced a smile across her face.

"Girls!" she chuckled, holding their backpacks in mid-air. "So, who is ready for school?" she continued. Her mother looking on could sense that something was off about her daughter and chose to intervene.

"Nyema, honey, why don't I take the girls to school?" she sympathized, placing her hand atop her daughter's, Nyema trembled now as Marvin and Irving entered the kitchen, the young boy coming face-to-face with the girls and their grandmother, holding in his hand tightly the novel *The Power of One* by Bryce Courtenay. Everyone exchanged looks, Nyema embarrassed as she quickly looked away, beginning to walk the girls out of the door, but this was proving itself to be rather difficult considering both Marvin and the girls were excited to see one another. Jumping in their father's arms, both Asha and Amara were smiling and laughing with glee as he tickled them, Irving looking on.

"Young man, what is your name?" asked Nyema's mother, who was interested in learning more about the boy—thinking to herself just how handsome he was. Unable to bend far, the seventy-four-year-old woman simply slouched as she awaited his response. But Irving was afraid to speak, draped in his father's white t-shirt which hung a little past his ankles, Irving was nervous and wanted only to eat and return to his new hiding place under the bed. Nyema was waiting by the door, her purse in hand and her jacket on as she insisted that the girls come along, her mother watching could not understand why she had not mentioned a word to the young boy, let alone offer him food.

"Nyema, Marvin, who is this handsome fella? Is he your nephew, Marvin? And where on earth did he get this book?" she asked innocently, but the room grew quiet, both Asha and Amara now outside buckling themselves in the back seat of their grandmother's Chrysler.

"Mom, can we please go?" Nyema droned. Marvin reached out to give Nyema's mother a hug,

"Miss Margaret, it is always nice to see you, how were the girls? I hope they ain't give you no trouble or nutting crazy." Marvin laughed.

"No, no, they were good, good babies, but, um, Marvin, I will see you later," she said nervously as her daughter anxiously awaited her by the front door.

"Mom!" she screamed.

Alone now, Marvin noticed there had been no leftovers for himself or Irving, resulting in him deciding to take Irving to work as he slammed the cabinets, noticing the uncleaned dishes, he was wondering if Nyema was going to return, especially after disclosing the true identity of Irving to her mother, who he knew would certainly not approve. But Marvin was seeking to turn a new leaf, raise his son and be there for him the best he knew how, he saw something in him, from the tender age of five as he was growing into his looks and assisting his mother. Church on Sundays was helping Marvin to heal, helping him to forgive his own parents who had abandoned him at a young age. Uncertain of what Irving could wear, Marvin simply lifted him, walking his son over to the Camry—barefoot wearing an oversized t-shirt. Irving strapped himself in the backseat, reopening his book as he continued reading, Marvin pulling off.

Heading into work, Rose feared she was going to be reprimanded for her actions the day before—logging her trip for mileage purposes, weekend house calls were strictly for category one families with children pending placement, however, she could not help herself, she wanted to ensure Irving was being treated well. Hearing her name called into the conference room startled her.

"Rose!" Reggie shouted, sticking his head through the glass doors.

Annoyed, she turned answering, "Yes."

"May we see you for a minute?" he replied. Rose made a U-turn, heading back down the hall, entering inside she removed her coat as she sat on the left side of the table, Reggie accompanied by two other managers sitting beside him across from her. Taking a seat, Rose noticed the papers sorted before them.

"Rose, how are you doing?" Reggie asked politely.

"I am well," she responded.

"Great, so the team and I were discussing and considering the fact that you have been with us for quite some time, we would like to have you placed on more challenging cases, specifically category one files. I see how passionate and knowledgeable you are and we by no means want to see your talents wasted," Reggie said.

Rose responded, bewildered, "So, are you taking me off the Houston case?"

"Well, yes, only because he is now in the care of his father, we are still going to investigate his father, I forget his name, but, as such, a case like this is now merely a category four, if that. So, we want to make sure we are utilizing your skills," he said. Rose was not pleased—the disappointment was written across her face.

"You put me on this case years ago, when the first incident happened. The school called because he went in with what appeared to have been a dislocated shoulder and then after one visit you convinced me we weren't needed; now look, two years later and his mother threw herself from a window just above his bed, he had bruises, infections, obvious signs of neglect. If we do our job correctly this can very easily be a category one case," she pleaded.

"Perhaps, however, we feel you may be becoming too attached the child," he admitted, the gentlemen beside him nodding in agreement. "We will assign someone else to the case to conduct the family interview, review any criminal history, and then, if it is determined that this is a category one, then maybe we will ask you to carry out the case further. But until then, we would like you to focus primarily on category one cases.

"But Irving is a category one case, at least a pending one. I do not understand why you are removing me from this case; I mean goodness, can we find some means to mitigate?" Vocalized an intimidated Rose.

"My dear, you are a brilliant woman, graduated top of your class from Yale and then came here to work, for this we are grateful, but we do not want you spending so much of your time predominately making house calls and sitting around in interrogation rooms. We want you in the courts, fighting, drafting petitions, and actively utilizing your skillset. We truly feel a case such as this is simply below your intellectual capabilities." Reggie said. "Rose, please, I am asking that you trust the process. We will discuss further as we look to get you acclimated," he added. This concluded their conversation, Reggie having hoped Rose would simply understand, and she did. Standing now, retrieving her things, she made her way out of the dismal conference room.

Rose sat at her desk reviewing the information she had currently on the Houston case, her first time meeting Irving two years prior, she was told he would be taken to the hospital to treat his injured arm, but as she scrolled through the documents on file, she could find nothing supporting this to be true. There were no medical records uploaded or criminal reports despite the bruises she found on him recently and the ones she saw on his mother upon first meeting her. Rose was stuck, with no documentation and no concrete evidence of neglect or abuse she would have no case and there would be no hope of Irving landing into a category one. Rose sticking her head above her cubicle watched as the woman exited the conference room, her coworker

Alissa. Alissa was a recent college graduate, and Rose wondered whether or not her case had been given to her; locking her computer, she began making her way to the opposite side of the office where she greeted the younger woman,

"Hey there!" The woman looking up from her cubicle, curious as to why she was there, they had never exchanged words before today. "I was just curious, did Reggie put you on the Houston case?" Rose continued.

"He did," Alissa replied as she resumed her typing.

"So, this case is new and you know we pretty much have a short window, thirty days to prove his case to be a category one. Are you going to do a home visit today?" Alissa chuckled.

"You don't have to school me on how to do my job and the general specifications. I know the timeline, but Reggie asked me to desk this one for a few because he's in his father's care now and doesn't require an imminent investigation," she said pretentiously. Rose began feeling helpless and grabbed a seat from the empty cubicle next to her.

"Listen to me Alissa, two years ago I was where you are now, and because the state has limited resources we are pretty much being asked to give up on this kid, when the truth is, he needs us. This is the second incident in two years, and that's just what we know of, if we don't fight to get him at a category one and out of their care, we are doing him an injustice and that is not what we signed on to do," she reasoned. But Alissa remained disinterested as she restarted working, answering emails and filing away documents.

"Look, I don't make the rules, I just follow them. He is in the care of his biological father, who from what I am told has two kids of his own and there hasn't been a single incident reported to us. Sure, the state is low on resources and of course funding, so realistically we cannot help everyone; therefore, we have to make these prudent decisions. Also, his primary abuser is no longer here to bring him any harm, so technically if you ask me, he has already received the results of a category one intake," she said. Rose stood now drawing a long sigh before walking back to her cubicle where she found a large stack of folders on her desk all labeled "*Category One Case Files.*"

As the day progressed Rose noticed the janitor making his three o'clock rounds, bringing her to remember the name she heard from Irving, Mr. Samuel. The reorganization of her case files was a daunting task, one she was in no mood to complete. Rose gathered her belongings as she stepped hurriedly to the elevators.

Rose arrived at the public housing projects where she wandered aimlessly before coming up to the place where Michelle's corpse was found, small stains of blood still decorating the concrete floors. She had no idea exactly what she was looking for or who she was trying to speak to before realizing she could speak with Marvin's supervisor; she saw emerge from the basement with two large garbage bags in his hands. The short Latino male wore an ivory jumpsuit with horizontal lines and a name badge hanging from his chest pocket that read Mario Velez.

She stepped towards him listening to him grunt and struggle to get the garbage bags into the blue dumpster just around the corner.

"Hi, my name is Rose Appleton and I am with Child Protective Services." Amicably, rustling around in her purse in search of her identification card. Once she had his attention, Rose continued, "I was wondering if I could ask you a few questions about one of your employees, Marvin Houston." Mario, raising one eyebrow, grunted.

"That son of a bitch," walking away now back to the basement, Rose followed him. Rose was terrified, the pipes were leaking and the basement freezing, the smell of urine hit her nostrils, and she rolled her eyes. She gripped her handbag tightly as Mario entered the tiny office in the basement. The office was small and devastatingly uncomfortable, there were pee stains on the chairs where he motioned for her to have a seat. However, Rose decided it best to remain standing, struggling to remove her pen and notepad, she stood awkwardly, trying not to touch the walls or furniture.

"How would you describe Marvin as an employee?"

"A punk bitch, he was supposed to work today and no call, no show! Punk!" Mario shouted aggressively—his Mexican accent making it hard to comprehend him.

"Okay, but what of his work ethic? Is he usually on time and does he work hard, do you know anything of his family?" she asked, noticing the change in his facial expression, a look of compassion swept across his face.

"His boy, you know, it's sad. I watch him late at night with the thugs and dealers, you know. But Samuel was helping," Mario said. Rose eyes widened, there went that name again.

"Samuel?" she questioned quickly, almost losing the grip on her handbag, "Um, can you tell me where I can find Samuel?" she asked with excitement.

"Aye, why? Why you so interested in Sammy? You undercover or sumptin? A fucking op, snitch? What are you, eh? First, you asking bout Marv and now you asking about Sammy eh, who the fuck you want?"

A timid Rose, now scared, trying to speak to him, stuttered, "I am so sorry, I did not mean to offend you, Mr. Velez, I a— am, simply just um—looking for Samuel, if you may. Also, no— no, no, I am not a cop or op. I showed you my badge; I am just a caseworker. Um, caseworker," she enunciated the second time, removing her ID badge once again, exchanging it with her pen and pad. "Simple caseworker, no cop or-or op."

Similar to that of a bipolar individual Mario then chuckled.

"Oh, okay, good. Samuel up in 2B." He laughed.

5

It was 4 p.m. in the afternoon when Rose made her way to the second floor, entering through the staircase. Using her handkerchief to turn the doorknobs and ensuring to sanitize her hands when she left, once out in the hallway, she listened as the hip-hop music blared loudly from the apartment to the rear. The lights flickered; the others dim. Rose moving rapidly in a pair of loafers she was sure not going to wear inside of her home after walking along the filthy floor as she dodged puddles of urine. The dilapidated housing projects did not appear to be welcoming.

Arriving at the front of his door and listening to the music playing just on the other side, Rose banged profusely, the music lowering. Inside a man bellowed, "Who dat?"

"I um, my name is Rose, I am from CPS, I am trying to locate a man named Samuel," she screamed, the sounds of a baby screeching now making its way to her, along with a woman shouting indistinctly.

"What the fuck is a CPS?" the man shouted.

"Child Protective Services," she responded.

A woman screamed, "Bitch, shut the fuck up!" Rose heard

someone yell from down the hall.

Rose looked around, as the locks clicked on the opposite side of the door. A Caucasian man opened the door wide enough for Rose to step inside of the apartment, standing behind her smoking a joint, the smoke blowing in her face causing her to cough. As she walked further inside the smoke filled the room making it hard to see anyone before her; following the voice of an elderly man she heard him say, "My name is Sammy, who may I ask are you?" his voice seemed groggy. Rose gripped her purse tighter now, the Caucasian man breathing heavily along her neck.

"Rose," she replied, removing her badge although she knew he would not be able to see it. The smoke continued to blind her, her eyes turning red.

"Rose, what brings you here?" the voice asked. He was articulate, aside from the grogginess in his voice. Rose began looking forward to speaking with someone who did not speak Ebonics nor have an incompressible accent.

"I am working on a case for a boy named Irving, I am wondering if there was any additional information you could assist me with," Rose stammered.

"Information?" he inquired, turning the music off entirely as the smoke began to clear. Rose noticed the African-American man sitting in a wheelchair—his legs amputated. The pants he wore were folded up to his knee caps and he wore a beige sweater with the hip-hop logo in the center. Rose continued looking on.

"I was interviewing Irving a few days ago and he mentioned a word he learned from you, I was wondering if you could tell me a little bit more about him, his family?" she said.

Samuel smiled, "I have been waiting for this for many years. That young man is special, he does not need to be in a place like this, among people like ours," Samuel wheeled his way to her, motioning for the man behind her to grab Rose a seat; the man unfolding a chair for Rose to sit, and she did.

"Robert, where are your manners? Samuel asked him.

"My apologies, ma'am, may I get you some water?"

"No, no, I am fine, but thank you very much for asking," she said, turning to face him. Rose was surprised by how quickly the people here altered their personalities. Twitching in her seat, she had not noticed the pistol facing her. Samuel held the butt of the gun just atop his armrest, aiming the barrel towards her stomach, a startled Rose hollered, "Oh my God!"

"Listen flower, I will not hurt you, but I let you into my home, I need to be sure you are not some undercover cop or prostitute, because I run a very successful business and the last thing I need is some flower trying to impersonate a civilian in an attempt to bring down my operation." Samuel said as Rose continued to stare down the barrel of the gun. She could not focus.

"I swear to God, I am just a caseworker." Rose, stammering once again.

Staring into her eyes for a brief second, Samuel then released the trigger, taking a long sigh, "Great, now let's talk about Irving." He smiled, returning the pistol to the rear of his chair. Robert lit a blunt, placing it between Samuel's wide lips, his eyes lowering.

"Sure," complied Rose, her hands shaking, making it difficult for her to hold her pen.

"Calm down, flower, we good now," Samuel whispered, taking another puff. But Rose could not calm down as she fought back tears, wondering if today would be her last to live.

"You want to know about the boy? Well, I met him when he was just three years old..."

Flashback

I remember like it was yesterday, that blessed day in 1984; the day started with a celebration, Reverend Jesse Jackson made it to The White House to meet President Reagan—a great day for the culture. After traveling to Syria to rescue Robert Goodman who was taken hostage, we weren't much to the White man then, but one of ours had made it. It felt like a new age was upon us, the Nuclear Age as Reagan liked to call it, but also, the age of the Black man.

It was never enough to learn the culture just from the television box—shit, they tell you what they want, not what you need to hear, not about the genocide, not about the plans to keep the Black man destitute, not about the issues plaguing our communities designed by the White man. Who you think brought the drugs here? But, see, we like to act like that's not the issue, making the issue the fact that the drugs remained here and we're allowing ourselves to die. I always tell the young boys, you got to learn from the *original gangstas* out on retirement; men like us, we don't sugar coat shit. I lost my legs in the streets and made good on my word that I would never allow my men to suffer the same fate, so when Jesse made it, the culture made it—and it was time to be a part of the solution.

The year before we had Junior in space, too, another moment in history, and as we continued to rise and make our mark, I lined my pockets from the eight balls I sold to them White boys up in Westchester. I then took my money and bought an apartment building offering section 8 housing for my impoverished brothers and sisters, providing them a place to lay their head at night and encouraging them down in the lobby about the importance of work and making an honest living.

I couldn't do much with the crack heads and the lazy folks who did not see it prudent to work, they were not going to devalue my investment, and so I had to teach them a lesson by sending them all out into the world to continue facing hardship until they were ready to change and then came Michelle. Michelle was slim, looking like she weighed about 110 pounds, with her box braids and a stank attitude. My boys kept an eye on her, as did I, but never to entertain her sexually, she was not my type. When I lost my legs in '77, I had to rethink the women I was going to allow in my life; me, I take a special kind of lady.

Seeing Michelle every day coming by the building just to hang out upset me, she was serving no purpose, only making my place look cheap, like a hooker lane, especially on the days when she brought her friends, and so I told her to go on, get going, don't anybody want no lackadaisical, unmotivated woman around here. We had women going to school—hustling to get their G.E.D. Pregnant women enrolling in college, working on the side, Michelle had nothing, and by nothing, I mean internal. She had no ambition, which only led to her being problematic and landing herself into the wrong hands time and time again.

I moved stealthy, I saw it all, from the women outside taking beatings to the men inside having sex with other men in the basement but returning home to their baby mommas. I did something for my community, I did what a lot of men don't do, but I had to ask myself, as I felt myself getting sicker by the day, who would continue this path I have created? Expand it, grow it, invest in other properties for our people so they wouldn't have to live in shelters or sleep under bridges? I waited a long time until I opened my door one day and was surprised to have seen Michelle making her way upstairs.

"What are you doing here, woman?" I asked her, because she knew better than to be there, surprised to see me. "I   changed my life, Sammy, I'm a mother now," she told me. I couldn't believe my ears, who would impregnate Michelle? Had to be a whole fool with nothing to lose, I thought. But I was happy she was a mother, her skin was glowing, she looked healthy, responsible, and I guessed she was doing well. I wouldn't allow my building manager to rent to her, so she had to have found her a man with some leg to stand on.

"Residing with whom?" I asked, only curious.

"Houston—Marvin Houston," she said proudly, almost as though she too couldn't believe he was with her. I did not know of this Marvin, but I disliked him already for bringing Michelle into my sector. But I decided to allow it, only instructed my henchmen to keep a close eye on her, and they did. One morning, as I was making my rounds, I found myself on the eleventh floor, I usually never make it past the seventh floor. But that day I did and as I rolled and Robert paced, we heard the cries of a young boy. I stopped my chair because I needed to listen keenly to determine where the sounds were coming from, and then we watched as the door flung open and Irving, a three-year-old boy, was thrown into the hallway and kicked in the stomach by his mother with the heel of her shoe, the door locking after she went back in. I never heard a cry that painful, that strong, that sharp. Robert wanted to do something, but I blocked him with my hand, watching that kid, I needed to see what he was going to do and you know what? After a few seconds, he stopped crying, rolling over, he sat along the wall staring blankly at the front door.

Robert knitted his brows. "He retarded, you think, OG?" he asked me, but I told him, "No, son, not even close." I rolled my way onto the elevator after instructing Robert to bring me the boy.

By the time they made their way downstairs, I was waiting for almost half an hour.

"What the hell took you so long?" I asked Robert. His face now covered in welts, "You let that toddler beat you?" I teased. Robert closed the door behind him and placed the boy down, he was hollering, kicking, biting, and would not stay still, I wondered if I made a mistake. As he sat on the floor, I looked him in his eyes, the little nigga had heart, he stopped crying.

"I am going to teach you how to change the world, how to help our people no longer be mentally enslaved, obedient to a system designed to aid in our demise and keep us as failures. I am going to teach you how to be a man of wisdom, logic, and understanding, do you hear me?" I told him, and as the words left my mouth, although only three, I could see him watching as my lips moved, his eyes widening and his face unreadable. He was not simply taking it in, he was allowing my words to resonate within him and that's when I knew I had found him.

No one looked for him, which disappointed me further, they did not deserve him, that Marvin and Michelle, the mother I understood, but the father, had it been me in my prime, I would have put money on his head—Black men raise your kings. Marvin was a father but not a dad. As the night went on and the boy sat on the sofa, he cried and cried and cried.

"Can we give him some water before he gets dehydrated and passes out on the damn couch, OG?" Robert asked me.

"Why are you acting like a dumb nigga? Do you know how long that boy would have to cry before his tears were to cause him to get dehydrated?" I shouted. "Let him cry!" I said switching on the television. That night he cried himself to sleep and as he slept, I read to him. The next morning Robert returned him home, claiming to have found him wandering the halls. Michelle simply dragged him inside, never questioning where he was, with whom, for how long or even how Robert knew that to be her son. I heard she grabbed him inside so hard, she hurt his arm.

A few months later, night after night he was coming down to the apartment, his clothes filthy, his hair uncombed, but I did not mind that, I am not a woman to care for his outside appearance, I am a man and as such, I fed his mind. Molded his character, we read books for hours on end while my phone buzzed, telling me a hit had been carried through. Our nexus was growing stronger day by day. At just three-years-old the boy was pronouncing words and solving math equations, I was instilling values, the importance of respecting the female mind and body. Aiding his mother in her day-to-day tasks—taking out the garbage, lifting the groceries, helping around the house, being the man of the house.

By the time he was five, we weren't seeing him as often, only about three times a week, maybe less because sometimes I had to handle my live wires; slowly looking to transition them from the street life once they made enough money to retire and not get caught. But he had a preeminent vocabulary, all from reading, no television, and conversations he sat amongst when my brothers from the street came to visit for poker. The boy was learning, he was growing, and I knew he was abused, but I taught him how to be mentally strong, that physical shit doesn't last long. He boxed with Robert, sometimes with me, he was growing so fast, we were eye level by the time he was six. But we taught him never to box on the street, never to fight the bullies back, and to remain humble.

As he grew, he learned things, caught on fast, and when the dealers would ask him to steal snacks from the bodegas, they knew better than to have me find out. Everybody knew he was my little man; he was respected and knew that my home was his home. That boy reads better than any fifteen-year-old I know, he is smart.

Rose continued to listen far more intrigued now.

"I need to get him from that house, but the system just won't allow me to do my job," she cried.

"That's incorrect, the system will allow you to do your job as long as your job does not exhaust the resources needed for children outside of the African-American communities. Ask yourself, how many Black children did the government aid these past few months?" Samuel asked, reclining in his chair.

"I am honestly not sure."

"There is your answer. But I am telling you, he is going to be great, but he needs nurturing and that is one thing I cannot provide." Samuel said.

Rose was now deep in thought.

Leaving the housing projects, Rose dialed her sister-in-law, praying she would answer.

"Hello beautiful," she sang. But Rose was in no mood for prattling.

"Marley, I need a favor," she begged, cutting straight to the point. Marley took a long, devastating sigh.

"It's nice to hear from you, too, I hope your evening is going well. Oh, Ryan, your brother, he is well. The children, they are well too, Rose, thank you so much for asking. Favor? Oh, wow, perhaps, how can I help?" she spoke sarcastically.

"Are you done?" Rose asked, growing impatient as she stood in front of her car.

"No, are you done? Rose, I do wish you would reach out more and not simply because you need something. This divorce has got you so messed up that you've completely shut us out, and it isn't fair. Michael still calls Ryan to discuss playoffs and rock bands and I can't even get you to be excited about attending a stupid dinner," she vented.

"Of course, he still calls Ryan, Jesus, Michael isn't the one who wanted the divorce, Marley, it was me!" she shouted.

"Why on earth would you end your marriage just to become a single bitter woman in her late twenties?"

"Because we grew apart Marley, and the verbal abuse was getting to be way too much," Rose sighed. "Oh, you're too tall, Rose, you should be knocked down a few inches, lower your voice, just because you look like your father doesn't mean you have to sound like him too," she mocked Michael, the memories all coming back. "Look, I have to go, forget about the favor." She hung up her Motorola flip phone, pushing down the antenna as she made her way into the vehicle where she sobbed.

Inside the two-bedroom apartment, Rose kicked off her shoes by the door before making her way to the bar where she poured herself a glass of vodka, neat. She was slowly beginning to regret having a bar at home, but the apartment Rose and Michael utilized for special occasions meant having a completely filled bar for their guests. At that moment, as she drew the shades covering the enlarged windows that granted her a view just above Brooklyn Bridge, she wondered if she was making a mistake.

6

That morning Marvin took Irving to breakfast, Irving reading and Marvin watching the game. Afterward, in Payless, Marvin purchased him four new pairs of shoes, and in Walmart bought him all new pants, shirts, undergarments, and toiletries. Marvin planned on asking Nyema later on what was to be used for the infection growing to the rear of his head, it sickened him to see the bald patches and it did not help that other parents were staring at him with disdain. Irving did not notice; he was however feeling tired as they made their way to four different local furniture stores where Marvin purchased different pieces of furniture. Mad at Nyema for he was clueless about what was truly needed or even style for that matter. Irving, trailing behind him, had changed into some of his new clothes, he was slowly beginning to look like a new boy.

Irving did not provide any input and he did not speak unless spoken to, buried in his book, turning the pages to new adventures. Just then Marvin snatched the book from him as they stood in the children's furniture section and demanded

Irving provide some kind of feedback or at least pretend to be interested.

"Goodness, can you at least act as if you care?" Marvin pleaded with his son.

"May I have my book back?" questioned Irving, staring into his father's eyes, but Marvin was not going to allow his son to be socially awkward.

"No," he said firmly, sucking his teeth whilst holding the book in his hand. Irving, walking around the store, was not enticed by anything, he was missing the characters from the story he had been reading.

"Can we go home?" he requested.

"No, we need to get you a nightstand, and do you want one of those racing car bed things? I mean you have to meet me halfway here, I don't know what I'm doin' and you don't even talk, like what the fuck!" he shouted, growing impatient. But Irving was not accustomed to this, for years he and his father had not exchanged more than a sentence and that was only on Sundays when they went to church. This being the case, Irving did not know how to handle their newfound relationship, although Marvin simply thought it would have been easier. Bending down to face him, Marvin took a long sigh.

"Look kid, iont want you going to the state and all that, this lady ain't come back yet, but she might, soon, so until then we gotta just try to get along, alright? When we get home you can meet your sisters properly and I can maybe get some pizza so you can live like a normal kid, aight? I apologize that I wasn't like this before, I wasn't the father you needed me to be." Marvin laughed, thinking to himself his confession was merely falling on deaf ears, rubbing his head he stood, "Yo, I don't even know why I'm saying all this nice shit, you don't understand anyway, you're a kid. But listen, pick a bed so we can go!" he said. Irving did not respond; however, he comprehended his father just fine, yet found no room in his heart to care and so, he pointed to the first bed within his view.

"That one, can we go now?" turning, walking towards the

register. Marvin watched him as he waved for an associate.

That evening when they arrived home Marvin was surprised to smell that Nyema had been cooking but figured perhaps there would be, again, no food for him and Irving. Shutting the door behind them, her mother approached quickly, shouting obscenities in her native language. She knew he understood nothing when she spoke Kiswahili.

"Kisingizio huzuni kwa mtu," her fingers waving in his face, Irving snatching his book, running upstairs to hide.

"Una mtoto juu ya binti yangu," she continued shouting.

Nyema now stood next to her, nodding her head, translating, "She's telling you, 'You are a sad excuse for a man, having a baby on me.' You need to hear this Marvin," she said. Her mother continuing to shout, clicking her tongue as she resisted the urge to smack Marvin.

"Dey boy! Dey boy cannot stay here!" she shouted, now in English. A traditional woman, Ms. Margaret always wore a long black dress called a buibui and her head almost always covered with the hijabu, which she only removed when inside of her home or that of her daughters'. Marvin continued to listen,

"You want my daughter, my daughter to raise your sex child? You must be crazy! Tuh, wewe mwana wa Malaya. Naweza kukuua, wewe ni mpumbavu na aibu," she continued as Marvin now wondered where his children were.

"Nyema where are the girls?" he questioned, whirling around to face her as her mothers' eyes widened—appalled that he would ignore her.

"Aye! You cheat, you have sex with someone else, you did my daughter wrong! No children until you stay and you fix things with dey wife, your wife, my daughter, you fix things with dey wife!" she repeated as she stomped her way through the front door, Nyema stood watching him, waiting for a response.

Rubbing his temple, Marvin, unfortunately, did not care to explain himself any further, he was trying to move on. "Nyema, his mother is dead! I understand you're mad, but we need to make some progress to move past this, we have children to think about. They need to grow up together, like, yo, I made a mistake," he quarreled.

"She came here! Okay? I did not tell you, but the night she died, she came here and she looked so hurt and disappointed that you had a wife and children!" Nyema sobbed, "Which means she had no idea. You kept our family a secret from a woman you call a mistake? And so what if she's dead, I am not a fool, that is what you do not understand. Marvin, you understand nothing!" she screamed, crying, her face drenched in tears. "You are disgusting. I see the bruises on him, I see the infection on his head, I see the neglect, but you did that out of guilt. The only reason you're so concerned and attentive now is that you no longer have to feel guilty about living a double life. You don't have to blame him anymore, you don't have to hate him anymore because you think you can just push him on us, on me! On your daughters, to alleviate your guilt. You are a selfish human being because that burden you were carrying slipping between homes at night that you now feel relieved of, was just transferred over to my shoulders to carry and I did nothing to deserve that!" she cried. "So you don't understand shit!" she screamed, breathing heavily.

Marvin knew she was correct, but he was not in the mood to quarrel.

"I just want my family back, we can order pizza," he said, stepping past her. "Oh, and please tell your mother I want my children home now! They all have school in the morning, and did you clean out the den?" Nyema stood, removing her apron she stepped outside, slamming the door behind her. Marvin following her as he wondered where she was going, but Nyema was infuriated and feeling unappreciated. she could not let him see her cry any further. She went for a walk around the neighborhood. Marvin prayed she would be calm by the time she returned as he phoned her mother demanding his children be returned home.

Sunday morning

It was a long week and although Nyema and the children had not returned since her walk, both Irving and Marvin took in the furniture as it came day by day. Each morning as he dropped his son off to school and headed to work to clean, Marvin pondered why he was so calm and at ease. He found himself enjoying the responsibility of truly having to raise his son, although he wondered why he was never asked by Irving to assist with homework or make small talk. Irving was militant, adhering to a strict schedule: walking home from school, homework, dinner, books, shower, sleep. He barely laughed, he barely smiled. Although he was no longer teased for his clothing, the children at school found something new to tease him about—*his dead mother*—all day long.

"I heard her brain splattered all along the concrete."

"No, my dad said she was falling and then splat! She died instantly, her buggers everywhere," a young lady snapping her fingers for extra emphasis.

"No one dies like splat! They die while falling, you have no mommy nerd!" another boy cried.

"His head is nasty; he has a disease!"

"Your mother was weak for killing herself, maybe you'll jump next," said another.

Irving did nothing but listen, he was not going to allow children to get the best of him, taking him out of character; mature for his age, these were his thoughts. The children around him were fools, mere degenerates as he remained studious, consistently getting good grades; he even pegged his father for a moron but dared not tell him, pretending to respect his authority.

Once inside, Marvin bellowed for his son. "Irving! Get down here," he called.

Irving made his way down the stairs, a new book in his left hand. "Yes?"

"Come on down here, we're gonna watch the all-star game, put the book away. You want Chinese or pizza tonight, buddy?" Marvin asked, making his way into the living room as he turned on the television. Irving rolled his eyes, he hated this, the sad attempt at bonding his father tried every evening. Marvin now snapped the top off his beer, looking at Irving he asked, "Want one?" extending it to him. Irving politely declined.

"Aight, but you don't know what you're missing, man." Taking a seat and tapping the empty space next to him. "Come on, sit down," he said, lifting the book his son was reading: *Lincoln*, by Gore Vidal.

"What is this shit?" he asked, tossing the book onto the floor, "Why must you always look so grumpy?" Marvin turned to ask him. Irving was now seated on the sofa watching as the commercials played.

"I believe the noun you're looking for is a curmudgeon. May we order pizza, pepperoni?" Irving asked, growing excited. The one thing he had come to enjoy about living with his father was eating unhealthily.

"Don't be a weirdo, say grumpy like a normal seven-year-old. Speaking of which, where the hell are you getting these depressed looking ass books?" Marvin observed, turning to face him.

"The cubby," Irving responded innocently.

"The one in the girl's room?"

"Yes," replied Irving, his eyes to the television. The game started, but Marvin could not help but wonder, *did the girls ever read these books?*

Convinced his father had forgotten his request, Irving looking up to him, whispered, "Pizza." Marvin quickly got up to dial delivery.

One week later as Rose made her way into work settling into her cubicle, she was anxious. Reggie had taken a vacation and was out of the office for a week—she desperately needed to speak with him. Watching as he made his way inside, she locked her computer, her loafers moving swiftly to his office before anyone else could enter.

"Hey," he looked to her, frightened. "My oh my you move

quickly, I haven't gotten stable yet, um, is everything okay?" he asked chuckling nervously removing his blazer and placing it to the rear of his chair.

"No, things are not okay. Did we close the investigation on Irving because we reached our quota for Africa-American children this quarter?" Rose asked with her arms folded, deciding it best to get straight to the point.

Reggie took a long breath. "It's far more complicated than that," nonchalantly speaking. Working.

"No, I need to know the truth," Rose demanded.

"Rose, you are one of my favorites here, but you truly have to stop this. Will it make you feel better if I sent Alissa out to do a house call this week? Perhaps check in and make sure things are going smoothly at the Houston residence?" Reggie asked, annoyed now by her persistence.

"Oh, my goodness, yes, please," remarked Rose, releasing a deep sigh as she now felt relieved. "But I need to know, are we limited on how many Black children we can take to a category one?"

Reggie looking at her, pity in his eyes, "Rose, unfortunately, yes. We cannot save everyone, and in this line of work you have to know when to detach yourself because every child is not going to be helped. There are many racial injustices in this world and it is not just within the prison systems for adolescents and adults, it begins as early as childhood," he sympathized.

"How many?"

"That truly does not matter."

"Reggie, please, how many?"

"As of now, fourteen; that's three, maybe four per quarter," he admitted.

Rose took a seat. "There's no way, just last month alone we took about thirty reports for neglect in some African-American communities, what have we since then done with those cases?" she questioned.

"This is not a discussion you and I should be having. But off the record, as a friend, I will say we set aside some case files to make room for the ones that technically matter," he said. "In those communities, Rose, let's face it, they don't want to be helped, almost 64% of those calls are fake—father and mother quarrel and then mother call CPS or the neighbors call, our phone number has become the *revenge line* instead of what it is truly intended for. A lot of those calls are from people crying wolf and we cannot invest our resources on wasted cases," he continued.

"But what about Irving? His case is not insignificant, there have been two incidents that we know of, both of which our office was present. That has to count for something. I have category one cases on my desk filled with Latino and Caucasian children, why aren't the African-American kids—the ones who truly need it—making it to a category one?" Rose said, her tone increasing.

"This conversation is over, Rose," Reggie dismissed, the bags under his eyes heavy from what appeared to be lack of sleep. Throwing his glasses on, he redirected his attention to his computer screen, but Rose was not through.

"The state is turning us into monsters, and if we are receiving funding for children we are not truly helping that is not only unethical but illegal," she continued.

"It is the cost of doing business, now get out please. We will not discuss this any further," he shouted, infuriated now that Rose was becoming so inquisitive.

As Rose sat in her cubicle contemplating her next course of action, she dialed the one person she'd fought to avoid.

"Hello," he answered.

Rose sat checking periodically to see whether or not someone was approaching as she crouched behind her desk, whispering.

"Ryan, I need to ask you a favor."

Shocked now, realizing who he was speaking to, Ryan said, "Rose! Rose! Oh man, are you okay? Can we talk? Why are you whispering?"

Rose grew impatient as she closed her eyes, praying he would simply concentrate and allow her to put forth her request,

"Ryan, I don't have time to really chit-chat, I just need to ask that you counsel a young boy for me. I know we haven't spoken that much, but I need this favor," she emphasized.

"Rose, this is insane. Is he one of your cases?" Ryan asked, beginning to worry.

"No, not anymore, but Ryan, this kid needs help and he won't get it where he is now, but my office won't allow us to assist him unless we can prove he's a category one case," she informed him.

"We have to discuss this later, but Rose, call me when you're free!" ...and just like that Rose received the dial tone.

On Wednesday, as Irving turned the doorknob to let himself inside, he noticed Nyema in the kitchen chopping up what appeared to be baby carrots and tossing them into a large steaming pot of water. The aroma arousing his nostrils as he began untying his shoelaces, he did not see it prudent to disturb her, but overhearing the door shut she called to him,

"Young man," she bellowed from the kitchen. Irving, who had been stepping lightly upstairs, turned to return to the hallway.

"Yes," he whispered. Nyema had returned home that morning where she found old pizza boxes, empty beer bottles, and cans along with unclean trousers and a pungent odor; the source of which still remained a mystery. She had cleaned, mopped, dusted, removed the garbage and vacuumed the carpets. It was devastating to see her art had been relocated to the basement, tossed into the corner like a pile of rubbish; Bordon did not mind as he found himself occupying only 70% of the space.

Nyema remained quiet, waiting for Irving to make his way to her, but he did not do so; Irving remained standing in the hallway, his back against the wall, awaiting further instructions.

Peeping her head into the hallway, Nyema stated, "When I call to you, you come. Understand? Have a seat. Are you hungry?" she asked kindly.

Irving, feeling apprehensive whispered, "No," but he was lying.

"You spent all day at school and you're not hungry?" she confirmed, finding his statement to be false. Nyema stared into his eyes where she saw a lost and confused boy. The girls were now returning home laughing as they entered inside, dropping their bookbags to the floor, kicking off their shoes and racing into the kitchen where they gave their mother a tight hug.

Asha, eleven and Amara, nine, had kinky hair braided into ponytails with beads that clacked when they walked, their skin as dark as chocolate and their eyes a hazel brown. Asha wore braces and dreaded eating; she would cringe with every bite and her sister constantly teasing her. Walking past Irving they both turned to look at him, astonished by how greatly he favored their father.

"What's your name?" Asha asked as she smiled rocking her body back and forth. She stood in front of her mother. Irving looking back at her, her mother and her sister as they all stood opposite him, wondering to himself whether or not he was the enemy, if so, why the interest in making his acquaintance and so, he remained silent.

Nyema intervened, "Irving is his name and Irving, this is Asha and Amara, your sisters, and girls, this is your younger brother," she said. Amara turned to face her, tugging on her apron as she looked up to her.

"But Mommy, where did he come from?" she asked, her voice soft. Nyema could not bring herself to reply, she simply suggested the children wash their hands before taking a seat at the dining table where she served them cookies and milk.

"Come, come now, no more questions, you all sit down for your snacks," she instructed. The children all did as they were told. Both Amara and Asha noticing the ringworm to the rear of Irving's head, looking away in disgust and whispering to one another, chuckling. Irving did not care, he simply ate and then removed himself—the sound of the wooden chair scratching along the floor startling Nyema; her back was turned as she continued working on dinner. The room was quiet as the girls and Nyema all watching him until he was out of view—walking upstairs into his room where he sat on the floor, pulling his notebooks from his book bag to begin his homework.

By evening Marvin was standing outside preparing to turn the key to his house, inside he could hear Asha and Amara quarreling over the television remote, this excited him and he raced inside, both the girls sprinting over to hug him as he knelt to grab them, kissing his daughters profusely.

"Daddy!" both girls yelled, smiling as Nyema stood by the kitchen threshold, preparing to clean the dishes she used to prepare dinner. Wiping her hands as she lean along the door frame watching them, their smiles genuine, the family she had come to know and love was all there before her. Marvin now stood, asking the girls to return to the living room so that he may speak to their mother alone.

The sweet smell of the soup she prepared now filled the walls of their home, inside felt perfect as she extended her hands to offer Marvin a hug and a kiss on the lips—surprising him.

"Is everything okay?" he asked, worriedly.

"Things are fine, go get cleaned up, dinner will be served in a few." Marvin decided to not question her further making his way upstairs searching for Irving who was seated by the corner of his bed, his knees to his chest, a book open in front of him, reading quietly.

Marvin entered the room where he took a deep breath before asking, "Boy, did you eat?" placing one hand on his hip—Irving looking up, nodding his head yes before resuming reading *Lincoln*. Marvin was concerned, noticing that his son was anti-social and not as engaging as he would have imagined.

"After dinner we gonna toss a ball in the back yard, understand? Burn some of the calories," he said sternly. Irving paid him no mind, "Boy! You hear me?" he shouted, startling Irving,

"Yes," Irving whispered, looking up at him.

"All these damn books and shit," Marvin mumbled as he

walked away.

By 6 p.m. Marvin, Asha, and Amara all gathered around the kitchen table where they feasted on the soup Nyema prepared along with baked bread and corn muffins. Marvin noticed Nyema taking her time to serve Irving his food, he too sat along the table while the girls ate and discussed their school day. Irving, on the other hand, remained quiet, patiently waiting, but Marvin did not question Nyema, he simply remained grateful that his family was finally together.

"Nye, we need to get something for his head," Marvin told her, Nyema agreeing as she realized the infection needed to be treated.

"I can get the lime and blue tomorrow afternoon on my way home from work." She smiled.

Marvin desperately wanted the evening to end, the children to go to bed, all for the chance to have a long talk with his wife, who he noticed was acting all too strange. She was always attentive; however, he wondered what could have possibly changed in only a week and a few days? There was no way she was simply accepting Irving without any further stipulations. A few moments later Nyema placed a plate before Irving and shortly thereafter, herself. Quietly everyone ate until there came a knock at the door, Marvin arose swiftly, he expected no one, advising the children and his wife to remain seated. Opening the screen door, he noticed a young woman standing outside holding a briefcase, a pen, and a pad—her brunette colored hair in a tight bun.

"Hello! My name is Alissa from Child Protective Services," she smiled, lifting her badge. "I was wondering if I could come in and possibly take a look around?" This bothered Marvin as he wondered why she was so chirpy; unlocking the screen door he invited the woman inside, motioning for her to take a seat in the living room where he joined her. Preparing to sit, Alissa dusted the crumbs from the sofa before taking a seat, where she opened her briefcase and began removing papers and folders.

"Is Irving here?" she asked politely. Marvin headed into the kitchen to fetch him, the girls and Nyema remained quiet; Irving stepped his way into the living room where Alissa greeted him with a smile.

"Hello there, Irving," she said, extending her hand to make his acquaintance. Although Irving reciprocated, he was in no mood to speak to the woman or anyone for that matter. Both Marvin and Irving took a seat on the chairs adjacent to her, their backs to the television.

"So, this is simply a regular routine visit following recent circumstances, and I am just going to ask a few questions to get an idea of how things are going here now." Smiling. both Irving and Marvin nodding their heads in agreement. "Okay, so Irving can you tell me how you're feeling?" she asked pleasantly.

"Fine." Marvin looking down at him.

"Sir, do you mind if I speak with Irving alone?" Alissa asked Marvin, who shot her a loathsome look before standing to make his way back into the kitchen where he stood with his feet apart, arms folded.

"So, Irving, tell me, how is school?"

"Fine."

Alissa taking notes, "Okay, are you happy living here with your dad and your sisters?" Irving did not respond. "Irving, you look clean, you're wearing nice clothes, are you uncomfortable? Is someone hurting you? You can talk to me." she added.

"I am fine." Irving said just above a whisper.

"Irving you don't have to say you're fine if you are not, I am here to help. Are you happy?" she asked again, this time concerned as Irving stopped making eye contact, his eyes falling to the floor.

"I am not happy, but I am not sad." he responded.

"Okay, so what are you?" Alissa asked, enticed now as he began speaking.

"I am growing accustomed," he whispered, biting the inside of his right cheek. His mouth twisting as his legs swung from the chair.

Alissa laughed. "Wow, you're a sharp one aren't you, where

did you learn that one?" she asked with intrigue.

"Mr. Samuel," he responded, his face lighting up with glee, smiling as she noticed the spaces between his teeth. Overhearing him, Marvin went stomping inside,

"Who the hell is Samuel?" he shouted. Alissa turned to face him.

"Sir, please, you cannot interrupt like that, I will have to continue speaking with him." As Marvin and Alissa exchanged words speaking over one another, Irving scurried past his father, making his way back into the kitchen where he took a seat to finish his meal, Asha staring at him.

"Mom, what's wrong with him?" she asked, afraid.

"I want you out of my house," Marvin shouted to Alissa, his anger stemming from the night Irving was caught kissing Kevin, the flashback giving him goosebumps, and now Samuel, he had no recollection of who that was, never hearing the name before because he was only familiar with the street name the OG went by, Mido. As Alissa took her leave, tripping out of the front door, Marvin slammed it behind her and made his way into the kitchen where he demanded that Irving go upstairs. Overhearing this, Alissa stood outside, trembling as she attempted to dial into the office, her fingers misdialing numbers, she only assumed Marvin was going to scold his child. "Shit." She whispered, dropping the phone, bending to pick it up, praying it was still working.

Trailing behind Irving, Marvin stumbled before reaching the top. Irving was petrified, unclear of what was to happen next. He stood by the threshold of his bedroom door watching his father retrieve his belt from the master bedroom. Irving fleeing into his room, but not quick enough as Marvin stepped behind him, folding the belt whipping him—Irving wailed; the metal from the buckle of the belt stinging him. Nyema made her way to the top of the stairs, grabbing Marvin by the hand to stop him.

"Jesus, he's a child!" she screamed. "You're hitting him too hard, you're going to hurt him," she cried. Marvin grabbed her by her collar, pulling her close.

"Don't you dare come between me and my boy when I'm scolding him, you understand me?" he grumbled before releasing her.

Standing inside and slamming the door shut in her face, Marvin turned to Irving who was now weeping uncontrollably. "Who the fuck is Samuel huh, you like you some niggas?" he shouted.

Nyema sat atop the stairs and listened as the belt whipped against Irving's skin, the screaming of the young boy giving her chills. As Marvin thrashed his son, oblivious to his own strength, he pondered to himself if he was truly angry, if so, why? Marvin whipped and whipped, the welts now turning to gashes as he feared the worst; a gay son. Although he never admitted it, that night in the park left him scared. Once he concluded, Irving crawled under his bed sobbing extensively, Marvin could not have prepared himself for what was to happen next. Listening as the doors banged, the girls holding onto one another standing in the kitchen as they cleared the table.

"Open the door, police!" a man shouted from the outside as the banging continued. Nyema rushed to the ground floor where she ran into the kitchen, grabbing her daughters and opening the basement door, she instructed them to go downstairs and stay with Mr. Bordon. Forgetting the belt in his hand, Marvin made his way downstairs, unlocking the door. In rushed three police officers, Rose, Alissa, Reggie, and another gentleman from their office. Rose stepping swiftly into the house.

"Where is he?" she demanded while briefly exchanging a look with Marvin. After frantically searching the ground floor, she began making her way upstairs as the commotion continued. The officers insisted that Marvin and Nyema take a seat in the living room where they awaited questioning. Rose located Irving under his bed—his uniform torn, the cuts in his skin bleeding through his pants.

Softly, she called to him, "Irving, it's me, Rose. Remember me?" Irving slowly turned to face her, his thumb in his mouth as the tears continued falling from his eyes; he could not understand what he had done wrong. He was afraid now to face any new adult as they had all proven themselves to be malevolent. Rose cried as Alissa stood at the top of the stairs, her jaw-dropping, watching Rose lie on the floor speaking to Irving under his bed. He remained stationed despite her constant begging, there was nothing getting him to move. She could not bring herself to tug on him as she decided on another method.

"Irving, I am going to take you to see Mr. Samuel," she said, smiling, and that was it, Irving crawled his way out from under the bed, flying almost, thrusting his arms around her neck tightly. The open wounds along his body burning, blood stains left on the floor, the boy quivering—Rose sobbed and Alissa stood wiping the tears from her eyes as Rose wrapped his legs around her torso. The evening moving slowly; she made her way down the stairs and out the front door, burying his head into her chest, careful to keep him from staring at his father. Marvin fought the police and the other men from CPS as he shouted for them to release him.

"Get off of me! That's my son!" he fought. Nyema could not believe her eyes as he behaved boisterously, making it past the little gates, watching as Rose placed Irving in the backseat of her vehicle, Alissa beside him as he lay down, closing his eyes to sleep.

The hospital waiting room was in an uproar, everyone speaking simultaneously as they argued with Rose.

"No, you cannot be granted provisional custody, that is not how this works," stated Reggie, taking a seat on one of the iron chairs. "He is going to be transferred to the state like every other child that's been removed from their primary residence, and for the record, what we did here today is never to be done again," he emphasized. It was after hours; the sun had gone down and it was time to make a decision on where Irving would be kept during their category one investigation upon his release.

Rose insisted. "Listen, I spearheaded this and if it wasn't for me, Alissa probably wouldn't have gone there in the first place. Reggie, you were going to put his file away and who knows, by then he probably would have been dead."

"Rose, while I do understand your stance on this, we cannot allow you to take him home, we will have to authorize his release to the state foster facility where he will remain for the duration of this investigation."

"I promised him, Samuel," Rose said sadly, everyone now turning to face her.

"Who is Samuel?" the room filled with muttering.

"Off the record!" she shouted, pointing her finger at everyone to ensure their compliance. Everyone nodded.

"He's some kingpin who raised him, I mean, it's like he imprinted himself on Irving and now he's the only person he wants. Believe me, I know it sounds crazy," Rose continued as she noticed the expression changing on everyone's face.

"So you want us to do what exactly? Send the boy to live with a drug dealer?" Reggie shouted, the murmuring continued.

"Listen, I know this is far—fetched, but this is a man he knows and respects. I feel like to establish some form of trust we should at least bring him to Samuel, I think that's a way better place for him than a foster home facility," Rose pleaded.

"Irving does show signs of depression, I don't believe it's mild, either," added Alissa. "However, Rose, I am sorry, but I have to disagree with this idea. The facility is equipped to handle situations like this, they have psychologists on call who can aid him if and when he needs it." Just then a male nurse came pushing through the glass doors, rushing inside he shouted.

"The young boy is having a seizure!" Everyone arose in fear, racing down the hallway into the room where Irving had been resting after having his wounds treated. Rose panicked as the nurses raced inside, turning him on his side helplessly watching the foam leave his mouth, noticing the back of his head where the infection continued to spread, she was sobbing.

An hour later, Rose, Reggie, and Alissa, all who had chosen to stay behind, were advised by a doctor after being instructed to return to the waiting room—it was a long night.

"Doctor, is he going to be okay?"

"The young man was definitely poisoned," the female doctor responded. A horrified Rose took a seat now, Reggie rubbing her back as Alissa continued to listen,

"The poison used was a small dose of ricin. It is usually hard to detect, but whoever gave him this served him in some form of liquid; he was vomiting soup. He will be monitored over the next few days, the dosage was not lethal, I assume whoever gave him this wanted to do so over a period of time. My guess, to make it appear as though the boy was simply getting sick," she said before concluding. "You all should head home and get some rest. You've done amazing work today."

"Thank you so much for listening to me, you saved his life," Rose stammered, speaking to Alissa.

"Honestly Rose, it was you. Had you not suggested a home visit I would have assumed things were fine. You really saved this kid," Alissa tapping her on the shoulder. "I'm going to head home, you should too, get some rest. You did well today." She proudly exited the waiting room.

Part 2

1991

R ose was nervous entering the courthouse, her documents in hand as she fumbled to keep them from falling. She was careful not to make eye contact, she had spent so much time in and out of court over the past two years that she was becoming a familiar face, one whom many parents did not favor. Although comfortable, the loafers on her feet were causing them to sweat, or perhaps it was simply her nerves. Always dreading these days when it was her against him. Stepping inside the empty courtroom, taking a seat at the plaintiff's table on her right, Rose removed her documents; bending down she found a run in her stockings, bringing her to panic considering the trial was set to begin in only a few minutes. She knew the importance of presenting herself in a professional manner—that meant appearance.

Distracted now, she fidgeted at the table for more than fifteen minutes hearing as the doors began to slam, entering were the bailiff and the defendant: Marvin Houston. Rose sat upright as Marvin entered, seeing him once every nine months was proving itself to be rather redundant. Two years later and they had still not come to a resolution that Rose found suitable. Reggie disliked trial days, especially for Rose, when she returned to the office she was never the same, something about her was always off—unhappy. Marvin did not look at Rose for he detested her, thinking of the rest he would take once he headed home. Marvin was exhausted,

"All rise for the honorable Judge Sherman," the bailiff bellowed—Rose and Marvin stood. The court recorder also made her way inside, taking her seat nearest the witness stand.

As the judge took her seat, she began by saying, "I hope we can reach some kind of a resolution today, lady and gentleman." Sluggishly, swerving her chair to face them as she removed the lint from her robe. "Shall we begin? Plaintiff?" she said, turning to face Rose.

"Your honor, as you know Irving has been in my care for the past two years, provisional custody. I am here today to request full custody of Irving Houston. I have enough evidence to prove that I am an adequate caretaker by providing up to date medical records, school progress reports, and notes from a licensed psychiatrist to show Irving's improvement, both emotionally and mentally, since being in my care," spoke an assured Rose.

"Bailiff," Judge Sherman called. The bailiff made his way to Rose, who handed him an envelope,

"Remove the documents, Ms. Rose, we don't need the envelope," Judge Sherman continued—Rose fiddled with the papers as she trembled, removing them from the manila envelope.

"I am sorry, here you go," she smiled nervously. She absolutely despised public speaking. The bailiff handed the judge the documents Rose had provided him, a brief moment of silence fell upon them.

"Okay, Mr. Houston, a pleasure to see you again, do you have any updates you would like to share?" Judge Sherman said, listening keenly.

"Um, your honor, I have been attending both AA meetings and anger management classes at a local church four times a week. I have a new job which pays me significantly more than I used to make, I am now making close to twelve hundred dollars a month, and—and I still have my house," he stuttered. Marvin was changing, it was not easy, but he was maturing and he was trying to change his life.

"And what of your daughters, Mr. Houston?"

"My daughters are with their grandmother—my wife's mother, your honor, I see them two times a week," Marvin replied.

"And what of your wife, Mr. Houston?"

Marvin took a deep breath before answering.

"My wife is still undergoing treatment at the psychiatric facility, your honor."

"Mr. Houston, I understand the importance of a parent being in the lives of their children, unfortunately for you this has not been the case for the past two years. However, I am pleased to see that you have been making strides and taking the necessary steps to turn a new leaf. I do recommend parenting classes in addition to the classes you are currently taking. Do you happen to have evidence to back up your claims stated here today?"

"Yes, I do, your honor," Marvin said, quivering. Marvin had decided to no longer allow his hubris to get in the way of his progress and evolution. After a few minutes of shuffling around papers, he handed the bailiff his documentation, proud of himself for the work he was doing and the growth he was experiencing; both as a person and parent. Once Judge Sherman received the documents she advised both Rose and Marvin that she would retire to her chambers to review all the information received, as such a one-hour break was granted. Rose, feeling like she could breathe again, let out a sigh of relief as she chose to remain stationed in her seat.

Marvin quickly made his way out of the courtroom as he proceeded outside to take in the hot summer air, bending over he placed his hands on his knees—his behavior peculiar. He could not understand the emotions he was feeling, all his life he was taught how to articulate anger and somehow thrived in negativity, but his life was changing, he was changing and learning new ways to combat his worries—deep breathing exercises and counting to ten before choosing to react. Marvin thought of Irving daily, underestimating the connection he would feel with his son once he realized he could potentially never see him again, this became one of his greatest fears.

One hour later, Judge Sherman was emerging from her chambers, both Marvin and Rose standing before her. The room felt cold as she prepared herself to begin speaking.

"Mr. Houston," Judge Sherman sat upright, placing her hands together, staring into Marvin's eyes. "I am appalled and disappointed in you as both a man and a father. We have been down this road before; we have been in this room and we have had many discussions on ways in which you can improve for the betterment of yourself and that of your child so that one day you may serve a purpose in his life. I contacted your sponsor, the one listed on the letter you provided, and he claims to have not seen you in over a month. Now, this letter is dated two weeks ago, which means his signature was forged—which was also confirmed," she said. A surprised Marvin knew better than to speak, and so he remained silent, shameful.

"Mr. Houston, take a look at the woman standing next to you." Marvin turned to face Rose before quickly looking away. "Your wife tried to murder your child and Ms. Rose here remained persistent in a case where the State neglected to do their job and your son is alive, thriving, and well because of her. Mr. Houston, not only did you commit another crime here today, which will further hinder your ability to see your child, but you are here to fight against a woman who has saved your child in more ways than one and continues to serve his best interest. I have been quite lenient with you in the past, however, that ends today." Judge Sherman reclined. Both Rose and Marvin exchanged a look of confusion,

"Mr. Houston, you are now mandated to attend the following: parenting classes, Alcoholics Anonymous, and anger management for six consecutive months, five days a week. Reports from officials will be mandatory and should you deviate from any of these sessions you will permanently lose all forms of custody, signing away your parental rights. You are not allowed visitation in any form or fashion to Irving Houston and are not to go within one hundred feet of the child or make contact. Rose Appleton, congratulations, you are now the sole and primary caretaker to Irving Houston and as of today are hereby awarded full custody." Judge Sherman advised Rose. Rose, taking a long, deep breath, smiled as she looked over to Marvin to see that his eyes were beginning to well. Marvin did not mean to falsify his documents, but with work and other classes being so demanding he was truly not getting enough rest and could not make time for it all. Saddened by the news he wondered now, *what is the point?*

"Additionally, Mr. Houston, for your misdemeanor today you are hereby fined two thousand dollars that you will remit to the court or face the possibility of jail time. I do hope that this will serve as a lesson to you and that you will make better decisions in the future. You are the father of two other children and it is because of them that you have eluded jail-time all together in this matter. It is significant to have a two-parent household, and with their mother gone, I am trusting that you will follow through with the schedule I have set for you and that you will do well," she stated before banging her gavel and standing to exit, the bailiff assisting her down the stairs and into her chambers.

A shocked Rose gathered her belongings as Marvin now sat with his head low, having no desire to move. But Rose could not bring herself to exit as she began to pity him, turning to face him, "Marvin, I know I am not your favorite person, or someone you even partially like, but may I give you something?" she asked him kindly. Marvin looked up to face her, his face now drenched in tears as he whimpered. Rose turned around to place her things on the table, she reached into her handbag where she removed a wallet-sized photo of Irving. A recent school picture where he sat upright, smiling. She handed it to Marvin.

"I promise you I will continue to love and protect him the best way I know how, but I assure you he is well and he is happy." She smiled. Marvin looked up at her, placing his hand over his mouth and nodding his head. Although he could not bring himself to admit it, he was grateful for Rose and thankful for all she had done and continues to do for his son. Sitting alone now, Marvin sobbed hysterically for the first time since he could remember.

Arriving home, Rose prepared herself before turning the key to the apartment she occupied in Yonkers, New York. Standing outside she could hear Irving laughing hysterically as the cartoons blared from the television in the living room. Once inside she stood by the doorway before placing her bags down watching Marley and Ryan sit along the couch, both rising as Irving continued laughing, paying them no never mind. Rose fought the urge to shout in excitement in fear of disturbing him as Marley and Ryan made their way over,

"He's mine!" she finally said, jumping and screaming, her hands shot in the air as she reached out to hug her brother and sister-in-law. They were all elated.

"Oh thank goodness! Rose, you did it, we're so proud of you!" laughed Marley. Ryan raced towards Irving, tickling him to the ground, chuckling and playing. Irving was having the time of his life. Marley and Rose were in the kitchen as Rose began to prepare dinner, pouring herself a glass of orange juice.

"How has it been going?" asked Marley, who took a seat on the kitchen table. Rose took a deep breath before responding.

"The drinking? It is going well I suppose. Now that the bar is gone and the plants are here, Irving has been helping me to water them and he's insistent that we get more. But anymore plants at this point will have our home looking like a greenhouse," she smirked.

"It's truly amazing what you've done for him Rose. I mean, Ryan says their sessions have gotten so much better. Irving is talking more, his depression now only mild and it's really all because of you," Marley said, staring at Rose. But Rose could not allow herself to take all the credit; she did not do it alone.

"Well, no, it's been all of us. I mean you and Ryan have been great, helping and watching Irving, taking him to school and helping me through the divorce. I think Irving and I both saved each other, I needed him too, he's brought me so much joy," she stammered.

The evening was filled with merriment, once Rose and Irving bid farewell to Marley and Ryan, Rose spent the evening explaining to Irving the details of the hearing and how things were going to be. Now nine-years-old, Irving had a better understanding of what was being told to him, he did not inquire further explanations, he simply comprehended that Rose was now his sole caretaker and he would not be seeing his father again.

"Okay?" he said tenderly.

Rose smiled as they sat on the sofa watching television; kissing him on the forehead.

Heading into work the next day, Rose was greeted with a round of applause from her co-workers and superiors. She stood by the door, amused.

"What is this for?" she chuckled. Reggie stepped swiftly to her, his suit wrinkled and bags under his eyes long, Rose desperately wanted him to get some rest.

"Well, we got the news. Congratulations on your victory in court and for being a stellar employee, we will be celebrating you later on this afternoon in the large conference room," he said as the applause began to cease. Rose felt honored as she thanked him abundantly, making her way to her cubicle. Alissa stepped over to her.

"I am so happy for you."

"Thank you, Irving is happy so that makes me happy," she responded. Alissa took a seat.

"How are things with his treatment?"
Rose nodded.

"The treatments are going very well. He is in counseling, he hasn't had any more outbreaks with the ringworm, and we've just been thinking of ways to renovate the apartment. He's doing well in school; he made the honor roll." Rose smiled, removing from her purse a bumper sticker that read: *My child is an honor student at Westchester Prep Academy* like that of a proud parent. Tapping her on the back, Alissa walked away. Rose stared deeply at her bumper sticker, reminding herself not to forget to place it on her bumper before heading home.

The Westchester Prep Academy was unlike anything Irving had ever experienced, he was too young to understand the antiquity behind racism and colorism, and therefore could not identify when it was practiced. Two years ago when Irving stepped onto a private transportation bus for the first time, he dealt with the alarming stares of his peers, all wondering why he was different from them.

A month prior, Rose dreamed of the day she would walk the halls of the preparatory school enrolling a child of her own, she was far more excited than Irving, even as the dean initially took little to no interest in the child. He too was alarmed at Rose for insisting that Irving attend his school, but Rose was guaranteed a large settlement from her divorce and was willing to pay whatever it took to get Irving the best education possible, and so Dean Christopher Royal was not going to turn her down. As they toured the building Christopher eventually noticed something about Irving, he was mildly intrigued by the art found in the halls, a first for one of his prospects. Christopher then made a mental note to keep his eye on Irving.

Once enrolled, Irving began his first day of school wearing his uniform and name-badge; his head bald now that he was undergoing medical treatments for the ringworm. It would hurt Rose to see him cringing and crying whenever they would conduct their examination and inject the medication into his scalp, but she consoled him every time. Feeling a little self-conscious and shy, Irving did not speak much, rather not at all often, causing teachers to wonder if he suffered from any developmental disabilities. But their cause for concern quickly ceased when Irving exceeded expectations by scoring the highest in his grade on a state aptitude test. Slowly Christopher began to cherish Irving as he eventually had Irving placed in honor classes, which to his surprise were proving themselves to be unchallenging for the young man.

It had been two years now since Christopher began eyeing Irving, who was now an honor student in the fourth grade. Christopher would take trips to his classroom where he stood just outside to watch Irving and he was always astonished to see the young boy comprehensively focused, undistracted and asking a multitude of questions, sometimes questions his teachers could not answer. It was Monday morning and Christopher was making his rounds, an elderly British Caucasian man with a head full of grey hair and a slender build—an imperturbable man, his demeanor cardinal in nature.

Interrupting one of his English teachers as he opened the door to the classroom filled with only nine children, he asked politely, "Mrs. Taylor, my apologies, may I please borrow Irving for just a brief moment?" Mrs. Taylor obliged as Irving stood, gathering his belongings. "No, no, young man, please leave your things. You can retrieve them at a later time." Christopher instructed. Irving stepped lightly to him and into the hallway—now nine-years-old, Irving was glowing as he heavily resembled a young Emmanuel Louis. Christopher stepped firmly, his head parallel to the ground, hands intertwined to the rear of his back as Irving struggled to look up at him. Walking along the empty halls in silence, Irving grew uncomfortable until they entered into a room where four Caucasian students all stood just in front of the chalkboard debating over the legalization of campaign contributions from corporate lobbyists. As Christopher entered the gentleman stopped speaking, respectfully awaiting further instructions.

"Irving, this is a public speaking assembly that I myself have meticulously selected. I would like to introduce you to Walter, Hensley, Patrick, and Johnson. These four gentlemen are going to teach you everything they know," Christopher said, his eyes darting between them all. The boys all turning to face one another,

"But—but Mr. Royal, with all due respect, this is a child," Hensley contested. An upset Christopher turned to face him.

"Mr. Hensley, soon you will come to think of this child as a peer, but please do not question my judgment call ever again," he said, exiting. The young boys perturbed.

"This nigger cannot seriously be one of us," Johnson snapped. "No one will respect us!" Irving took a seat.

"You're insulting me," he raged. Walter stood with his arms folded.

"Don't you have a class or something, and how old are you anyway?" Walter questioned.

"Yes, but I think this is more important, and I am nine," Irving replied. The boys all murmured, speaking amongst one another before turning to him again,

"You cannot be nine, talking like that, and what do you know about an insult?" Hensley asked. "Do you even know how old we are?" he then teased.

"An insult is a disrespectful word. You used the N-word, which is an insult to me because I am a Black boy!" Irving shouted.

"Alright kid, calm down. Look, we're a lot older than you and we just cannot have you in our group!" Walter laughed.

"Mr. Royal says otherwise," Irving said. Just then Patrick turned to face him. A slender boy with a face full of acne, greasy brunette hair and braces, he was not looking to get involved— he left. Walter then whispered to Johnson, who turned to Irving now, chuckling.

"Okay, you want to be one of us? I have an assignment for you," his laugh was sinister; he folded his arms.

2

A s Rose struggled to bring the large brown grocery bags into her home, Irving stepped swiftly to assist her. She was impressed by his chivalry—never did she have to ask to be aided around the house: he was tidy, responsible, and very helpful. Sitting the bags down on the kitchen counter, Rose turned to find an abundance of paper, textbooks, and her legal pads all along the floor. Placing her hands atop her hips, she turned to face the sitter who was now emerging from the restroom—startled to see Rose, the sitter noted she was home a little earlier than usual.

"Hi, Lisa, um, what is going on?" Lisa was a fifteen-year-old African-American girl with a fair-skinned complexion who resided with her parents in the unit just below Rose—she accepted thirty dollars a week to babysit Irving afterschool until Rose arrived home. Irving had grown accustomed to her as Lisa would fix him a sandwich and a glass of milk after school before assisting him with homework. But tonight was different.

"Ms. Rose, I am sorry, I have no idea what's gotten into him.

He didn't eat his sandwich and he wouldn't let me help with his homework. He told me I wouldn't understand the *complexities* of it," she said, her eyes widened. "And yes, he used the word *complexities*," she continued. Rose knitted her eyebrows as she made her way into the living room where Irving sat on the throw rug, papers in front of him, he was studying.

"Irving, darling, did you give Lisa a hard time tonight?" she asked kindly, placing her hand on his shoulder in hopes that he would face her, and he did.

"No, I need to study," he replied softly. Rose turned to Lisa as she decided it was time to relieve her of her duties.

"Lisa, thank you as always for coming by to assist, and of course I apologize for Irving's decorum. I will see you tomorrow." Lisa grabbed her backpack, smiling as she made her way through the door. Rose stood watching as Irving picked apart his books, using his finger to guide his reading while writing his notes aggressively and reading articles from a stack of newspapers she was sure weighed more than he did. But she did not question him, Rose cooked and cleaned before stripping the walls in the living room and prepping the surface. The television set remained off as Irving continued to read, Rose could not help but chuckle when he would stand, run to the kitchen to place food in his mouth, and then race back to his work area in the living room—this happening almost every ten minutes; the sounds of his little feet warming her heart.

The next morning came quickly, Irving racing through the door, Rose was surprised to see he had awoken before her, dressed in his uniform and made himself breakfast. Although the kitchen was now a catastrophe, she could not help but chuckle, calling to him, "Irving slow down!" she yelled from the apartment door threshold, watching him run to the staircase leading outside to wait on the bus from the Independent School District, but before he could step through the doors he called back to her.

"I will, Mommy Rose!" he screamed. It was the first time he called her mommy, the first time he uttered the word since she began taking care of him. Rose could not believe her ears, racing inside to dial her brother.

"Hello, this is Ryan."

"Ryan! Oh my goodness, he said Mommy Rose!" she screamed, dancing around in her pajamas. "Could that mean anything?" she continued.

"That is excellent news. I mean we've been making a great deal of progress, but that means he's slowly coming out of his shell and he's ready to identify with you on that level. You're a nurturer, Rose, and he feels that. This is truly great news," Ryan confirmed.

In school Irving attended classes, but he was not focused, he was too anxious for the meeting, thrilled to discuss all the wonderful new things he learned the night before. His mind bursting with new information he had otherwise not been privy to. His fourth-grade teacher, speaking slowly, began to irritate him. Irving was told that at 1:15 p.m. the boys would be in the music room for their meeting, but much to his surprise this was untrue. He arrived in the room but could not locate anyone, and so, he waited.

After forty-five minutes passed, Mrs. Taylor advised Mr. Royal that Irving was not in class. This upset him greatly as he despised having to leave his office, but the receptionist was instructed to always send calls straight to him whenever it concerned the boys from his group. Irving was now one of these boys. Inside the music room Irving stood, waiting, he did not grow impatient, rather intrigued, until the door swung open, startling him.

"Irving, why are you not in your class?" Christopher asked, standing before him, a cane in his hand aiding him to walk now that his knee was causing him pain.

Ecstatically Irving responded, "Walter told me to come here. I did my research, too, Mr. Royal, all of it. I learned about The American Civil War, I wrote the pages and notes and I even learned about slaves—" Irving was speaking so fast, stuttering as he fell to his knees pulling a stack of papers from his book bag with thorough notes and textbooks belonging to the teenage boys. Interrupting him, Christopher placed his palm to his face. Instantly Irving quieted.

"Go to class," Christopher instructed Irving sternly, removing the papers from his hands and walking out of the music room to locate his boys. This disappointed Irving. After thirty minutes, Christopher sat in his presidential chair until his receptionist called through his door, peeking her head inside.

"Mr. Royal, the children are here," she said softly.

"Send them inside," he replied, writing a memo. The office he occupied was large, the furnishings burgundy and brown with portraits hanging of his ancestors. Inside Walter, Johnson, Patrick, and Hensley were all anxious, with only two chairs, two of the boys remained standing.

"Hello, Mr. Royal," Walter whispered. But Christopher did not look to them, he was pondering, his head down as he continued working on his memo.

Finally, "Gentleman, what happened yesterday after I specifically gave you instructions pertaining to Irving?" he asked, lifting his head to face them now. "Walter and Patrick, stand," he instructed them. The boys all looked at one another standing consecutively. Walter speaking first,

"Sir, if I may speak candidly, we do not—"

"I did not give you permission to speak candidly. However, I did ask, what happened to my instructions yesterday?" his tone abrasive.

"We—we just wanted to have a little fun with him," said Johnson.

Christopher, raising his right eyebrow, firmly asked, "Fun? Do you believe it is okay to mock me? Because it is never okay to do something like that. I believe this assignment belonged to one of you fellows. No?" Christopher, removing the papers Irving scribbled on, his notes impeccable. The boys all exchanged a nervous look.

"The assignment was mine, sir," Walter said, stepping

forward.

"Good! Well, here is what I would like, I need sixty-five handwritten pages on the topic of The American Civil War. MLA format, do not skip lines and add thirty-two trusted sources, this is due to me tomorrow at 6 p.m. If you do not have the assignment you will no longer be a member of this group. I will also be checking in periodically with your instructors to ensure your work is still being completed and turned in. Rest assured, Walter, I will read every inch of that document and if it is not grammatically correct or contains fabricated information, I will have you rewriting it until your hands either begin to bleed, or you quit," Christopher threatened. Walter could not believe his ears, he stood in shock as Christopher placed Irving's notes into a folder before him.

"Tell me, how exactly were you planning to retrieve this paper from Irving? You allowed him to go back to the music room despite knowing no one would be there, no?" Christopher continued. The boys were confused as they had not thought through the details.

"You are all a part of an elite group and yet you behave so idiotically. I do not make mistakes; therefore, I was not wrong in selecting you, but I will be respected, otherwise, I will unleash a series of punishments that will have each of crawling back to your mummies and daddies, begging them to keep you home! Walter, you are dismissed." Walter fleeing hastily to the exit.

"Hensley, this week Irving is your responsibility, understood? You will find him during lunch, eat with him, teach him our ways, and thoroughly explain to him the purpose of this group. You are also dismissed," he continued.

"Yes, sir," Hensley agreed.

"Johnson, Patrick, you are dismissed," Christopher said. This did not sit right with Hensley.

"Sir, Johnson called him the N-word!" he blurted.

"Snitch," Johnson shouted. There was a brief commotion, meanwhile, Patrick remained standing.

"Stop it!" Christopher shouted. "Johnson, is this true?" he

stood, outraged, the boys now quivering. "Patrick and Hensley, go to class." His eyes widened; the boys off to the exit.

"Johnson, you are suspended for three days, I will have your paperwork drafted in the upcoming hour, however, you will be in attendance for our meeting, understood?" Johnson appalled.

"Sir, I—I can't tell my parents I've been suspended, I will be in so much trouble!" he cried, pleading now as Christopher took a seat, his head buried into his computer where began typing his memo. Johnson knew there was nothing more he could say as he turned to take his leave.

That evening, Irving went home feeling sad, watching Lisa wait for him outside of the apartment only reminded him that he was a child, which only aided in his disappointment.

"You don't have to babysit me, I am not a kid," Irving said as he turned the key,

"Well, you're also not an adult, which means you don't make the rules. Your mommy does," Lisa replied, stepping inside. Irving raced up the stairs. "Do you have a lot of homework, Irving?" she bellowed, but Irving was in his bedroom after slamming the door behind him. Lisa decided to simply work on her own homework assignments.

By Wednesday evening the boys were all sitting inside of the music room when Christopher stepped inside. They were sitting next to one another; he was interested in speaking to Walter to see what he had retained from his assignment, which was surprisingly turned in on time and flawlessly written. Christopher began pacing, the boys seated in front of him, their notebooks on their laps.

"As you all know this group is tailored to develop young leaders. Every one of you sitting here today, in front of me, can someday look to lead this country, the free world—" Walter, Hensley, Johnson, and Patrick all sat with a confused look on their face,

"Sir, do you mean President of the United States?" Johnson asked apprehensively. Christopher shook his head to confirm, just then the boys all leaned forward simultaneously to face Irving, whose feet swung from the chair; who was confused by their gawking eyes.

"Is there a problem?"

"No sir, we're just thinking maybe you forgot about a certain someone in the room," Walter said, nudging his head in Irving's direction. Christopher was growing impatient.

"Racism, what is it? Johnson, twenty-two seconds to answer!" Christopher affirmed, turning on the timer. Johnson stood and recited in a matter of seconds an elaborate definition of the term and its history, during which he decided that Irving was owed an apology. Completing his monologue in a mere fifteen seconds, he turned to Irving.

"Hey, sorry about that," Johnson apologized before taking a seat.

Christopher paced back and forth. "Write," he screamed, the boys preparing their pens and notepads, shuffling around.

"Twenty seconds is how much time you have to deliver your message, inform your audience, and hold their attention long enough for them to care about anything else you must say after those twenty seconds have ended. Racism can by no means be defined and thoroughly discussed in the allotted time I previously allowed. However, that is enough time to hook your audience," he concluded before taking a seat, his cane to the front of him, placing his hands atop the handle. "Irving," he called, his voice startling the boy. Irving struggled to stand, 52.2 inches in height, Irving most certainly looked his age, although he felt like he could stand up to the even the brightest of men, he was simply that confident in his intellect. Irving stood, his hands behind him as his palms began to sweat. Although he was self-assured, he feared to upset Mr. Royal as he had come to cherish the thought of learning from such a prestigious man.

"Yes," he whispered. Christopher's eyes burned through him like a ray of sun. Irving began to sweat.

"Ten ways to ruin a presentation. Ten seconds, go!" Christopher said, turning on his timer. Irving stood, his posture poor, his head unapparelled to the ground and his fingers fidgeting behind him as he rocked back and forth on his tiptoes. Christopher grew irritated as Irving stalled, searching his mind for the answers, the boys' feeling a mix of emotions: angry, scared, disappointed, frightened, unsure of how they would be punished.

Just then Irving began, "Unexplained…points, bullets, and importance…" he mumbled nervously, the timer buzzing. Christopher stood as Irving lifted his face.

"Hensley, what was your assignment?" he asked him. Hensley sat upright, pondering his answer, his palms sweating, his face a beating red,

"Sir, I did—teach him," he stuttered. Christopher drew a long, deep breath.

"…and yet, he stands here, unable to answer my question," Christopher grumbled. "Irving! You will not mess up again, do you understand me? You will pay attention to the lessons you are taught, and you will retain said information for better practices, do you hear me boy?" Christopher shouted.

"Sit down, open your books, today we will focus on eloquently speaking, the importance of delivery, our tone, our timing, our enunciation. Your knowledge is only two-tenths of the battle. When you choose to speak, the order in which you speak, those are all vital elements, but none of it matters if the people you are speaking to remain unmotivated and unconvinced." Christopher stood in silence, watching as they all jotted down his dictation.

"Irving, eloquence. Ten seconds, go!"

A startled Irving stood, his books and papers all rustling to the ground, annoying Christopher.

"Boy, sit. I will not teach under these conditions." Mr. Royal griped, taking his leave, his cane banging ferociously atop the wooden floors. Afterward, the boys all turned to face Irving, angry, shouting.

"What the hell!" screeched Johnson.

"Irving!" screamed Hensley, guilt-ridden; his eyes widened.

"If you aren't going to take this seriously, then you shouldn't be here," Walter hollered.

"Calm down!" Patrick shouted, standing in front of Irving. "Gosh, he didn't ask to be here, alright? Hensley, if you did a better job teaching him, we wouldn't be in this mess. Show him what we've learned these last four weeks and maybe, just maybe, he will catch on. I mean, have you shown him anything?" Patrick asked disappointingly.

Hensley feeling pressured responded, "Well, no. I mean, what help does he need, he's supposed to be some prodigy kid right?" he said, jealous. "I mean, why should I miss my lunch to go sit and eat with a bunch of children just so this twerp can learn about missions and posture?" Hensley continued. Walter and Johnson folded their arms in discontent before grabbing their backpacks and heading out the door; Patrick remained seated as Irving watched on.

"Listen, I would do it, but unfortunately Mr. Royal told you to do it, so, if you don't want us all getting in trouble or having to come in on a weekend, then I suggest you start taking this a bit more seriously. I have a date Saturday. I can't afford to run laps because of your disobedience," pleaded Patrick. Hensley wondered *who would possibly date him?* Shaking his head back to reality, he looked around the room, noticing a pitiful Irving still remained seated.

"C'mon twerp, let's go," said Hensley, grabbing his backpack. Irving remained seated.

"Go where?"

"My place. I have a car." Irving jumped from his seat.

"No, no, I have to go home, Mommy Rose will be mad," he said, terrified.

"Nothing is worse than seeing Mr. Royal mad, now, we have a choice, either anger him or anger your dear old Mommy Rose. I think the choice is easy. Now let's go!" he demanded, slamming the door behind him. Irving was already worried about how he was going to explain coming home at five to Rose, but anything past that would require some serious thought. Running through the double doors, Irving managed to catch up with Hensley, climbing into his lipstick red 1989 Honda Accord.

Arriving at Hensley's residence, Irving was intrigued. He found his abode to be quite large, the inside décor ornate. Hensley was not wealthy, a young boy with blonde hair, beady eyes, and bold legs, his parents separated, residing now with what appeared to be his father. The middle-aged man greeting them once inside.

"Hey there, kiddo," his father said, bewildered as he stared at Irving who was standing in the foyer taking in the home's ambiance.

"Hey dad, I'm busy okay, I have a lot of work to do," Hensley replied, motioning for Irving to remove his shoes and head upstairs. The brown carpet beneath his feet was immaculate. Irving, removing his shoes, made his way upstairs, following Hensley into the first bedroom on the left. His father decided to not question him further. Plopping himself onto the twin bed, his room a Teenage Mutant Ninja Turtles theme, his favorite turtle: Raphael. Posters of the turtle hung everywhere. Hensley prided himself on idolizing the turtle as he too felt himself to be a dynamic visionary, always imagining his future. As Irving mindlessly let his eyes wander, he noticed how filthy Hensley was: piles of books, laundry, dishes, and an unorganized collection of tape cassettes all falling from his nightstand.

"Okay kid, let's get started."

Two hours, two sandwiches, and some milk and cookies later, Irving learned a lot from Hensley—from body posture to new vocabulary, to highlights in history and the names of the presidents in order. Most of the information was all new to Irving, he'd heard of some of the information but never thought to retain it. Surprisingly enough, much of the material in relation to the presidents he had already come to learn through his reading of *Lincoln*. Hensley was impressed and also taken aback by Irving's strong focus. He was not easily distracted. Hensley's father was kind enough to bring Irving home—the clock read 8:09 p.m.—once he arrived, slamming the car door as he shouted *thank you* while running towards the apartment entrance.

Outside he missed the marked car parked by the street, stepping up the last step and pulling the door open he noticed Rose standing just outside speaking to the officers. Tears flowing from her eyes.

"Officer, he's—he's just a baby, I mean he's my baby, he's about yay high," she said placing her hand palm down by the middle of her thigh. "Please, you don't understand, he's so quiet and anything could have happened to him." Rose stood sobbing and sniffling as Irving approached, squeezing the straps of his backpack.

"Mommy Rose," he said softly, the officers turning to him.

"Are you Irving?" one officer asked, Rose pushing them both to the side as she raced from the threshold, falling to the ground and squeezing Irving tightly.

"Oh, thank God!" she cried, examining him, "Did someone hurt you? Are you hurt?" she continued. Irving struggled to speak as the officers took their leave.

"Young man you get on inside, ma'am," they said tipping their hats as to indicate their pending absence. Rose lifted Irving, scurrying inside where she examined him further after placing him on the couch, drying her eyes before beginning her interrogation.

"Jesus, Irving, where on earth did you go?" she cried, pacing now. She was craving some form of alcohol, a shot maybe to soothe her nerves. The worry becoming too much as Irving had become her everything, she could not fathom the thought of losing him but came to realize her paranoia was beginning to frighten him as he sat, watching her, his eyes empty. The post-trauma setting in—Momma pacing, frantic, angry, distraught, could only mean one thing: punishment.

In two years, Rose had not found herself reacting this way, she was always pleasant, a new normal for Irving. But today, she was hysterical and Irving had learned to associate this behavior with a scolding. Quivering as he sat upright in the couch, his knees curled to his chin, his face lowered as a tear fell from his eyes, preparing himself mentally for a whooping. Realizing this, Rose knelt to console him.

"Oh, my baby boy, I am so sorry," she cried, taking a seat next to him, his head falling into her arms, and then his body, she rocked him back and forth. The sniffling from his nostrils and the tears she felt running along her arms causing her goosebumps; cradling him she whispered, "Irving, I would never hurt you, I love you so much and I am so sorry. But, please, please don't ever scare me like that again," she begged him. After a short while, Irving slowly fell into a deep slumber, his legs hanging over the arm of the sofa.

3

S lamming the oak door Rose marched in her loafers—
her fashion tomboy style aiding her today as she was
able to move swiftly and without attention into the
office where she watched as Christopher stood looking
out of his window as the children began piling into the
building—his arms behind his back, his posture, perfect. He did
not turn to face her, his receptionist bellowing from the door,
"Sir, I tried to stop her," she cried. Without turning,
Christopher simply swatted her away.

Rose now stood ready for war, angry as she cried,
"Christopher, I want answers. My son was out until nine in the
night and I had no clue where he was! How dare you?" she
screamed. "Look at me," she demanded.

Christopher turned slowly, taking a seat he waved his hand,
inviting Rose to do the same, to which she obliged.

"My dear Rose, you look rejuvenated, it is always a pleasure
to see you here, although it's seldom. How may I help you?" he
asked nonchalantly.

Rose was growing impatient from his need for ridicule. "My son, my son came home at nine in the night yesterday, I—I ended up calling the police. When I was putting him to bed and I asked him where he was, he told me he was with your group. What group?" she screamed as she feared the worst—molestation.

"I see Irving did not come off the school bus this morning, is he in class?" Christopher inquired, now reaching for his Baoding Balls, placing them in his left hand, reclining.

"No, my son is just outside these doors waiting for me. Now stop evading my questions, I want to know what exactly is going on."

"My dearest Rose, pretty soon you will receive a piece of mail from our office, in it you will find a letter. I have a newfound respect for you, for you see, that young boy who you've decided to bring into my quarters is not merely a bloke, he is extraordinary. I can pull for you his test scores, his reading levels, his grades, his paperwork. I began watching him very closely. I believe about four months after his enrollment his teacher at the time—I believe you were familiar, Mr. Price—he brought Irving to my attention. He is gifted, he is going to be someone special one day, but you cannot coddle him—nurture, but not coddle. I understand the boy had been through some tumultuous times, I see the scars; however, those things have built character and we must use that to our advantage," Christopher said.

"I am not following, nor does any of that explain why my child came home at eight in the night," uttered an impatient Rose.

"A group, Ms. Rose, a group of elite, fine gentlemen whose ages range from twelve to sixteen is the reason for Irving's late arrival last night, I am sure, and for that, I apologize. I've thought about a group like this for years, a group of men who, with proper training, mentorship, and guidance could one day change the free world. Then, I found them, and shortly after that, I decided to include Irving. I was skeptical at first. But then he was sent home to complete an assignment given to him by a sixteen-year-old, at which he excelled, above and beyond even my expectations. His notes were impeccable, his penmanship legible, he is a fourth grader who can write in script," Christopher said, handing Rose the papers he removed from the bottom drawer in his mahogany desk. Rose looked through them.

"A few pages, he did scribble, but after I carefully reviewed them, those were merely questions he later answered one by one. He wrote sheets of information, I myself was not knowledgeable of. Ms. Rose, your son is different, in a good way, and with your permission, of course, I can make him a momentous individual." Christopher continued.

But Rose remained unmoved, throwing her bag over her shoulders. "I want my son home at a decent hour, I am not sending him here to be your science project or help you fulfill some hobby in your downtime. I know he is intelligent, and he will, of course, be great one day, but not like this."

"Of course, you leave me gutted, Ms. Rose. But I hope for your sake, and for the sake of that young man, you will one day soon reconsider," Christopher articulated as Rose stepped through the door, slamming it behind her. Rose escorted Irving to his class where she squatted to face him.

"Irving, honey, you cannot be a part of this group anymore, do you understand me? You have to come home at a decent hour, and this sounds like it could be too much for you at your age. I want you to have fun, we'll go see a movie this weekend, alright? Maybe go to an arcade, you have to enjoy your youth," Rose said, her voice cracking as she could see the distress in his eyes as he gripped his back straps.

Rose could not stand to watch him anymore, as she stood to her feet kissing him atop his head, a saddened Irving opening the door to his classroom disappearing inside.

As Rose got into her car, she began to question whether or not she made the right decision, wondering if Irving was going to resent her—desperately she wanted a drink, although the day had just begun. Rose decided to skip work, making the decision to call in sick upon arriving at her brother's house. Marley would be home, considering she was a stay-at-home mom. Approaching the Long Island residence, she neared the front lawn, perfectly trimmed. Marley was such a perfectionist; with four kids she still managed to keep an immaculate home and make time for her husband. Ryan had no complaints as far as Rose could tell. Ringing the doorbell, Rose waited patiently for Marley to greet her.

A few seconds later Marley appeared—her blonde pixie cut suiting her just fine as she heavily favored a young Mia Farrow. Elated that someone had come to visit her, an adult, she was thrilled to let in Rose,

"Rose!" she smiled, her maxi dress flowing freely behind her. Their Long Island one family home was small but cozy, three-bedrooms, two bathrooms, upstairs, downstairs, and a basement. Marley, being the eclectic woman she is, decorated their home using antique furniture and a vintage layout.

"Hi Marley. May I borrow your phone? I need to call out of work." She removed her bag, hanging it on the coat rack inside the foyer—considering the warm weather, the closet had no other use during this time.

"Yea, sure. I was just in the basement doing some pottery, why don't you come on down when you're through?" Marley said, gracefully shutting the front door. The call between Rose and Reggie lasted all of six minutes, Reggie was already growing concerned for Rose, advising her to take all the time she needed. Entering into the basement Rose stepped lightly as she heard the sounds of "Strange Fire" by Indigo Girls playing in the background. Taking a seat, she watched Marley mold the clay.

"Marley, I think I did something wrong today. You—you and Ryan make parenting look so easy, I just thought anyone could do it. I mean, I feel like I'm in way over my head here," Rose said, sounding defeated.

"Oddly enough, I went through the same feeling. Rose, parenting is not easy, sometimes you have to be the bad guy, the mean mommy," Marley stated as she molded—her hands now brown.

"I want to be firm, but it's hard considering everything he's been through. But if I'm not then I'll just be spoiling him and I know I cannot do that."

"You're right, you can't. Want to tell me what happened?" asked Marley, concerned now. Rose contemplated before agreeing,

"Well, Mr. Royal, the dean for Westchester Prep, um, he wants Irving to take part in some elite group or something because of how smart Irving is. Which of course, it sounds great, fantastic, but Irving is still a child. He needs to enjoy his childhood, spend time with his cousins here, play, fall, have accidents, bruise his knees," Rose cried. Marley could not console her as she concluded her molding.

"Rose, I understand how you're feeling, but what do you feel is going to make Irving happy? The whole point of your working so hard was to take him away from a household of mental and physical abusers who wanted to stifle him. Is he happy being a part of the elite group?" asked Marley innocently. Rose nodded her head.

"I know he is, the look on his face when I told him he couldn't go back, it broke my heart," Rose sobbed. "But he was always with someone, Mr. Samuel and—and now Mr. Royal, someone is always trying to teach him and mold him into becoming the next Martin Luther King Jr., and I just want my little boy to be a little boy," she continued to cry. Marley sympathized.

"Well Rose, if learning makes him happy, then don't deprive him of it. Just find ways to implement playtime at home. Maybe two days a week, find some balance," Marley said, shrugging her shoulders.

Rose nodded, "You're right," she smiled.

By 3:30 p.m. Rose was home, she advised Lisa that Irving would not need babysitting but promised her an evening worth of wages. Rose cooked, cleaned and bought games such as

Scrabble, Chutes and Ladders, and chess for her and Irving to enjoy along with a new G.I. Joe action figure. She even cooked his favorite, meatloaf with rice and beans with pink lemonade for his drink.

As the key turned in the door Rose grew excited as though she was awaiting her husband or best friend, she had not felt this nervous in quite a long time. Irving stepping inside and wondered why Rose was there. Rose smiled.

"Hello there handsome, I made your favorite and I bought some games for us to play tonight!" Rose, pointing to the living room center table where the games were meticulously placed. Standing in the kitchen, she watched as Irving removed his shoes and his backpack, walking slowly over to her.

"How was school today?" she asked nervously as Irving took a seat at the kitchen table.

He took a deep breath before responding. "School was good." Rose brought over his snacks and he prepared to dig in.

"Now Irving, don't eat too fast, you're going to have dinner at 7, okay?" Gladly, Rose set down his sandwich and milk. Irving did not speak, rather he nodded his head slowly in agreement.

Rose wanted him to speak, he was not being his normal self; taking a seat beside him with a cup of tea, she asked, "Irving are you upset with me?" the warm cup in hand as she watched him take small bites.

His eyes wandered. "No," he whispered.

"Irving what did we say about lying?"

"I am not mad, Mommy Rose," Irving spoke softly, taking another bite. Rose now bit the sides of her cheek.

"I bought you a new G.I. Joe too, so once you're done with your snack you can pick a game." She smiled.

"But what about my homework?" he asked, looking up at her as she now stood. Rose felt confused.

"Um, we can do that too, soon—after we play games," she stuttered as the doorbell rang. Her eyes enlarged as she was not expecting company. Rose was not feeling like herself walking towards the door, looking through the peephole, turning to

Irving and knitting her brows before unlocking the door—a tall gentleman stood before her.

"Hello." Irving now peeping his head out to see who was in the hall.

"Hi, um, my name is Keith Davis—I live next door. I just wanted to come by to ask if maybe you had some extra sugar you could possibly spare?" The Caucasian man appeared to be in his late forties, slender, with brunette hair and small facial features—he looked strange to Rose. But what she found even more disturbing was that he was asking her for sugar.

"Yes, um, I do, can you give me a second?" Rose asked, shutting the door and turning the locks. Rose would never admit it, but she was paranoid. Afraid all the time that someone, anyone, could come and bring harm to either herself or to Irving. She'd made a promise to herself to protect him with every fiber of her being, and so she was skeptical of just about everyone.

Irving, after finishing his meal, ran behind Rose as she reached into the cupboard removing sugar and pouring some into a Ziploc bag.

Returning to the door, the man was still there, standing in the hallway. Rose handed him the sugar before proceeding to close the door when he asked, "May I take you to dinner sometime?" Rose stood, shocked, Irving now chuckling.

"That is not funny," she mouthed to him before re-opening the door. "Um, I don't think that's a great idea, I um, I have a son and—um, I appreciate the gesture—"

As Rose fumbled through her refusal, Irving shouted from behind the door where he had tiptoed, "She will go!" A shocked Rose couldn't help but laugh.

"It's a date then! And thank you for the sugar," Keith taking his leave quickly before Rose could decline. Rose remained jaw-dropped, closing the door as she chased Irving around the house, playfully tackling him and tickling him as they laughed the night away and later enjoyed a game of chess. Rose was feeling blessed beyond measure and secretly happy that she had a date.

"Checkmate," she laughed hysterically, proud she had

beaten the boy genius.

"I let you win," Irving joked.

Their night was memorable.

By the weekend Rose decided to enlist Irving's help with the renovations she kept putting off, the walls needed repainting, the floors needed buffing, and the bedrooms, Rose thought, could use a room-lift. Some new furniture and perhaps a larger bookcase in Irving's room, amongst other things. The settlement from her divorce and the alimony she was receiving was enough to cover the cost of the renovations, keep Irving enrolled in school, and assist Rose in starting his trust fund. As Marley and Ryan stepped inside, along with their four beautiful children— Andy, Ally, Monica, and Tyler—Rose found herself catering to a cluster of children that was proving itself to be rather tiring as they all retired to Irving's bedroom. Irving periodically stepped outside to assist Rose and Ryan in carrying in the supplies she purchased from Home Depot before their arrival.

Ryan asked, "Wow, is he always this helpful?" out of breath as he carried four large cans of paint up the stairs. The elevators had chosen a fine time to be out of order.

"Yep, always," Rose struggling to give Irving a kiss on the cheek as he fought to make his way up the stairs holding bags of supplies. Rose felt like the luckiest woman in the world, her child was unproblematic, intelligent, and already a Godsend at the tender age of nine. As everyone took breaks between their trips, the remainder of items stayed in the lobby in a corner, Rose was somehow confident they would not be taken. Pouring lemonade and passing out mini sandwiches with the crusts cut off, the kids were having the time of their lives upstairs, enjoying Chutes and Ladders, but oddly enough Irving did not engage them. Rose wondered if this was a norm,

"Marley, when you would babysit Irving on the weekends, was he always so sequestered from your kids?" she asked, her eyebrows knitted. Marley licked her lips before responding.

"Well, yes, I mean he just wants to either read or sleep, but he usually doesn't play with them," she said, trying not to sound awkward. A shocked Rose turned to face her.

"Marley!" she shouted.

"Rose, listen, okay, he just feels like they're different from him and he has a right to feel that way. Irving is not an idiot, he knows our kids are not his actual cousins; they're White and he's Black, so, I mean, he just doesn't relate, I guess. I—I honestly don't know. Okay, Ryan says one day he will come around and to not make such a big deal about it; Irving's ASPD is only mild," Marley concluded as she removed the paint brushes from their packages. Ryan brought up the remaining bags as Rose stood in the living room downstairs, watching as Irving sat just outside of his room, engrossed in a book. Rose shook her head in disappointment.

"I can't believe you didn't tell me this, Marley," Rose griped as she grabbed a hold of the blue painters' tape.

Ryan, again out of breath, walked in, "Hey, what's going on?"

"Rose is upset that we didn't tell her that Irving doesn't play with the kids," Marley said.

"I mean, we um, I didn't think that was something we needed to necessarily bring up, I mean he's making such great progress in other areas," Ryan stammered.

"Mild Antisocial Personality Disorder doesn't equate to progress. Ryan, you're his psychiatrist, things like this are something you tell the parent. I am the parent, so tell me that my child is a social deviant and doesn't want to play with his family members, who according to your wife, because she knows more than me, as per usual, is because he knows they're White and he's Black," Rose argued. Ryan shot his wife a look of disdain.

"Listen, we are all finally on good terms, I know in the past this was an issue, me confiding in Marley about things pertaining to you or your marriage that I should not have done, but to be honest, Rose, I made a business decision in not disclosing this information," Ryan pleaded. "Just please, don't shut me out again," he begged.

But Rose was not happy. "Again, you two pull this shit again?"

"Rose, listen, these past two years you have been dealing with a lot. The divorce, your drinking, getting custody of a kid! I mean, the last thing we wanted to do was burden you with something so minuscule. This is not something he can't grow out of," Ryan said.

"Ryan, you are my baby brother, okay? Stop treating me like a child. I know there are things that I wish I had, as you do, but it just didn't work that way and I am dealing with it. But when it comes to my child, and anything that pertains to me, you need to tell me, you have a moral obligation to do so," she cried. Rose found herself growing emotional, praying now that Irving would simply go into the room and that he had not heard them in their attempts to whisper.

"I think the two of you should leave," Rose said, washing her hands in the kitchen sink. Ryan and Marley exchanged a look.

"This is ridiculous Rose. They're just children," Ryan scoffed.

"They are children, yes, but it's the betrayal with you that I can't seem to get past. You kept Michael's cheating a secret from me a whole month before I married him. Then accidentally let it slip over drinks and wings during a boxing match, oh, but Marley knew, you knew, and as my brother, my own flesh and blood, you let me marry a man who you knew was cheating on me. This isn't just about Irving, it's about the way history continues to repeat itself and you can't seem to see where you keep going wrong. Now, please get out." Rose said firmly as she stomped her way up the stairs, walking past Irving who continued to sit outside of his room, a book in his lap, reading.

Rose dived face first onto her mattress; although her clothes were unclean—the overalls they all wore stained with paint from test colors she was trying on the living room wall—she could not stand. She simply needed a moment to gather her thoughts as she wondered whether or not she was overreacting. Listening to her brother bellow the names of their children and hearing them all make their way out the front door, shutting it behind them, brought her relief. Peeling herself from the mattress, Rose stepped into the hallway on the grey carpet where she no longer saw Irving sitting outside of his bedroom, knocking before she entered, she took a seat next to him on his twin bed where he was sitting turning the pages to *The Joy Luck Club* by Amy Tan.

A worried Rose asked, "Irving, where on earth did you find this book?" She laughed.

Irving arose, climbing down from his mattress and lifting the bed skirt from his bed, inviting Rose to join him. Underneath was a collection of books; Rose could not believe her eyes.

"Irving," she gasped, reaching for the novels. There they were, at least fifty books stacked neatly in piles of five fitting nicely under his bed, "Where on earth did you get these?" she inquired again.

"Mrs. Taylor," Irving said quietly, laying on the ground now, his voice angelic, the look in his eyes innocent and restful.

Rose rubbed the back of his hand. "Irving, I have some questions to ask you, do you promise to be one hundred percent honest with me?" Rose asked—her feet dangling through the door, past the threshold.

"Yes," Irving answered as he now sat upright. Drawing a long breath, Rose asked,

"Do you want to be in the group with Mr. Royal?"

"Yes," Irving replied quickly; his hands tucked under his legs which were draped in denim.

"Okay, also, why don't you play with your cousins? Irving, I know that you believe you are different because you are African-American, but sweetie that doesn't mean you should sequester yourself, understand? You are my son, and we love you just like we love Andy, Ally, Tyler, and Monica."

Irving fought for his turn to speak, panicked. "No, no, I want to play, they won't let me," he said softly, his tone slightly increased. "They—they pushed me, Andy, and—and Monica. They say I'm too young and we are not family," Irving said sadly. Rose now sat up, gripping his shoulders.

"Irving are you sure they said this? When did this happen?" she asked firmly, staring into his eyes.

"When you were sad and I went to Uncle Ryan's for a while," Irving now rocked himself back and forth.

"Irving, get your shoes on, we're going to Uncle Ryan's house," Rose snapped as she stood to race downstairs. Irving stepping lightly behind her.

Arriving at the Long Island residence, both Ryan and Andy were on the lawn tossing a football, their clothes unchanged. Rose felt herself coming unhinged as she wondered why she had chosen to drive to their home rather than simply calling, but she was infuriated and oftentimes found herself making illogical decisions based on her temporary emotions. Motioning for Irving to step out of the car, she and Irving made their way onto the lawn. Andy, noticing them, stopped tossing the ball and pointed to Rose, his father turning around.

"Rose, come on now, what is it?" Ryan asked whimpering like an exhausted child. But Rose simply ignored him as she turned to face her twelve-year-old nephew. "Andy, I have a question for you. Did you push Irving?"

Ryan threw his hands in the air out of frustration now, "Rose, what is this? What—have you lost your mind?" he shouted. Irving stepped backward. "Listen, Andy, don't answer that; Rose maybe you should consider getting some professional help—" Just then Andy interrupted him.

"Well—I did because he's not normal," Andy said, fretful, his eyes darting back and forth, Both Ryan and Rose turned to face him, he seemed fearful that he would be reprimanded. Ryan turned to face him slowly.

"Andy, why did you push him?" he asked, his arms folded.

"Because he wanted to play with me and Monica, but there weren't enough toys and we didn't want him to play with us.

He—he said we were family and—and he isn't family, dad, he—
he is too dark," cried Andy, feeling confused. Ryan placed his
hand atop his son's shoulders and turned to Irving, apologizing.
Rose, on the other hand, was still awaiting her own apology.

"Maybe you should get your son some therapy," Rose
grumbled, taking Irving by the hand.

4

T he weeks for Irving were no longer the same, every Thursday morning he found himself waiting by the front door of their school building for Hensley to bring him notes and a detailed report of their group meeting. Irving was taking the information home, reading, and begging Mrs. Taylor to fetch him new books as per the assignments assigned from Mr. Royal. During their group meeting, Christopher took notice of Hensley taking notes for two, but this made him happy, knowing Hensley could have simply been passing the information to Irving—who was always delighted to have it. A month came and went while Rose finished painting the living room a bumblebee yellow.

Rose contemplated allowing Irving to continue with Mr. Royal as she noticed how engrossed Irving had become with his learning, but as she watched the children play on the playground in the apartment complex she wanted desperately for Irving to join them. Keith visited, but he and Rose never quite made it on that date. As Rose gathered her mail from the mailbox, she watched Keith standing beside her doing the same.

"Wow, what a month, huh?" he asked bashfully. But Rose knew not whether to reply or simply ignore him, he was unreliable and clearly inconsistent, and so she chose to ignore his advances for conversation. "So, I know we were supposed to go out a few weeks back, but if you let me make it up to you I would really appreciate that," he pleaded, handing her a card with his number scribbled on the back.

Rose wondered; *did he always just keep a random card hidden in his back pocket?* But she went against inquiring realizing it was a business card and decided to take it as she was feeling rather lonely between work, home, and raising a child, she needed some form of companionship. Keith was happy she took the card, despite her not responding.

As Rose's hair grew longer—now flowing freely to the center of her back—she considered cutting it, perhaps a pixie cut or a bob to her cheekbones. As she admired herself in the mirror in the upstairs bathroom, she wondered what she would do. Her hair a flaming red, her skin pale and the bags under her eyes heavy—only thirty-one years old, she was beginning to look a lot like fifty. Rose desperately needed a change, to smile more, to laugh and simply enjoy life as she had initially planned. That day after receiving an early dismissal from work due to a building violation, Rose cooked and dialed Lisa, asking if she would be so kind as to babysit that evening—Lisa obliged. Rose then dialed Keith, who answered on the third ring, and informed him that she was his date for the evening and to be at her place by eight.

As Rose stumbled across the apartment, Irving sitting adjacent to the television set, it was powered off. In front of him Rose noticed she had carelessly tossed the letter received by Westchester Prep from Christopher on the coffee table, she prayed Irving would not grab hold of it. A typical night, Irving sat in front of the blank television screen, racing to and from his dinner, only this time Rose was preparing herself for the first date she had in almost three years—Irving paid her no mind.

Every fifteen minutes she found herself standing before him, questioning him, requesting his take on her outfits, and surprisingly, he was interested in assisting her.

"No straps," he said to one of her gowns. "That dress is too flashy, it's only dinner," he remarked about another. "Too many buttons," he softly commented on a dress she purchased while thrifting that buttoned in the front. Finally, Rose suggested that Irving simply join her upstairs. Gathering his books, papers, pencils, and her notepads, he struggled to make his way up the steps and into her bedroom where Rose had thrown clothes everywhere. The dresser, floors, mattress and door frame were all covered with articles of clothing. Irving sat on the floor nearest the bedroom door, intrigued.

"You're a pulchri-tudi-nous woman, Mommy Rose," Irving stuttered, Rose turned to face him as she struggled to fit into her cargo pants, laughing.

"Where did you learn that word?" she asked, smiling.

"From my vocabulary list," Irving laughed, however, he quickly stopped, realizing this was his list from the elite group and Rose would soon begin to question.

"Your vocabulary list for fourth grade consists of the word *pulchritudinous?*" she questioned; her eyebrows knitted. Gasping, Irving quickly stood, gathering his books as he raced down the hall into his bedroom, closing the door behind him. Rose called to him as her doorbell sang.

"Young man, we will finish this talk later!" she bellowed. *A pulchritudinous woman?* Rose whispered to herself as she made her way downstairs to let in Lisa, who was unusually happy. Standing by the front door, she removed her bag, setting it down on the floor.

"I know tonight is a school night and very much appreciate you deciding to come by so late, I will be back no later than eleven, or perhaps ten," Rose assured her as she raced upstairs to grab a button-down shirt. Considering the amount of weight she'd gained, she simply did not feel confident enough to wear a dress, and so she went with her regular outfit of choice: tomboy chic and her perfect loafers—throwing her hair into a messy top bun to apply her makeup and eyeliner. By 8:01 p.m. the bell dinged, and Lisa called to her.

"Ms. Rose, you have a guest!" she bellowed after opening the door. Rose moved hastily grabbing her over-the-shoulder bag and making her way down the stairs.

Coming face to face with Keith, her jaw dropped in amazement. He wore a three-piece black suit and tie—Rose felt completely embarrassed as she placed her hand atop her head, but Keith was a gentleman.

"Don't worry about it, maybe I'm just overdressed," he smiled nervously. Rose took a huge gulp, shutting the door behind her after bidding Lisa a farewell.

That night Keith took Rose dancing at a small restaurant just on the outside of Yonkers on the border of Mount Vernon, it was a beautiful neighborhood with great music. Rose had not had so much fun in years, even when she was married to Michael. Both her and Keith dancing and singing karaoke until she completely lost track of time. By half-past ten the shop was taking their last orders and preparing to close. Rose stood anxiously, ready to go now, but she could not help but feel proud of herself for not having any alcohol.

A curious Keith inquired, "Why don't you drink? I noticed you didn't have a drop all night?" he asked, lifting his tuxedo jacket and placing it over her shoulders. Apprehensive at first, Rose decided on responding.

"I was honestly never a drinker before I met my ex-husband, and then as our marriage prolonged there were so many things happening and he's such a socialite, we were going out all the time and then eventually I picked up a bottle to deal with my emotions. Our fights became worse, he was spending a lot of time outside of our home and there was information that I wasn't privy to prior to our wedding that I learned about, which just sent me over the edge. Then when we separated, I got the apartment, he stayed in the house and there it was—me and the bar. Every evening, one drink turned into two and eventually two turned into three, and then our office found Irving and I've just decided to quit cold turkey. I haven't had a drop in twenty-six months," Rose said proudly. Keith nodded his head, he was happy to hear her story, moved even as he leaned in to kiss her before opening her side of the door, Rose reciprocated this act, feeling like she could finally allow herself to release some of the tension she had been feeling.

The time read 11:02 p.m. as Rose turned the key to her apartment, Keith standing just outside, kissing her goodnight, inside she found a sleeping Lisa on the couch snuggled under a blanket, the television blaring.

Turning off the television, she shook Lisa slightly, whispering, "Lisa, I'm home honey." Lisa wiped her eyes, smiling as Rose walked her down the hall and to her apartment thanking her profusely. That night Rose lay awake after checking in on a sleeping Irving, showering and changing into her nightwear, *could Keith be the one?* she thought, dozing off.

The sound of Irving's beatific voice awakened Rose by 5 a.m., causing her head to hurt.

"Mommy Rose," he shouted, jumping atop her on the mattress, "I've lost my teeth!" The young boy opening his mouth wide for her to see, but Rose could barely see anything, her eyes fluttered to open and everything was a blur.

"Irving, sweetie, I thought you were done losing your teeth," she grumbled, stuffing her face into the pillow beside him, wrapping her arm around his torso, swinging his body around and begging him to return to sleep. Irving obliged, placing his new tooth on the nightstand and closing his eyes.

In school, Irving was growing tired of the redundant school work, no longer feeling challenged by his academics, he requested additional books from Mrs. Taylor.

"Mrs. Taylor," he walked up to her desk.

Smiling, she laughed, "Oh my, look who is officially a big boy! You've lost another tooth? And right in the front."

"Yes."

"Well, you know what they say about nine-year-old children who still lose their teeth," she teased, taking a seat as the children now cleared out for lunch. Irving's eyes widened with intrigue, "You're a big boy and can officially conquer the world," she continued, pinching his nose, her words music to his ears. "Would you like me to walk you down to the cafeteria?"

Irving quickly said, "No! I'm a big boy, remember, and I need more books, Mrs. Taylor. Big boy books!" he shouted, racing through the doors and down to the lunchroom.

Mrs. Taylor pondered long and hard before deciding to bring along her daughter's old college textbooks and workbooks for Irving—her daughter had graduated one year prior, she figured, *what harm could it do?* Plus, she knew he was growing bored and impatient, always the first to complete his assignments and never receiving anything below an 'A' on exams. A calculus textbook, *Public Speaking* by Stephen Lucas, *The Principals of Economics,* and an SAT prep-book was the best she could do at the moment; she removed them from the trunk of her car as earlier that day she decided to thrift them. Mrs. Taylor figured that perhaps Irving could seek to increase his vocabulary and begin teaching himself in his spare time or even when he went home. Irving loved this!

Lisa was always worried seeing Irving and the heavy book bag he carried; stepping inside, Irving removed his bag, the loud thud startling her.

"What do you have in here, boulders?"

Irving ran into the kitchen where he struggled to open the refrigerator, stretching to the top where he grabbed the cold cuts.

"Hey, hey, hey," Lisa called to him, dropping her bag to the floor, "You know the rules; I will make you a sandwich to eat. Now, please go wash your hands and start your homework, Irving," Lisa said, mildly irritated. But Irving did no such thing.

"You're not the boss of me, I am a big boy now, see!" he shouted, showing her his missing tooth, "So I can make my own food and you, you can go home!" he continued screaming at

Lisa. Lisa felt sad, his words upsetting her.

"If you want to make your own food, then fine, but I can't leave you alone," she said, sounding disheartened. "You're smart enough to know that, but just too young to care," she continued. Irving did not feel guilty; Lisa retreated to the dining area where she sat doing her homework as Irving struggled to make his snack and pour his juice, but as persistent as he was, he refused to ask for help. Pouring the milk and hearing it splatter along the floors, Lisa could not help but get distracted. Irving removed his backpack from the ground, placing it on his back, the books no doubt weighing him down as he grabbed the cup and plate with his sandwich and began struggling to make his way up the stairs. It was the hardest thing for Lisa to witness; however, she decided to say nothing, and the mess he was making along the carpet was of no concern to her.

Rose entering into her home felt something was wrong, again the television set had not been turned on, Lisa was preparing to leave, the kitchen unclean and the stains on the carpet had her feeling perturbed.

"Lisa," Rose called.

"Yes," she responded, her tone displeased and agitated.

"What on earth happened here?" Rose asked politely.

"Irving happened, I have no idea what's gotten into him lately, but he hasn't really been himself and then today, he yelled at me and told me that he doesn't need a babysitter because he's a big boy now. Ms. Rose, I understand you're his adoptive parent and all, but Irving is spoiled and now, quite frankly, a bit rude. Maybe I should rethink whether or not I want to come back," Lisa said, opening the door and making her way into the hall, disappearing as Rose bellowed.

"Irving, get down here right this second," But, Irving did not come, rather, he remained seated, his cup and plate empty, mindlessly kicking them around his bedroom. Rose waited at the bottom of the stairs, for what felt like five minutes before deciding to straighten the kitchen; Rose removed her cardigan, planning what she was going to make for dinner. She decided not to worry, she simply could not bring herself to, although after Irving she convinced herself never to bring work home again, she was getting swamped and now falling behind. Category one case files were now being continuously postponed by the judge due to her lack of preparation. Rose was feeling overwhelmed, wondering now had she taken on too much, too soon.

Work was no longer an escape for Rose, it had slowly become a place of burden, and now with Irving beginning to disobey her, she was not sure exactly how much more she could take. The night was beautiful as she walked to the open window, staring outside as the chicken baked and the rice simmered. Irving was quiet, almost too quiet, but she was in no mood to scold him. After all, by now, how could she? Rose knew she was too lenient, but considering all Irving had been through she could not bring herself to reprimand him. At the beginning Rose had known the approach she was going to take with Irving, and in the beginning it had been quite effective, but now that he's getting older, she needed something new, *but what* exactly? She thought.

Two hours later, dinner was ready. Rose made her way upstairs to fetch Irving, knocking on his bedroom door, lifting the door hatch handle, she allowed herself inside.

"Irving," Rose called, unable to locate him, but he remained silent.

"Irving!" she called again, this time a little louder, opening the closet door and then looking under his bed to find him reading a textbook. Rose took a long sigh.

"Irving, why didn't you answer me?" she snapped. Irving slowly turned to face her.

"I am reading," he said softly.

"Well, hello to you too, and dinner is ready. Also, what happened with Lisa today, Irving?"

"I don't want a babysitter anymore," he said. Rose switched positions to lay next to him, opening the door wider so her feet could hang past the threshold. Irving's bed was right next to the door entrance, but he slept with his head away from the wall towards the window and had positioned himself under the bed the same he would had he been sleeping on top of the mattress.

"Irving, we have to stop meeting like this, and you cannot be rude to the babysitter. You are a brilliant young man, this is true; however, you cannot be disrespectful towards adults, is that understood?"

"Lisa is not an adult, she is only six years older than me, she isn't equipped to babysit, she needs a babysitter, too," he cried, a baffled Rose now struggling to find a rebuttal.

"Listen, I am the adult and I made the decision to have her here, understand? She is going to watch you while I work, Irving, that is the plan," Rose contended. "Now, come downstairs for dinner." She sat up before standing and walking downstairs where she overheard him,

"I'm not hungry," shouted Irving. Rose could not believe her ears.

"Irving, you get down these stairs right now!" she screamed. *Silence.* Rose was getting a migraine as she fought the urge to behave belligerently.

"Irving," she called again to no prevail. As she stomped up the stairs now, Irving heard her and began wiggling his way out from under the bed, rushing to close his bedroom door, upsetting Rose further. "Irving, I have no clue what on earth has gotten into you, but I will not tolerate this kind of blatant disrespect in my home!" Rose shouted. She was shocked at herself for speaking to Irving in such a tone, but he stood listening. "You are under my roof, and so you will do as I say. Do I make myself clear?" she asked, pointing her finger at him after re-opening the door and staring into his eyes as he remained standing before her.

"But—but, I am a big boy and big boys don't get in trouble! Big boys do what they want!" Irving screamed, backing up into his study desk.

"Oh no, no, no, you are a young man, still growing up. Okay, you lost your tooth, this does not give you the right to be disrespectful," said Rose.

"You're alone, Mommy Rose, and you're alone because—because you're divorced and sad," he stammered. "But a big boy can help; if I am big then I can help," Irving cried. Rose fell to her knees.

"Listen to me; my burdens are not yours to bare, do you understand? I am not alone or sad or needing you to grow up before your time so you can help me. I am fine, and with Lisa here to help we will be fine together, but Irving, Lisa is only here to help your Mommy Rose, she only wants to make it better. Also, ignoring me does not help me, getting an attitude and being rude, does not help me," Rose pleaded.

"I just ignore you sometimes because you don't let me do what makes me happy," Irving confessed sadly. "But I know you saved me, but I just want to be happy too." Rose was confused.

"Irving, are you not happy, what have I not done to make you happy?"

"You keep taking people away from me and giving me things I do not like. Lisa, I do not need Lisa. I need Mr. Royal and Mr. Samuel, but you take them away. You take away everyone who makes me happy because you're divorced and sad."

Rose stood, disappointed in herself as she had not realized the damage she was causing. Lifelessly, she said, "Dinner is on the counter, if you're hungry you can get something to eat, okay? I am going to sleep." she exclaimed sadly after taking a huge gulp. Rose stood, walking out of his room. Her eyes filling with water, closing the door behind her, Rose fell onto the mattress as she cried herself to sleep that night.

LISA K. STEPHENSON

5

"It just feels like I'm losing my mind," sniveled Rose. She had decided to call out of work; she sat on the couch in her living room, the spring sun shining brightly through her windows as Reggie sat adjacent to her.

"I understand this may be a rough time for you; I have Alissa covering your caseload. But Rose, I am not sure how much longer I can cover for you. I've been explaining your excessive tardiness and absences as family emergencies," Reggie said, sounding worried. "Be honest, what's really going on?" Gripping the cup with his tea tightly, he had not removed his cardigan for the weather today was cool; he was unsure of whether or not he should get comfortable.

"Reggie, I thought this was going to be easier, I thought we were going to have the time of our lives: parks, trips, hanging out, I thought—" Rose drying her tears.

Reggie interrupted her. "You thought Irving was going to be your new companion? Well, obviously not in a sexual way, that would be considered pedophilia in which case I would have

117

to have you arrested," he joked, but Rose did not return the jest. Reggie always had a strange sense of humor, what he found comical was merely offensive—Rose now second-guessing whether or not she should continue to confide in him.

"A companion, I suppose," she reluctantly agreed.

"Rose, what did you do after your divorce was finalized. I mean, did you talk to anyone?" Reggie asked, concerned.

"No, I did not," admitted Rose.

"I can recommend someone, how about it?" Reggie asked, removing a pen and small card from his inner suit pocket. "His name is Alan White, oh and interestingly enough, his daughter wants to be a psychologist, too," laughing now. "Danielle, she's quite the firecracker, that one." But Rose remained unmoved, deep in thought as she pondered her next course of action for the day.

"Sure."

"So, what are you going to do once you set up your appointment? You know, if you tell him you know me, he may get you in today! It's still early, give him a call," Reggie said standing and preparing to exit. "In the meantime, kiddo, take care of yourself." And just like that, he was gone, closing the door behind him.

Rose decided to contact Alan, she figured what could it hurt to speak to a professional. As she dialed his number and reached his voicemail, she decided against leaving a message. Listening to her voicemail messages, the majority of which were from Marley and Ryan pleading with her to call them back, Rose could not bring herself to forgive them yet.

Arising from her place of comfort, she decided to take a walk over to the window where she stared outside at the large back yard, jungle gym, and parents playing with their toddlers. Rose was always jealous of her brother, and seeing families was always a reminder for her and a reason she could not get over her unhappiness, but meeting Irving that day when he was only five-years-old made her want to change. She'd dreamt of holding him in her arms ever since that day. Meanwhile, she was entertaining guests and serving as a trophy wife to a wealthy physician. But Rose needed more, she craved it, and now she was inadvertently projecting her emotions onto the one person who meant her life well.

Her younger brother, married to his high school sweetheart, having child after child, his wife never working a day in her life. But they had it all, all before her. She had studied rigorously to earn a good degree to make a lucrative living only to find herself smitten by an egotistical man who wanted absolutely nothing to do with the thought of children—at first, she thought this true of herself as well, finding it comical that they had that in common. Then she met Irving and the conversation of children came up, but Michael remained adamant about never wanting children. The news to Rose devastating to her, their fights becoming worse and as a result brought along his infidelity, and so she filed. Rose thought this was her only way out. After touching Irving's hand that day, he changed her entire life without even knowing it, and for that she was determined to make things right.

Picking up the phone again, Rose dialed Alan, who answered on the third ring.

"Hello, Dr. White's Psychologist office, my name is Danielle, how can I help you?" a woman said politely.

"He-hello," Rose began clearing her throat, "My name is Rose Appleton and I am a friend of Reggie Helms. I am calling today to set up an appointment with the doctor."

"Sure, give me one second whilst I grab his schedule. Do you prefer mornings, afternoons, or weekends?"

"Um, weekends preferred."

"Perfect, we have an opening for this coming Saturday at 10 a.m., does that work for you?"

"Yes," Rose lied, she had no idea whether or not that would work considering Irving's unpredictable behavior.

"Great! I have you down. We look forward to seeing you. Have a great rest of the day," Danielle said before Rose heard the dial tone. She felt relieved slightly, Rose was growing tired of keeping her emotions contained.

Rose was not accustomed to spending days at home, as she flipped through the channels on the television realizing nothing good was on, considering at this hour people were supposed to be at work, so she decided to catch up on assignments—something she promised herself she would stop falling behind on. As she tugged on her hair she remembered she was considering a change. Rose hopped out of her sofa, ran to her room to change her clothes and struggled to locate her earrings. Searching the house, she cleaned up along the way, cleaning the kitchen and Irving's bedroom until a faint knock came to the door—wondering who it could have been at 10 a.m., she opened the door and was surprised at who she saw.

"Good morning, I heard your footsteps so I figured I would drop by—I hope this isn't a bad time," Keith said. A perplexed Rose stood wondering what to say. She had not seen nor spoken to Keith since their date the other night and sort of found herself at peace with that. She wondered if she was truly ready to begin dating. "I know my dropping by is sudden, I apologize, I seem to be doing that a lot lately, which isn't too attractive I suppose. But um, I am next door if you ever want to swing by for a chat," Keith continued as he grew worried; he'd thought their date was absolutely phenomenal, only her reaction told him otherwise.

"No, no, sorry, I just have a lot on my mind, and with my son, things have been a bit crazy. But I am fine and I appreciate you stopping by. I was actually on my way out, not sure if maybe you'd like to join me?" Immediately following her invite Rose wondered why that last sentence left her mouth. But it was too late; Keith accepted her invitation, joyfully letting her know that he would return shortly. Closing the door slowly, running her fingers through her hair, Rose had failed to tell Keith how she planned to spend her day, hoping he would still be okay with the arrangements.

Thirty minutes later Rose and Keith arrived at a nearby hair salon where she waited her turn to be seen, Keith making small talk.

"So what are you planning to have done today?" he asked, smiling. Still, Rose could not understand why he was so willing to accompany her.

"I am just looking for a change, thinking of doing a short cut. What do you think of a short hairstyle on me?" she asked, lifting her hair and turning her head from side to side, hoping to make it easier for him to see the vision.

"Well, I think because you have such strong facial features, maybe not to go too short. Maybe try stopping at your jawline." Rose began to feel insecure; *strong facial features.* She resumed flipping through pages of a magazine. Keith, sensing a change in her decorum, "I mean, you're beautiful the way you are and by no means was I trying to offend you," he panicked, but he was speaking on deaf ears. Shortly they were greeted by the stylist.

"Good morning, what can we do for you today?" the charming woman asked.

"A short stylish cut with a sweep, and let's go platinum blonde," Rose said assertively. Keith stared at her.

"Wow," he chuckled.

As Keith waited patiently for Rose, he went and purchased them both water and snacks. Rose realized now that Keith was both kind and attentive; and although she valued his input, this day was after all about her and her mental health. As the beautician massaged her scalp Rose drifted off into a light sleep where she imagined how different her life would have been without Irving. Maybe she would have traveled more, went hiking, fishing, or even visited her parents in Ireland since they decided on moving there upon retirement—blessed to have been able to retire early.

Two hours later, as she admired herself in the mirror with Keith looking on, Rose felt like a new woman. Her hair now inches above her ears, a platinum blonde color, no more red and no more boring—the beautician, Lydia, stood behind her admiring her work.

"Now all you need is a good tan and you will be good to go." Keith could not believe his eyes.

"You look fantastic," he told her. "Do you want to get something to eat?" Rose was ecstatic.

"Of course!" she smiled, popping up from her seat and completing the transaction, she headed out the door, staring at herself through every store window they passed until they came to a diner only a few doors down from the salon in the plaza. But as Rose prepared to enter, her cellular phone rang. Raising the antenna, she answered; it was Mrs. Taylor.

"Good afternoon, may I speak with Ms. Appleton?" her soft voice asked.

"This is she," Rose grabbing Keith by the arm to stop him from walking inside.

"Ms. Appleton, Irving did not return to class after lunch today. I was wondering if maybe he had a doctor's appointment I did not know about."

"No, he did not," Advised Rose as she struggled to locate her car keys, panicked. "I have to go," she said to Keith, hanging up the phone, her eyes welling.

"What's the matter?" Keith shouted from behind her as he too made his way towards the car, begging her to calm down, he asked again, "Rose, breathe, what's the matter?"

"Irving, he isn't at school," she cried, stepping into the car. As Keith entered inside, she turned the wheel so hard the tires screeched out of the parking lot.

That morning Irving attended homeroom long enough for his attendance to be taken and then he begged Hensley for a favor after tracking him down during his lunch period. Irving stood in the hallway with his backpack on, his eyes searching frantically inside the lunchroom and then, there he was, Hensley, sitting amongst a group of girls from his class. After taking several deep breaths, Irving stepped viciously towards him, praying no one would tease him—or worse, assault him.

Face to face with Hensley, who was now embarrassed to see Irving, he immediately stood. "What do you want?"

"I need your help." Hensley walked him towards the

emergency exit to the rear of the cafeteria.

"Help with what?"

"Can you bring me to Mr. Samuel?" Irving asked politely. Hensley was confused.

"Look, my dad lets me drive from school to home, technically, I'm not even supposed to be driving. I don't have a permit or a license, dude, I'm fourteen. But, if you tell me where you're trying to go, I can give you some money for the bus," Irving nodded in agreement.

"Okay!" he said with excitement. Hensley couldn't believe he was doing this, reaching into his back pocket he pulled out two dollars and a few quarters, placing it all in Irving's hands.

"That's all I have, okay?" he said to Irving before walking back to his table. Irving raced through the front doors, past the gates, and down one block to the W60 bus.

Three buses, two hours, and fifteen minutes later, Irving arrived at the housing development. He had not been there in over two years. Everything appeared different now, especially in the daytime. As he walked, he noticed there was no one standing outside, only the women and men passing through. He waited by the steel doors for someone to open them, he did not have a key card anymore to swipe. After standing around for almost ten minutes, a woman began making her way outside, struggling to open the door as she held a toddler in her arms and the stroller contained an infant she was looking to pull out onto the concrete. Irving was happy to assist.

Once inside he took the stairs to the second floor where he wandered around, listening for the loud music to blare and—it did. It came from apartment 2B. Irving banged on the front door, elated. The locks clicked on the other side, and the man opening the door holding a gun just above Irving's head, but this did not frighten him. As the man lowered the pistol a sharp shriek filled the hall.

"Little man!" Robert shouted, lifting him from the ground. Irving found it hard to recognize him as he walked Irving inside.

"Yo, Mido, look who I found in the hallway, man. It's little dude, but he ain't little no mo' doe." Robert placing Irving on the ground as Irving searched the room with his eyes to locate Samuel, and he did. Straightening his uniform and tossing his backpack to the ground, Irving ran to him, leaping into his arms. Taller now, he could no longer fit in his lap, but Samuel's smile filled with glee.

"Boy!" he shouted. "My little man, how have you been?" Samuel asked putting out his blunt into the ashtray. Nothing changed since Irving had last been in their apartment. He only noticed that Samuel lost a lot of weight.

"Why are you so small?" asked Irving. Samuel smiled from ear to ear.

"Boy, you talk so well, good and articulate. The White people doing you well, huh? Stand over there and let me look at you." Samuel wanted to get a good look at the young boy. Irving complied, stepping over to a corner where he stood with his hands to his side. His navy-blue school uniform fit him perfectly with a pair of black dress shoes to match, his hair trimmed nicely and his skin clean. Samuel wanted to cry, but could not bring himself to shed a tear, "Irving my boy, have a seat," Samuel instructed him. "I am sick, you hear me boy, and so, I won't be here much longer. But I don't want this life for you, what I want though, is for you to know the system so we can adjust it," he said. A bewildered Irving could do nothing but focus on the change in his voice—croaky. He was dying now, stage four cancer. Irving did not understand as their joyous union had turned into a sorrowful one.

"Change it how?" Samuel motioned for Robert to assist him.

"Come on youngin, we gonna go for a walk, aight?" Robert said, pushing Samuel's wheelchair out into the hallway. Samuel was indeed elated to see Irving, thinking now that it was destiny he would return at such a crucial point in time.

"Okay," whispered Irving, standing and walking alongside them. "Mr. Samuel, why don't you buy medicine to get better?"

Irving asked, fearful of losing Samuel, he could focus on nothing else.

"Ah, Irving, I done bought all the medicine in the world," he said going into a coughing fit. Irving backed up, Robert caressed his back and handed him a bottle of water from beneath the wheelchair as they waited for the elevator light to ding.

Once outside Samuel could not wait to take in the nice cool breeze, he closed his eyes, tilting his head back, Irving finally seeing him in the sunlight and raced over to give him the tightest hug he could muster. Patting his arms Samuel smiled, "You don't have to worry about me, Irving. I am stronger than I look, I promise. I'll be here a bit longer," Samuel smiled. His eye sockets were sinking into his head, dark circles formed under his conjunctiva.

As Robert wheeled Samuel away from the housing sector and down to the houses a few blocks over, the gentlemen all walked and talked.

"Irving, as we walk out here, tell me, what do you see?" asked Samuel, Robert behind him pushing slowly. A timid Irving, unsure of how to answer, knew with Samuel that questions and answers were never so transparent.

"I see a neighborhood divided," whispered Irving. Robert stopped as Samuel turned himself to face Irving, who stood in front of a fire hydrant just ten feet from their initial destination.

"Face me," Samuel instructed him. Irving did as he was told.

"Look to your right, what do you see?" Samuel asked Irving.

"I see the *public housing building*, home!" Irving smiled as he read from the sign stationed just outside the entrance to the housing sector.

"Look to your left, what do you see?"

"I see houses."

"Look behind you, what do you see?"

Irving struggled to turn. "I see Starbucks." He nodded, assure of himself.

"What you are seeing here, is called The American Class System," Samuel said. Irving took another look around, bewildered.

"What does that mean?"

"It means there are the rich, the poor, and the middle class. This also means there are givers and earners and the people in between who both classes take from, so let's call them the takers. We live in a country where our class is based on our socioeconomic conditions," Samuel said, leaning forward, Robert standing against a pole as Irving stood before Samuel soaking up his knowledge like that of a sponge. "We start with the upper class, the earners, the owners of mass production and most of the country's private wealth. They earn because they provide a service or produce goods that are beneficial to the people who drive the economy. Are you following me?" Irving nodded profusely.

"Good, earners have mastered the difference between generating income and acquiring wealth. Income is a sad salary, what the owners can choose for you, while wealth, wealth is your goal, wealth is the total value of all your assets, without your debts, and so income is what you make, also known as what they tell you-you can make, while wealth is what you have. You're no fool, tell me, the person who works at Starbucks, does he have income or wealth?"

"Wealth?" Irving said, guessing. This upset Samuel. "Sorry, no, income, the worker has income because his salary was chosen?" Irving asked, unsure of his response.

"Do you want income or wealth?"

"Wealth?"

"Wealth!" Samuel said, gritting his teeth. "Income earners live from paycheck to paycheck, if they were to stop working, they would become destitute. You need to learn the importance of frugality, investments, property and—" before he could finish he entered into one of his coughing fits.

Robert quickly came to his aid, handing him the water he drank earlier. Samuel felt better, resuming, "Irving, remember this, someone can bring in a high income and not be wealthy, meaning, they earn a lot of money but have no investments, making them *new money*. I want you to be new money, so your children's children can be wealthy, do you understand me?" Samuel emphasized as he motioned for Robert to push his chair. Irving nodded, as he did understand.

As they strolled in the neighborhood, Samuel continued his lesson on the social classes advising Irving, "Middle class, listen carefully, son, because when the time comes, it's these people who you have to convince that you are good enough to represent. They are divided, but they are the same. Just as the upper class, they too are divided, you have *new money* and *old money*. always remember, *old money* equals wealth, *new money* equals high income." Samuel coughed again, although it was not as bad as before; he was growing weary.

"Maybe we should head back, Mido. Tomorrow another day," said Robert. Coughing still, Samuel replied no as he continued.

"The upper middle class, their professions, most likely the white-collar man—lawyers, physicians, accountants and so on, typically, the college graduates. The lower middle—blue collar, police officers, electricians, truck drivers, plumbers."

"But why aren't the plumbers just the lower class? They live in public housing?" Irving inquired.

"That's because they working son, they work! And I am speaking about the ones who are on the books, books mean taxes," Samuel responded. They arrived in front of a church; a large building taking up an entire block in the Bronx.

"Irving, my days on this earth are numbered, but this building here, this church, I am leaving it to you," Samuel said. "I understand you are young, but I worked hard to invest in properties so that one day, my offspring would acquire wealth. Unfortunately, while chasing the money, I lost the ability to reproduce, but then you came along, and although you are not my blood, you are my protégé. I want you to carry out my mission here on earth Irving—building more wealth for the Black Man. Right now, with this building, you are not *new money*, you are well on your way to wealth, do you hear me?"

"…and I got you lil homey, just like I've had him," Robert interrupted. Samuel nodded his head in agreeance.

"You are not going to die tomorrow!" cried Irving.

"I have a few months, Irving and then I'll be gone, the doctors say, so you came back just in time. But the lawyers would have found you. Money is power Irving, and with it you will teach the Black Man the importance of investments and how to acquire wealth, not for himself, but for his children's children. A lot of these youngins, they're doing' it all wrong." Irving could not help but cry.

"You can't go!" he sobbed, grabbing Samuel's arm, "You just can't go! I am happy with Mommy Rose, but she isn't us, she isn't this, you can't go!" he screamed. Samuel turned his chair to face Irving as the sun began to set.

"Listen to me, get some tough skin. Alright!" Samuel scolded him. "And knock out all that crying shit, you about to be one wealthy Nigga. Can't nobody tell you anything, do you understand me? You walk with your chest high, your eyes dry, and handle your shit, but you will do so in a sophisticated manner. The White folks raising you are educated, so you listen to what they got to say and you pay attention, do you understand?" Samuel continued as Irving dried his eyes, standing upright.

"Yes, sir."

"Let's get back to the housing, I need my medicine," Samuel instructed Robert, who gladly obliged. Irving stood across from the church, taking it all in. An entire block, in a middle-class neighborhood, a church building, his to own, his mind still could not fathom this.

6

Night came down quickly as Robert wheeled Samuel back to the building, all out of water now, Irving feared another coughing fit but they were close. Arriving at the building, a group of gentlemen stood outside, Samuel motioning for them to move as he struggled to preserve his strength. Once inside, Irving lagged behind them, trying to see if the men were at all familiar, remembering the night he met Kevin. Irving ran back outside, Robert was not quick enough to stop him as he chose to prioritize Samuel, who needed both medicine and rest. As the elevator door closed along with the steel doors—Irving stepped back outside. He looked up to see the window from where his mother had jumped, ending her life so prematurely. Irving was basking in the nostalgia, although there were many horrific memories here, there were still a few he wished he could have held onto.

Irving remembered when the dope peddlers would flee at the sight of Samuel, now, due to his illness, they seemed to pay him no never mind, simply counting down the days to when he would be no more. Irving then wondered, who would be in charge of the housing projects, as he pondered this, making his way towards the street light, a shadow stood behind him, startling him.

"You all groomed now and shit," said Marvin, barely able to stand—staggering. Irving's eyes widened; he took a large gulp. The oversized Hennessey bottle in his father's hand was a sure sign that he was inebriated, the dope dealers all high and out of focus as Irving stood fearing for his safety, but no one could see the terrified look on his face,

"So, you ruined my whole fucking life yo, you a little shit for that. I tried to take care ah you and what you do? Huh? Fuck around and tell these child people all types ah shit. I told myself," he said now, tossing the 750ml bottle back and forth as he spoke, slurring his words, his sentences incoherent.

"My wife all locked up and shit, but here the fuck you are, new uniform, haircut, and rich shoes, out here just looking fresh to motherfucking death. But you don't know death, you fucked up my whole shit, everything I had going for myself, you ruined it. I had a new job and couldn't focus cause of yo ass, lost my shit, had to come back here and look at the coincidence, huh!" Marvin shouted, still no one took the time to notice how close Marvin was stepping to him, Irving continuing to back up, praying he could simply run away, but he felt trapped as Marvin teased him, stepping to the left and to the right, making it obvious that anywhere Irving ran he would grab him.

"What do you want?" whispered Irving.

"What do I want?" his father replied, the look in his eyes hateful. "I want you dead. Fucking dead, do you hear me?" he grumbled. The men behind him all scattered as Irving now stood alone, Marvin stepping towards him Irving lifted his hand to protect his face, emptying the last drop in the bottle onto the concrete, Marvin stepped hastily towards him, knocking Irving upside the head until he fell. With the butt of the Hennessey bottle, Marvin bludgeoned Irving to the rear of his head, blood beginning to splatter as the blue Nissan pulled up just outside,

Rose and Keith both exiting. Rose fell to the ground, tripping over her feet. The night happening in slow motion as Irving slipped into an unconscious state. Rose screaming and Keith ran towards Marvin as he continued to bash Irving's head in, feeling no remorse—the look on his face possessed.

Just then a loud gunshot was heard from the steel doors. Cocking the gun once more, Robert stood by the threshold, letting off another bullet into Marvin's chest. He fell, the Hennessey bottle ornate with Irving's blood rolling on the concrete, the cracking of the concrete resonating, Marvin's eyes left open as he fell to the ground, blood everywhere. Rose screamed, the sound of her voice echoing at least three blocks away as she cradled Irving, his blood leaking through her fingers. Rose quivering as she struggled to stop the bleeding, covering the gash in his head; Irving's body was beginning to feel cold— life leaving him. Rose continued to cry, listening distinctly as the ambulance sirens blared along with the police officers. Arriving now, the EMT lifted Irving onto the gurney, only a few feet from where his mother's corpse once lay. Robert was taken away in handcuffs, his face unreadable. Rose could not defend him, she simply raced to the back of the ambulance where the world seemed to resume.

"Oh my God, help him please!" she screamed. "Is he going to die?" she cried. Keith sat beside her, trying to console her, but she was constantly fighting him. Feeling as though this was his fault, she wished she was home. Rose held herself accountable, fearing that she may lose him; she drenched herself in tears, unable to fight this feeling of shame as she found herself feeling lightheaded, the mere thought of Irving dying bringing her to a dark place.

"Ma'am, he has taken quite a beating and there seems to be some serious damage to his brain perhaps, I can't tell you for sure, but I promise, we will do everything we can to save your son." The EMT continued to apply pressure to his open wound.

Inside the hospital moments later Rose had fallen asleep. Her eyes fluttered open to see the buzzing hospital lights above her head. Rose was now in the visitors' room with Keith standing above her, a cup of coffee in his hand and forms to complete—he'd been instructed to provide them to Rose.

He handed her the coffee first, "You might need this."

A confused Rose replied, "Where is he?"

"He's been in surgery for the past three hours." Rose sobbed. Try as he may, Keith could not calm her as she grew hysterical, fearing the worst.

"What if he's dead?" she stood, crying. Placing the coffee down, Keith stood to hold her—the room empty and dismal. Reggie called to Rose as he entered the waiting room where he was led by a nurse from the nurse's station, removing his suit jacket.

"Rose, oh dear God," he said with compassion. Rose stepped away from Keith as she turned to face him, quivering, she was at a loss for words. Knowing this, Reggie simply gave her a hug. Rose sobbed until she could not find it in herself to cry any longer, the flashbacks of the evening haunting her as she looked down on her clothes to see she was still covered in blood—his blood. As she sipped her coffee and took only small bites of the coffee cake handed to her, considering her appetite was gone. She could feel the onset of tears beginning to form. They heard nothing for hours, no update, no news, which only resulted in there being no peace.

Rose's mind was racing, grateful for both Reggie and Keith as they both continued to wait patiently. Their story now breaking news as Rose overheard the television set outside by the nurse's station describing the events of the night, the reporter holding her mic standing just outside the housing projects where an outline was now drawn for where Marvin had been found dead.

Tonight, we bring you coverage of the latest tragedy to hit The Bronx, a little boy was beaten unconscious by his father right here just moments ago. Behind me, you will find the body outline of the aggressor, his father, shot and killed by one of the residents here at Bloomfield Housing projects. We are told the little boy is in critical condition at t—" Rose screamed as she jumped up and exited the waiting room to enter the hallways by the station. "Shut it off!"

The announcement of Irving's condition was now public news as though he was being mocked as the reporter so nonchalantly spoke. Five hours and still nothing. Rose was growing tired as the night pressed on, Keith requesting a blanket to cover her as the disturbing sound of a cane tapped against the white floors. Looking up to see Christopher, Rose launched towards him, grabbing him by the collars as she cried, punching his chest. Keith and Reggie, both appalled, struggled to restrain her.

"Jesus, it's your fault, you were supposed to be watching him!" she cried. "I left him in your care and you let him leave! Why wasn't anyone watching him?" she screamed as she struggled to assault him.

"Rose, stop this before you begin falling apart. Irving needs you to be strong!" Keith said. Reggie leaving to make a phone call as he apologized profusely to Mr. Royal, who continued to stand by the door, his knit shirt now wrinkled and a button missing from the shawl-collar cardigan he wore. But Christopher did not allow this to faze him—his uptight militant character did not allow for such trivial matters to take precedence.

After six long hours a doctor entered, the completed forms in an uncomfortable pile in an empty seat next to Keith, everyone now fast asleep. Clearing his throat, the doctor stood, hands together, facing forward.

"Ahem," he called. Rose opened her eyes to see everyone still there, Samuel had appeared, a strange man behind him. Rose resisted the urge to attack him, feeling nothing but pity as she noticed he was slowly beginning to perish. Now that the doctor was in the room, she shook Keith to wake him. He stretched his arms as everyone now sat upright, the sun beginning to rise behind them.

"Good morning, who is the parent?" the doctor asked calmly. Rose stood quickly.

"I am," she stuttered, preparing herself for the worst.

"Please follow me," the Doctor turning to leave, Rose trailed behind him. Standing across from the nurses' station, the doctor spoke—an African-American man in his mid-thirties, tall and slender with a small afro and green eyes.

"Ma'am, at this time we were able to stop the bleeding."

Rose knew better than to be excited, his tone was melancholy, as though he had more devastating news to bestow upon her. She listened keenly. "However, he is comatose; we can't say for how long. He has good eye movement, but the concussion will need time to heal considering there was so much trauma to the brain." As Rose listened, she began to cry. "I understand this is a lot to take in, but I don't want to give you any false hope here, his brain is a lot more fragile than older patients, and this will not simply be an in and out of consciousness ordeal. There are scales we use to measure our comatose patients, categorized by motor responses, verbal responses, and eye responses. As such, he may open his eyes one day, but that does not mean we get excited. Our scale is in-depth and trustworthy, and we will do our due diligence in maintaining him here," he said.

"May I have a copy of the scale?" Rose begged.

"Absolutely," the doctor replied; his name tag reading Harold. "As of right now he's undergone an intense surgery, but as the weeks go by we will have to do more. We've removed the entire right side of his skull and put it back together; he is wearing a special pair of preventative net gloves for his protection. This is to keep him from pulling the bandages off and perhaps disturbing the skull." Rose shook her head in disbelief.

"So—so what do we do now? Can I see him?"

"Ms. Rose, I strongly recommend that you go home and get some rest; allow the news to marinate and take care of you, because I assure you Irving will need you now. Also, I do not mean to sound insensitive, but do some research to learn about exactly what you are dealing with, a large percentage of comatose patients die within the first month—now, if such a case were to happen, I strongly recommend considering organ harvesting, and there are many other options," he said, placing his hand on her shoulder. Rose could not believe her ears.

"Get your Goddamn hands off of me," she grumbled before walking away. Returning to the waiting room where she stood now staring into the eyes of those around her: Christopher, Samuel and the strange man who accompanied him, Keith, and Reggie, Rose was feeling drained.

"Thank you all for staying with me and supporting Irving." Rose was no longer seeking to blame anyone, aside from the monster who put Irving in this position. She knew their support would mean a lot to him. "I have just learned that he is in a coma and there is no guarantee that he will ever wake up again—" her eyes began to well, unable to continue, Keith stood to console her as he spoke.

"I do think everyone should head home and regroup and possibly come back tomorrow to check on Irving," he said, facing Rose as she buried her head into his chest, the tears flowing freely now.

That night Rose could not sleep, she found herself cradled in Irving's bed holding tightly his books, the one he was currently working on, she sobbed as Keith went home to shower and prepare for a day's work at the construction site.

By Saturday morning Rose was staring at the desktop computer screen down at the local library, trying to find the words to search online to learn more about Irving and his current state but had no clue on where to begin. Beginning to feel discontented, she decided to make her way to the liquor store across town where she purchased two 375ml bottles of vodka and a bottle of dry wine to which she went home to take shots by 11 a.m. Seven shots of vodka and one tall glass of red wine later, Rose was fast asleep.

Christopher called for an emergency meeting Saturday morning; the boys were accustomed to coming to school on a Saturday whenever they were in trouble and found that they would have to be performing some form of intense physical training. But today was different.

"All your base belongs to us!" mocked Patrick as the boys conversed in the music room, waiting for Christopher to make an entrance. They were reenacting scenes from their video games.

"*Zero Wing* is so awesome, man!" shouted Hensley, portraying one the characters.

"Sega-Genesis for the win!" exclaimed Johnson as he and Walter continued to horseplay. Christopher made his way inside, standing by the door, the boys scrambling to find their seats, all dressed in sweat suits and sneakers, ready for their day, but Christopher had a more pressing matter to discuss.

"Irving will not be joining us for some time. Not in the group and not in school." he was indifferent. The boys all chattered amongst themselves. "The boy is comatose, and I do encourage each of you to try to stop by and pay him a visit, young Irving is staying at the Bloomfield Memorial Hospital," he continued. They were shocked.

"Bloomfield? That is the destitute part of town," Walter exclaimed. Christopher scoffed.

"Walter, I will need two laps around the track please," Christopher making no eye contact. Johnson, Hensley, and Patrick all grabbed a piece of paper from the mahogany desk to write down the name of the hospital as Walter exited, making his way to the track. "Gentleman thank you for your time, that will be all," he continued, walking towards the back yard to ensure his orders were being carried out, and they were.

Standing in the hallway after work, banging on the front door of Rose's apartment, Keith wondered where she had gone, why she was not answering as he continued to knock. Rose startled awake, noticing the pitch-black apartment as she stumbled to the door to open it—one eye opened, her voice unsteady.

"Hey," she whispered. Keith pushed his way inside as he suspected Rose was not well.

"Have you been drinking?" he asked, demanding answers, which he found once he entered to find the empty vodka bottle and the wine bottle half empty. Rose stood, one hand above her hip and the other behind her hand, playing in her short hair—missing her long hair.

"What are you going to do, huh? Scold me?" But Keith was at a loss for words, feeling in over his head.

"Look, you clearly have a lot going on, and I by no means want to interrupt your life or bring you any additional stress or issues. But, not even as a potential mate, but as a friend, please listen to me when I say you are heading down a road to destruction," he said sympathetically. Rose simply swatted him away.

"Just go! I have no desire to date right now, I can barely raise a kid—one that was given to me at that. You would think it would be easier, him being a little older, but no, all I've managed to do is take him from a world where he almost died and introduce him to a world where now he will. Maybe he was just better off never having met me," Rose sighed as she felt along the walls, switching on the kitchen light before slamming the freezer door after removing a container of ice cream and a spoon from the drawer. Her hangover was getting worse.

"Now you're just being overly dramatic. I don't know the history with this kid, but he sure does seem to make you happy. Our walls are paper thin and there are times when I hear you two over here laughing, joking, and just having the time of your lives. I can't imagine that he would have been okay having never met you. Rose, maybe you should think about Irving. You say you love him, but how would he feel if he knew this is what you were up to when he needs you the most?" Keith pleaded. Rose began to sob profusely, her tears falling into the melting vanilla ice cream.

"I just—I just don't know what I'm doing," whimpered Rose.

"Rose, maybe you're just scared," Keith said as he made his way over to her. "But you have nothing to be afraid of. Irving is not some puzzle you need to figure out, you've told me so before. He is articulate, he tells you what he's feeling. Rose all you have to do is listen to him." Rose knew he was right as she nodded, pushing away the ice cream, frantically searching the cabinets for a Tylenol to soothe the headache from her hangover.

"I have to get to the hospital," she said, pacing around, distraught.

"Whoa, I don't think that's a good idea," Keith advised her. "I mean, maybe some more rest will do you good. I can grab you some sleep medicine if that will help, probably won't be as easy to go back to bed now," he continued. But Rose would hear of no such thing.

"No, I have to see him, what if he's awake or-or reacting to stimuli and yet I'm not there to see any of his progress?" she rambled now, confused on what to do next. Keith grabbed a hold of her shoulders, begging her to calm down.

"Rose, if Irving was showing any kind of progress the hospital would have called. Also, it's pretty late now, it's after six, why don't I just get you some food, you shower and relax?" he suggested. Reluctantly she agreed, as Keith released his grip of her, promising her his return in less than an hour, "I will be back soon with medicine and some food, okay?" he asked, the questions rhetorical as he stepped into the hallway, slamming the door behind him. Inside, Rose waited until he was gone, stepping upstairs to see her face in the mirror of her bedroom. Adding light foundation, fluffing her hair, and straightening her blouse, hoping that she looked presentable as she crept outside to make her way to the hospital.

Rose tried to remain inconspicuous and stepped past the nurse's station once she arrived at the pediatrics wing with her head held down and the front of her cardigan wrapped tightly around her torso, her loafers assisting her to carry out her plan. Inside of the small room, there he slept, his eyes closed. Rose stood as the tears fell from her eyes: Irving's left eye was completely swollen, the tracheostomy helping him to breathe was an unpleasant sight to behold, the IV chords, PIC lines, catheters, and feeding tubes plus much more all bringing her to her knees. Never did Rose imagine seeing Irving look this way, he appeared to be dead, there was no movement. Rose kissed his hands as she removed his gloves to feel his soft skin against her face—closing her eyes as her sobbing grew louder, the sound alerting one of the nurses who called for the doctor.

"Ms. Rose," Dr. Harold called to her—surprising her. Rose gasped as she stood, releasing her grip of Irving's hand, her headache growing worse, as Dr. Harold approached her he could smell the alcohol seeping through her pores. Disgusted, "Get out now, before I call security, you are drunk."

Rose knew the reason for his threatening tone as she turned to face Irving bidding him a farewell, but she lost her balance as she attempted to step out of Irving's room, inadvertently walking into a wall and struggling to regain her posture, she could hear the doctor indistinctly telling the nurses to call security and to find her a ride home.

"Ms. Rose, did you drive here?" he asked with concern. Rose turned to face him.

"Please, you don't have to pretend to care. I work for the government and I know how these things go, so, you're going to file some mandated report now about how unfit of a parent I am because I came to see my son inebriated, or perhaps slightly drunk, because the truth is, I just haven't eaten." Rose taking deep breaths as she concentrated on standing. The longer she stayed awake the drunker she felt. She wondered why she had not slept it off, or if her nap was not long enough.

Dr. Harold grew impatient, calling to the nurses, "Where is security?" he screamed.

One girl timidly responded. "They say they're understaffed, sir, but will be right up when they get the chance," Keith ran off the elevators to hold her—his timing almost impeccable as he lifted her head to look into her eyes.

"Sir, doctor, sir, I am so sorry!" he said nervously, holding onto Rose as she buried her head into his chest, her eyes closing, "I will bring her home immediately, please, I am sorry, this won't happen again and she's just going through a lot," he pleaded as the doctor continued to stare at him, unmoved.

"She needs rest and please do not allow this to happen again," Dr. Harold said sternly.

Part 3

1992 – AGE 10

T he nurses, Rose, Keith, Christopher, and Doctor Harold all gathered together in the therapist's office, surprising Irving with a birthday cake in celebration of his tenth birthday.

"*Happy Birthday to you, Happy Birthday dear Irving, Happy Birthday to you*," everyone sang in unison, clapping their hands and smiling. Irving sat upright in his wheelchair, preparing to blow out the candles. Everyone applauded in excitement, Rose felt relieved, nervous but excited that he had awoken for his birthday. *January 8, 1992.*

As Rose and Dr. Harold exited the room, Rose kissed Irving profusely, promising her swift return. As they entered the hallway in the basement, Dr. Harold began by saying, "Well, this looks like it could be permanent," he smiled.

Rose grinning from ear to ear, "Are you sure?" she questioned, fighting back tears.

"Yes, we conducted a CT scan and everything looks good. His brain is functioning. I know we've had some bumps in the road, him going in and out of consciousness these past four months, but I feel pretty confident that this time he's here to stay with us," the doctor said. Rose jumped to hug him.

"Oh, dear God, thank you so much for that news!" she cried.

"Rose, I don't want you to take for granted just how lucky Irving is to have survived this; the damage to his brain was severe, and now that he seems to be conscious this will require even more work from you, his friends, and his mentors." Doctor

Harold seemed hesitant in having this conversation with Rose, especially on a day like today, but knew it had to be done. "While it does look like we've made it past the sleep/wake dichotomy, there are still all sorts of layers of consciousness a patient will go through on their way to recovery, and although he is in a conscious state, that does not mean that his memory is fully intact or that his brain will ever function the way that it used to," he continued.

Rose listened. "I understand, Doctor, and of course I am prepared to do whatever it takes, but what about his weight, I mean he's lost so much and he's so small, should I be worried?"

"Well, this is typical of comatose patients to wake up and look almost completely different than they once did. I know on television there are usually little to no changes in a comatose patient, but the reality of things is far different. The feeding tube we had him on is not designed to have him gain weight, and it is a system that will leave patients emaciated. The tube is simply there to provide the necessary nutrients for survival. But rest assured, if this is it, then he will be eating like a man who has been deprived of food for years. I wouldn't be surprised if he's eaten that entire cake by now." He chuckled, hoping to lighten the mood, and that it did as Rose felt somewhat relieved.

"Will he walk again?" she asked, immediately reverting back to a state of worry.

"Rose, yes, but unfortunately that too may take some time, he will need to relearn how to grasp the intricacies of his muscular system, but for now, standing will feel abnormal to him, his balance will be off and he may be swayed at times from feeling weak. But as aforementioned, this is the part where you will be needed the most—your time, your patience, and of course your nurturing. He will not get through this without you," Dr. Harold emphasized. "But please don't let me frighten you, you look a bit worried. We are all here to help; in the interim, today is his birthday and I am sure he is missing you in there, so go on and have fun," he said, smiling.

As he turned to walk away, Rose stood, perturbed, gathering

herself emotionally before returning to the room where Irving, in fact, did eat the majority of the cake, everyone else enjoying a small slice—this amused her greatly. A few hours later Rose wheeled Irving back to his room, she wondered what he was feeling considering he barely spoke a word that morning.

Last year...
Four weeks after the incident, Irving opened his eyes for the first time, finding beside him a sleeping Samuel, but Irving could not decipher whether or not he had been dreaming or experiencing a memory. Trying to speak, he realized this was impossible. As Samuel looked up to see him, the swelling from Irving's left eye gone and aside from the tubes, he was looking like himself.

"Hey," Samuel said. There was a man seated behind him, but Irving could not speak. Panicked now as he took a look around, he was lying in a hospital bed with walls of netting on all sides. The room zipped shut from the outside so when it closed he could not escape—he was physically tied to the bed. Samuel then bellowed for a nurse, the strange man awakened, sitting up straight. Irving cried, his eyes darting back and forth, terrified as his breathing increased along with his heart rate—immobilized. He could not move. Samuel, noticing the fear on his face, bellowing again, this time a little louder.

The strange man now stood, throwing his hands in the air, motioning for the nurses to assist them. a young man in scrubs finally made his way over, unzipping the cage and letting himself in, trying to calm Irving as he placed his hand atop his chest.

"Sorry, we're pretty short staffed here," he said, racing inside—Samuel backed away as he watched in horror, Irving struggling to breathe through his tube and panicking. The nurse now considering whether or not to sedate him,

"Irving, I need you to calm down," the nurse begged him, his heart rate increasing, beeping loudly on the cardiac monitor. "Can one of you speak to him, he doesn't seem to be responding to me and if this continues, he can go into cardiac arrest?" the nurse begged. Samuel rolled to him.

"Irving," his voice groggy. "Irving, listen to me, you're alright, just relax, I'm here and you're gonna be alright, kid." Irving sobbing as he turned to face him, unbeknownst to Samuel, his words were incomprehensible. But Irving recognized his face, and this was enough to calm him, his heart rate slowly decreased. The nurse now faced Samuel.

"Thank you, sir," Cautiously, he removed his stethoscope to check Irving's heart and lung function. "I have to let the doctor know he's awake, but for now, you can try having a conversation with him to see if he remembers anything. It's highly recommended," the nurse advised before walking towards the exit.

"Wait, why is he all restrained like this?"

"The other night a few nurses caught him sliding off the bed; it's just protocol, and these measures are strictly for his safety," the nurse reassured them. "My name is Andy, by the way," he said, extending his hand to shake Samuel's and the strange man's. "I will be back shortly," he exclaimed, leaving now.

Rose sat at her cubicle that morning going through the motions. She was slowly beginning to give up hope as she checked the internet for solutions and outcomes for comatose patients. For weeks now this was all she could do, having yet to find one success story—patients were either dead or permanently disabled. Crying every single day, her appetite gone and her hair falling out due to an increased amount of stress, she refused to give up and Keith remained by her side, giving her advice, always encouraging her and coming by in the evenings to cook her dinner as she rummaged through textbooks and studied all night long.

Some nights she lay awake dreaming it was she who had pulled the trigger instead of Robert. She wanted Marvin dead, again—whenever she attended cases for her category one patients, she would check the court board to see if Robert was going to be present for his hearing. News got back to Rose that he was facing up to twenty years in prison for possession of a concealed weapon, involuntary manslaughter, and drug trafficking, but he had the absolute best lawyer money could buy, which left Rose bewildered by how he could have possibly afforded the retainer fee. But she knew better than to pry.

Day in and day out she worked long hours trying to keep her mind occupied, but the more children she saw, the more interviews she conducted, and the more neglectful parents she encountered, the more she grew to hate the world she lived in. All of these extrinsic factors directly contributed to her drinking; she was ashamed that she had to keep her liquor cached under the kitchen sink, promising herself it would only be for emergencies, but the longer Irving took to wake up was the more each day was feeling like doomsday.

Keith frequented Rose's apartment—four times a week, cooking and tidying up as she rested, reading and waiting patiently by the phone for it to ring. In the beginning, Rose went to the hospital daily, but when Reggie had her convinced that her job was on the line she decided to reduce the amount of time she spent there with Irving. Rose loved watching him sleep, but hated that it was for this reason. She missed his smile, his laugh, and even when he scolded her. She missed him so much it was beginning to hurt.

"Hey, I can make the mac and cheese you have in here." Keith treaded lightly; although he wanted Rose to love him, he knew she was incapable of that right now—at least for him— and so he decided on another approach: providing her with care. The phone rang; hurrying to answer it, Rose bumped her toe on the coffee table, letting out a loud cry as she grabbed the phone off of the hook.

"Ro-Rose," the voice stuttered.

"Yes, this is she," Rose replied, praying it was a nurse, but it was not.

"It's me, Marley," her voice calming. "I know it's after seven and you're probably busy with Irving and getting him prepared for school tomorrow, but I just wanted to tell you how sorry I am. I feel like us not speaking these past few months was truly just awful," she said sadly. Rose ran her fingers through her hair as Keith looked on, thinking too the nurses had called to deliver some good news.

"Marley," Rose sighed, Keith resuming his work in the kitchen as he prepared the macaroni and cheese, "Irving is in a coma," she acknowledged, biting her bottom lip. Marley remained silent before screaming to Ryan.

"Ryan!" she called, "Rose, we will be there as soon as we can. I am so sorry this happened." Marley in a state panic bringing Rose to listen to the dial tone. Keith could not help but overhear.

"Who was that?"

"My sister-in-law," Rose said solemnly.

"You didn't tell them?" Keith inquired.

"No," Rose rubbing her hands together as she took a seat. "No, I didn't tell them. I mean, I shouldn't have had to tell them. Ryan is Irving's counselor and has been for almost three years, every other Sunday he meets with him and for months he hasn't gone and not once did Ryan contact me to find out why," Rose complained. "As usual, he sends his wife."

"I don't know your brother, but perhaps they do genuinely care and you could just be pushing them away," Keith said. Rose looked up at him.

"What makes you think that?"

"Well, you kind of did that to me, too."

"I wasn't always like this, I swear. I know I have my faults, but I just find it easier to avoid my problems sometimes, even if that means avoiding the people closest to me."

"You're a great person Rose, and lots of fun to be around when you're not being so defensive, don't beat yourself up too much. I think with some patience and time, we'll get it right."

"You talk as though you're in this for the long haul," she teased.

"I mean, I don't go around boiling mac and cheese for just anybody you know," he grinned—both Rose and Keith laughing at his sarcasm. He strained the boiled macaroni and cheese as he finished preparing it to serve Rose. A few moments later he said, "My dearest lady, your gourmet meal is ready." Rose made her way into the kitchen.

"You know, I really appreciate this, but you don't have to cook when you come."

"I know, but you deserve it," Keith leaning towards her; as they prepared to kiss, the doorbell buzzed. Rose threw her head down as she stood to answer it, both Marley and Ryan stepping inside.

"Rose, oh my God, what on earth happened, when did this happen? How has he been?" Marley said energetically. Ryan removed their coats and placed them on the coat hangers.

"This isn't fair, Rose, this is an emergency and you keep this from us!" he scolded her. They wanted answers but would not allow her a chance to speak.

"Jesus, you cut your hair too, what on earth has been going on?" Marley questioned, looking around to see Keith standing awkwardly in the kitchen. Her eyes darted back and forth. "Are Ryan and I interrupting something?" she asked, praying the answer was no.

"No, listen, you are both right and I apologize, okay, I just had a lot going on and I was angry with you both, and so I didn't involve you."

"Angry? Rose, you don't get to do this! I apologized the last time we were here and had a conversation with both Andy and Monica. Now, instead of forgiving us, you chose to hold onto this malice even through such an emergency. I am shocked, and I am pissed, Rose," Ryan shouted. A speechless Rose continued to listen.

"I have no problem admitting my wrongs, and yes confiding in my wife before speaking to you is wrong, Andy's behavior was also wrong, and yes, I should have taken more of an interest in Irving's interactions with the children—or the lack thereof—and should have been paying more attention, but that does not mean I love him any less than I do my own flesh and blood. We deserved to be here for this! We are a family," he continued. Rose had not heard Ryan speak this much since they were children, indicating his level of thoughtfulness.

"Stop shutting me out, stop shutting us out! We want to help you," he concluded. Ryan stepped to remove a bottle of water from the refrigerator and introduced himself to Keith.

Rose remained standing as Marley asked, "What happened, Rose, and when was he admitted? Last night? Was it school, did he fall? I mean, my goodness, this is serious."

Rose refused to answer as she knew her response would only trigger another uncomfortable wave of emotions. But Ryan, knowing his sister, knew there was a reason for her silence.

"Rose?" Ryan taking a sip of his water, Keith looking on, unsure now of whether or not he should stay.

"He's been in the hospital for about four weeks, um, and Marley, um, his father actually did this to him, he beat his head in with the bottom of a liquor bottle one night when Irving decided to skip school to see one of his mentors, Mr. Samuel," Rose revealed awkwardly. "...and um, I think that's it, don't think I missed anything." She concluded, grabbing the dish from the counter as she began eating.

"Wait a minute, did you just say four weeks, as in one month, as in, Irving has been lying in the hospital for one month in a coma and you didn't think to talk to me about it?" Ryan said, placing the water down on the table, his eyes beginning to well. "Why do you hate us so much?" he asked, feeling fed up.

Marley interrupted him. "Sweetheart, don't do this, let's just go," she pleaded, standing by the front door.

"No, I won't leave. You smile in our faces, you begged us for help so you could win this custody battle, and then when you did, you just toss us away over something so minor. Rose, you forget I'm a child psychologist, so when children are acting abnormally, I know. Your behavior these past few months have been very unbecoming, is it jealousy? What is it? Why are you like this?" he asked, sounding distressed.

But Rose remained unmoved as she turned to face him.

"Ryan, we will never be the same again, you and I. You chose the bro-code over the family code a long time ago!" She said dispassionately.

"Jesus Christ, is that still something you're holding onto? Rose, for goodness sake, let it go. You married an asshole and yes, I apologized for that as well, but how would you have felt had I told you on your wedding day, '*hey sis, don't marry him, I just found out he cheated on you a month ago?*' You would have hated me for ruining what was supposed to have been the happiest day of your life, and now you're still harboring that resentment towards me?"

"Just go!" Rose, slamming the plate on the coffee table began making her way upstairs.

"Yes, go ahead, have a temper tantrum, reminds me of Ally when we scold her for lying and behaving foolishly," he yelled.

"Ryan, stop this, please, both of you," Marley interrupted.

"Get out of my house!" Rose screamed slamming her bedroom door closed. Ryan and Marley both listening as they grabbed their jackets, preparing to leave. Ryan, turning to Keith, asked, "What is the name of the hospital where Irving is staying?"

"Bloomfield Memorial," Keith responded.

"Thank you." Ryan and Marley exiting, Marley waving to Keith goodbye.

Keith thought about leaving but decided against it as he stood in the kitchen quietly, waiting for Rose to emerge—ten minutes later she did, wearing a pair of pajamas. Startled by him, she stood at the bottom of the stairs. "Jesus, I thought you were leaving."

"I was going to but then I decided to stay."

"Why?" Rose asked standing now with her arms folded.

"Rose, you're damaged, and although you did a wonderful thing by helping Irving, you need someone to help you, too. Maybe a change in location will do you good, maybe counseling, which I do highly recommend." Rose was beginning to lose her patience,

"I am sick and tired of everyone telling me that I am this abnormal woman all because I am feeling emotional about the things that my son is going through. I mean, God, am I not allowed to feel? Also, not to mention a man was shot and killed right in front of me!" Rose cried. Just then Keith bent down, removing the vodka Rose hid under the sink.

"Your dishwashing liquid is also under here, so you know I wasn't snooping. Rose, you're hiding alcohol, this is a serious issue and the thing with your brother, it's way deeper than you're letting on, and if you continue like this, then even when Irving does wake up, emotionally and mentally you won't be in a good space to help him." Keith said as he watched the tears flowing from her eyes. Walking over, he opened his arms, pulling her close, hugging her, his chin settled on top of her head as she sobbed, caressing her slowly, he continued, "I'm here to help."

The next day Rose arrived to work feeling rejuvenated. Keith spending the night gave her the comfort she needed; she had a smile plastered across her face. Inside her cubicle, she could hear Reggie screaming her name from his office. Alissa raced to her desk.

"Irving is awake!" she said, smiling. Rose could not believe her ears, "the hospital called here since they couldn't reach you at home," she continued, jumping for joy—their coworkers beginning to stare. Rose paced heavily to the front of the office, sticking her head into Reggie's office where he was laughing.

"Don't stop here, go, go to the hospital, he's awake!" his hands motioned for her to leave. Rose felt like she was dreaming as she raced along the highway, heading to The Bronx. Inside Bloomfield, she made her way to the coma ward on the other side of the building where she waited for a nurse to sign her in. Growing impatient, she simply walked past the nurses' station and into the confined room Irving occupied. Tossing her purse to the side, Rose could not believe her eyes, there was Irving sitting upright, having a Jell-O cup, it was the most beautiful thing she had ever seen.

Rose was crying now as she stepped towards him, calling his name and rubbing his back, but Irving did not turn to face her—it was almost as though her presence was non-existent.

"Why isn't he excited to see me?" she asked, looking up at the nurse.

"I think the doctor will be in soon, Ms. Rose," the nurse replied as she continued to feed Irving. Rose could not mask her excitement as she continued smiling, kissing him copiously. But Irving did not seem to register what was going on around him. Dr. Harold then made an appearance, his eyes wide.

"You've arrived." The sound of his voice making Rose uncomfortable. Rose could not understand why Irving was giving her what felt like the cold-shoulder.

"May I speak with you for a moment in the hallway?" An apprehensive Rose followed him, pulling her jeans up—she was losing weight.

"Hi," Rose entered the narrow hallway, her arms folded.

"Hi, so, I want to let you know that the young man you see in there is Irving, but he is still very much unconscious. He woke up yesterday around noon—" Dr. Harold said; Rose interrupted him,

"I'm sorry, what? Yesterday? Did I receive a call? How come no one called me?" she cried. Dr. Harold took a deep breath before responding,

"We did not want to alarm you, however, when he reacted to the presence of a Mr. Samuel, emotionally, it took us some time to run a few more tests before reaching out you, we did not want to give any false hope in regard to his recovery." Rose paced.

"Samuel was here?"

"Yes, a Mr. Samuel, his mentor, I believe. He was here when Irving woke up," the doctor said, his tone annoying Rose because it was as though he felt no compassion, no empathy.

"Why was I not called the second he opened his eyes?" she screamed.

"Ma'am, please lower your voice, we are trying the best we

can and Irving was not alone when he woke up, which is truly all that matters; otherwise, yes, we would have immediately contacted you."

"That is such bull-crap! What kind of doctor are you? Why would you think after waking up from a coma he wouldn't want to be with his mother, or-or hear my voice?" she cried.

"Ms. Rose, please, can you calm down? You are unfortunately missing the bigger picture here." But Rose could not allow herself to get past the hurt of knowing that she missed one of the most important moments of his life, a time she was sure never going to get back. She stood taking long, deep breaths, trying to catch hold of herself.

"Okay, okay, so what now, huh, he's unconscious still, is that what you're saying?" she inquired while breathing shakily.

"Yes, but we did take him for a walk today with the assistance of one of the nurses, and we are encouraging all friends and family to begin bringing in photos, anything that you feel will jog his memory and help him in his recovery," he continued. "But we aren't sure how long he will remain awake; we just know that right now his brain may go to sleep again."

Rose was finding it hard to follow him as she wondered, "Well, why bring in photos if we don't know when he's going to go back to sleep?"

"Well, because it's best that we see whether or not he can identify the people in his life through photographs. Also, if he sees a loved one before falling into a state of unconsciousness he may very well dream of that individual, which will increase the likelihood of him remembering them when he does come to." Rose simply nodded, thinking only to return home as fast as she could to gather old photos and bring them back. But Rose decided against this, fearful that she would lose him before having the chance to return.

"Thank you, doctor." Worriedly she made her way back inside. Rose spent the entire day with Irving, he did nothing but eat and rest as she took naps and forced herself to drink coffee and have snacks. She assisted him with his meals as she tried her best not to cry, she just wished her baby boy would return back to her. At 7:14 p.m. Irving went to sleep—entering into another unconscious state as Rose tried waking him to read him a bedtime story from a book she purchased in the gift shop. But he did not respond.

Five days later Rose felt like she was back to square one, visiting the hospital daily, leaving work before her shift ended and fighting the urge to drink again. As she took another day off from work, standing in the kitchen making breakfast, she heard her doorbell buzz. Rose stood in the kitchen in her pajamas, hoping they would go away. The door buzzed again, this time longer. Rose scoffed before making her way to the other side of the apartment, removing the kettle from the stove.

"Coming!" she shouted. Unlocking the door, she opened it to find a man standing adjacent to her holding a briefcase and wearing a business suit. "May I help you?"

"Yes, I am looking for the guardian for Irving Houston," the sound of his voice monotone.

"Yes, I am she," Rose growing impatient. She was feeling dehydrated and looking so as well. Her skin dry and peeling, the bags under her eyes palpable.

"May I come in?" he asked politely.

"What is this in relation to?" she asked, hesitating.

"Your son's inheritance, ma'am."

2

1993 – AGE 11

One year later and Irving was making an enormous amount of progress. The therapists, nurses, Ryan, Marley, and the boys from Westchester Prep visiting often, reading him a list of words or numbers and having him recall as many as possible. Irving hated those exercises but knew they had to be done. He felt like a young child having to relearn arithmetic and feeling like a complete failure—day in and day out he kept getting discouraged.

"This work is for elementary school children," Irving pouted, his words slurred; sitting in the wheelchair wearing his favorite pajamas and socks. Rose stood next to him, opening the curtains in his room as they prepared themselves for the big day.

"Irving, I have pretty much put this off for as long as I could, okay, so we have to get you ready, we're meeting with the lawyer today, alright, so please put a smile on your face and try to be optimistic," Rose smiled, although she was not hopeful. "You're a big boy, we all know that, but you have got to try and be a little more appreciative considering how far you've come," she continued as she folded his clothes.

Rose prepared to lift him. "You know the drill, grab my shoulders and hold on tight," she smiled as she lifted, imitating an aircraft blasting off, vibrating her round lips. She smiled, but Irving did not reciprocate. He was so big now, reaching her shoulders when he stood. Seating him on the bed, Irving scooted himself over as Rose folded his wheelchair, placing it behind the hospital bed.

"Knock knock," the man entered. Rose greeted him with kindness.

"Hello, um, Mr. Hartford, this is Irving," Rose said, presenting him.

"Please, no need to be so formal, call me Paul," he extended his hand to greet Irving, his eyes honoring his presence. "Young man, it is definitely a pleasure to finally meet you. Do you know why I'm here?" he asked, turning to face Rose, who immediately responded.

"No, no, he doesn't. I just, um, thought it would be best if you simply explained everything," she laughed tensely.

"Absolutely." Paul was well-groomed, his suit tailored, standing about 5'6 with a dazzling haircut and a pleasant smile. "Irving, I have a lot of news to share with you today. It is to my understanding that you are still recovering, so if I am saying too much, or I've said something you don't understand, then feel free to stop me, okay?" Paul then taking a seat in one of the chairs found in the room.

"Sure, as long as the information isn't something that can be taught to a two-year-old," Irving snapped.

"Irving, please behave," Rose pleaded as she pulled a chair next to Irving's bed where she too sat down. Paul opened his suitcase, placing stacks of papers along the top of it. Paul chuckled.

"This kid is a sharp one, huh? Well, let's begin. A little over a year ago, your mother and I had a brief discussion in regard to your inheritance. Mr. Samuel Phillip Moore died on the 9th of November two years ago in his home. In such an event you were named his one and only beneficiary," he said. "Now, Irving, it is because you are a minor and we don't seem to have any reputable relatives on file, plus Rose has proven to the court that she is both fit and responsible, that she had been appointed the legal guardian of your inheritance," he continued handing Irving and Rose both a piece of paper reiterating his last statements.

"So, until you're eighteen, you won't have access to the money or the business. I bet you're wondering, 'What business and what money?' well. At this time, we've gone ahead and set you up with what's called a UTMA account, which is pretty much an account for minors who have been gifted an inheritance. Right now, in this account, there is a total of two million, three hundred and ninety-seven thousand dollars and seventy-seven cents. In addition to that, you now own the—" Rose and Irving exchanged a look of comfort as Paul rummaged through his paperwork. "Ah, yes, you own Bloomfield Housing Projects, the sector is yours, so you will eventually be responsible for paying the taxes and collecting the rent, which of course you can simply pocket, it's lucrative income." Paul shrugging his shoulders. "Also, there is a Starbucks location that you now lease as well, however, considering you're still a minor, Rose here will have to operate these businesses until your eighteenth birthday. Do either of you have any questions for me thus far?" Irving shook his head no, Rose as well.

"Fantastic, so, the Starbucks, you are now the franchise owner of, you have a license to operate, and lastly, a church, the church is in a one point seven hundred-million-dollar building, of course, churches are a non-profit so you would do well to remember that. However, the building itself is large enough to host functions, rent office spaces and much more to earn a very profitable income as well and um, that is that. Rose, you're familiar with all of this, I know this is a lot to hear and of course a lot to handle considering the circumstances, but our offices are here to help."

"I know absolutely nothing about running a business, or building or anything like I've told you before, I—I just work for the state," she said nervously. Paul smiled at her.

"Rose, that is perfectly understandable. I have a team who can assist you with property management and handling the finances. I assure you, you have nothing to worry about. I've been working with Sammy for years, I have a good team," he said confidently. This put Rose at ease as Irving knit his eyebrows.

"Why should we trust you," asked Irving; both Rose and Paul turned to face him, bewildered.

Paul knew that the things Samuel told him had to be true, standing to close the doors for privacy, "Well—um, I have been cleaning Samuel's money for years," he said.

Rose tilted her head, "Cleaning?" she asked, needing clarification.

"Yes, laundering the money through the businesses." Rose stood, outraged.

"Jesus, you did not mention this before. Do you want to give my kid drug money? Is that what this is, drugs? I didn't want to say anything at the risk of sounding racist, but I was wondering how the hell a man like Samuel could have possibly afforded all of this, and now-now the answer is clear. Look, we don't want your drug money, okay!" she quarreled.

"Lower your voice, I could be disbarred over this; now I wondered if you could be trusted, and Samuel told me he had a talk with you and you seemed legit," Paul said, his tone changing.

"Listen, I just want us to live a normal life, and can you blame me? I almost lost him. If you think for one second, I am going to knowingly put my son in that sort of danger again you are sadly mistaken," she screamed, now standing.

"There are no dangers here, the money is 100% clean, I made sure of this myself. I counted thousands upon thousands of dollars with my bare hands for Samuel, okay! I would not put my livelihood in jeopardy over something like this. The kid is free and clear," Paul assured them—clearing illegal drug money being one of his many specialties as a crook attorney.

Rose was not content with that response as she ran to the door, sliding it open and calling for security. She was frantic. Irving struggled to stand as he yelled to her.

"Stop it, Rose! Stop!" Rose stood by the door, silenced.

"Did you just call me Rose?" she sniffled.

"That's your name," replied Irving. Rose realizing he had not addressed her by name at all until now.

"But you used to call me mommy," painfully the words left her mouth.

"I—I can't remember that," Irving admitted. "But—but, you have to calm—calm down," he stuttered, growing weary. Rose, taking a deep breath, simply exited the room leaving behind both Paul and Irving as went out to light a cigarette. With her alcohol now tamed she needed a new substance to abuse.

Rose felt like she was diminishing, losing herself, her youth taken from her along with her happiness. Keith grew distant as they found themselves quarreling daily. Although the air was cold, Rose was burning up, she was losing faith in everything. Deciding to go home, she left the hospital, having no interest in what was being discussed between Irving and that crook, she raced home where she slammed the door behind her, startled to find that Keith was inside removing ingredients from the refrigerator—from the looks of it, preparing to cook.

"Hey," he said, wiping his hands clean using the apron.

"What are you doing here?" asked Rose—their last encounter unpleasant.

"I know you've been stressed and I just wanted to come by and cook your dinner, I hope you don't mind," Keith said. But Rose did mind, she was not happy with Keith.

"You yelled at me," she fussed, reminding him of why she could not simply accept his pleasantry. Keith felt ashamed.

"Yes, I know, but I just wanted to help and try to mend the relationship with you and your brother. The truth is, Rose, no matter how much time we spend together or how much we say we love each other, I find it hard to believe it the longer you stay mad at your brother for something he did years ago involving your ex-husband," Keith admitted. "You're still allowing your past to dictate your future, and sometimes I don't even know where I stand. Our arguments are deeper than you wondering why I haven't called all night while I'm at work—a construction site at that," he pleaded. Keith was beginning to feel hopeless.

"I know I have a lot of changes to make. I will see a therapist," she said. That night, Rose and Keith made love, promising one another to communicate better and spend more time loving one another.

A week later Rose entered into the office of Dr. Alan White; a licensed psychologist stationed out in Connecticut—she dreaded it. But she knew for the betterment of her relationship she needed to speak to someone. Irving and Rose were now at odds, he was unremorseful, snappy, and at times downright rude to her. His frustrations growing as he could not remember photos or walk on his own, continuing to fall to the floor, he was feeling like a failure. The nurses would take him on short walks and at later stages begin to exercise with him, but due to the severity of his muscle damage Irving was quite skin and bones, he was also beginning to complain about his inability to breathe on his own—his walks were bizarrely hard.

Rose feared she would lose her mind after the third rice pudding cup was thrust at her head by Irving out of complete rage. She tried to empathize with him, but the doctors, nurses, and witnesses to Irving's tantrums all suggested she take some time away to recuperate, a few weeks if needed because Irving was not going to recover as fast as one would have hoped. Rose did as she was told, but as the first week went by without any visits to the hospital, she realized it was the perfect time to visit Dr. White.

Inside the office, Rose sat nervously tapping her legs. The office, although small, was comfortable. Once inside the glass high-rise building, Rose followed the signs that led to his office on the ground level. Stepping past the glass doors, there was no one by the receptionist desk to greet her. Rose rocked back and forth, moving her hair to the rear of her ears as it now extended past her shoulders, her roots turning orange.

A strange man stuck his head out from the back office, calling to her. "Ms. Rose," he called. Rose abruptly turned.

"Yes, yes, that's me," she said nervously.

"Fantastic, please, this way," the doctor motioning for her to step past the receptionist desk and into his office. He was strangely upbeat, charmingly, he made slight arrangements around the room. Removing throw pillows and placing them on other sides of the sofa, stepping back to admire his work, lighting candles and turning down the lights as he straightened the tissue box.

"Oh, don't be startled, darling, have a seat, loosen up. Can I get you some water?" He was moving so quickly Rose did not know where to sit or what to say next. Alan was flamboyant and clearly suffered from OCD as he then returned to the lights where he turned them up slightly, illuminating the room, asking Rose once again, "Would you like some water darling?"

Rose again politely declined. As she watched him pace along the room before taking a seat in the single sofa cushioned adjacent to her, she wondered if perhaps he was an escaped patient. But then she took notice on her left his degrees from university hanging from the walls along with some family photos of him and his lovely daughter, who Rose assumed was Danielle.

Finally, after pacing around, Alan took a seat, his business attire worn with delicacy as he removed his suit jacket, placing it meticulously behind him, he asked, "How are you Rose?" Rose felt out of place as she took a deep breath, trying to get comfortable on the couch.

"I am okay, I do wish I was better," she admitted.

"I love an honest patient, as I believe the only way to truly get the most from our sessions is if we are completely transparent with one another," he said. Just then the door flung open, a young lady stepping inside, out of breath, the soothing sound of her voice dreamy,

"Daddy, you have a two—" she stopped speaking after realizing his session had begun, "So sorry," she said, quietly closing the door. Alan chuckled.

"My apologies, that is my daughter Danielle, she is here working part-time as my receptionist—or at least that's what I hired her to do, but you know young men and women these days," he laughed and finally Rose did too.

"She's beautiful." Complimented Rose.

"Thank you, all praises to her lovely mother," Alan responded. "So Rose, tell me, how are you feeling and what brings you in today?" Rose was stumped as her smile quickly turned into a frown.

"I am trying not to lose my sanity or my family."

"Okay, tell me more about that."

Rose spent an hour speaking with Dr. White; she discussed everything from adopting Irving to the issues with her brother and his wife, but as she spoke, listening to herself out loud, she felt childish. Realizing that her anger was never really due to the fact that Ryan kept such a secret from her, it was because deep down inside she was jealous of him. Ryan and Rose grew up in a suburban neighborhood where their mother was a doctor and their father a pharmacist. She had big plans on marrying a wealthy man and being whisked off into the sunset where she would have two children of her own and live happily ever after, as her parents did. Instead, she found herself working a dead-end job, marrying a cheater, and watching her brother have his first child and marry his high school sweetheart all while she sat at home with a man who despised the idea of having children.

But Rose came to the realization that she was simply settling because she envied the way their parents praised Ryan for being the first to give them a grandchild, and although now she felt foolish, years ago she felt robbed of an opportunity. Rose began to fear that her parents would never love her children the way they loved Ryan's, and then came another and another and another, and still Rose had not given them one. She felt betrayed by her emotions and working for a system where children were her primary focus, she was losing a handle on things, nothing was making sense, her life was falling apart, and then came Irving—the first time she met him. It was his tiny hands, the innocent look in his eyes, and yet he was so brave despite all he had been through.

Alan listened as Rose detailed her encounter with Irving down to the strands found on his head, which worried him.

"Rose, you sound to have a deep infatuation with this young man. Do you notice that?" A bewildered Rose looked up to face him replying, "No, it's not an infatuation, it's love," she corrected him.

"Rose, you ended your four-year marriage based on one encounter with this baby boy," Alan resumed. Rose chuckled nervously.

"So what are you saying, I'm some pedophile or-or I'm obsessed with my son?" she asked laughing nervously.

"No, maybe not to that extreme, but you've projected your feelings onto him. Perhaps the reason for your meltdowns, alcoholism, and crying fits is not the fear of losing a son, but the fear of losing an attachment. It sounds to me like you've grown to become co-dependent on a child," the revelation shocking. Just then the buzzer rang, frightening her; just like that one hour came and went. Rose now left with her thoughts to decipher on her own.

"Ms. Rose, it was an absolute pleasure speaking with you today." Alan stood, extending his hand for Rose to shake, but she could not bring herself to do so, she felt attacked.

"I don't see how this helped me; I feel worse than when I walked through the door initially. I—I don't feel like we accomplished anything," Rose stammered.

"Ms. Rose," Alan moseying his way to her, taking a seat on the love sofa. "If I may be forthright, we have quite a long way to go. I do understand that as of right now you are feeling confused, but therapy is not a sprint, it is a marathon. You cannot rush through the process. I promise you weekly you will begin to see things more clearly. Now, are you having any type of anxiety or lack of sleep? I can always refer you to a doctor for prescriptions," Alan said. But Rose would hear of no such thing.

"No, I don't need medication to sleep. I think I will be fine." Alan did not push her further, stepping into the hallway he asked Danielle to schedule Rose another appointment, one week from today. Alan disappeared into his office.

Danielle sat smiling.

"So, does a Wednesday of next week work for you?"

"Sure," mumbled an apprehensive Rose after drawing a deep breath.

"Great, you're all set, see you next Wednesday at two." Danielle confirmed as she handed Rose a business card—her appointment written in.

That night Rose and Keith made passionate love, avoiding the topic of her therapy session, she had no desire to disclose the information that Dr. White had revealed to her, afraid that it would chase him away. Before Keith could go to sleep, Rose turned to face him.

"Can we have a baby?" she whispered as they lay upstairs in her bedroom, the room a pitch black. Rose felt her way to him, rubbing her hands across his chest. Keith opened his eyes and responded.

"A what?" His reply shocking, Rose could not take this form of rejection once again and so she decided to turn over, pretending as though she had said nothing, ashamed to have even mentioned it. But Keith insisted, sitting upright now, turning the switch to the lamp next to him on the nightstand, staring down at her. "Rose, what did you say?" Rose pressed her head against her closed palms, which were placed under her head atop the pillow.

"I just asked if maybe you wanted a baby," this time her voice lowered. Keith raved with excitement.

"Do you mean it?" he asked. "Like a baby-baby? Little feet, *Johnson & Johnson* lotion baby? Crying all night and we can't sleep baby? That kind of a baby?" ecstatically he spoke, Rose turned to face him, comforted by his enthusiasm.

"Well, yes." She laughed.

"Hell yeah! Let's do it. Baby it is!" he said, grabbing a hold of her as he began to kiss her passionately. Rose felt anxious, knowing her reasons for requesting they have a child was merely to relinquish herself from any guilt or torment she may have been feeling in regard to Irving and her co-dependency. She also decided that in the morning she would finally make amends with her baby brother.

3

1994 – AGE 12

As a seventh-grader Irving was feeling the true pressure of his recovery; packing his bags as he prepared to leave the hospital—this moment bittersweet. Administrators were kind enough to bring along his school work so he would not fall behind. But the honors curriculum was proving itself to be rather difficult for him, a feeling he loathed as his pride felt damaged. Surprisingly, Patrick spent a lot of his free time with Irving at the hospital as he too began sneaking him assignments from Mr. Royal whenever Rose would leave for work.

Rose was now working two jobs as she found herself managing the buildings and completing the expense reports each night when the Starbucks franchise closed for the evening. She contemplated hiring a store manager but decided against it considering she was interested in earning the additional income. Keith and Rose were trying hard for their dream baby, but it devastated her that she was not pregnant yet after working at it for a little over a year. After a tremendous amount of doctor visits, it was determined that she did not have any fertility issues and neither did Keith, however now that she was in her thirties, she was having a bit more difficulty in conceiving the natural way.

Rose continued her visits with Dr. White who helped to mend the issues between her and Ryan; Marley was elated to learn they were both making strides towards building a better relationship, which ultimately strengthened Rose's own romantic relationship as Keith no longer felt insecure. Rose was slowly returning to her happy place, so much so after returning home one night she noticed on the coffee table a letter—it was the letter from Christopher concerning his elite group. The note was vague, printed on the Westchester Preparatory Academy letterhead, the body read:

This letter is for the parent and/or guardian to Mr. Irving Houston. I am writing to inform you personally that your child has been elected to take part in the work of a new elite group where he will be to be mentored, trained, and educated in an advanced learning capacity. The aim is to one day have your child serve our country's Armed Forces and from there on, proceed to become one of this nation's top government officials. As Rose read on she now knew why Irving was so engrossed with this group and the idea of taking part—his intellect was challenged. Rose decided to clean the document, rubbing away the coffee stains, and the dust that had built up over the years, signing her name to the bottom. She secretly prayed this would make Irving happy, but she had some stipulations of her own.

Entering into the office of Christopher Royal was always an experience, he was a classy gentleman, well poised, and sometimes intimidating. As Rose stepped past the receptionist, she stuck her head inside the door.

"Christopher," she said—her voice low.

"Yes, how may I help you?" The last he had seen Rose she was assaulting him, which still did not sit well with him, he now viewed her differently—unhinged. Rose stood before him gripping the letter, ripping it almost.

"First, I want to apologize for the way I behaved the last time we were in one another's company. You were kind enough to take the time to visit Irving and I should have been more appreciative of that," His eyes pierced through her, and Rose became timid. "I know how much this group means to Irving and how hard he's worked ever since he joined, I can only guess when that was, considering the change in his behavior at one point, but I'm rambling, sorry," she said, handing him the signed note, which he slid towards him using the tip of his signature pen—the paper crinkled and unclean. Christopher looked at the form with disgust.

"Whilst I do appreciate you taking the time to come here, Rose, offering both an apology and an executed document that was sent to your attention two years ago, I will say I am not interested in your apology and whether or not you would provide me this documentation of approval, I would have continued my work with Irving. The child is simply remarkable and I simply pity the fool who would think otherwise or fail to see this for themselves. But considering the fact that you are here," he said, rolling his eyes, his tone condescending, "I will advise you of the new arrangements I will have put in place upon his prompt return. He will be picked up in the mornings, along with his peers, in a black town car, please see my receptionist for additional details on licensing and registration. Additionally, dropped home in the evenings after school—this is to avoid the young man skipping away and taking buses to ungodly places— and I have arranged that he begin treatment at the Veterans Affairs hospital for his therapy. I will let you decide when that will officially begin, again, reception is in possession of further details." Rose could not believe her ears—speechless, she simply turned, nodding her head as she prepared to walk away feeling entirely too grateful.

"As you can see, Ms. Appleton, I take my work here very seriously and I've allowed myself to fail him once before, but it will never happen again," he said sternly. Rose was shocked that he would take such accountability. But still, he seemed to dislike her, as he made very little eye contact and appeared to have been scolding her rather than conversing.

The next morning Rose arrived at the hospital bright and early, making her way inside to Irving's room where she found him sitting on the edge of his bed, dressed in a pair of jeans, sneakers, and a green t-shirt. Rose kissing him plentifully, Irving begging her to stop. As she kissed his little hands and playfully nibbled on his neck, she was happy he was coming home and could not stop laughing—this moment joyous. Just then the nurse came walking in.

"It's been a long journey," Andy said. Irving nodded. "Alright, little man, so you know you still have a lot of work to do, right?"

"Yes," Irving confirmed, swinging his legs. Rose caressed his back, bringing him comfort. Andy then handed Rose a packet which contained about two-hundred pages of material.

"Okay, this is the review packet for him to study. Just try asking him specific words—"

Rose interrupted him, "Well, um, in regard to the cognitive therapy I believe his mentor made other outside arrangements," Rose speaking cautiously, unsure of herself.

"Oh okay, well, I mean, that's good, it's just the insurance he has is good for here, so you wouldn't be paying anything out of pocket. I mean realistically, a private therapist can cost way more."

"No, no, I completely understand," she said, wishing Andy would simply go on.

"Okay, no problem, so Irving I guess all we need to focus on is your gait. So we will see you Saturday morning bright and early in the basement, he's familiar with it down there."

"Yes, I know where that is," Rose smiled as Andy handed her over discharge papers, a referral, and an appointment track sheet. "Andy, I really appreciate all the work you've all done for us here, I mean truly," Rose hugged him, a first for Andy as he contemplated whether or not he should reciprocate. Irving struggled to stand.

"Oh, no, no, I will grab him a wheelchair," Andy said, racing into the hall and seconds later wheeling in a chair. He and Rose both lifted Irving, aiding him to step inside and sit down. Irving was so skinny now that the chair appeared to swallow him whole, Rose held his hand as she wheeled him to the elevator—the nurses all telling him goodbye. His duffle bag was across Rose's shoulders. Once outside, Rose could sense that Irving was unhappy.

Sliding her hands along the armchair beside him, squatting, "Irving, honey, what's the matter?"

Irving was crying now. "I can't remember anything," he cried, sniffling.

"Oh sweetheart," Rose cradling him, "I know, but the doctor says it's temporary okay, it won't be forever, and with your therapy that's going to help too, I promise," Rose said kissing his forehead. Rose felt helpless as she stood wheeling him out into the parking lot and into her vehicle, strapping him in the backseat.

Rose hated that Irving was so sad. As she drove along the highway, she noticed a Ferris wheel coming into view, which could only mean that a carnival was nearby. Rose took a glimpse at Irving sitting in the back seat; she turned off the highway, following the Ferris wheel until they drew closer and closer. The spring weather felt great and Rose was in no hurry to return home. Keith, after all, was working. Arriving now, she parked, Irving lifted his head to see an abundance of people walking inside: children, mothers, fathers all making their way towards the festivities, Irving sat moping.

"I want to go home," he said pouting. But Rose would hear of no such thing.

"Even if I have to drag you inside kicking and screaming, we are going to have some fun. You've been cooped up in that hospital for so long." Her hair now long enough to fit into a ponytail as she searched her car for a hair bow, locating it around her wrist—pulling up the sleeves of her cardigan she proceeded to aid Irving out of the vehicle. Irving felt uncomfortable, but no matter how hard he tried to be disinterested, there was something inside of him causing him to smile. He grabbed hold of Rose as she assisting him with his walking, he was swaying slightly, off-balance, but concentrated on catching himself. He was working really hard and this made Rose happy, realizing now he was excited, walking slightly faster than she did, he could not wait to get inside. The music blaring, the smell of cotton candy, the children laughing, the rides and the thrill of it all, Irving was taking it all in.

Basking with joy, Irving took a large chunk of his cotton candy and thrust it into his mouth, Rose periodically warning him to slow down, but he was so elated—his eyes lit up with glee. Rose playfully teased him as they rode the merry go round, the teacup, and played games, winning him stuffed animals. Irving ate hotdogs and funnel cake, and tired now after five hours, Rose lifted Irving and carried him to the car as he had now fallen asleep. Irving was slim now, so Rose did not have any trouble holding him and oddly enough she enjoyed this moment. As she laid his body down gently across the back seat where he could sleep, she began their journey home.

Rose had no idea just how tired Irving was feeling, arriving inside she carried him up the stairs and into his bedroom to sleep; deciding against waking him as the door slammed shut. It was Keith making his way inside—they now lived together.

"Rose," he called to her. Rose raced from Irving's room, placing her index finger vertically on her lips asking him to quiet down.

Whispering to Keith, she said, "Can you get the bags from the car please?" He quickly obliged, turning around and heading back out the door after grabbing the keys from the mantle. Rose began undressing until she suddenly felt nauseous, running into the bathroom she vomited everything she had that morning. Rose was overjoyed, thinking now that there may be a possibility of a baby growing inside her. She had been on edge for months, taking any sign that her body gave her as a sure sign of pregnancy; this time, she once again wanted to be sure as she ripped open a box from under the sink which contained a few pregnancy tests she put away. Rose proceeded to pee on the test, placing the cap on top of the absorbent strip afterward, her hands trembling as she waited nervously for the results—the test producing a positive. Rose remained stationed; she could not move. She was in such a state of shock that when Keith now entered the bathroom preparing to shower she did not notice him, but he noticed the test, turning to her as he lifted it to see the results.

"Oh man! Baby! We're pregnant?" he asked joyfully. Rose screamed, "Yes, oh my God, yes, we are." She smiled, hugging him. Keith and Rose exchanged a passionate kiss. As Keith turned to shower, Rose could not help but rub her stomach, as she exited, now making her way into Irving's bedroom, she sat on the corner of his bed watching him sleep—gently removing his hospital wrist band. He was home and their family was growing.

Monday morning Rose walked Irving down to the all-black town car that awaited him outside. A confused Irving was unsure of why he was not taking the bus as the other children, but Rose politely explained to him that he would now be picked up every morning and evening. The driver turned to face them.

"Ma'am, I assure you he is in great hands. I've worked with Mr. Royal for the past nine years," the man said. He appeared to be in his fifties, and continued talking as Rose kissed Irving goodbye, closing the car door and waving, she stood by the edge of the sidewalk. It had been three days since Rose learned of the news about her pregnancy and decided to spend the day with Marley, finally breaking the ice.

Inside the school building, Irving struggled to keep his balance, but the shoes he wore were especially padded for such circumstances. He walked slowly, an easy target for the other children to pick on him, but everyone knew better; it was no secret that he was a member of the elite group, and while some children envied him, others respected him. Patrick raced behind him as he exited his town car.

"Hey!" he shouted to Irving before Irving could make his way onto the elevator. "Glad you're back," he said, smiling now. But Irving was in no mood to converse, he was struggling to piece together his memories from yesterday and even some parts of breakfast.

"Listen man," Patrick said to him, "I know this is hard, I can see the discomfort all over your face. But take solace in knowing that you lived. My mom says that's rare." Patrick concluded before walking away. Entering into his seventh-grade class for the first time, his classmates and the instructor all cheered, Irving felt warm inside as he smiled before looking at his instructor who motioned him on where to sit.

"You're right over here Irving." The sound of her voice fragile—her name was Mrs. Vencer. She was short, late twenties, 5'0, with long brunette hair and inviting ocean blue eyes, her complexion pale. Taking a seat as his classmates ceased their applause, Irving was ready to seize the day, or at least try. By noon Christopher was standing in the hallway where he patiently awaited Irving once the bell tolled for lunch. Irving formed the line just outside, and spotting him, walked over.

"Hi Mr. Royal," he said looking up at the elderly man.

"You will have lunch with me today?" He and Irving now making their way down the hall, the other students staring at Mrs. Vencer who now begged them to focus their eyes forward. Irving sat across from Christopher at a small round table located to the left of his office just under the large windows; Irving watched as the chef removed containers of food. For Irving, a small dish of rice and baked salmon. Unfamiliar with this type of meal, Irving sat poking into it with his fork, before taking a bite.

"Yum, yes," Christopher chuckled. Irving's eyes widened in adoration.

"Yes!" he said as he ate quickly.

"Slow down, young man, we don't want you choking." Fifteen minutes later Irving was through and thus it began.

"Irving what are ten ways to ruin a presentation?" Christopher asked him. A startled Irving stuttered before responding.

He could not think of the answer, one he used to know all too well. He was stumped, he was confused, his head was beginning to hurt. "I know the answer," he screamed, rising to his feet, growing agitated that the words were not coming to him, "I know the answer, I promise," he begged.

"Time!" Christopher yelled, Irving now stood, swaying, his fists balled—frustrated, resisting the urge to toss the empty container across the room.

"I know the answer!" he sobbed.

"Wipe your tears at once!" Christopher beckoned, stomping his cane to the ground. "Are you exercising your brain? If not, then you are not ready to be elite again. I need to know that you are serious, Irving, this is not a game. Your training, your education, these are all vital to your overall wellbeing. You need to focus! Now, tell me, what are the ten ways to ruin a presentation? Go!" Christopher screamed. Irving stood fighting tears, his eyes turning red as the bell tolled once again, indicating his return to class, Christopher simply stood. "You best be on your way," he told Irving, disappointed. Irving began to hyperventilate, breathing deeply, quickly, the tears falling from his eyes as he continued standing, he wanted to scream, but instead, he stuttered,

"Ja—ja—jargon, unexplained, tech—tech—nical jargon," his heavy breathing decreased. "Lots of text, memory recital, no-no eye contact," he said as he continued to struggle, pleading with his brain to cooperate as Christopher now stood, walking away.

His back to him, he said, "Tomorrow we try again, go to class," Irving exited the office, rejoicing as he made his way down the hall, praying he could run because that's all he wanted to do. He was feeling great! Irving now spent the remainder of the day concentrating heavily on regaining his memory.

Arriving home, Rose was having a small get together with Ryan, Marley, Keith, and a few of Keith's friends, along with Reggie, all gathered for finger foods, smooth jazz and champagne—which Rose could not have, she helped herself to Sparkling Cider and decided to share the update amongst everyone except Marley, who was already privy to the news of her pregnancy. As Irving entered inside everyone turned to greet him, Ryan lifting him and giving him a tight hug.

"Little man, how's it feel to be home?" Ryan smiled as Irving removed his shoes, his walking corpse syndrome worsened due to his anxiety as he made his way to his bedroom. But Rose, witnessing his poor etiquette, was not amused. Ryan insisted that perhaps he just needed some rest, but Rose could not allow that.

"No," she said, "he knows better than to not address the adults in the room, that was completely rude, Ryan." Placing her glass down now as she lifted her maxi dress slightly and began making her way up the stairs—everyone paid her no mind.

Rose entered into Irving's room where he was rummaging through his bookcase, searching frantically.

"Young man, you march right back down those stairs and apologize to your uncle and greet the adults," Rose said sternly. Irving wasn't listening as he continued to toss around books, whispering to himself, *where is it?*

"Irving!" Rose called to him. *Silence.*

"Irving!" again she called, this time a little louder as she stomped her way over to him, grabbing a hold of his wrist, "Irving stop this," she screamed.

"Get off of me," he yelled, pulling his arm free, standing now. The music in the living room decreased as everyone overheard the commotion. Ryan racing up the stairs, shouting to him,

"Irving, knock it off right now!" Ryan now standing by the threshold—the look on his face menacing. Irving stood still as he cried.

"I just want my notes!" He tossed his hands in the air filled with discontent. Rose was shocked, unable to move, she could not process what was going on. Irving was becoming so aggressive.

"Rose, give us a minute," Ryan said, shutting the door as she exited.

Rose made her way back downstairs feeling distressed, "By the way, everyone, we're having a baby," she stated out loud—sarcastically. "What a great night, huh? I can't even raise the first one right and here I am having a baby!" she shouted now as the tears fell from her eyes, Marley racing to console her. Everyone now felt uncomfortable and slowly began making their way out, Keith's friends congratulating him as he prepared to clean, Reggie carefully stepping out into the hallway. Rose massaged her head in anguish.

"Rose, please stop being so hard on yourself all the time. Not too long from now you'll have a teenager to raise and I can assure you, it only gets worse from here," Marley sympathized, wiping her tears as they both chuckled now sitting at the foot of the step.

"I honestly don't think I'm ready for that."

"As of right now, no, but you will get there. The doors are going to slam, he's going to be dating, he isn't going to confide in you at all, and it's going to sometimes feel like you're living with a total stranger. But Irving is your kid, and as such you have to just always remember he's simply coming into his own and so his intentions aren't malicious," Marley continued.

Meanwhile, Ryan took a seat on Irving's bed, motioning for him to join.

"Want to explain what happened back there kiddo?" Irving stood with his eyes to the ground.

"I just want my notes," he said innocently.

"What notes?"

"The notes from Mr. Royal. Rose said I couldn't go anymore and so Hensley brought me notes," Irving felt guilty for prattling on about Hensley but he knew he had no choice but to tell the truth.

"Why were the notes so important, Irving, you were very rude today."

"I remembered, Uncle Ryan, I remembered things today, from the notes I studied and I haven't been able to do that since I was in the hospital. I was just really excited and wanted to see if I could do it again," Irving said, excitement building in his voice. Ryan began to sympathize, wondering if perhaps his sister was just stressed.

"Irving, may I ask you a question?"

"As my doctor or my uncle?"

"Uncle," said Ryan. "Are you happy?" he continued. But Irving did not know how to answer.

"I am content," Irving nodding. "But I just want to study and learn without feeling guilt-ridden, and Rose won't let me. I'm not like the other kids, but I'm okay with that; she isn't." And with that, Ryan had heard enough as he stood.

"You're not a bad kid, but you hurt your mother's feelings, so maybe you should apologize, Irving," Ryan unlocking the door he noticed Marley and Rose sitting at the foot of the stairs, he bellowed to her, "Rose." She turned, placing her hand atop Marley's shoulders for support and making her way up the stairs. "Can we talk for a second?" Ryan pointing Rose in the direction of her bedroom.

"What's going on? Did he tell you anything?" Her eyes widened, curious as she folded her arms.

"He's not a bad kid, but maybe you can consider possibly just easing up a bit with the expectations." Rose scoffed, unfolding her arms and turning away from him.

"Me? Ease up? I mean, what am I still not doing right?" she asked, sounding fed up.

"I understand he came home and he didn't greet us, I do understand that was impolite of him, but did you ask him what he was looking for, I mean the reason he didn't greet us?" Rose, now bewildered, answered, "I'm the parent, was I supposed to care about why my kid was being disrespectful or only the fact that my kid was being disrespectful?" she said.

"But this is unlike him is what I'm saying, and because the behavior was abnormal, towards you, me, Marley, hell, even Keith, then maybe your approach could have been different," Ryan pleaded, but Rose would not hear of it.

"Don't talk to me like some psychologist, okay, you spend five minutes with him and he's managed to manipulate you to the point where you decide now that I deserve to be reprimanded," she screamed.

"Rose, just calm down, I am not reprimanding you, but he remembered things today and that is a big deal for him—and so, out of excitement, he waddled to his room to find the papers where the memory stemmed from," Ryan said, his palms together as if to beg his sister to comprehend. Rose lowered her shoulders and took a seat on the mattress.

"I'm just really bad at this parenting thing, and I'm pregnant Ryan, maybe I should just give this baby up for adoption," she said, covering her face. Ryan now knelt before her, placing his hands on her knees.

"No, you're a savior in his eyes, Rose. He loves you, and that's such great news, congratulations to you! But Irving, he's wired differently and you just have to try and accept that. It seems as though sometimes you're ready to, but then, you feel like you're losing control and you try to pull on the strings again. He has his own mind, he's eloquent and you've instilled some wonderful morals in him. But it seems that this is one kid who isn't going to put the book down."

"That little angel growing inside of you could possibly be the dream child you've always wanted or envisioned yourself having, but Irving isn't it—he doesn't want to play board games with mom, or play dress up, or go shopping, or have you knit while he plays around on a jungle gym. Yet you still have to love and accept him for exactly who is he, which I know you can do," Ryan continued. Just then Irving appeared. In his arms, he held tight his notes!

"Excuse me," he whispered politely. Ryan lifted his right brow, standing, allowing Irving room to enter. Irving now jumped on the mattress alongside Rose, feeling giddy.

"Mom! I found my notes, I have to tell you what happened today, it was so amazing!" Irving rambling as he smiled. Ryan took his leave.

"What happened, sweetie?" Rose turned to face him, ecstatic to hear of his good news.

"...and by the way, I am sorry for upsetting you." Ryan stepped downstairs to find Marley and Keith conversing over a glass of wine, the kitchen now immaculate.

"You're quite the cleaner-upper," Ryan joked as he mocked the infomercial.

"I think you and I both know why that is," he laughed as Ryan now took a seat at the dining room table, Keith handing him a beer.

"Wow, a baby, is it your first?" he asked Keith.

"Yep. Forty-seven years old and this will be my first," he chuckled.

"Wow man, what made you wait so long?" Ryan asked, Marley now relocating to sit on his lap as Keith continued to stand by the counter.

"Never quite found the one, and at one point I honestly just gave up looking." Ryan nodded to indicate his understanding.

"You don't sound like you're from here," Ryan then said. "No idea how I missed that accent before."

"Nope, born and raised Texan," Keith replied.

"Super awesome dude!" Ryan raising his beer to salute. "Well, a special congratulations from me and the wife here, you're in for a treat. So, have you been getting along with Irving?" Keith took a moment to respond.

"Um, well, to be honest, I haven't been quite getting along. I mean I try to stay out of his way. He's a young fella, but, uh, he's a little intimidating. Plus, the last thing I want to do is upset Rose by upsetting Irving for whatever reason." The couple listened; however, Marley did not understand.

"How do you intend on having a family then, if a twelve-year-old intimidates you? I mean, he's a part of Rose, comes with the package." Her laugh suspicious.

"Yea, well, packages are meant to be opened—you throw out the box and keep the gift," he said, taking a sip of his wine. Ryan and Marley exchanged an uncomfortable look. Noticing their exchange, "Look, I just want to make sure Rose is happy."

"Irving—Irving, makes my sister happy, and that's all there is to it," Ryan voiced, taking a deep breath and tapping Marley on the buttocks for her to stand. "We should get going, we have a long ride ahead of us."

"Yes, Keith, today was amazing, thank you for having us," Marley said, standing by the door as she and Ryan exited.

Once they were walking down the hall, she asked, "That was bizarre, no?"

"Yes, but we'll keep an eye on that one," Ryan replied as they stepped onto the elevator, allowing Marley to step inside first.

4

1997 – AGE 15

R ose continued therapy after officially quitting her job
and making the commitment to run the businesses full-
time until Irving himself was able to do so. She was
learning quickly that owning a license for a Starbucks
franchise was no easy task, flying out to their headquarters in
Seattle, Washington for chairman meetings, franchise host
parties, and luncheons were exhausting her. Now that Ivy was
turning three and her relationship was on solid grounds, she also
decided it may be time to relocate, perhaps buy a house.

Seven years later and Irving was still undergoing intensive
rehab and making intermittent visits to the hospital. Now in the
tenth grade, Christopher did not let up, he was not giving Irving
any special treatment, which irritated Rose, but she knew better
now than to butt into their affairs, especially considering how
much Irving liked being treated equal, oftentimes scolding her
for suggesting that Christopher go easy on him. A wounded

brain has pride, too, and as such Irving was not going to be counted out. He wanted to be reprimanded, run laps, and make his way through the obstacle courses just as his peers did.

Hensley, now twenty, Walter and Johnson, both twenty-two, and Patrick—who was always closest to Irving in age was turning eighteen and preparing for his high school graduation. Irving frequently took trips to West Point Military Academy where he, Patrick, and Christopher would visit the other boys, Patrick was preparing for his time there which angered Irving as he hated the thought of them separating, but Christopher was looking forward to this, he needed to get Irving by himself so he could truly look to educate him and work on unlocking his full academic potential—whatever that meant for him and his own expectations for Irving. Christopher viewed Irving as a prodigy, a young boy destined for greatness with a legacy that would one day outlive him and his grandchildren.

Graduation activities began that Tuesday as Walter and Johnson were on campus, but Irving was not allowed to attend. He had therapy and school, and Christopher was not going to allow him to miss a day. Commencement Day, held in the Michie Stadium that Saturday, was when Irving was picked up by the stretch limo from his home. Rose waved him goodbye. Christopher was exhausted as he spent the entire week with Walter and Johnson, attending marches and exercises, superintendent receptions and awards reviews, baccalaureate services ceremony, graduation parade, banquet, and hop all requirements for firsties, which is now what Walter and Johnson were to be called. Irving missed Christopher in school despite the fact that he was only away for a week, Wednesday Irving looked forward to their meeting, but when he and Patrick showed up to the music room studying their tasks from the week prior—the room felt empty.

Arriving on campus at 07:00, Christopher dressed in his colonial uniform, Irving and Patrick both instructed to dress in unison: black pants, a black long sleeve dress shirt, black dress shoes, black belt, and a bow-tie, their heads shaved bald. The other students were jealous as both Irving and Patrick walked alongside Christopher who was known to them as Lieutenant colonel. The students wondered why they were receiving special treatment, especially a young Irving who was still struggling to walk, much to which therapy was utilized. But in an effort to blend in with his peers he struggled through the pain, walking upright and standing for hours on end once the ceremony was underway. Irving watched as the men and women all marched in a straight line down the football field, not one person, hand, foot or hair out of place—he was mesmerized by their discipline.

With his short-term memory still a blur, Irving found himself awakening at night with night terrors, reliving those days when he was physically abused. He was still learning how to process his emotions, taking into account all that had transpired in his life; oftentimes he found himself flinching whenever Christopher would raise his voice, and today was no different. Christopher, stepping past them as he made his way to the podium, tripped over Irving's shoelace which had come undone on their way to their seats. Christopher turned to him, his eyebrows knitted, embarrassed, he lifted his cane to assist him in regaining his balance, but to Irving he thought the cane was going to be used to harm him, and so he raised his arms in fear, blocking his face as he had many times before as a little boy.

Patrick, witnessing this, felt bad for him, and although Christopher was a stoic man, he could not help but pity him. Grabbing Irving by the wrist he walked him down the stairs, onto the field and near the stage where he was to deliver a farewell speech—a young Irving standing beside him facing an audience of over 2,000 consisting of friends, family, and alumni.

Christopher stood in front of his audience delivering a powerful, motivating speech spanning over forty-five minutes long. Eloquently speaking as Irving listened on, emulating him—his tone, his posture, and the inclined vocabulary he utilized. Irving was like a sponge, taking in all that he could, the men and women standing behind them all fighting the urge to gossip among one another, astonished by the fact that

Christopher had been showing favoritism to an African-American boy who from the looks of it appeared to be mentally disabled. Irving still struggled to grasp his muscles—standing required a great deal of effort and concentration. Infrequently Irving began experiencing impaired cognitive function, losing short moments during the day, his brain shutting down, unaware of when this would happen, Irving equipped himself with a notebook and pen jotting down details of the day and the emotions he felt, whether temporary or not, he needed to know it all. This kind of rigorous detailing assisted him with his recovery.

Indistinctly, Irving listened to Christopher,

"The U.S. Military Academy at West Point's mission is "to educate, train, and inspire the Corps of Cadets so that each graduate is a commissioned leader of character committed to the values of Duty, Honor, and Country and are prepared for a career of professional excellence and service to the Nation as an officer in the United States Army," he said as the men and women stood at attention.

Concluding his speech Christopher made light mention of his elite cadets—both current and future, calling on Hensley, Patrick, Johnson, Walter and young Irving who he turned to face, making distinct eye contact, the audience now murmuring as he bid his farewell by introducing their keynote speaker, General Donald P. Walker Jr. who stepped aggressively towards him. They shook hands, raising their right hands to salute one another. Christopher now turned to Irving, instructing him to walk alongside him. Irving scurried past the adults as he made his way off of the stage and onto the grass. The ceremony lasted for five hours—graduates receiving their bar pins ecstatic as they walked across the stage, pumping their fists in the air. Irving envisioned himself up there one day draped in the full dress coat's 44 gold-plated buttons, the 16-ounce wool grey uniform, the 32-ounce wool in the black parka, the zippers, shoulder pads, the sleeve heads, and all 300 or so other raw materials that go into the uniform—watching his peers walk across the stage only motivated him further as he now looked forward to returning to therapy that upcoming Monday.

Inside school Irving could not sit still, fidgeting all through his tenth-grade class, his teacher now growing impatient.

"Irving, are you okay?" Ms. Mooney asked.

"Yes," Irving responded with glee as he waited patiently for the bell to ring at approximately 3:30 p.m., the time now reading 2:17 p.m. Irving got lost in a book he received from Mrs. Taylor. Mrs. Taylor was one of the few people who found herself in tears when the news reached her about Irving's health, once he returned she vowed to do the one thing she knew would make him happy: bring him textbooks. Although her daughter completed college, she would visit local bookstores after school purchasing new books for the sole purpose of providing them to Irving, knowing her money would not be wasted. Irving often times burning through seven-hundred-page textbooks in a matter of days. The only thing Irving hated was his inability to retain the things he had read; his memory was now failing him.

As the bell tolled Irving raced outside, locating the black town car that would pick him up in the mornings and evenings bringing him to and from school—three days a week, bringing him to therapy. Irving was average height for most boys his age, standing at 5'6, but he was reserved and as such often times mistaken for being somewhat younger than he actually was, his driver, for instance, did not believe Irving to be the average teenager—he was not interested in dating, video games, music, or even small-talk. Irving was mature for his age, but did not appear so physically—slender and conservative was what he was, which to most do not seem to be typical for most teenage boys.

Christopher recommended that Irving be transferred to a military facility to receive his on-going care; Rose did not fancy this, she loathed the idea of Irving joining the military. Having little to no education on the matter, she only assumed it meant war and the possibility of losing her only son prematurely. But Christopher felt the need to teach Irving from a young age the history of the United States Armed Forces.

Irving stepped inside of the Veterans Affairs Hospital gripping the straps of his backpack as he made his way to the seventh floor entering into the office of Dr. Mitchell Moore, a licensed psychologist who specialized in assisting coma patients on their cognitive journey to recovery. Today Irving was enthusiastic and looked forward to his session; the one had been attending for the past three and a half years after leaving Bloomfield.

The office was small, Dr. Moore stepping past Irving to offer him a bottle of water which Irving refused. He took a seat across from Irving now and removed his legal pad and pen.

"You seem anxious," mentioned Dr. Moore, tapping his chestnut colored Oxfords along the wooden floor. Irving could see that he was tired, his button-down shirt missing buttons, his hair uncombed, the bags under his eyes heavy and the constant rubbing of his forehead as if he were fighting off a migraine were all indications of same.

"No, just excited." Dr. Moore was intrigued.

"Wow, it's the first I've heard you use that word to describe your emotions—any particular reason?"

"Yes, Mr. Royal has been telling us about the importance of getting a valuable education and why studying is vital for West Point, and Saturday I realized exactly what he meant."

"Really, and what's that? Also, who is *us*? You mentioned that word," the doctor jotting down notes.

"My friends," Irving responded. "Doctor, I want to be fixed, healed, I want to read and retain the information. Lately, I've been having these flashbacks and none of it seems to make sense," he continued.

"Tell me a little bit more about the flashbacks," Dr. Moore said, again jotting down notes.

"I remember things, unpleasant memories from my childhood I suppose—when I as much younger," Irving said sadly.

"How do those emotions make you feel," Dr. Moore asked

again, this time uncrossing his legs.

"Grateful," replied Irving.

"Why is that?"

"I get to see my mom every day and now I just want to make her happy that she saved me," Irving immediately changing the subject. "I have some words for us today, can we work on them?" he asked, removing a stack of papers from his backpack.

"I can see, because it depends on how difficult the words are, Irving."

"No, I want these words, I want to learn them so that I can do well on my SAT's and ACT. I have to get into West Point," he said with assertion. "I want to be a man of erudition, earning my way into West Point so I can one day make my mother proud of me, and my sister. This is important," he emphasized, his eyes staring deeply into Dr. Moore's, who quickly turned away.

"Irving, you cannot expedite your treatment. You're still very fragile despite the fact that it's been three years, and to make matters a bit worse is that you were so young when it happened. You lost a few months that were indeed important to your overall cognitive development. We have to start small, the basics," the doctor pleaded. "Out of the fraction of people who survive comas and recover physically, a quarter are permanently mentally disabled and even those without a permanent disability usually start with impaired cognitive function, which is what we are here to work on," he continued.

"Can you just look at the words," asked Irving, growing impatient—they were words he once knew but could not recall. Dr. Moore now looked down at the papers, realizing the small handwriting he reached for his glasses, stretching his right hand behind him, using his fingers to feel for the lenses—grabbing them he placed them on his face as he proceeded to read the words aloud.

"Vituperate, cumbersome, supine, avaricious, noisome, extemporize—um, Irving," he said, removing his glasses. "We are not on this level yet. We need to focus on getting you refamiliarized with simple verbs, compound words, nouns, words like climate, anguish, resistor, village, twine, those are some words we can work on today, and arithmetic—"

Irving interrupted him. "Those puerile words are an insult to my intelligence; I will not pass the standardized tests learning such child-like vocabulary. In the past three years we've done nothing but discuss geography, the difference between an island and a peninsula, and words that are designed for the mind of a third grader. There's no stimulation for me aside from school. But what good are you doing me if you are not going to help me be the best that I can be cognitively? We are wasting our time," he said in an unpleasant tone.

"Well, it sounds to me like you've been doing just fine with growing your vocabulary, who has been helping you?" the doctor asked as he crossed his legs, reclining in his chair.

"Patrick," Irving admitted. "But Patrick is busy and you and I have time carved out of our day for this specific function. I would like to utilize our time a bit more wisely."

"I see," Dr. Moore replied.

"I cannot continue to live being condescended to like a child," Irving concluded, this statement causing Dr. Moore to widen his eyes. He was shocked and of course, impressed. Most civilian comatose patients who do recover, based on his experience, typically give up in pushing themselves, but not Irving, his motivation was unmatched and unlike anything he had ever seen.

Throwing his glasses back across his face, Dr. Moore went through the papers handed to him once more, finding not only an extensive vocabulary list but deductive and inductive reasoning examples, logical reasoning, general calculus, and analytical reasoning. "Mr. Houston, are you by chance planning to attend law school? I ask considering the nature of this curriculum you've handed me," Dr. Moore chuckled.

"No, but in addition to knowing the law, it is important to know how both law and government officials think," Irving said, sounding vague. Dr. Moore now nodded as he prepared himself mentally for the adventures to come—his smile internalized.

Thus, began a new working relationship between Dr. Moore and Irving. Monday, Tuesday and Friday at 4:15 p.m. until 6 p.m. and Sundays remained reserved for muscle training at the hospital. Irving underwent an additional form of cognitive training in addition to discipline. Dr. Moore wanted to see Irving thrive and was more than willing to aid him in doing just that. A young boy with ambition and a love for education was not something to be taken lightly. Irving was assigned writing assignments from his teachers, Christopher, and Dr. Moore, managing to complete them all within the allotted time. He did not play with the children in the neighborhood as he had no interest in wasting such precious time.

As the weeks pressed on Rose thought she could now relax considering Irving was in good hands. She had come to trust Christopher since he made good on all of his promises and she and Irving were getting along far better. She learned to listen to him, but the reality was, she admired him for all of the efforts he was putting into his recovery. Rose was an honest woman, putting herself on the payroll for the Starbucks branch where she began to manage full-time, periodically checking into the housing development and the churches, she now had a great relationship with the pastor and the overseer of the premises. As Irving's wealth increased, Rose thought long and hard about the possibility of relocating, a conversation she feared having with her son, who by then only had one focus—school. She arrived home that evening to find Irving and Lisa sitting at the dining table completing their homework—after greeting Lisa, Rose made her way upstairs where she ran the hot water while undressing herself. She could not stand the scent of coffee bean reeking from her clothes. Ivy was spending time with Ryan and Marley as they insisted on having her for the weekend and had yet to return her home that Monday night.

Fifteen minutes later Rose emerged smelling and feeling gracious as she made her way downstairs, Lisa preparing to leave.

"Hey Lisa, thanks for letting me take a quick shower." Rose knowing very well Irving no longer needed a sitter but something about having Lisa with him gave her peace of mind, something Irving now did not mind as he would utilize Lisa with assisting him to learn new words from the flashcards he created. Rose took a seat where Lisa had sat, she was a few pounds heavier since her pregnancy so she adjusted the table slightly.

"Irving, how was therapy, baby?" she asked politely. Irving was buried in his books.

"Good, mom?" prying his eyes away from the books to face her—Rose looking completely shocked that he lifted his head—this was unlike him.

"Ye-yes?" Rose stuttered.

"We should move into a house," said Irving, staring at her. Rose licked her lips nervously.

"We can't really afford that right now, Irving." The sound of her voice melancholy.

"We can, I have money," he said. "Let's buy a house," he continued. Rose did not know whether to thank the heavens or simply cry. She was dreading the conversation as the money from her settlement was beginning to dwindle and the salary of a Starbucks manager, although slightly higher than when she worked as a social worker, was not making it easy to save. In addition to Keith now only working part-time to stay home with the baby, things were surely a bit rough.

"Irving, that money is yours to have when you're of age, sweetheart. Keith and I, we're adults, we have to figure it out." Rose rubbing his bald head as she stood. "What do you want for dinner?" she asked, wrapping the robe belt around her torso.

"I hear you crying at night. I can't remember everything, although I am trying, I remember your face, mom, when I was lying under the bed and you came and took me out. I'll never forget that, you love me and the money is ours, without you I probably wouldn't be alive anyway." His voice soft; Rose tied her robe, trying to not face him, placing her shoulder-length hair behind her ears.

"Okay," she said. Her face a beating red, "Okay, baby, we will buy a house," forcing herself to smile—she was unsure of why, but she felt guilty.

5

2000 – AGE 18

Opening his eyes at the West Point Military Academy, Irving felt blessed to have seen another day—one week and four days and he was already accustomed to his routine. Beginning his day at 05:30 a.m. for physical training, Irving rolled out of bed, taking the things he used for sleeping and locking it underneath his bed—the actual sheets never slept on, making them good for inspection. Irving then grabbed a hold of his shorts and t-shirt—the words ARMY written across the chest. At age eighteen he was expected to perform 42 push-ups, 53 sit-ups and a two-mile run under sixteen minutes, but Irving pushed all boundaries, exceeding his own expectations and that of his superiors. In the two minutes allotted Irving was performing 61 push-ups, 77 sit-ups and running a two-mile at twelve minutes, earning him a gold-star and the recognition he well deserved. Irving took his training very seriously, exercising in his room, reading and actively working on assignments that were due weeks later.

By 06:55 a.m. he stood in uniform after returning to his quarters to shower for morning formation, waiting around until 07:00 when it was time for breakfast. The cadet uniform he wore consisting of khaki Dickie pants and a khaki dickie shirt, black leather uniform shoes, black socks and undershirt accompanied by a 1 ½ inch black belt. Irving always ironed his clothes the night before, so he would have no problems with his superiors. The mess hall was filled with his peers, Patrick sitting with the *cows*—junior class—who occupied the upper right corner of the hall. New, Irving found himself sitting amongst the *plebes,* also known as the freshman class.

"How's it going?" Patrick asked, startling Irving as he walked up behind him. Now twenty-one, Patrick had no more acne, he was 5'7 now with an athletic build.

"Going," responded Irving; now a man of few words.

"Awesome, what classes do you have today? We're going to the river around 3, you should come," Patrick said.

"American Politics and sure, will do," replied Irving, nodding his head in agreeance, Irving and Patrick exchanged a handshake as Patrick now turned to walked away, not noticing the young man walking past behind him, Patrick bumping him causing his food to fall.

"Watch it!" the teenage boy cried; his tone extravagant.

"Hey, sorry man," Patrick replied. "Jeez, just go and get some more food," he laughed, walking away, turning to face Irving and shrugging his shoulders as if to indicate its insignificance. Irving is now a conventional man, old-fashioned and uptight, an intellect and at times pompous. He did not act aloof, nor did he behave irresponsibly, taking each moment as an opportunity not to be wasted on trivial matters. Irving was thorough, pristine and maintained a clear head, never using or abusing any substances as he would often times see his peers do. Irving was respected, Christopher ensuring this having solicited personal recommendation letters for Irving, Patrick, Hensley, Walter, and Johnson from Congresswoman Krista Gales who was a personal friend of his. As Irving had come to later learn, Christopher was the program director for American Politics here at West Point, his time split between two campuses.

As the young man walked away after clearing the floor, Irving noticed his walk, flamboyant, swaying his hips from side to side, but he did not care to speak, although it was expected that the freshmen stick together, Irving had no such desires— looking down on them considering the fact that he and Patrick were like brothers and the classes before them knew of Irving as he attended the graduation of both Walter and Johnson and later on Hensley, where he had the pleasure of meeting other upperclassmen. A lot of the women and men in the freshmen class envied him for this reason.

Preparing himself to exit, the loudspeakers erupted, instructing students to make their way to the auditorium. Irving made his way outside to see the young man from earlier standing with a piece of paper in his hand, appearing to be lost. The cadets all piled out of the dining hall, stepping hastily to the meeting area in the adjacent building, Irving resisting the urge to make small talk, but later decided to proceed.

"Irving," he said, facing the young man who was African-American with profound features. Handsome, Irving thought.

"I thought you were too good to speak to us freshman," he answered. Irving now felt embarrassed.

"I'm not that amicable."

The teenage boy scoffed, "Oh please, I heard about you, you're the inheritance kid and the Lieutenant colonel's pride and joy, nothing to do with amicability, you have a superiority complex,"

Disinterested in his blather and backhanded insults, Irving asked, "What's your name?"

"Shawn," the teenage boy replied, smiling.

"Good, I'll see you around, Shawn," Irving pushed his way through the crowd to get a good seat in the auditorium. Inside the seats were filled to capacity, some students still pouring in and having to stand towards the rear. A few moments later, second Lieutenant Johnson G. Love took a stand by the podium;

Johnson, who was now twenty-five years old, having graduated two years prior, is a respected leader and director of the United States Secret Service.

"Cadets," he began speaking, the room quiet. "I am here today because it has been brought to my attention that one of our students will not be returning in light of recent events taking place off campus over the weekend. We are now issuing a lockdown beginning this coming Friday. No student is permitted to leave campus grounds for any reason at all; your weekends and all leisure time will be spent on campus until further notice. We have been getting complaints from the local business owners, which as you all know is unacceptable," he continued.

"Fuck it, parties on campus," one boy whispered to the girl sitting next to him. Irving overheard them, both chuckling. Irving then redirected his focus to Johnson, who was wearing his Army Service Uniform: a dark blue coat and pants with a black belt for all general officers, his secretary of defense badge conspicuous. The murmurs grew louder as everyone sat wondering what could have taken place, but the answers were vague, his announcement short, and before they knew it everyone was instructed to return to their respected classes to continue their day.

Irving remained seated, waiting for everyone to exit to avoid the crowd, Patrick now approaching him.

"This sucks." He said taking a seat.

"It must have been something serious," responded Irving. Patrick tapped his shoulder.

"Come on man, it's starting to look empty in here."

"Cool," replied Irving as Johnson ran from the stage calling to them,

"Houston, Rogers!" he shouted. Both Irving and Patrick turning to face him, elated as they all exchanged hugs.

"Well if it isn't Mr. Love," Patrick teased.

"I liked you better when you didn't talk," Johnson said. "Houston, how's it going, man? I see you looking sharp!" he complimented.

"Yep, things are going well," Irving said.

"Nice! You see anything sweet yet?" Johnson asked winking.

"I'm not following," Irving laughed.

"A girl man, something sweet and just between us," Johnson looking around ensuring they were alone. "It was Marcus who got busted, rape charges from a girl he met at a bar not too far from here. Shit, that's why I had to speak, everyone is in meetings with lawyers and press." He shook his head in disappointment.

"That happens way too often, when do you leave for D.C.?" Irving asked, his hands now in his pocket.

"Tomorrow, I have a hotel, you guys should come by, maybe get some drinks and for you Houston, find you some women!" he replied, teasing.

"It baffles me how you think I am incapable of finding women on my own," Irving said in his defense, they all began moving.

"Finding a woman is not your issue man, bedding them is. I know you're still a virgin." Both Patrick and Irving simultaneously turning to face him.

"Love, what the fuck man," said Patrick.

"Rogers, come on, he's way too uptight to not be a virgin. Look how starched his suit is, I mean Jesus," Johnson joked.

"Look, who I bed is my business, understand?" said Irving sternly.

"Chill out man, it was a joke."

Friday morning Irving awoke to complete his morning routine. He decided against heading to the river with Patrick on Wednesday, insisting that it was best he study. By 07:30 he was sitting in Research Methods—day 2, as his day one days differed slightly. Irving loved day-2—he had boxing class and enjoyed learning new physical techniques that would, later on, prove itself to be beneficial. After class he had to return to his dorm where he dressed in his physical training uniform before sprinting back across campus; Irving had been running so fast he did not recognize Shawn passing him, stopping to get a better look, he bellowed, "Hey!"

Shawn, wondering where the sound came from, began looking around, spotting Irving on the other side of the freshly cut grass, he waved his hand.

"Hey yourself," he smiled. Irving nodding his head as he continued on running to class, 08:40 there he was, learning and practicing the fundamentals of boxing. Two weeks now, Irving attended this class a total of six times, each time getting knocked to his feet and landing on his back by one of his peers. Irving hated to lose but knew it was all mind over matter, his use of willpower was going to be needed to overcome such a situation. The physical release did him wonders, he needed an outlet and between boxing and playing on team Echo for the athletics company he was finding ways to relinquish his aggression in a positive manner.

Once 09:35 came around Irving was released from class. As he walked along the path heading back to his dormitory he decided to take a seat on the freshly cut grass just below the Statue of President Eisenhower. Students were seen jogging along the paths taking in the last few weeks of summer. Lying down, Irving felt the presence of someone approaching him.

"You looking really tired," her soft voice said. Irving sat up to face her.

"Is that so?" he responded, before laying back down. She was beautiful, her uniform fitted, her hair pulled back into a tight bun, small studded earnings that shined brightly, with smooth features standing at 5'5—her complexion melanated.

"My name is Shani," she smiled, gripping her textbooks, "Seems as though we're both plebes," she laughed, "I can't figure out how they came up with such a stupid name," she continued. Irving ignored her.

"I rather not have a conversation right now." He continued to lay down, his head to the sky, eyes closed, and his arms extended.

"So I guess the stories were true, you are an asshole." she said walking away. But Irving did not care about the things people had to say about him, his grades were excellent and he was on his way to becoming one of the most single, successful men in the world. The last thing he needed was people in his life who were there for the wrong reasons—his first day on campus, Christopher introduced him to a group of incoming freshmen, speaking his praises and when the questions began swirling about his childhood it was casually mentioned in conversation the inheritance he received. Keeping that in mind he was always skeptical about the new people he would meet, the conversations they would start or any interest they would show in him. African-American students attending West Point was not that common.

One hour passed as Irving continued to lie on the grass, realizing that he had class in fifteen minutes, he jumped to his feet, making his way to his dormitory at a sprint. The room he shared was large enough to hold two twin beds, two wardrobes, two dressers and two nightstands, his dorm mate, Robbins spent little to no time there as he seemed to always be with his girlfriend. Robbins had been there since the summer so he was very comfortable—some of his things spilling over to Irving's side of the room, but he didn't mind.

Next class, 11:00 a.m. Chinese.

It was noon and lunch formation was starting, the mess hall large enough to accommodate all 4,400 students and so everyone stood outside at attention for what felt like five minutes before piling inside. Lunch was a bit longer, lasting about forty minutes, with six lines the servers moved fast, the cadets, even faster. 12:55-13:40 was study time for Irving at the library. Learning a new language was very difficult, especially Chinese and so, he would carve out some extra time to review the curriculum. Inside the library Irving swiped his badge, passing the turnstiles he made his way to the second floor where he spotted Shawn in one of the meeting rooms studying, knocking on the door Irving entered inside.

"Is there room for one more?" he asked slamming his back bag on the steel table—four chairs surrounding it. Shawn looking up startled.

"I did not tell you yes—here you go again with that self-entitlement," he said playfully, his eyes squinting seductively.

"I do not think I am entitled," Irving laughed. "Also, why do you keep insulting me?"

"Insult? Wow, such a strong word, I offend no one," Shawn smiled.

"Well, I must be no one then," Irving replied removing his books from his backpack, a photo of Ivy falling to the ground.

"Oh my, she's so gorgeous." Shawn admiring the photo having tilted his head to get a better look.

"Yea, that's my baby sister," Irving responded, Shawn immediately looking up at him, "My mom is White, okay, she adopted me when I was younger," he concluded.

"Oh!"

"Let me guess, you think my so-called self-entitlement comes from the fact that I was raised by a White woman?" he asked, curious now.

"No, not at all, but the rumors about you have definitely begun making its way around campus," Shawn replied gently biting the tip of his pencil—flirting.

"Rumors, I've been hearing that word often, I wonder why though, why the infatuation with me?"

"Well, people see how much Lieutenant Royal favors you, I mean you call him by his first name, you barely speak to anyone and your friends with upperclassmen who are practically untouchable, not to mention you're a Black man. I hate to state the obvious but—"

"Well, that's interesting, but how about we put the rumors to rest and you work on getting to know me for yourself huh?"

"I would like that very much," Shawn said as he looked Irving up and down, fascinated by him.

From then on Irving and Shawn meticulously coordinated their schedules so they would meet one another after and before classes, attend events off campus once they were permitted to leave campus again. Shawn did not consider inquiring to Irving whether or not he thought of him as a romantic interest, he was simply not that forward and truthfully feared being rejected. Five months later the boys were preparing themselves for winter break and returning home. Irving was very mature for his age so Rose did not question whether or not he would be coming to their new home in Long Island. He was free to go wherever he pleased and so, he decided to head to Washington, D.C. to be with Shawn and his family.

While studying for finals in his dormitory Irving would dial Rose, checking in on his mother and his baby sister weekly.

"Hey mom." His hands flipping through the pages of his textbook while taking notes—finals were approaching, Rose answering him.

"Hello darling, how are classes? We miss you!" The happiness in her voice exciting him,

"Things are really good, classes are great. How is Ivy doing?"

"She has a little cold, but other than that she's doing great. Irving honey what are you doing for Winter break?" Rose asked him. Irving remained silent as he wondered.

"Um, I'm not sure yet to be quite honest with you," he said scratching his head—lying.

"Did you meet a special young lady?" she teased.

"No," Irving quickly replied, "It has nothing to do with that, I just may travel to some new places that's all. Well, unless you need me, how are the businesses running?"

"No, no, things are fine—" she spoke as a knock came to the door, Irving allowing Shawn inside, instructing him to be quiet. "Our third quarter numbers have been phenomenal for the Starbucks. But with the housing, I did have some ideas for the building; possibly doing some renovations, painting and changing the flooring in the hallways." But Irving was not liking the idea.

"Renovating how? Gentrification?" he asked sternly. Shawn took a seat on the mattress as he listened. Irving was beginning to turn him on.

"No, my God, no. But Irving, honey, if we fixed up the

building we can earn a lot more money. I mean you have some tenants only paying three-hundred dollars a month. Sweetheart, with that you're only covering the costs of taxes and some mechanics but there isn't much of a profit there." Rose advised him.

"Mom, if that's what they can manage, then that's what they'll pay. If doing renovations means the people who live there can't continue to do so while paying what they can afford then we don't need to make any changes for now."

Reluctantly Rose agreed, their call ending after exchanging their *I love you's*.

As always, Irving was happy to see Shawn, who was now staring at him with esteem. Irving wondering why Shawn was staring.

"Why are you looking at me like that?" he laughed.

"Because you're just so…kick ass, it's so cute," Shawn no longer able to hide his affection. "Irving, we should talk, I mean, I think you know how I feel about you," he continued. But Irving did not want to listen.

"Look…" Irving said, but unable to find the words without hurting Shawn's feelings. "I don't know how I feel or if what I feel is even appropriate. I honestly just try not to think about it, and if you're about to say what I think you're going to say, then it's best we do not have that conversation." Shawn lowering his head, saddened.

"…and here I was thinking you were different, but you're ashamed."

"Ashamed of what?" Irving replied, annoyed.

"Of who you are and who I am and what we could possibly be together. I mean, you spoke to me, surely you-you knew I was gay," Shawn was feeling outraged, but his personality would not allow for him to speak aggressively.

"You being gay doesn't bother me, you assuming that I too might be, does."

"I see the way you look at me," Shawn responded quickly as he stood tossing his books aside. He and Irving now face-to-face, "Tell me you feel nothing and I will never bring it up again," he said breathing heavily, passionately looking Irving in the eyes. Irving could not bring himself to look away, eighteen and still finding himself he thought this was just a mere experience as he kissed Shawn slowly. An ecstatic Shawn reciprocated for what felt like one minute until he stopped, lowering his body and unbuckling Irving's pants as he pushed his body against the desk on his side of the room. Irving confused, but erected, he did not stop him as Shawn firmly placed his mouth atop Irving's penis shaft, motioning his head up and down. Irving tilting his head back, moaning, his hands pressed firmly against the desktop.

Seventeen minutes later, Irving came, his cum dripping from Shawn's lips as he stood to kiss Irving, who then asked, "Can you go?" Irving said zipping up his pants hastily. Trembling now, as he could not believe what had just taken place—his mind swarming with confusion. Shawn stood wiping his lips, hurt, that he was now being tossed out like a hooker, allowing his tears to fall, but Irving did not care as he motioned for him to make his way through the door. Shawn was emotional because he was such a caring and loving individual—his discontentment palpable.

Irving had no contact with Shawn for three days, the first time in five months, their non-communication now feeling foreign to him. But Irving did not how to handle his emotions, he was not used to feeling them. Irving felt numb to the idea of dating a man, let alone having sexual intercourse with one, but wondered what his friends and family would think of him, what Christopher would think. He had hopes of one day becoming the leader of the free world and feared this would now be impossible, as he made his way to the mess hall where he arrived late, missing formation, but was not scolded.

Irving was avoiding Shawn and was successful until Shawn had enough of being given the cold shoulder, made his way over to him, just as Patrick stepped towards him, greeting Irving first.

"Hey man! We have training this evening, but I think I lost my knee padding. Do you have an extra pair I can borrow?" he asked but Irving was paying him no mind afraid that Shawn would cause a scene he kept his eyes on him, Patrick wondering why he was being ignored.

"Hey Irving man, are you okay?" he snapped his fingers.

Shawn now spoke. "You can't keep ignoring me." Holding his notebooks tightly after discarding his food tray. Irving stood frozen between both Patrick and Shawn, feeling terrified until Shani made her way towards them heading for the exit. Irving stepping past Shawn and Patrick grabbing her hand, Shani reluctant at first smiled as she watched Irving greet her amicably, tossing his free arm around Patrick walking away. Shawn left standing alone.

"Dude, what was that? You know that faggot?" Patrick teased.

"Nothing and no, I don't. I don't know what he was talking about. Anyways Shani, how about dinner this weekend?" Irving nonchalantly asked her, Shani grinning.

"Yes, of course!" she fidgeted tensely, looking him up and down. Standing outside in the cold, Irving said,

"Great, I will find you later." As the words left his mouth, he felt disgusted and unsure even of how he was going to find her. But she knew better, removing a piece of paper from her notebook, pressing on it she wrote her phone number down, folding the paper she handed it to Irving as she walked away. "Bye you guys," she said politely.

Once she was out of view, Patrick completely forgetting his initial question cheered on Irving, "Way to go, man! She's a good catch too, nice body and big tits and here we were thinking you'd never get your rocks off," he smiled patting Irving on the back. But Irving did not feel like a winner, he felt guilty.

By the time the weekend came around Irving could think of no one but Shawn. Returning to campus from his date with Shani—dinner and a movie, Irving tossed a baseball in his room as he lay in his bed throwing it in the air and catching it after walking Shani to her dorm, not kissing her which left her feeling confused. Standing now, he made his way to the seventh floor where he stood outside of Shawn's dorm, palms sweating, his peers wandering aimlessly about; everyone dressed casually. He was nervous he could feel their eyes on him as he lifted his hands to knock, Shawn's roommate answering.

"Oh hey," said Lopez as he was making his way out. "Shawn's inside," he told Irving smiling. But Irving did not reciprocate his kindness as he stepped inside to see Shawn laying down in his bed, his back turned to the door. The posters that hung on his wall were of his favorite boy band, *The Backstreet Boys*. Irving stood clearing his throat, Shawn turned, immediately sitting upright, fixing his boxers and straightening his shirt while using his hand to flatten his hair, "I look a mess, why didn't you tell me you were coming here?" he asked nervously. But Irving did not answer him, turning the lock behind him, praying his roommate would be gone long he walked over to Shawn kissing him. That night they had sex, Irving losing his virginity.

6

2007 – AGE 25

S tanding by the front door Irving browsing the internet as the realtor and Shani made their way around the 3,500 square foot house. Cathedral Heights, D.C., Irving was planning for his new family to have a life where he now considered running for Mayor. As a second lieutenant and business owner, he was making a lucrative income, one in which afforded him such luxury. Shani now seven months pregnant waddled her way up and down the winding stairs.

"Irving," she called to him. "You haven't even looked around, what do you think?"

Wearing a three-piece suit with an all-black trench coat and top hat, Irving lifted his head.

"We've seen almost four houses today, I think they all look the same, can you just pick one?" he insisted, lowering his head to resume browsing the internet, he was reading articles on past presidents and texting Hensley who too resided in the D.C.

Metropolitan area. Shani now frustrated asked the realtor for privacy to which she obliged, rubbing her round stomach she turned to Irving,

"Can you please not be such a jerk, I understand this isn't what you wanted, but we can at least try and make the best of things Irving," she uttered passionately. Irving placed his phone in his pocket.

"What would you like my input on?"

"Do you like the fixtures; do you think it's spacious enough? I mean, just what are your thoughts?"

"The house has five bedrooms and two bathrooms, I think there is more than enough space, we are having one child, one!" he emphasized.

"No, what if I want more?"

"Shani, no, we talked about this," he replied. Slowly he was growing intolerant. Shortly thereafter, the realtor returned from standing outside.

"So, have we decided?" she benevolently asked.

"Yes, we'll take it," Shani confirmed, forcing herself to smile as Irving turned to leave, dialing a number on his phone and walking along the garden just outside, after two rings a voice answered.

"Irving!" he shouted. Irving knew he would be in trouble. "Irving, where the hell are you? I've been sitting in this airport for two hours now!" he exclaimed.

"Shawn, baby I am so sorry, I know I said I was going to be there earlier but Shani is looking at houses and it's taking longer than I thought." Irving pleaded.

"What do you want me to do?" asked Shawn as he took a disappointing sigh.

"Call Brandon and have him pick you up, you can stay at Bloomfield until I get back." But Shawn was anything but pleased.

"The Projects! You want your henchman to take me to the projects?" he screamed, the patrons in the airport now looking at him, bewildered. "I thought you were on a flight, why has it even taken you this long to call me?" he continued, pacing now as he placed his hand atop his freshly groomed head. But Irving had no excuse, he was simply trying to avoid confrontation and did not want to call Shawn until Shani had decided on a home, which would have given him a better idea on when he could return to New York.

"Shawn, I will be there in about four hours. I am going to try and find a flight now." Irving said calmly. "So, you won't be at Bloomfield long, I promise. Plus, I have a surprise for you that I know you're going to love." But Shawn did not reply, he simply hung up the phone, which was no surprise to Irving because Shawn was always dramatic. He prayed that Shani was ready to leave as he browsed the internet in an attempt to book a flight. Shani was privy to Irving's affairs but decided against fussing.

"We have to sign some papers," Shani said calling to Irving noticing how worried he looked. Irving stepped with purpose, signing wherever he was told as quickly as possible. The realtor congratulating them on making a decision, promising to speed the process along so they can be settled in before the baby would arrive, but Irving was lost, paying them no mind.

"Alright good, so we're ready to go?" he asked, clapping his hands together indicating that their time had come to an end and the deal was finalized. Shani stepping behind him as he made his way back outside, climbing into the drivers' seat of his black 2006 BMW X3. The car ride was silent as Irving drove Shani to Silver Spring, M.D. back to the two-bedroom apartment they occupied; having recently deciding to relocate. Shani did not question him, thirty-two minutes later they had arrived, Irving turning to face her as she climbed out of the vehicle.

"I should be back on Monday." Slamming the car door Shani made her way inside the luxury apartment building, the concierge kind enough to open her doors.

Arriving in New York Irving was greeted by Brandon—their first stop, Bloomfield. The sun was shining bringing Irving to remove his trench and top hat; leaving them both in the back seat of the black town car with tinted windows. The men, women, and children were just outside playing and conversing, a young man struggling to remove the barbeque supplies from the back of his commercial vehicle. The neighborhood was thriving, everyone greeting Irving and acknowledging him respectfully.

"Kara!" he called to one young lady as he walked along the pavement, the fifteen-year-old African-American girl racing over to him, hugging him tightly as she smiled from ear to ear.

"Mr. Irving! I can't believe you're here," she said removing her braids from her face.

"Yep, how are you doing?"

"Good, just going to school but I really need a job." she sadly confessed.

"See Brandon alright and he'll work something out. In the meantime..." Irving said, removing his black wallet from his back pocket. "...here's a little something for you and your mom, don't go spending it too crazy," handing her four hundred-dollar bills—his voice just above a whisper, her eyes lighting up with glee.

"Oh my God, thank you! I will give this to my mom! Thank you so much, Mr. Irving." Her arms outstretched hugging him again. Irving reciprocated, hearing Kara mention needing a job at such a young age in the projects only meant one thing.

"Alright, go on now, looks like a barbeque starting soon." Irving walking away as Kara ran inside. Brandon moving distinctly behind Irving throughout the neighborhood—men, women, and children all treating him like royalty, recognizing all the good he had done for them and continued on doing. Stories from the elderly men of Irving and his youthful struggles, his story an inspiration to them. Brandon was proud of Irving, working with Samuel as he accompanied him to the hospital to visit Irving during his coma was when he knew Irving was going to be special.

"He's here," Brandon murmured to Irving as they stood outside of the apartment—3A. Irving unlocking the doors as Brandon waited outside, his arms folded. The apartment was vacant, but Shawn was provided food, water and managed to occupy himself with games on her cellular phone as he sat on the kitchen counter patiently waiting for Irving to arrive. Five hours later Irving was there and although Shawn wanted to despise him for having him wait so long, he simply could not bring himself to be upset, instead, he leaped from the countertop diving into Irving's arms kissing him profusely. Irving was now the happiest he had been in weeks.

"I missed you so much baby," Shawn said. The sound of his voice harmonious. Irving wanted to make love to him but decided against it, he instructed Shawn to gather his things, informing him of a surprise he had in store for him. Shawn loved surprises especially gifts from Irving. Once he gained access to his inheritance, he did nothing but spoil Shawn: new luggage, clothes, couple vacations overseas, the works! As the men exited the housing sector more people were gathered outside, the sun began to set as the music blared, the chicken cooked, and the women served water and snacks. Everyone comfortable and having the time of their lives.

Irving and Shawn sat in the backseat after Brandon loaded his luggage into the truck. The couple kissing and flirting for the duration of their ride which lasted about forty-five minutes. There they were in the heart of Harlem, Brandon finding a spot by the curb to park their car just under a large tree with orange leaves. As Irving and Shawn stepped out, Shawn wondered what the surprise could have been.

"Baby, what is it?" he asked flirtatiously.

"This" Irving said smiling as he pointed to the large Yellow Brownstone in front of them. The only brownstone on the block that was painted yellow on the outside with a pink door. "Surprise," he continued as Shawn looked on, shocked. Irving kissing his neck, moaning. He was horny and couldn't wait to get inside.

"What's this exactly?" Shawn asked him as Irving took him by the hand stepping inside the little black gates onto the stone steps and past the plant pots. The children were heard just outside playing in the streets, the sidewalks covered in orange tree leaves, the scenery exemplary and absolute perfection. Standing inside Irving felt proud.

"So, what do you think? There are two floors, an apartment upstairs and another downstairs, there's a finished basement with its own entrance and an exit just outside under the stairs. I mean, this is great right?" Irving smiled.

"Are you expecting me to move here?" asked Shawn as he stood with his arms folded.

Irving took a deep breath before responding, "Look, I have to start getting things in place and preparing for my run, I know this isn't ideal—"

Shawn interrupted him, furious, "Irving you're not running for President for another decade, why on earth are you trying to move me away from my family, my friends? I had a life before I met you and that life is in Washington," Shawn pleaded.

"Listen, I know, okay. I know, but as soon as I announce that I have an interest in running—which Mr. Royal and I plan to do soon—the media will begin to dig. Even if it is ten years from now, I can't have them finding out anything about me that could possibly jeopardize my chances of making it into the general elections."

"So, you're hiding me?" Shawn said, his eyes beginning to well. "We don't have to be ashamed of who we are Irving, you're gay, just accept it and let's move on. Why can't you run with me standing by your side?" he asked, his heart beating quickly. But Irving was in no mood to quarrel.

"I am a Black man trying to sit in the Oval Office one day, the people I love will have to make sacrifices and this-this is just one of those sacrifices. The brownstone is yours; you can rent out the two units and earn an income. Maybe I should come back once you've calmed down." Irving preparing to leave.

"No. don't leave," Shawn hated himself for saying that. He knew Irving was being cruel, but he loved him and chose to put Irving's needs above his own, "What about Shani?"

"Shani is going to have the baby and she decided on a house

today in Cathedral Heights," Irving replied.

Shawn now huffing and puffing, "Did you honestly have to have a baby with her? Are you going to continue fucking her? You told me you didn't love her, Irving," he said, feeling heartbroken now.

"These things have to be done. I love you. She's there for the public, not me. But Shawn I love you and I will do my best to make sure that you continue to feel that I do. But as of right now, my goals are my focus. Now can we go upstairs and christen the apartment?" Irving flirtatiously biting his bottom lip. Shawn folding his arms as he pretended to be angry, sucking his teeth and rolling his eyes at him, but Irving knew this was all an act as he approached him, his penis erected, unfolding his arms and kissing on his neck gently, Shawn moaning, "Let's go."

Two hours later Irving stood, getting dressed and buttoning his shirt as Shawn lay naked across the queen mattress. Irving making his way downstairs into the foyer where he brought up their luggage; Brandon had been kind enough to bring them in before retiring for the night. The mid-century modern apartment was fully furnished. The top floor brought in amazing natural light—relinquishing an airy feeling. Inside there were two bedrooms and one bathroom, a large living and dining area annexed to the kitchen. The living room had a small brick fireplace, above it hung a one of the kind *Renaissance Art* painting by Archibald Motley.

Next to that was an empty bookshelf and along the walls between the wide windows were additional traditional paintings from Jacob Lawrence, Kara Walker, and Alma Thomas. The hardwood floors recently polished, the kitchen appliances brand new and modernized along with the leather sofas and plush throw pillows producing a moody atmosphere created by the rich tones lining the windows. Additionally, the built-in window bench is not only a beautiful detail of the apartment but also provides seating without taking up precious floor space.

The bedroom contained two wooden crates for additional storage, hanging plants, a bedside lamp, dresser, molded plastic chair, antique rub, a wall mirror and hamper. Irving did not do any of the decorating, deciding it best to hire an interior designer who was kind enough to fill the apartment with plants, she knew Shawn would absolutely adore and he did. Lying in bed taking it all in now, Shawn began to realize just how lucky he was—a man who loved him, a home to live in and finding his place in the city that never sleeps.

"Maybe I should think about pursuing my actor career now. What do you think?" he asked Irving who was now in the kitchen preparing a snack.

"You want a sandwich?" he bellowed to Shawn who too was getting out of bed.

"A sandwich? Boy, what kind of food do you have here? Hopefully something decent so I can make you a good meal," Shawn said as he moseyed over, the crème colored sheets wrapped around his hips leaving his chest exposed. Irving was enjoying every moment of this, for the first time he and Shawn were finally going to enjoy living life on their terms, like the couple he knew they would always be, despite the restrictions he had a positive outlook on things. Leaving Shawn to cook, Irving stood, watching him, smiling with his eyes, his arms folded.

"You're possibly the best thing that could have ever happened to me," he said. Shawn smiling. That night Shawn and Irving spent the evening laughing, watching television, eating and enjoying one another's company. Irving was different with Shawn—he was gentle, caring and absolutely smitten by him and his benevolent personality as he would sneak kisses randomly during shows and movies. At times showing his feeble side so Irving would be inclined to assist him but this did not bother Irving, he loved Shawn for allowing him to be a man and never taking away from him a chance to be the provider and protector he was destined to be.

Morning came quickly as the sun made its way to greet them. Irving upheld his discipline going for a jog around the neighborhood at 5 a.m. wearing a tracksuit he removed from his duffle bag, showering afterward. Shawn remained sleeping as

Irving gathered his belongings, leaving a note on the nightstand and five-hundred dollars instructing Shawn to spend the day shopping. Irving dialed Brandon as he walked to the corner of the block to a nearby deli ordering two breakfast sandwiches and a cup of coffee. He stood waiting for Brandon to arrive.

Rose spent her morning assisting thirteen-year-old Ivy to prepare for school. Ivy was bright, seemingly following into Irving's footsteps although she was not selected for Christopher's elite group she was regarded as a bright student in the academy, which for Rose was enough. The new house she purchased in Long Island not too far from Ryan and Marley was breathtakingly beautiful. Standing outside Irving arrived just in time to see off his sister and greet Rose who was standing in the driveway preparing to take off.

"Irving," Ivy shouted as she climbed from the back seat, her brunette strands flowing in the wind. Rose could not see her, running as she sat in the driver's seat, preparing to take off—startled.

"Ivy, Jesus Christ, why would run out of the car like that?" she screamed noticing Irving making his way up the driveway, cradling his younger sister who fit perfectly in his arms. Ivy smiling from ear to ear, "Irving, oh my goodness!" Rose shouting, elated to have seen him. Irving loved family visits especially since that meant spending quality time with his loved ones.

"Hi mom," he said still holding Ivy, extending his right arm to wrap around Rose, she reciprocated.

"Irving, you look like a gangster," Rose staring him up and down, the all-black getup and hair cut was not sitting well with her, "Why are you dressed like this?" she then asked. Irving was confused.

"Mom, what on earth do you mean?" he chuckled. But Rose was not tickled, deciding to change the subject.

"How are Shani and the baby doing?" Motioning for Ivy to return to the car so she could be taken to school.

Irving looked suspicious as he responded quickly, "They're great," kissing Ivy atop the head.

"I cooked some breakfast, you can help yourself until I get back," Rose said climbing into her jeep. Ivy waving,

"See you later Irving, please stay until I get home" she begged, her voice soft. Irving waving goodbye as he made his way inside, motioning for Brandon to join him—Rose disappeared from view down the road making a left at the stop sign just inside the cul-de-sac.

When Rose returned to find Irving showered wearing a pair of Keith's sweatpants, she could not help but laugh, her son had become a grown man right before her eyes, but she had a bone to pick with Irving, one that could not be excused by his evolution.

"Irving," she called to him, slamming the front door and making her way into the living room where she took a seat on the crimson sofa. Irving stepping inside, his plate filled with strips of bacon, scrambled eggs and toast. "I went through the expense report and checked the business accounts," Rose said deciding to waste no more time. "There was a significant increase in both your spending habits and the amount of money you have coming in—I'm talking thousands of additional dollars in as short as four months. For example, last quarter the church made $178,000.00 and the housing development, $268,000.00, the Starbucks generated, $88,000.00 in profits and yet, the accounts went up tripling those amounts. Where is this extra money coming from?" She inquired, afraid of the answer.

Irving taking a deep breath as he listened on, his lips pursed, "I have another business and it's lucrative." Rose shot to her feet.

"Listen to me, if this is at all what I think it is, please stop! You are way too intelligent and you risk losing so much." Rose beseeched him. But Irving simply listened.

"Years ago, when you mentioned that I should get the house with your inheritance, I felt so guilty because I knew where the money came from, and Irving, I have tried so hard and have cried and have had many sleepless nights praying and wishing that you truly be one of a kind and so, I will not judge you, but I am asking that you stop whatever it is that you are doing. We have more than enough."

Irving stood as Rose stepped rigorously towards him, grabbing his biceps, "Irving, do not ignore me, I am still your mother." Irving turned to face her as he spoke slowly,

"Mom, I love you and I promise you I will not allow anything to happen to anyone I love, please, you have to trust me," he said bending his knees slightly to look her in the eyes. Irving was now 6'3, muscular and his chocolate complexion free of imperfections, as Rose stared into his eyes, she could do nothing but trust him, nodding her head yes,

"Okay." She whispered.

Shawn woke up to find himself sleeping alone as the sun shone in on his face. It was ten in the morning and although Irving had gone Shawn did not fret, he knew Irving would be home later on. Rising to stretch and make his way to the kitchen where he prepared himself a hot cup of coffee, Shawn decided to take a tour of the brownstone. As the coffee brewed, he took glimpses of his naked body all throughout, realizing the abundance of mirrors they had.

Shawn favored actor Larenz Tate, a man whom he had grown to love and adore and it didn't hurt that he was his celebrity look alike. As he puckered his lips to take selfies to upload to social media, he noticed the nightstand and the money that was left there, chucking to himself, thinking of how wonderful Irving had been to him; he couldn't help but smile. Biting his bottom lip, he raced to the bathroom where he showered quickly, removing some clothes from his suitcase, dressing, excited now as he had other plans for that money. Shawn was quite the fashionista, favoring pieces like Chinos pants and Hensley tops, some cologne and a pair of laced chestnut oxfords. Pouring his coffee into a canister, Shawn was ready to take New York by storm, tossing his bag over his shoulder, he stepped confidently outside.

Seconds later he realized his key was locked inside, as two women approached him, appearing to be quite young, Shawn rolling his eyes in annoyance.

"Hi!" one girl said, her look bohemian chic, the other, sexy. Shawn pushing on the front door could not get inside.

"Hi," he replied back walking down the stairs choosing to finally give up. He did exit from behind the little black gate but stood just on the opposite, the girls smiled with glee, introducing themselves.

"My name is Frances and this is my best friend Jade." Spoke the young woman. Shawn remained unenthused.

"Okay, yes, how can I help you lovely ladies?"

"Well, we're looking for an apartment and we're just trying to go door to door, it would be awesome if we found an apartment inside of a brownstone—that's like, always been my dream," Frances said, her natural hair combed into a high ponytail. Shawn thought she was absolutely stunning but could use some foundation. Frances handed him a flyer with her number annexed, he wondered, *was everyone in New York this carelessly stupid?*

"Well of course, if I hear of anything I will give you lovely ladies a call," Shawn forcing a smile as Frances and Jade made their way to his new neighbors.

7

2009 – AGE 27

I rving had the community in his back pocket, a slew full of civilians ready to go to war for him as he not only began aiding those who were destitute with finding means of employment but also teaching the middle class how to properly budget and maximize their spending. The church officials and congregation members came piling into the church building every Saturday night at 8 p.m. sharp to listen to Irving give his powerful and influential speech on wealth versus income. A curriculum he learned very early on in life. This intrigued members as the economy was depreciating and everyone was looking for ways to save, capitalize on their earnings and learn new ways to invest—Irving had the credentials, he was, after all, a wealthy man.

By twenty-seven Irving managed to open one additional Starbucks location; three in total considering the second he purchased two years ago, ultimately deciding to renovate the housing projects and expand the church, now renting two sides inside of one. When Rose questioned his spending habits and the abrupt rise in revenue Irving decided not to disclose this information because Rose had yet to learn of Shawn and the money he used to take care of him. Irving had a plan, utilize the church to expound on his public speaking skills and then take his knowledge and curriculum higher once word began to spread that such a local man of wealth existed. Careful, Irving did not think to squander his money, he was frugal and prudent, thinking twice before making a purchase and looking at each monetary gift as a tax write-off.

Christopher and Irving grew increasingly close over the years, Irving had met his wonderful daughter, wife, and his son, Jasper, who did not fancy Irving too much. Christopher and Irving spent a lot of time at the Larchmont County Club golfing whenever Irving was in town—the two gentlemen discussed politics, wealth, investments and Irving's journey to the Oval Office,

"You've come a long way young man," Christopher said to Irving preparing himself to start a game out on the open field, deciding to break the ice. The summer breeze feeling wonderful against his skin. Both Shawn and Jasper accompanying them, however, Shawn and Irving had yet to disclose their affair to anyone. Irving and Shawn were beginners, holding in their hands a 6-iron club with a regular flex and a stiff flex shaft—the only thing Shawn knew was to swing fast and swing with aggression never once taking any time to practice.

"Thank you, sir," Irving said, his attire similar to Shawn's.

"You boys are no longer in the academy, no need to dress alike," Christopher chuckled, now in his late sixties, he moved a lot slower than usual, allowing Irving and Shawn to often times find themselves walking ahead, unintentionally of course, but Jasper did much observing of their decorum as he had grown accustomed to his father's leisurely gait learning just how well to pace himself. Jasper—5'9, tanned, short brunette hair strands resembled his mother, Katherine. His facial expressions always unpleasant as he spent many of days wishing his father would pay half as much attention to him as he did the children who either attended the preparatory school or West Point. Jasper did not fancy those things which no doubt disappointed Christopher—his only son not wanting to follow in his footsteps.

As the gentlemen made their way down the cautiously maintained and challenging 18-hole championship golf course with unparalleled gold practices Christopher made small talk, a little annoyed that the boys were not having a good time,

"Irving, how are things with the locals?" Irving turned to face him, his all-black Adidas shorts rising up his thighs as he walked—constantly tugging on the bottom of them pulling them down, Shawn whispered, "Looks like somebody is gaining some weight." He teased. Irving swatting him away,

"Well, the congregation is beginning to enhance their political views and bringing along more questions and concerns as it relates to their wellbeing," he said. "Which is good for me to know of course—"

"—and why is that?" asked Christopher interrupting him. Every moment spent together was a teachable moment for Irving,

"Because then I can gauge their troubles, implementing them into my political campaign, which can only strengthen my numbers when the time comes for me to answer to the constituents," Irving said with confidence.

"Yes, yes and when is this?"

"In two weeks, sir."

"Good—good, I will need a thorough breakdown of your plan on attack, and Benedict Mitchell III will be running for office in 2012, so we will have to get you a spot on his campaign, before the elections. This will ensure you get a chance at the 2016 elections—understand?"

"Yes."

"Good, now get off the course, all of you whimpering youngsters are depressing me." A relived Irving made his way back up the hill, Shawn scurrying behind him; Jasper remained at his father's side.

Shawn struggling to keep up tugged the glass doors, the doors slamming behind him, irritated now, Shawn followed Irving past the main dining room equipped with bordered French doors and boasts hand painted wallpaper complimenting the elegant feel of the clubhouse. Shawn beginning to feel like his time was being wasted climbing inside the black town car, sitting beside Irving who immediately removed his phone to begin working.

"Irving, what is going on?" Shawn asked setting the gold clubs down on the floor in front of him, the car driving off. But Irving said nothing, only angering Shawn further, "Irving!" Shawn cried, removing the phone from his palm.

"Shawn, what are you doing?" Irving shouted.

"What's gotten into you?" Shawn demanded answers, his eyes squinting.

"Nothing," replied Irving, "I need my phone. Now!" he shouted, Shawn, placing the iPhone back into his palm as he turned to look through the window taking in the scenery atop the mountain as they made their way down.

Inside the brownstone Irving undressed, leaving himself unclothed, he took a seat on the sofa stretching his legs and reading an article he found online, Shawn went into the bathroom where he let the water run preparing himself for a cold shower. Shawn was beginning to feel lonely, although Irving would visit every other weekend, he was beginning to feel as though it was simply not enough, he wanted him to himself, he wanted him all the time. As he pondered their arrangements a lightbulb went off in his head, the cold water beating against his naked body, Shawn stepping swiftly from the tub, water dripping everywhere.

"You're sleeping with Shani aren't you?" he asked Irving standing by the bathroom threshold. "That's why you're acting weird and—and giving me the cold shoulder, huh? You've been fucking her," he said again, this time his eyes welling as he tapped

Irving atop the shoulder; slapping him—his hit delicate.

"I don't—I just don't know what to say," Irving replied solemnly. He was never going to tell Shawn, but his behavior could not be hidden, he was growing to love Shani, watching her raise their son, had done something to him, something he could not explain. Shawn sobbed as he threw his right hand across his mouth, and placed his left hand atop his hip, turning to face the large windows that overlooked the queen mattress. He could not believe his ears, Irving stood to place his hands on his shoulders, kissing him lightly, "I'm so sorry. I made a mistake and I didn't know how to tell you; I promise I wanted to though, I did," he said turning Shawn to face him, but his face was drenched in tears, his eyes could not open as he continued standing. Irving felt awful.

"You promised me," Shawn cried, the tears trickling between his lips as he salivated. "Leave," he ordered a few moments later as they both stood in silence.

"I don't want to leave you like this," said Irving fervently.

"Please, I cannot stand to look at you right now, I've uprooted my entire life for you and you told me it was just for the public Irving, you said she meant nothing and now you sound so unsure," Shawn bellowed. "My entire life!" Screaming now. "Get out! Go home to your precious Shani!" he continued tossing Irving his tennis shorts and the white t-shirt he wore. Irving backed towards the front door, opening it, he let himself out. Dressing now, Irving decided it best not to anger him further as he made his way downstairs and out of the pink double doors.

Shawn spent hours upstairs pacing and sobbing until night came, listening as his new tenant made her way inside, her keys jingling to her front door, dressed now, Shawn opened the door, calling to her.

"Frances, is that you?" he asked, sniffling. The young woman's voice responded softly, "Yes, hi Shawn," she smiled.

Shawn decided to rent the first-floor apartment of the brownstone considering he would need income and was having a tough time finding employment in the big city. Deciding on Frances because she was polite during their first encounter and after having invited her back for a follow-up conversation they seem to have hit it off pretty well; ultimately this was a no brainer, she was young, educated, gracious and most importantly, responsible. Shawn was devastatingly heartbroken, he spent years loving Irving and only prayed that one day their love could be public. He had become a lover in hiding, no longer respected by his parents as they soon learned his true reason for relocating.

It was all too overwhelming as he and Frances now sat upstairs in the living room, enjoying the view accompanied by a hot cup of tea and the wonderful smooth sounds of jazz to which Frances grew curious.

"This music sounds amazing." She closed her eyes to take it all in; the ambiance and the sweet smell of incense burning.

"Honey, this is the sophisticated way to live, get with it," Shawn said. Little did he know, she would one day do just that.

Irving decided to head back to Washington, D.C. where Christopher assured, he too would soon arrive. Their plan was simple, get Irving elected Mayor—considering the District did not have Governors, soon after, run for President. Irving studied his competition, watching his debates, learning of his livelihood and his stance on politics, Benedict Mitchell III was a born to be a politician. Coming from an affluent background, he was destined to one day sit in the Oval Office. Christopher landed shortly after Irving, making his way to the nation's capital in uniform having plans to meet with Johnson, who was now a military captain and remained the head of Secret Service.

Johnson was not pleased to hear of Christopher's intentions with Irving; he was currently employed in The White House full-time and was just too busy to entertain what he felt to be an impossible feat.

"We already have a Black man for President, do you honestly think the nation is going to allow that to happen again?" spoke a pessimistic Johnson to Christopher as he entered into Johnson's office, taking a seat in the leather chair; Johnson shutting the door behind him, alerting the receptionist to hold his calls.

"Johnson, we are the nation, what goes on behind these walls is what we allow to happen. I understand the Oval Office is currently occupied by a man of color; however, we have another man who I feel will do wonders for this country. We need a filibuster, however, Mitchell, he can win the 2012 election and then we bring along Irving for the 2016 run. I feel this can be done," Christopher said.

"Republican?" Johnson asked taking a deep breath.

"Mitchell, yes—Irving democrat," he responded. "Perfect, no?" Christopher continued.

"What is Irving bringing to the Oval Office?" Johnson asked. "I mean, what can he do that the Black man currently serving our nation cannot? These are the questions my superiors will ask, the attorney general, the state senate, how do I respond?"

"Listen, just get the word out that Irving is a rising politician and I will handle the rest. Meet with Walter and have him cover the press. You are all in place for a reason," Christopher said, standing. A bewildered Johnson nodded in compliance.

Irving, later that day contacted the District of Columbia Board of Elections Office where he confirmed his registered address and his intent to run for Mayor—the clerk verifying him and his qualifications taking nearly an hour to complete. Arranging soon after for his receipt of the nominating petitions from the Board of Elections, where he would be expected to earn fifteen thousand signatures. This exciting Irving—it was July 10, 2009 and with only six weeks to submission on August 21, 2009 for the general elections taking place in November, Irving was now racing against the clock. As an independent candidate, Irving knew better than to sit around twiddling his thumbs and so concluding his call he headed downtown where he would meet with Christopher for lunch, but he was late.

Christopher made his way across town in the black stretch limo where he found Irving sitting inside the coffee shop reading old articles he carried with him daily tucked away in the jetted pocket of his suit jackets. The maroon suit he wore today was tailored nicely, his shirt a crème colored Harris Wharf design. Stepping inside, Christopher took a seat across from him, as he bellowed for the waitress.

"You need a haircut young man," he began by saying, Irving simply shaking his head.

"I've registered and will pick up my petition form tomorrow morning," Irving informed him as the waitress made her way over, the expression on her face benevolent.

"How can I help you gentlemen?" she asked smiling, a pad and pencil in her hand.

"Nothing for me, thank you," said Irving.

"A hot cappuccino for me please with a caramel swirl," Christopher asked smiling—elated. "Irving, may I ask you, how are things with your girlfriend?"
Irving grew uncomfortable as he began thinking of Shawn and the way he was forced to leave things between them,

"She's fine," he grumbled, "I was thinking of attacking these districts first," his hand affixed to a brochure mapping out their territories as he hoped to change the subject.

"Irving, focus, your girlfriend."

Irving, now irritated, responded, "Why—why do we need to discuss Shani? She is home with our son and, that's that."

Christopher was skimming as he slowly became aware of the disdain Irving showed for his live-in girlfriend, realizing this first years ago when he and Shani were invited to their home for a lovely dinner. Irving made little to no eye contact and displayed no signs of affection.

"You were smart enough to conceal who you truly are by shacking up with a lovely woman. But you will need to do more than just that," observed Christopher as the waitress meticulously placed his coffee in front of him.

"What do you mean?" Irving asked, pretending to be aloof.

"I mean, you will need to marry her, although this may be against your will and you will need more children and please for the love of God at least pretend to give a damn about the woman when asked of her existence," Christopher snapped.

"My personal life is none of your business," he snapped.

"Your personal life is business Irving. Nothing but, you will be heavily monitored by the media come August and if all your ducks are not aligned you can kiss this opportunity goodbye. You must be a model citizen, this means house, wife, children, pets, no scandals—"

Irving interrupting him, "I do not want my family involved in anything I do, I want this to solely be about me—marriage? Does she have to be my wife? I thought the mere fact that I was dating a woman was enough."

"Ah, there it goes," a cheerful Christopher lifting his cup to take a sip of his cappuccino. "You are a gay African-American man who will one day run for the Oval Office, this will be no easy task, we have a Black President and as Johnson mentioned earlier today, what is going to set you apart? What is going to make the nation want to know Irving Houston?" he continued.

"I have no idea," Irving replied, for the first time finding himself without answers.

"Oh you know, you just refuse to admit it to yourself. You will have to use the people in your life to be a catalyst towards your greatest accomplishment to the world."

"No, I will not involve them," Irving said.

"Not yet, but one taste of power and you will. Love is transient; we will lose the people we care for one way or another, either to death or their own free will. But power, power is unmatched. You'll marry the girl, one day have more babies. Until then, I will be by in the morning to begin our petition run." Christopher, removing a fifty-dollar bill from his pocket, tossing it on the table, "...and bring along Shani, I will have the prenup drafted for her execution as well," standing now to take his exit.

On the way home, Irving pondered his conversation with Christopher, arriving inside to Shani and their two-year-old son running about.

"Irving is that you?" Shani called to him from inside the kitchen. Irving closing the door behind him as their son Kwame stood before him, wearing a diaper, a shirt and holding a bottle to his lips. Loosening his tie, Irving stepped to him, lifting him as they made their way into the kitchen following the sound of her voice.

Shani now five months pregnant with their second child was showing through her clothes as Irving leaned down to give her a kiss on the lips—she was after all very short. Exhausted, she thanked God for his arrival.

"I'm so happy your home, but I thought you weren't coming back until Monday," her hands pressed together as she cleaned.

Irving was paying her no mind, replying with the first thing that came to mind, "We should get married," he told her.

Shani could not believe her ears and so, she repeated after him, "We—we should get married?"

"Yes, but I have to be honest with you." Placing Kwame to sit on the counter top, his body blocking him to keep his son from falling. "We will have to get a prenuptial agreement and—and, um, I am in love with Shawn, while I do love you too, it is not the same type of love. I love our children; I love our friendship and I have the utmost respect for you—"

"Stop talking!" she screamed storming out of the kitchen, ripping the apron from around her hips, as she stomped upstairs to their bedroom. Irving calling to her, but Shani did not respond.

After making dinner Irving showered Kwame, bringing him to his room where he read him a bedtime story, hours later and Shani did not make an appearance. Sitting downstairs in the living room Irving began going over business expense reports and pertinent documents for the building. The church, and the franchise realizing the mistakes he continues to make in regard to their profits and gross. Things were flowing smoothly outside of that, after hiring the necessary team members to properly manage and market his properties.

Irving contemplated calling Shawn, he spent the whole day thinking of it, just then Shani appeared, draped in a silk negligee, her hair in a bun, she took a seat on the couch adjacent to him, as they both watched the fireplace wood burning.

"I'll do it," she said. "Under one condition, I am not signing a prenuptial agreement," Irving knitting his brows as he turned to face her.

"Are you crazy?"

"No, you're gay and you need me, and for the sake of my children, I need you too and so I need to be sure that they will always be taken care of, as will I," she said.

"No, we get a prenuptial agreement, however, we can negotiate the terms and fees."

"Irving, no! I will not be publicly humiliated. I asked you when we first began dating if you were done experimenting with Shawn, or-or exploring that side of you and you told me yes," she screamed.

"Goddamn it that's because I was, I couldn't accept who I was then, I didn't want to accept it, but now I have no choice. This is who I am," he replied beating his chest with the balls of his fists.

"Fine, then go be gay, alone! Let the public see that you're a gay man who likes taking it up the ass," she hollered with resentment.

"Watch your mouth!" he said stepping to her face. "I will not be disrespected or ridiculed in my own home. You wanted this life and you knew I could give it to you so stop acting like a child and stand up and be a woman about it. You want the money, we have it, you want the fame, and you will soon have it. But what you won't have is the ability to ever tell me what to do or what you will or will not do. Notice, Shani, I did not ask you to marry me; I told you we should get married. This isn't about being in love, it's about being in business," he shouted, walking away. "Wear something nice, we leave for the courthouse tomorrow morning," he continued, bellowing from the top of the stairs. Shani sat sobbing quietly to herself.

Irving felt remorseful, but was far too angry to apologize, his respect for Shani spanned as far it did for his mother. But, he was not going to be insulted, not even in the slightest. The next morning Irving awoke for his morning run, returning home around 7 a.m. where he showered and began making breakfast for his soon to be wife and their son. Irving enjoyed doing things for Shani, she was typically kind-hearted and treated their son with such care that Irving could not help but feel grateful— especially considering the nature of his past. Kwame did not sleep late as he crawled his way down the carpeted stairs startling Irving by 7:45 a.m. rubbing his eyes. It was Sunday morning, the perfect time to find civilians at home, resting with their families and enjoying their day.

Their bedroom massive and the blackout blinds helping to keep the sun out but this was an issue when it came time to wake up in the morning. Losing track of time Shani jumped up, rubbing her eyes she noticed Irving standing by the doorway, a tray in his hands and Kwame sitting atop his shoulders, having his bottle of milk. Bending slightly careful not to hit his head on the door frame, Irving entered inside, impressed with his ability to balance the tray and his son, Shani could not help but smile. The light from the hallway shining inside as Irving placed the tray along her lap, grabbing a hold of Kwame's legs, bending over so his son could crawl on the bed now. Turning around Irving flipped the switch in their bedroom, illuminating it.

After breakfast Shani showered and got dressed, finding a beautiful dress she purchased a few years ago while thrifting with her friends. It was a 1950's inspired, blue lace belted bow tie dress and a pair of silver heels. Straightening her hair for the first time in months, she allowed her natural hair to flow freely down her back. She looked gorgeous. Irving did not dress for their wedding; he dressed for his first day of campaigning. Irving was feeling delighted, energetic and optimistic. As the car horn beeped outside for them one hour later, Irving was placing shoes on his son's feet, lifting him out the front door. The black stretch limo double parked outside, just on the other side of their picket fence excited Shani as she slid inside. Christopher there to greet them and amongst him were signs, posters, pins, pens and other merchandise for Irving's campaign.

"This looks amazing," said Shani lifting a pin with Irving's face on it. Irving was surprised, he had no idea this merchandise was purchased, he was also confused about where the photo of him had been taken from.

"Where on earth did you get this picture?"

"Captain Photo, a year ago," Christopher said as everyone sat inside, his back to the driver's window, tapping it gently to indicate they were ready to move. He handed out pins to both Irving and Shani.

"Put these on," he commanded them as he reached into his back pocket to remove a set of wedding bands and a solitaire cut diamond ring for Shani and then came the papers.

"We need signatures on here, you will find the places where you are all to sign, now-now come along." Irving glimpsing past the clauses did not bother to read anything, signing along the dotted lines. But Shani could not read the forms as the car moved along the bumpy roads. Kwame sitting quietly with his pacifier watching them as Shani continued to hesitate.

"What if I can't sign this?" she asked. "The dates are pre-filled from a week and a half ago, and notarized, isn't this illegal?" Christopher grew angry.

"You will sign those documents; do you understand me? You will not ask one more question and you will one day soon be the very best First Lady this country could have asked for," he said to her, reclining back in the chair. Irving reclined as well, staring through the window as Shani stared at him, taking a huge gulp before scribbling her name. A happy Christopher rubbing the top of Kwame's head with joy, "Your mummy and daddy getting married aye boy,"

Arriving at the justice of the peace, Irving remained seated as both Kwame and Shani made their way outside and up the steps to the courthouse. Inside the limo Christopher handed him the wedding bands, a wedding certificate and rings, advising him that his campaign manager could be found inside and that he, Christopher would be heading to the attorney's office to prepare the docs for filing.

"I'm too old to go door to door for campaigning, but I will be wearing my pin," he smirked. "The limo will return in an hour, Mr. Mayor," he teased, he was all too happy as Irving now climbed outside chortling.

Part 4

S hani and Irving stood with their heads bowed; standing beside them was Zoey Colquhoun a second-year law student interested in politics—assertive, vivacious and talented having successfully coordinated three government campaigns in the last two and a half years alongside her father, William Colquhoun. Christopher knew to invest in Irving's campaign was going to be costly, but it was worth it as he looked to hire the best in politics.

Stepping outside now husband and wife Irving could not bring himself to enjoy this joyous moment as Shani and Kwame took photos, shouting for Irving to join them. Shani was elated, although apprehensive at first she was now a married woman and could not wait to tell her parents the wonderful news. Despite the rift that came between them when Shani did not re-enlist for the military after her four years in the service her father was still happy she managed to find love and took a liking to Irving. He was even more ecstatic that Irving was a millionaire and could afford to care for his daughter. Shani remained painstakingly beautiful, having barely aged a day—retaining her youth she stood smiling, cradling her growing baby bump.

Irving was ready to hit the campaign trail, growing weary after ten minutes of snapping photos he was making his way down the stairs towards the limo that returned for them.

"Let's go!" he shouted to everyone, Shani tossing Kwame on his hip as Zoey aided her down the stairs.

"Can we maybe go out for lunch, you know, to celebrate?"

asked Shani nervously. But Irving would hear of no such thing, it was time to pick up his petitions board and head on their way.

The cellular phone and email engrossing his attention, he replied, "No, I will have the chef come and make lunch and dinner for you both, I have to head out," he replied, never making eye contact. Zoey knew the drill, work before family, and so, she instructed the driver,

"Home for the wife and child please," tapping the window slightly, this pleases Irving as he sent a text message to Shawn, asking him to prepare himself for a flight in the next four hours. Irving sat booking Shawn a flight to D.C., he was indeed excited but wanted to celebrate after work was complete with the love of his life because he was making strides towards his dreams, no matter how he would get there. Irving struggled with trying to figure out the best way to break the news to Shawn, he thought of dinner by candlelight but felt that to be cliché and so, he waited until his wife and child were out of view and inside their home to ask Zoey.

"I need to be able to trust you with my life, can I do that?" he questioned, tucking his phone in his back pocket once Shawn complied with his request by way of text message. Zoey reached into her briefcase highlighting their hot spots for the afternoon.

"Sir, absolutely you can." Irving could tell she was power-hungry; he could see it in her eyes and hear it in her tone.

"If a man did something that was completely unforgivable, such as betraying your trust, what would he have to do to earn your forgiveness?" Irving was knowledgeable, but when it came to his relationship with Shawn and trying to balance the two, it was becoming hectic. Zoey looked perturbed.

"I'm not sure, your wife looks extremely happy to me," she said. "Plus, if it's an unforgivable offense, how can you expect to be forgiven?" She asked, confused.

"My wife is for the world, the person I am speaking of— that person is for me, and I have managed to hurt the person that is for me," Irving said trying to remain as discreet as possible.

Taking a deep breath before responding, "Do you love your wife, Mr. Houston," she asked boldly.

"The people will love my wife; I think that's all that matters."

"When you hurt the person you love, you change the behavior, then you do something grand, something that makes them feel untouchable, like your love for them is unmatched— mistake or no," she said. Irving had an idea.

After receiving his petitions form, door to door they went, Irving and Zoey both taking sides of the sidewalks, campaign pins annexed to their clothing. Irving did not know what to say, he simply explained why he should be elected Mayor citing the issues he would fix beginning with the foibles within the school systems, children failing their aptitude exams and being held back more than once, Irving played to his strengths speaking on his outstanding academic achievements despite his tumultuous childhood, one family mentioned having a child who too had been held back by the school system three times despite having the basic academic skill, but lacked good test-taking abilities. Irving swore to change this, demanding a regulation such as this is asinine.

Zoey did extensive research on where to go, which neighborhoods to visit, checking for demographics and specifically speaking on the needs of the neighborhoods. Surprisingly, Irving was making great progress, after only two hours earning himself 102 signatures in support of his proposal—Zoey earned them 82 signatures. It was the highlight of his day when one gentleman asked that Irving place his law sign outside, and of course, they obliged, also taking from him a pin and some pens. The veterans in the neighborhood instantly connecting to him as he mentioned working towards better employment for veterans' returning home, and strengthening community programs needed for their reintegration into society. Some veterans were tired, tired of hearing the same promise from every candidate, but Irving spoke passionately, swearing that this time would be different because he too was feeling like a pariah once he returned home, no longer attending West Point. But there was nowhere to go, nowhere he felt comfortable enough to express his fears or concerns—just like that, the people were hooked, convinced that he meant well.

Irving stacked his credentials all throughout district one. By the evening they were both exhausted, Christopher checking in, calling Zoey to get the status of their efforts, Zoey was happy to report they were on to a good start—by the days end together they had earned 864 signatures. Feeling optimistic Zoey calculated that by the end of six weeks they would far exceed the numbers necessary for him to enter the running.

"If we continue at this rate, Irving, you can enter the running twice," Zoey said. But Irving felt beat, asking, "Is there no other way?" Zoey nodding her head yes.

"There is, of course, we will do community outreaches, get back to New York and set up church events, have the members in the congregations contact their families and so much more. This was just scratching the surface, we have a long way to go and with numbers like this, this only means you have the talent it takes to get there. Christopher is going to love this!" she smiled—her eyes obsessive.

"Okay great, I need to get to the airport and we have to make a stop before that," Irving told her. Zoey quickly obliged.

Irving stood in the airport alongside Zoey who was busy crunching numbers and paying him no mind as he waited at baggage claim for Shawn to arrive. He was feeling nervous about removing his wedding band. As the passengers from flight 2578 coming in from LaGuardia Airport all made their way into the baggage claim area, he noticed Shawn walking down wearing a pair of men's Princeton horse bit-detailed floral print Gucci sandals, a Gucci printed twill shirt and a pair of navy Caspian cropped logo-jacquard cotton pants and fashionable sunglasses. Irving was shocked to see how well Shawn managed to put himself together. Standing face-to-face now, Irving wanted so badly to kiss him but refrained from doing so, considering that they were in a public setting.

"Which is your bag?" Irving asked him.

"I don't have luggage; I won't be staying the night. I'm catching a red-eye back to New York. But wanted to see what exactly it was that you needed," Shawn said bluffing—his intentions were to have Irving eat his heart out for his disloyalty. Irving amused; his smile perfect.

"Wow, and you didn't want to just call and ask?"

"Nope, and have you miss seeing my sexy ass in person, and I've been doing my squats," Shawn teased, his heavy upper lip puckered as he began making his way through the sliding doors. Zoey stepped lightly behind them. He stood lowering his glasses to stare her up and down, "Eh," he muttered, deciding she was not pretty enough to compete with him.

Standing outside Irving handed Shawn the bouquet of flowers as they all climbed in the back of the stretch limo. Shawn desperately wishing he had hair to flip, but rather had to settle for his dark Caesar.

"You have four hours of my time and then I have to be back for a 3 a.m. flight," Shawn articulated while clenching his roses. Irving reclining in the limo to admire him, the Balenciaga tote bag he carried looking new.

"So, how are you affording all of this?" Irving asked as the driver took off, chuckling to himself overhearing the theatrics.

"Well, I was angry and I went through your clothes looking for her number and found your AmEx," Shawn admitted staring down at the bouquet—his lips pursed.

"You're beautiful." A lustful Irving laser focused on him. Shawn felt flattered; his plan was working. Thirty-five minutes later of champagne, music and catching up the limo they arrived at North Potomac, Maryland where Shawn was born and raised. It was late at night but Irving could see Shawn's face lighting up as they made their way down the block of his old neighborhood stopping in front of his home. Shawn turned to face him.

"What is this?"

But Irving did not respond, instead, he asked Zoey to move over slightly as he exited, stepping outside grabbing Shawn by the hand. The house stood alone in the affluent neighborhood, all the lights inside illuminated, as one girl yelled, "he's here," Shawn could not believe his ears, as his eyes began to well. He and Irving making their way up to the lawn as though they had been making their entrance into the inauguration ball—a moment Shawn dreamed of at night. The front door unlocked, Shawn's dad greeting them, Irving stepped inside exchanging hugs with the family, the house filled, Shawn's mother, sisters, father, nieces, and nephews were all present, the home nicely decorated, the smell of food cooking arousing his nostrils.

Everyone speaking indistinctly as they all smiled making light conversation. This moment meant everything to Shawn, when he decided to leave Washington, D.C. he and his family stopped speaking, his father appalled that after all they had sacrificed for Shawn, he would relocate, leaving his family and life behind they could not agree with this abrupt decision. But Shawn missed his family, so much it was painful for him to know there was a divide amongst them, Irving realizing he was the cause for this, decided his grand gesture would be to reunite them.

As the family conversed and prepared for dinner, Shawn could no longer stay mad at Irving, kissing him tenderly, once they were alone.

"You are the best," said Shawn as he made his way into the kitchen lifting his niece. Irving thought long and hard about breaking the news to Shawn, but before he did, he moseyed into the kitchen where everyone gathered, split between the kitchen and the living room, the couches all filled with his cousins and their spouses, the children jumping up and down watching television. Irving tossing back a shot of tequila as he fell to one knee, Shawn still turned the opposite direction, his family and friends standing, smiling, a few of his cousins crying tears of joy as he turned to find Irving on one knee. Shawn gripping his niece, could not believe his eyes, placing her down gently.

"Turn that television down," one woman beckoned.

Irving kneeled, in his hand a black box containing a Men's I CT. T.W. Diamond Solitaire Step Wedding Band in I0K Two-Tone Gold. Shawn could not believe his eyes, sobbing as Irving spoke.

"This ring is my commitment to you, I have spoken with your family and I have laid all of my mistakes on the table, I will have to come clean with you too, but I needed them to accept me first. I needed them to understand my faults and to know that despite everything my heart beats only for you. I love you, Shawn McDonald, more than the words I can say, you are my rock, and my best friend—I would die if I ever lose you and so, I ask, will you accept my commitment to you?" Shawn said yes, unhappy that it was not a proposal, but still grateful for the effort Irving made, due to his hubris that could not have been easy.

Shawn later learned that night that Irving was conversing with his parent's way before his arrival, and his parents now apologetic for the time they allowed to pass without speaking to their son. Their union blissful as the music from the speakers now blared and the living room filled with friends and family laughing and dancing in celebration.

As the clock stroke midnight, Shawn was preparing to take his leave, packing away his to go plate as his friends and family all bid him safe travels. He could not help but admire the new accessory he wore, the one that complimented his skin and his manicured fingernails. As Irving and Shawn walked down the long driveway, Shawn was not happy, he was appreciative of all the work that Irving had done but he was not satisfied, questions still lingered in his mind.

"What are you not telling me?" he asked abruptly as they took a seat in the back of the limo. Zoey was gone; the driver had taken her home whilst they were inside.

"To the Graham Georgetown Hotel," Irving said, tapping the glass gently as he has seen done before many times today. The drive awkward, Irving refusing to tell Shawn anything as he sat quietly with his eyes closed preparing himself for the worse—having to spend the night with his new wife once Shawn kicks him out of the hotel room. Shawn squinting his eyes, noticed something about Irving was off, but sadly he could not enjoy this moment because there was something he did not know, which was beginning to eat away at him.

"If I guess the mistake you made, will you tell me? Shawn asked playfully, but he was not playing, he was not joyful, his heart was beating a mile a minute and his hands trembling. Nothing could prepare him for what was going to come next. "Irving you're scaring me," he said, telling the truth. Irving was eerily calm and although he appeared so on the outside, inside he was worried. As the car halted in front of the Graham Hotel, the concierge opened the door taking Shawn by the hand escorting him inside, Shawn held on tightly, in his hand, both his leftovers and his tote. Irving stepping outside, tipping the concierge graciously.

Inside Irving and Shawn made their way up to the eleventh floor, a suite he reserved. Walking inside there were rose petals along the ground, soft jazz music playing in the background, the lights were dimmed low and although Shawn wanted to appreciate his efforts, he could not, Irving was withholding information—in other words, lying.

"When you withhold information or omit information, you are lying to me. You are showing me, that you cannot be trusted Irving. I want to appreciate this so badly, but I can't until I know what I'm up against," Shawn pleaded as he placed his food on the island just by the bar. Irving taking a few steps backward, where he stood blocking the exit. Taking a deep breath removing his shoes and socks to get a firm grip on the floor—to leave, Shawn would have to get through him first. He was ready.

"Shani and I are having another baby and we went to the justice of peace this morning to get married," he whispered. Standing now, his chest rising and lowering, its movement palpable, Irving felt his chest tightening, his arms flexing and his eyes fighting back tears as he spoke quickly, removing his wedding band from his pocket tossing it onto the throw rug beneath Shawn's feet, "It means nothing to me," he continued. "As a child, I had one goal, become a leader and, now that goal is at my fingertips, I never intended to fall in love," Irving said, as the words left his lips the tears fell from Shawn's eyes, he was in shock as he took a seat on the arm of the sofa—feeling empty, lost even.

"I cannot lose you, especially now. I love my children and I pray one day you will too, but I try to see it as we can't have them ourselves—"

"Don't you dare!" Shawn screamed. "Don't you dare make excuses for this!" he cried. The room grew silent, there was no movement, no dialogue, nothing but two vessels who were feeling empty hours later. Shawn sliding into the sofa after crying himself to sleep and Irving sliding his back down the front door, having made up his mind that he would sleep on the floor if it meant ensuring that Shawn did not leave—and so, he did. His eyes heavy as he fought to stay awake, at least until 2 a.m. knowing Shawn had a flight to catch, but Shawn remained sleeping, and Irving knew better than to wake him, he too falling into a deep slumber.

The next morning breakfast arrived; Shawn had awoken, showered and spent the morning in the wide basin trying out every type of water pressure from the nozzle head. Finding himself on the verge of masturbation before stepping out and pouring himself a glass of champagne; Shawn slept until 9 a.m. and was driven to drink, by a man he loved more than anything else in the world. Because of this Shawn was not through getting his revenge, pouring the remainder of his alcohol atop a sleeping Irving, who awoke gasping for air curled into the fetal position by the front door. The towel wrapped around Shawn's torso greeting him as his eyes fluttered open. Struggling to stand Irving slipped, groaning as he finally managed to crawl onto his two feet.

"How long are you going to punish me?" he asked making

his way to the bar where Shawn was re-heating his leftovers.

"Oh, that, I'm not sure of, how long do you plan on staying married?" Shawn asked sarcastically.

"Oh God," Irving groaned.

"Do you know how many men would kill to be with someone like me? Huh, do you? I am fabulous, I am toned, I have skills, I am intelligent—I mean fuck, I went to West Point. I cook, I clean, I suck a mean cock and—and I have an amazing personality. But, some of that you wouldn't know, right, because you're so busy keeping me locked away like some circus freak. What's my favorite color Irving?" Shawn asked banging his hand on the kitchen counter, his right hand pressed firmly atop his right hip as the microwave beeped.

"Turquoise," Irving responded, struggling to lift his head as he listened to Shawn's bickering.

"Favorite movie?"

"Anything with Molly Ringwald, but you especially loved her in Sixteen Candles," Irving responded. Shawn's eyes widening.

"Favorite thing to do?"

"Journaling and jazz," Irving said quickly, he liked this game. "I know you quite well and your favorite food before you ask is Cajun shrimp with dirty rice," Irving laughed hysterically, his face and arms feeling sticky as Shawn removed his food from the microwave, angry that Irving was correct—he did know him, but he would not admit it, watching Irving boast was making him sick. Shawn moseyed back to into the bedroom shutting the door behind him, Irving shouted, "I know everything because I love you!"

"Go to hell!" Shawn yelled.

After several messages between them, Zoey arrived downstairs, Shawn and Irving making their way to the stretch limo. Irving asked Shawn to come along for his campaigning, although he did not know what they would be working on today, as long as Shawn was by his side this would minimize any speculation of wrongdoing on his part. Shawn obliged.

This was a step up for Irving, he was treating Shawn like royalty—by the time breakfast arrived Shawn had already eaten his leftovers but was adamant about saving food until later. This was not his most attractive trait, but Shawn simply hated the idea of wasting food, often times explaining to Irving that once elected they would take trips to feed starving children. This, he was passionate about.

Inside, Zoey read from a long list of to do's she had written on her phone.

"First, we have a photoshoot over in Georgetown. Next, we will head to a ministry event where Christopher arranged for you to give a speech on the importance of business investments—"

"...and shopping, may I please get some clothes?" Shawn interrupted—Zoey exchanged a look with Irving who simply nodded his head yes.

"Sure," she sighed.

"We'll both need suits, actually," Irving added.

"You do not, the stylist is at the photoshoot with fittings, all you need is to get there," Zoey said to Irving, her tone blunt.

Shawn scurried into the Men's Warehouse not too far from Georgetown where he and Irving shopped for a three-piece suite. Locating one, Irving swiped his card and off they went. The empty gallery was immaculate and the setup fit for a king. William and Christopher were present, William was a short man with blonde hair, an eccentric mustache, and a dapper style—he was very well dressed. As Irving entered inside he took a look around noticing the three racks of clothing that were lined up for him, a table filled with shoes, accessories and to the corner, hair, and makeup. Shawn felt out of place, Irving decided to make it known to his team of professionals that he was, in fact, a homosexual man and Shawn is his partner, Christopher quickly advising that everyone on set sign a non-disclosure agreement to which Irving disagreed. Making his way to the center of the room.

"I am not ashamed of who I am and the road in which I plan

to travel, I just know that who I am may be too much for the general public to handle. I want to make sure that the men and women in this room are here for the long haul. I do not want a revolving door, and not to change stylist every other week. Let's be a committed team; we are not stopping at Mayor we are going straight to The White House. With that said, let's get started," everyone nodding in compliance as Christopher motioned for Zoey to make her way over to him.

"I want the attorney to draft NDA's for every man, woman and child who comes anywhere near Irving to work, understand. Oh and get one for the partner," he whispered, referring to Shawn. Zoey quickly agreed.

"Yes, sir."

Five outfits, two hours' worth of fittings and a plethora of images later, Irving was taking his leave, Shawn by his side, as they made their way over to the church by 2 p.m. The congregation filled with men and women from all over the country; Irving had never spoken to a group that large—the most 300. People were shouting as his campaign photos hung everywhere, excited to be seeing a politician, most for the first time. The megachurch goers and visitors swarming inside for the start of their week-long business convention, and Irving was to be the first act on the list. Nervous, as he looked out to see the 10,000 people sitting in the audience. Irving wished he had more time to prepare himself, his speech, but Christopher would hear of no such thing.

"I've trained you damn near your whole life for this; this is what you were meant to do! What are ten ways to ruin a presentation?" Christopher asked, his question rhetorical as they stood just off stage. Shawn was trembling, he could not believe that Irving was going to speak to such a large crowd, but was impressed by how fearless he appeared to be. Turning to him as the host sang his praises during an introduction, Shawn and Irving exchanged a passionate kiss, everyone around them looking on and wearing pins. Irving then stepped on stage where he delivered the most persuasive speech of his early career. In the interim Zoey was taking calls, scheduling appointments and booking Irving for additional conferences simultaneously monitoring press releases via email.

William and Christopher strategized while listening to Irving, formulating new ideas for him to acquire additional signatures predicting only less than half would be obtained today. But they were wrong, Irving was charismatic, amicable and as he spoke of his past members began to sympathize, viewing him now as a rags to riches story—their interactions incredible and it did not hurt that Irving too was having the time of his life. On stage the—me to you delivery felt effortless. The crowd cheered, standing to their feet once Irving concluded forty-five minutes later. Whatever qualms he had about speaking engagements immediately went away as Irving now felt like he could conquer the world.

"Your future Mayor, Mr. Houston everybody!" the host said making his way back onto the stage, grabbing a hold of Irving's hand as he bowed before exiting stage right—that day his speech landing him 8,798 petition signatures. Backstage Shawn raced to Irving, standing beside before hugging him tightly; Irving felt an influx of emotions: happiness, gratitude, bravery and high-spirits—but this was only the beginning.

2

As Irving campaigned and gained more signatures he also found himself with a large number of volunteers, working from home conducting interviews, production teams taking over both upstairs and downstairs of his house once he completed his final step—completing all additional paperwork and filing them, having all his docs submitted 90 days before the deadline guaranteed him a place in the general primaries to advance to the general election.

The more he worked, the more comfortable he became speaking to large crowds and delivering his messages across the state. Donations were coming in as Zoey continued her door to door campaigning, with other volunteers; this was moving rather quickly, faster than anyone could have anticipated. A pregnant Shani having to sit through hours of fittings, photo shoots and interviews about her marriage, much of which she found herself lying because Irving was barely home, so calling him a hands-on father and loving husband was not the easiest thing to do. She felt overwhelmed—their marriage feeling strained.

Four months later Irving made it to the general elections, speaking candidly during his debate, much of which aided him—the crowd receiving him well. He spoke to having the essential skills necessary for turning civic vision into civic reality as resting on vision alone is not nearly enough. The grandiose visioneering worked to get him noticed, but Irving was careful when he spoke of such visions, speaking to his strengths in management—his time spent at West Point, the multiple successful properties and businesses he owned, all of which playing into his favor. As time pressed on Irving began to realize the Mayor's job is big and sprawling, a lot harder than he initially imagined, before the votes were finalized Irving found himself receiving twenty to thirty thousand emails daily, and he was not yet elected.

Iyana Houston stared into her father's eyes as he sat in the living room feeding her a bottle. Irving could not take his eyes off of her. After winning the elections, Irving was now the Mayor of the District of Columbia earning him over two-hundred thousand dollars annually. Now that Irving was the highest official within the executive branch of Washington, D.C. he was responsible for proposing budgets, signing legislation and overseeing city operations, the feeling was bittersweet as he was now forced to spend more time with his wife and children: Kwame now three years old and Iyana, three months. Irving pondered what he would do for his birthday, wanting badly to spend time with his family and Shawn in New York, but struggled to find the time.

As the media continued to dissect his personal life, Irving was told to remain as far away from Shawn as possible and so, he and Shani were photographed on dates, outings at the park, visiting museums and attending press conferences where Walter was now lobbying for Press Secretary. Christopher was a genius having placed each of his elite group members in valuable positions where they would all have a significant role to play in Irving's climb to the Oval Office.

Shani was beginning to show signs of postpartum depression as Irving spent less and less time at home and she was always alone with the children, the help she received from their live-in nanny was not enough, she found herself spending more time wondering about her husband's whereabouts rather than focusing on the children. That morning while Irving was feeding Iyana her milk, Shani made her way downstairs.

"I want to see a counselor," she said softly.

Irving stood, pacing back and forth bouncing Iyana slightly, her hair wrapped in a tiny turban and a matching onesie.

"Counselor?" he asked, Irving was looking far more mature and attractive as his facial hair began to come in, connecting to his goatee. Shani hated him for not loving her the way she loved him, using her almost. Every other day it was photo ops, meetings, conferences and them having to pretend to be happy for the public, it was devastating.

"Yes, we live this fake life like we're happy and we aren't. You and I don't even sleep in the same bed, you've been in the guest room for months now and every night you're on the phone with Shawn!"

"What do you want from me? You're the Mayors' wife, you can go out, you-you can start a non-profit organization, you have help. I feel like you're spending so much time thinking about our relationship because the truth is you're bored," he said laughing—but Shani did not find anything amusing.

"Bored? Did—did you just tell me I'm bored like I'm some child? I'm not bored! I've become a puppet, a doll!" She screamed. "How dare you speak to me so condescendingly?" Shani continued, crying.

"Lower your voice," Irving said as he placed Iyana over his shoulder to burp her. Kwame approaching them. "Look, why don't I have Cheryl take the kids out for the day, this way you can go to the spa, go shopping, go do whatever it is that women do, to just relax. My birthday is this weekend and I'm going to head to New York, work on some projects—"

"Fuck your boyfriend," she shouted, standing with her arms

crossed, Kwame staring up to her, the look on his face innocent. "You always seem to so conveniently leave that part out," lifting Kwame and tossing him on her hip.

"Well, yes, spend time with my boyfriend. Listen, while I'm gone just play nice and please don't get wrapped up in any scandals. It's only been four months, after about six, the press won't care about us this much and we won't be under so much scrutiny," he sighed. Irving knew he was not supposed to be around Shawn, but he missed him terribly and the late-night phone sex was no longer cutting it. It had been six months since they'd last seen one another and Irving was adamant about not sleeping with Shani.

Irving had an epiphany, realizing he could not anger Shani and so he said, "Look, I apologize alright. We have a long way to go, I mean eight years for Mayor and then four years in The White House. I know right now things feel almost impossible, but if we both just focus on our individual lives, come together for the children and the GP, then I promise you, Shani, this will begin to feel like a walk in the park," he pleaded, placing Iyana in one of her bassinets located in the center of the living room, tickling her.

"I don't want to be with another man, I just want us to be a normal happy family," her voice just above a whimper. Irving was unsure of what to do, as he stood watching her, his mind elsewhere.

"I mean, Shani, we talked about this."

"That was in college," she sniffled, "How could you not have expected my feelings to change, we have two beautiful children and a life we've created here for them, you want me to apologize for falling in love with you? I will not do that," she continued. Just then Irving's phone rang; it was Rose looking to confirm his attendance to her engagement party the next morning—relieved by her timing he stood answering it,

"Irving honey, I was just calling to remind you please don't forget the champagne you promised." Irving taking a deep breath before replying, he completely forgot that his mother was having a party to celebrate her engagement.

"Yes mom, I will be there and I will have the champagne," he said disappointedly.

Shani now finding the strength to play with her children as Irving wrapped up his call, turning to face her.

"We have to go to my mother's engagement party." Irving was crushed as he imagined a peaceful weekend with Shawn, but all family functions required their presence—a rule heavily enforced by his public relations team.

"No, I am done playing this game!" Shani refusing to make eye contact.

"Shani, this is not a damn game, this is our livelihood, this is how we will feed and take care of our children. If you don't want to be a part of this, then there is no possible way you can love them. All of this is for them," Irving said hoping to change her mind.

"No, you're already a millionaire; you don't need this, what's a measly two-hundred grand a year to you? Your housing sector makes quadrupole that! You just want the fame; to be loved by strangers, meanwhile, the people who love you the most all you do is hurt them!" she screamed. "I will not be your freaking trophy anymore!" she continued before grabbing Iyana and making her way up the stairs, calling to Kwame to join her. Turning to face Irving,

"Bring your whore with you to Long Island." But Irving could not bring Shawn, both for political reasons and his family had not yet met him or knew of his existence.

While Irving was pondering his next course of action he made his way down to the office where all new faces were there to greet him. The campaign volunteers all removed once Christopher decided it was best to hire professionals, nothing but the best—those with campaign management experience, quantitative and technical skills all filled the room; new faces meant new changes and effectively introducing them. Irving was happy he did not have to be the one to tell campaigners their time had come to an end, both Zoey and William were proactive in taking those steps and finding their replacements. Irving was still getting acclimated, his office located in the John A. Wilson Building in downtown Washington, D.C.

Every morning Irving would run his hands across the large mahogany desk, taking it all in, his new photos plastered against the walls as he stood between the nation's flag and the Canadian flag.

Irving needed to organize the Mayors' office from scratch, advising his staff that everyone will have to put in long hours, hitting the ground running in an attempt to put into effect the policies and changes promised to his supporters. Meanwhile, none of the daily demands of the job slowed down, he was thrown into a position that was never truly vacant—it was time to continue building his team and ramp up fast in order to catch up, some of which he elected to do remotely.

As the office filled and everyone prepared to begin their day, the sound of a door slamming shut just outside could be heard on the top floor. Irving removing his suit jacket took a look outside to see Christopher and Jasper making their way up from the black stretch limo. As Christopher stepped upstairs with assistance from his son and the cane he carried—his body beginning to turn on him. Everyone stopped working, standing promptly to greet him, the receptionist walking to the rear where Irving's office was located letting him know of Christopher's arrival.

Irving nodded.

"Well, well, well, look at the champion," Christopher boasted, taking a seat in the leather chair adjacent to the mahogany desk. This was the first time he had been by to visit the office since the election went underway, he was proud, to say the least.

Irving stepped to the front of his desk where he leaned on the desktop just slightly.

"This is it, wouldn't have made it without you," he said. Jasper stood by the exit, his arms folded—it was evident he envied Irving despite his many efforts to conceal it from his father.

"Mr. Royal, I have an issue."

"Ah, what seems to be the problem?" Christopher said, his hands pressed firmly atop his cane now upright between his legs.

"Shani, she's having some problems adjusting and wants to see a counselor." Christopher sucking his teeth.

"I don't blame her, I blame you. What have you been doing?" Christopher snapped. Irving was confused.

"Huh? Me?"

"Yes, you, for goodness sake she is your wife. You have to treat her like it. I mean yes, given the circumstances, it may not be idealistic for you, but for the people, for her, you have to make an effort. Have you been staying away from that boy?"

"That boy is the love of my life and yes, I have, but it's killing me and I'm sure he's quite angry too. I mean, I respect Shani, and I know that there have been times when I've slipped up—we have two children. But I don't want to lose Shawn."

"We've talked about love; love does not exist in politics. This is business, we are here for a goal and a purpose and before I take my last breath, Irving, you will stand in that Oval Office with Shani by your side, do you hear me?" Christopher said, Irving drawing a deep breath before complying as he stood, looking through the window, his hand in his pocket.

"What about Shawn?"

"Forget about him, loving him will only prove itself a distraction and will ruin you, if you allow it," Christopher replied.

"I have to fly to New York later this afternoon for an engagement for my mother, I have to at least end things in person."

"...and the media? Will Shani be accompanying you?"

"She won't come because of Shawn, but I need to figure out the best way to combat this. It seems that ending things with Shawn is to make everyone else happy except for me, it's not fair."

"Life isn't fair my dear boy, but, fly to New York, stay for a month or so, we'll tell people you're there running your businesses, which is a fine excuse, get as much playtime as you possibly need, end things and return home to your true life," Christopher demanded as he arose. "There's a White House photo opt next month, you meet President Obama, you two start building a bond of some kind so he can endorse you during your run. You have to take care of yourself Irving, your home, your family and your health. This is no easy task, but we will overcome," he concluded.

In the meantime, on page 9 of *People's* magazine, there they were, *America's New Modern Family*, the headlines read. Mayor Irving Houston and his beautiful wife, two children and their new life in the District—turning the pages, Shawn sat reading, having a cup of orange juice as he and Irving had just ended their call that morning. He retained all the media releases, newspaper articles, and magazines, brooding over all that he had seen and despising Irving for not seeing him for months and avoiding him at all costs. A late night phone call with some pornographic material and masturbation was all he had been reduced to. Irving's political rise to the top was all happening so fast, every news station, every radio broadcast, every magazine he was front and center and there she was, smiling from ear to ear, happy.

Shawn did not speak on their relationship, he feared sounding insecure and ultimately losing Irving if ever he were to sound childish or lose his confidence. So, he kept to himself. The past six months was proving itself to be hectic and although Shawn had a new hobby volunteering down at the Boys and Girls Club of Harlem and was slowly coming into his own, he still felt a part of him was missing. All of the media coverage Irving was receiving was unbelievable, labeling him 'The Golden Mayor' due to his rags to riches story which became instant phenomena. Men and women from all over the county were watching his videos on social media platforms, his family photos going viral and now—he was everywhere and yet nowhere simultaneously.

Later that day Shawn received a text message from Irving

stating that he was coming to town but would be heading to Long Island for an engagement. Which only meant one thing, Irving was going to be in town, but unable to see Shawn. Disappointed again, Shawn decided it best not to respond and so, he was done waiting around. Getting dressed to head out for lunch, Shawn dialed up a few of the friends he made while volunteering at the Boys and Girls Club to join him for mimosas, three out of five agreed—two hours later they were all meeting up at The Silver Fish block over on Frederick Douglass Boulevard. A strip of restaurants and bars filled with Gay establishments that were open for brunch.

Shawn was happy to have friends he could share his life experiences with, growing up a gay man was not the easiest, but with laws now in place to bridge the gap between homosexuals and heterosexuals, it was slowly beginning to feel less complicated to have open discussions and display public acts of affection. Yet, Irving was hiding him, as he sat at the table inside with his friends explaining to them the nature of his relationship, their feedback was hard to digest. Shawn being told all sort of things.

"This man you speak of honey cannot possibly love you, I mean why pretend he does—just to have his cake and eat it too," Darren said. A school teacher and part-time volunteer, he was 5'6, adventurous, born in South Africa relocating to the big city at the age of thirteen. "I can't have a man trying to hide me, what for?" he continued. But they were not all as flamboyant as Darren. Except for Alex who was the prima-donna—over the top, narcissistic and showy. In just twenty-two minutes he was already on his third glass of mimosa, never politely waiting for the waitress to return but calling to her while placing his glass in the air, indicating he needed a refill. Alex was Caucasian, a personal trainer who loved his job, always gloating about his wonderful views and never missing a chance to show off his biceps.

"Bye! This man is obviously just not that into you. You sound like a woman who sees the signs, ignores them and then cries to her girlfriends. We don't want to hear it, Shawn. You're new to the Big Apple but, the men here are recycled—no one is certified fresh. Every one of their excuses, the same. Lies, the same. It's like they have one big douche bag book they all read from—"

"Stop being such an asshole," Darren said interrupting him. "We're here to support you, Shawn," he continued. But Shawn simply listened—saddened as his thoughts consumed him.

"You look like shit," Connor said; the circuit queen, Connor did not have a full-time job but enjoyed volunteering because it gave him purpose. He was taken care of by a "daddy"—an older man who was well off financially, so all Connor had to do was stay hot. He attended parades, festivals and even considered himself a gipster at one point in his life. He was well tanned, waxed and has a body filled with tribal tattoos; a party animal he is, slowly growing bored that this outing was not filling with men gyrating on one another. Shawn took a deep breath before breaking his silence.

"I get where all of you are coming from, but he is married with two children, so I can't expect to have him all the time. I have to be understanding, right?" he asked despite already knowing the answer. Everyone gasping in unison.

"Um, no, he's dead weight cut em loose," exclaimed Alex as he held his glass in the air again, waiting on a refill.

"Shawn, you have the body of ten Gods, you're always fashionable and you can make it in life. Don't let this one guy bring you down," Darren added.

"You're right," Shawn said.

By 10 p.m. the lights got low and the bar was filled with men and women from all walks of life. Eight hours later and the men were all inebriated—they had so much to drink the night was slowly becoming a blur. Shawn danced and danced, the sweat drenching his clothes as he made his way over to Darren pushing his way through the crowd, kissing him. Darren reciprocated as he found himself attracted to Shawn but dared not tell him considering how vulnerable he was now. The two danced, lip-synched, kissed and had the time of their lives.

At 1 p.m. Darren and Shawn were making their way outside, Shawn inviting Darren back to his house calling for a taxi. When one quickly arrived, Darren and Shawn kissed profusely in the back seat resisting the urge to strip one another of their clothing. Shawn was erect, praying they would arrive home soon. The soft kisses Darren planted on his neck put him in an ebullient mood; missing this feeling, he felt alive. Once the taxi parked in front of the brownstone Shawn and Darren staggered their way inside after Darren tossed the driver forty dollars. Shawn struggling to open the doors, as they continued kissing, knocking down the brooms in the hallway, giggling now, the liquor seeping through their veins, they stepped into the dark apartment, Irving watching them, calmly he sat in the living room just under the windows.

Now, clearing his throat, switching on the lights; Shawn was startled, fixing his clothes, buttoning his shirt and zipping his pants, Darren following suit as they both stared fearfully into Irving's eyes. Shawn facing Darren, who asked, "Holy shit aren't you that politician?" he shouted ecstatically—never having seen a celebrity before, upsetting Shawn.

"Leave!" he screamed to him shoving Darren through the doors. Irving stood, silently, his hands in the pockets of his Dolce and Gabbana pantsuit. The trench coat covering him, his hands not inside—his look stylish.

"I'm not apologizing," spoke Shawn with assertion. "You have some damn nerve showing up here like this, and I was told you were going to that engagement party thing, oh and course, with your wife and two kids I assume," Shawn continued.

"Shut the fuck up!" screamed Irving. Shawn's eyes widened. "You don't get to humiliate me like that!" he continued.

"Humiliate? Meanwhile, I'm locked away like some caged animal. How are on earth can I humiliate you, no one even knows of my existence?" Shawn bellowed.

"Jesus, you and Shani are going to send me to an early fucking grave. I can't please you both, I just can't. Shawn, this is how it is, this is my life now. I have enough cons stacked against me, adding that I am a gay man to the republic will only do more harm than good. It's about painting a picture, selling a story!" Irving screamed as he threw off his top coat, stepping heavily into the bedroom where he located boxes and magazines of his photoshoots with Shani, "Why are you keeping these? Huh? To hate me, because of what I have to do, because of what I'm forced to do! My job!" he screamed tossing the photos and magazines to the floor.

"Well, your job is tearing us apart," cried Shawn, the tears now flowing freely down his cheeks. Irving Paced.

"They don't want us together; they don't want me to be happy. What I've realized today is that if I don't do it for myself then I will only regret it later. I'm supposed to end things with you," Irving admitted. Shawn gasped.

"What?"

"But I deserve to be happy, I do all of this, I work hard every single day and I want to be happy. You make me happy. The important people know, the people who matter Shawn, they know about you and about us. All I know is, you make me content, when I think of your smile, when I think of the little kisses you give me even when you're mad at me, you love me through it. If I can't have you while doing this, then I won't do it," Irving said. "It's selfish of me to ask you to live like this, no family, no social life and then just beg you to take my word for it despite seeing me on television or in magazines kissing a woman my heart doesn't beat for, I know it's hard. But tell me please what do I need to do, what do you want me to do?" He was feeling defeated as Shawn made his way to him, hugging him.

Shawn stepped backward, straightening Irving's shirt collar, standing on his toes to kiss his forehead.

"I want you to one day be the best damn President this nation has ever seen. I want that for you. I want you to be pleased and I'll be here to make you happy," Shawn struggling to speak through his tears. Exhausted, fighting to stay up with Irving after they both showered together and made love passionately until 5 a.m. when the sun began to rise.

His hangover got the best of him the next morning, Shawn slept in while Irving made his way into the kitchen cooking them a superb breakfast by 10 a.m. no longer able to complete his morning run fearing to be seen by the media. The engagement party set to begin at 1 p.m. giving him just enough time to spend the morning with Shawn and await the crate of champagne he scheduled to have delivered to the brownstone from the UK. In his pajama pants, Irving kneeled on the floor by Shawn's bedside watching him sleep. Shawn was perfect in his eyes. Irving thought of how different his life would have been if he and Shawn were given the chance to be open about their affairs. Now that he was regarded so highly such a scandal would for sure ruin him.

Women from all of the state were writing into Shani, speaking on how beautiful she was, how lucky and praised her for having met such a wonderful man. If Shani were to ever tell the truth of their marriage or even disclose the fact that Irving was having an affair, she would skyrocket to fame, leaving Irving in the dust to scoop up whatever would be left of his career. Irving knew how quickly things could turn and although he loved Shawn, was not ready to make such a sacrifice despite having said so the night before.

Irving showered as Shawn slept once he realized the crate arrived, he dialed Brandon who within twenty-five minutes awaited him outside.

Paparazzi swarmed his mother's home—careful not to step on the lawn or make their way onto the driveway where Irving and Brandon pulled up, two cars across the street awaiting them his security detail stepped outside. Johnson was always on top of things, receiving news from Walter on Irving's whereabouts and placing men where they were needed. Irving did not know how the mechanics worked; he simply went about his day. As the guests were arriving, they all stared, wondering who he was and why he was accompanied by security, some taking photos, and others simply passing by locking eyes with Irving and whispering amongst one another.

The cul-de-sac where Rose now lived was absolutely beautiful, they had a pool in the backyard and a tennis court within walking distance and inside was the home theater she had constructed. Keith and Rose finally decided to tie the knot, although long overdue she was in no rush to get married again Rose wanted to be sure that Keith was not in it for the small fortune she was earning by working for her son, she now managed all of his estates, books, and operations. She was by no means going to put that in jeopardy for a man.

Rose, now fifty, and Keith turning fifty-two in a few weeks was still as beautiful and handsome as the first time they met. Ivy, now fifteen, raced over to her big brother giving him the tightest hug she could muster. The backyard filled with people as security entered behind Irving who had become the center of attention, people asking him for photos, autographs and others making small-talk—all of which he obliged. Ivy was slender, gorgeous with long flowing red hair like that of her mother— her features reminding Irving of Molly Ringwald, ultimately reminding him of Shawn.

The day was beautiful, the weather gracious as by now there should have been snow, but the warm weather continued. Rose and Keith were lucky considering the weather would alternate frequently between freezing cold and spring-like temperatures. Brandon removed the champagne from the boxes as Rose made her way over to Irving.

"Oh my goodness!" she said happily. "You're so tall. Where are Shani and the kids?" she asked, her tone disappointed.

"They honestly couldn't make it mom, I'm really sorry, I know you were looking forward to seeing Iyana."

"Well, I want to see them both!" Rose advised him watching as Ivy made her way to them.

"So, you're like famous and I have to take lots of pictures with you so everyone at school can stop calling me a liar." Ivy wore braces and had her hair in a messy bun wearing a pair of baggy pants—her style simply the girl next door, a pair of converses with a quarter sleeve top.

"Of course," Irving said as she took out her phone, turning the camera.

"Totally a selfie." The music blaring playing rock/pop from the early '90s. Rose interrupting them as she made her way past the guests who were helping themselves to finger foods and conversing among one another, Keith standing on the opposite side of the house with his friends and some neighborhood bandmates.

"Irving, I need you inside for a second," Rose, grabbing a hold of his hand. Irving hovered over his mother, she appeared to be shrinking. Stepping inside the house Irving waited patiently for Rose to let him know what was going on, helping himself to an apple, security following behind him standing by the patio doors. Two women making their way downstairs, turning into the kitchen, Rose following behind them. One of them heavyset and the other tall and slim. A perturbed Irving asked, "Mom, what's going on?"

"Irving," Rose stepping in front of the women, "These are your sisters, Asha and Amara."

3

Irving felt uncomfortable, he did not know what to say—and so, he said nothing.

"Irving, please don't be rude, they're family and they are not their parents, just like you are not yours," Rose sympathized. Asha stepping to him, elated.

"I know this is very awkward, um, we've spent years trying to find you but it was so hard until you were everywhere. Magazines, television interviews and we have the same last name we heard of your story and your adopted mother and hired a professional to find you Irving—"

"It's true and we'll take any lie detector test to prove it, we don't want you to feel we're lying to you," Amara interrupting her sister. "Also, please we don't want you to feel this is about money, Asha is a lawyer and I have my own textile company, we both live right here in Long Island, just about seven blocks over, which is why when we heard that Rose lived here, we almost died, it was such—such..." Amara began to cry, unable to finish her sentence.

"It was great news," Asha said completing her sentence, she too weeping now. Rose caressing their back, consoling them.

"It's alright, no need to cry."

"No—no, you don't understand, we're just—just so grateful to you Ms. Rose, you've been so kind," Asha expressed. Irving looking on, Rose praying he would say something, anything. Deep down Irving simply wished his sisters had not resurfaced. They would only serve as a constant reminder of the gritty past he worked so hard to move on from. He thought about politely asking them to leave, but decided against it knowing this would upset his mother. Irving was not just standing silently. He was thinking.

"Maybe, this isn't such a good time. Irving, I know you probably need time to digest this, which is fine, we can just go," Asha leaned in to hug Rose, who would hear of no such thing.

"Absolutely not. You are family and so, you will enjoy all the festivities our family has to offer. You do not have to go, maybe we can just head outside and leave Irving to his thoughts." Rose grabbing them by the hand, escorting them outside. Irving wished his mother was not a recovering alcoholic, there was absolutely no liquor in their home and he desperately needed a drink.

Hours later as the sun began to set Irving remained stationed in the living room, the temperature dropping as everyone wished Rose congratulations, cutting the cake, singing and dancing, the night still young but only their immediate family choosing to retire inside. Amara searching the bottom floor to locate her brother, but he was gone as everyone began piling indoors. Rose hosting. Irving went upstairs, making his way into the den, he and Shawn texting. Amara peeking her head inside.

"Hey," the sound of her voice loving. Amara strongly favored their father, she had his dark complexion, large nose and was quite taller than the average woman.

"Hey," Irving finally spoke, scooting over a bit for her to join him on the grey padded sofa. In the large den was a desk for working, study chairs and some dilapidated boxes.

"I commend you for staying," she said. Irving looking at her. "Me?" he scoffed.

"Well yea, I mean, you ever see those movies where the celebrity family member gets ambushed at a family event and they just—like, leave," she chuckled nervously. But Irving was not amused.

"No, I've never seen that."

"Oh, well I'm a cinephile so I've seen just about everything, but I was just trying to ease some of the tension here. As kids, we didn't really get a chance to know you or have much of a relationship, our mother sought to that. But me and Asha, wondered about you every day since meeting you. You were so small and mysterious, we were kids though Irving, so I hope you don't hold any grudges against us for not being more sociable. We didn't know any better," she pleaded.

"I don't have any grudges, I am just trying to—" Brandon interrupting them, knocking on the door as Irving motioned for him to come inside, Brandon stood whispering to Irving.

"Can you use the details car?" he asked him. Brandon nodding his head. "Just look out for any papps and I'd like the restaurant closed for the evening," he instructed him. Amara confused as Irving text Shawn telling him to be ready for dinner, Brandon would be arriving soon. Brandon exiting.

"Wow, you're quite the Mr. It guy."

"Right, but no, I don't have any grudges nor do I seek to castigate you or your sister. I just never intended on reopening old wounds by staring into the eyes of familiar faces from that part of my past," Irving confirmed. "My life changed and I have a new family, nothing personal against either of you," he continued.

"Gotcha," Amara affirmed, her feeling sad. Noticing, Irving felt remorseful.

"Do you have children?"

"No, and neither does Asha, and neither of us is married," a long pause between them. "Just a pair or worker bees," she continued.

"That's not good. Maybe I can set something up with some friends of mine if you guys are ever in the district." he said.

"Is that so? Are you sure they'd even go for women like Asha and me? We don't seem to fit the color bill these days for the brothas," she exclaimed, tossing her right fist in the air. Irving knitted his brows.

"I have heard about that, is that seriously a thing?" he asked, confused.

"Of course, it is, I mean, just at this party alone how many interracial couples did you see? Black men, White women, that's the new way of the world—the trend."

"Hmm, well that's odd."

"Where is your wife from?"

"Shani is of Jamaican and Dominican descent, but she's darker than you and I, and I would have never thought to be prejudice towards a woman based on the color of their skin.

"Well, that makes you and about one hundred other men who are so vocal about that via the internet and yet, Asha and I can't seem to meet one," she laughed.

"Those men are filled with self-hate," Irving said before his phone dinged, receiving a text message from Brandon, alerting him that Shawn was picked up and they were in transit to the restaurant. Irving stood, Amara too.

"Well, it was definitely a pleasure seeing you." He wondered whether or not to shake her hand or give her a hug, but she decided for them both. Stretching her hands, she gave Irving a tight hug as she smiled from ear to ear, inhaling the sweet smell of his cologne.

"Here is my cell," she said removing a piece of paper from her pocket, searching the room frantically for a pen.

"Here, just put your number in my phone, Asha's too," handing her his cellular phone. Concluding, Irving stepped past her as he made his way down the stairs, his trench coat trailing behind him. Downstairs the remaining guests were playing a game of charades as the night came to greet them. Irving locating Rose, tapping her on the shoulders, Amara and Asha now grabbing their coats preparing to leave, Ivy making her way over.

"You're leaving? I need more photos!" Irving smiling as they all said their goodbyes.

"Why don't I take a photo of all of you?" Rose suggested as both Asha and Amara were making their way through the door after thanking her profusely for the hospitality. Surprisingly, Irving agreed. Everyone stepped swiftly onto the lawn, the sounds of the paparazzi cameras flicking behind them.

"Those people are vultures Irving," Rose said as she stepped back preparing herself to take the picture. There they stood all together: Irving, Asha, Amara, and Ivy.

That night Irving was driven to an upscale restaurant in downtown Harlem where he and Shawn had dinner, alone. They had the restaurant to themselves after Irving paid for the establishment to be closed once 8 p.m. came around. Shawn loved when Irving did nice things such as this, their nights out feeling like a scene from a movie. For one-month thereafter, Irving remained in New York, corresponding with his sisters daily and finding new ways to put a smile on Shawn's face. The feeling was different, coming home to Irving every day as Shawn did not give up his volunteer work, he was not going to stop working on something that made him happy to once again to appease Irving—uprooting his life was enough.

Irving loved being home, he visited the churches where he gave speeches, the housing development where he spent time with the new tenants and assisted Rose in the Starbucks location closest to the development. He visited the others, making his acquaintances with the managers, he had never met them entrusting Brandon to run the offices, hiring and firing as needed. Brandon was an asset to Irving, more than the man behind the wheel, he had two master degrees, one in marketing and advertisement and the other in sociology. However, he was a man of the streets and after all that Samuel had done to help him, he prided himself on taking care of those he loved: that being Irving.

Everywhere he went he was regarded with the utmost respect. Inside the Starbucks, the teenagers and patrons all wanting photographs, autographs, and advice from Irving who was always willing to oblige. However, Rose did not like this, they were taking away from the work that needed to done and after one week politely asked her son not to return. Irving understood this. He was not an authoritarian—so the methods his mother needed to use were all comprehended.

Day in and day out Shani grew to despise Irving, back in D.C. she was called upon to do interviews, one after the other while both Zoey and William were present. In one month, she was feeling exhausted, coerced into attending fundraisers where she was always a sloppy drunk by the end of the night. Two to three nights a week, there was no privacy except in the bathroom, her live-in nanny always around, she tried firing her but was told by Christopher that she cannot be the one to do so. Her life felt like hell, while to others it was grandiose.

In the office Irving was receiving thousands of emails a day, many from the local churches inviting him to join them for their breakfasts or luncheons, some of which he would personally respond to promising his attendance and then asking Zoey to make note in his personal calendar. When the day came for him to leave, Shawn made peace with it, peace with himself and their relationship. He was feeling satisfied, having had Irving to himself for a month was spectacular. Their last night was spent on the rooftop where Shawn brought along two lawn chairs; it was mid-February, Valentine's Day vastly approaching. Shawn missed Irving for his birthday and decided to make it up to him now. Both Shawn and Irving exchanging gifts, Shawn decided his gift should be from the heart, giving Irving an original 18"x 24" Vintage NY Harlem Renaissance Jacob Lawrence Manner Tempera Painting—African American Social Realism Modern Art Jazz Musicians worth thirty thousand dollars.

Irving could not believe his eyes, removing the blanket that covered them, "Shawn!" he exclaimed before smiling, "How did you even get this? How—how did you afford this?" he asked, rubbing his hands over the canvas in complete admiration.

"I won it at an auction. I have been bidding on it for months," Shawn laughed. Irving could not believe his eyes. Shawn's first bid was the money Irving left him their first night in the brownstone.

"This is unbelievable," Irving grabbing Shawn by the rear of his neck pulling him forward, kissing him, their lips pressing tightly together. He was ashamed to show Shawn his gift, just another piece of materialistic rubbish. There was nothing he could gift Shawn that would even compare.

"I'm actually ashamed to even give you my gift," said Irving, "It's nowhere near as thoughtful as this," he continued.

"I appreciate anything you give me, even if it was just time." Shawn kissing him. The night filled with promise as they sat, kissing passionately, Irving no longer wanted to leave, he was so happy that he finally found true love and yet, time and time again he had to walk away, leaving it behind. Love making was special for them that night, Irving was gentle, making Shawn feel special, the alpha male in their domain and Shawn loved every moment.

Years passed and with Irving going back and forth between New York and Washington D.C. things were getting easier and far more manageable. Shani was dating a man who Irving had yet to meet or know of, but it did not bother him, he preferred it this way. Their marriage felt perfect, by no means idealistic but it was working for them both—working on this campaigning, managing the legislature and the locals all loving Irving for his hands-on approach. There were two mistakes he could have made: show up and react only to what landed on his desk or in his inbox, becoming what politicians liked to call a reactive Mayor or issue orders, directives and commands trusting that his staff would follow.

Irving became a professional at multitasking, amid the din he needed to be strategic, leading with grace, attending business launches, exuding wisdom, and of course humility and authenticity. Irving created a new policy, analyzing it from scratch, this required many sleepless nights. His vision for the city and its future was slowly coming to fruition and now women and men from all over the country began showing interest in Irving, drawing in more publicity, more eyes, and press which only hindered his ability to travel to Shawn. But Irving was starting to see the importance of his welfare and how beneficial it all was. Raw managerial talent, that was his strength, he was succeeding where others have failed.

By the fifth year, the people expected Irving to fall short, following the stigma that the longer a Mayor remained in office he or she would be less likely to drive change. Irving fought hard, choosing to not be a statistic in any aspect of his life. Every other week it was the same, Irving entered into a room where the cabinet meetings were held, pushing the envelope and getting his voice heard over every other man or woman, their rival egos posing him no threat—having never lost the engagement of the cabinet. The detailed reports he received from their departments were all publicly disclosed so during press conferences Irving chose his words carefully, millions of people were now waiting for his downfall, but as he triumphed month after month their views changed.

Managing the four-billion-dollar district budget was far harder than he would have imagined. A head-spinning array of funds and pockets watched over by the city budget office and it's nearly thirty intense number crunchers. They were sensors, planners, measurers, and enforcers, effective in large swaths of time given to them by Irving—his attention needed there, always. Implementing higher school budgets was the most challenging issue for Irving, while the Mayor only executes, the council legislates, and Irving was slowly learning this. Now, using Shani to set up play dates with the wives of the councilmen, five was all that was needed to earn their vote for his bold visions. Landing Irving in a position where his visions were not only trusted but often times implemented.

Christopher no longer came around, bed-ridden suffering from both macular degeneration and cystic fibrosis, but

Christopher was a fighter, choosing to not give up as he listened to the news, reveling in Irving's success. As the clock struck twelve at midnight there they were on the rooftop of the Baccarat Hotel counting down as the ball dropped on New Year's Eve. Shani and Irving draped in the finest for this black-tie affair.

"Five, four, three, two, one," everyone shouted in unison as the ball touched down in Time's Square the sound of everyone cheering resonating through the New York City streets. Irving was happy to be home and while Shawn too was in attendance, he made sure to stay away from Irving, their thing was to now get Shawn into events, but to remain inconspicuous until they both were able to sneak away. This worked on many occasions. Everyone made their way back downstairs, the ballroom filled with Mayors, governors, senators, the Vice President, journalists and much more. It was the event to start the new year and with Irving turning thirty-two in only seven days he felt this the best way to jump-start his birthday week.

Shani retired as she had many times before as Irving made his way across the room, networking—a woman by the name of Isabelle Bianchi, wife to Robert Bianchi asking Irving,

"Where is your darling wife? We have to set up a play date for our little ones," she asked, she was gracious, Italian-American, 5'5, long brunette hair and a smile that was nothing short of perfection. Irving could not miss this opportunity; every function was a chance for him to grow closer and closer to the inner circle of the legislation now that the presidential elections were slowly approaching. And so, he searched, frantically for Shani, looking into bathrooms, hallways, staircases, and nothing. Finally, he located Shawn, enlisting his help—Shawn and Shani still never formally met.

"Help me find Shani," Irving told him removing the glass of champagne from his hand. Shawn turning instantly to assist him,

"Babe, slow down," he cried, Irving was moving hastily as he feared the worse—she left. But he knew that would have been impossible as she was now wanted by one of the most important figures in his life, especially at this crucial moment. Slamming doors and stepping into the bathrooms, both gentlemen and ladies, he listed keenly, Shawn now behind him to the excessive moaning taking place inside the storage room down the corridor just steps from the ballroom. Pushing the door open there they were, Shani and Johnson, having sex amongst the cleaning supplies.

"Such an embarrassment," sniped Irving. Shawn standing behind him with his jaw dropped as he ran back towards the ballroom to avoid anyone spotting them. Irving stepped inside the storage room—slamming the door closed.

"Of all the fucking politicians and ordinary men, you choose my friend?" he screamed. Both Shani and Johnson speaking simultaneously as she struggled to pull down her dress, pulling up her panties and Johnson buckling his pants. "Let me be clear, I don't care that you're fucking, it's who your fucking that has me upset!" he continued. Shani and Johnson grew quiet.

"It shouldn't matter," she screamed.

"Get out! Mrs. Bianchi is looking for you, and let me make myself clear, you screw this up I will see to it that you are far more miserable than you could have ever imagined," Irving warned her as she turned the lock to head outside, now pushing Johnson in the chest,

"Dude, listen, you're my brother, alright. She came to me, said she was lonely and that you treat her all crappy and stuff, I felt bad, alright—it won't happen again. I promise, it's only been a few months, but I will end it. I just thought you wouldn't care," Johnson whimpered. Irving looked intimidating; he was devilishly handsome—dapper and majestic. Irving was not only liked for his intellect but single women enjoyed throwing themselves at him. But despite this, he remained humble, staring into Johnson's eyes he knew he was sorry and knew he felt worthless compared to Irving.

"Just stop fucking her," Irving bellowed forcefully, fixing his suit jacket unlocking the door and making his way back into the ballroom.

Retreating to their suit Irving and Shani had an altercation that was heard all throughout the seventh floor. Pouring herself a glass of vodka straight—slowly becoming a lush she removed her dress, moseying around in her bra and panties before a taking a seat by the piano.

"You don't care," she screamed. Irving having a bottle of water and loosening his tie.

"If you're having sex with another man, no, but yes, I care when you're having sex with one of my friends," he said. "Did you schedule the play date with Mrs. Bianchi?" he demanded to know.

"Yes, her and three others. I am doing exactly what you want me to do. I—I am rubbing elbows with the higher-ups, cooking dinners, attending luncheons, sitting through boring ass galas and smiling every time one of these reporters wants to sit in my living room and shine their bright ass lights in my face! Yes, King Irving, I am your humble slave doing as you command!" she shouted, her mascara now running from her eyes.

"We were fine, for years I thought we were fine," he asked, confused.

"No, you were fine, you've been fine. I've just come to accept this—"

"Then why are you so mad?" he questioned, not allowing her to finish her thought.

"Because Johnson, Johnson made me feel good, he helped me to understand the situation, he-he bought me flowers, he took me to dinner, he was the husband I wished I had and so I just thought of him each time I had to complete one of those daunting, mundane tasks. I thought of him and told myself that instead of you, I was doing it for Johnson, doing it so he and I could continue to be together," she cried. Shani was trembling now as she took a sip of her drink.

Nonchalantly Irving mentioned, "Just seven more years, anyone but him," he said exiting the room, motioning for his security to begin moving, walking outside he heard the glass shatter against the back door— Shani let out a shrieking cry. Six minutes later Irving stood outside of Shawn's door, knocking faintly as the security guards stood on each side, Shawn unlocking the door as the jazz music blared from the stereo, journaling about his evening—one of many.

4

Inauguration Day
January 20, 2017

I t was a not public holiday, but it was a day of celebration. The days leading up to Irving being sworn in as the leader of the free world had everyone on their toes. Winning the election by both popular votes and a unanimous vote by the electoral college, Irving was proud. The world rejoicing around him.

Irving spent that morning getting fitted for his appearance at noon. His Vice President, Robert Bianchi. Shani, Isabelle and their two sons, Raymond, and Angelo along with Kwame who was now eleven and Iyana, six all ran about playing in the yard. Robert and Irving made an amazing team. Democrats who were looking to pose changes in relation to gun control laws—their opposition to the carrying of same as policemen are shooting and killing unarmed African-American boys. This was top of the list for Irving, as he himself had a son to protect. The death penalty, taxes—progressive tax system forcing the rich to pay higher taxes. As a wealthy man, Irving considered it greedy to hold onto finances where there were many other children and women in need, as such he was going to work hard to see to it that employment went down and homelessness in the United States, a subject often neglected.

Irving was excited as he stared through the window of the Victorian home that both Robert and his wife occupied, their lives all changing for the better. Champagne during fittings, stylists, and barbers coming to meet them at their door. Security then made their way inside, escorting Shawn, Irving now rushing over to kiss him as his tailor grew angry.

"Good morning Mr. President." An elated Shawn teased, handing Irving a small box—but it was empty—removing his shirt, Shawn turned his arm, "That's because the gift is on me. It's your name in Japanese," he leered.

"You got a tattoo of my name?" Irving asked, "You're ridiculously silly."

"Yes, but it isn't in English, you know just in case we ever break up—"

"We're never breaking up," Irving interrupting him, kissing Shawn again.

"Look, love birds, we have a fitting to finish and Shawn, please don't let Shani see you, she'll lose her damn mind," Robert said. Robert was tall, athletic build, caramel complexion with brunette hair, scars along his face, he was not that easy on the eyes, but he was a hard-working, scholarly and unproblematic individual.

"I love you," Irving professed to Shawn as he made his way out of the door.

"I love you too," Shawn shouted back.

"Boy, you two love taking risks huh, how did he know Shani wasn't in here?" Robert asks, stretching his arms while the tailor measured their length.

"I told him to come in quickly to give me a kiss, demanded

it rather, since I'm now the President," Irving laughed.

"Down boy, we still have three hours to go," Robert laughed.

A few moments later Shani and Isabelle made their way inside, out of breath.

"You both need showers, quickly," shouted Zoey from the center of the hallway. An attorney now she was bossy, owning her own law firm only a few blocks away from the capitol. Standing in front of Irving she took a long look at him.

"Well, look who it is, you've grown up kid." Zoey taking a look around, returning from her four-year hiatus to strictly practice criminal law.

"Yea, and it seems you haven't replaced me at all, may I? I promised myself I wouldn't return to politics unless you made it into The White House and now, today is the day," she asked as she pointed to herself.

"Whatever position you want, it's yours. Your father did one hell of a job in your absence by the way." Irving said.

"Well of course he did, he's the one who taught me everything I know," she smiled.

"Did he teach you how to catch stray bullets?" laughed Robert—he had a strange sense of humor.

"Excuse me?" Zoey asked.

"Apparently there's some rumor that I'll be shot today on the hill by some hillbillies. Another Black President, so soon at that, some people are outraged," Irving revealed tenderly, making light of the situation.

"I mean all jokes aside, we are all worried," Robert intervened.

"Well thanks for the heads up," Zoey said winking to Irving, "I'll take care of it, you just worry about looking and feeling like the new President that you are," she continued as she exited.

Irving stood reminiscing on the year before, the countless meetings he had with William and a public relations team he hired on the off chance that anything could go wrong. Kenneth Anderson became Irving's leading man for all matters involving public relations. Irving knew he was in great hands but as he stood in the large room, cathedral inspired, he could not help but fear for his life. Despite having a wonderful team working with him and no scandals or fires to put out he was afraid. The red states all having a hard time accepting his win, especially the unanimous vote from the Electoral College. Arguments now posed that the votes were rigged, citizens demanding a re-count and further investigation.

A vast majority of the general public was outraged to say the least. Robert caught the look of worry on his face.

"Listen, man, we're all going to be there and today is going to be great," he told Irving as the tailor wrapped up his measurements and alterations.

"Yea—yea, no, I mean you're right," stuttered Irving.

The swearing-in ceremony drew a large crowd, people from all over the county were there—thousands all gathered. By noon, Irving, Robert, Shani, and Isabelle were all making their way out of the capital doors down the stairs where reporters lined up, Irving stood waving at the large crowd of people shouting his name. Shawn amongst the crowd along with Asha and Amara. Rose, Ivy, and Keith all stood on the capitol steps nearest Irving and Shani's family were in attendance as well. Proud of their daughter and how absolutely gorgeous she looked.

In and around Washington, D.C. that afternoon was a considerate amount of disruption, both on inauguration day and days before. Irving had been planning for this ever since his name was announced on the television in November the year before. Security was everywhere today, protestors, demonstrators all shouted from the rear of the crowd. It was safe to say that Irving was not going to be harmed—snipers were on top of buildings and police officials stood on every corner.

Robert was sworn in first at exactly noon, immediately following was Irving, who once he stepped up to the podium, could hear the sound of men and women shouting his name in the distance, a wave of applause following. After swearing in, both Robert and Irving received four ruffles and flourishes. The ruffles are played on drums and the flourishes on bangles—simply brass instruments with no valves. The ruffle and flourishes form a fanfare before a performance of the President's anthem, "Hail to the Chief," and the Vice President's anthem, "Hail, Columbia." This excited Irving, as he leaned in to kiss Shani on the lips, upsetting Shawn who stood in the crowd. He was simply too elated not to share this moment with someone, also, he was grateful for all that Shani had done leading up to this moment.

Following the musical piece, there is a 21-gun salute from the howitzers of the military district of Washington—Christopher watching via facetime from the Apple phone Zoey held. He was no doubt proud as he lay in bed struggling to remain alive.

Following the ceremony Irving stood for a few moments taking it all in, Shani resting her head on his chest as he placed his arm around her to comfort her, kissing her forehead, the crowd went wild. Shawn stood forcing a smile as he looked on. Irving and Shani exchanging a look of passion before turning to walk inside—the couple's fashion complimenting one another, the donner flapper look accompanied by pearls and fresh manicures with her hair slicked to the back. Making their way inside to attend a luncheon where they were regarded as the guests of honor given by Congress. Shani had never shaken so many hands or taken as many pictures in her life as she did that afternoon.

The great hall where the luncheon was held was magnificent. The tall ceilings making her dizzy as everyone continued cheering, Irving stepping off to the side with Robert for a photo opt with Benedict and his family. The room was joyous, filled with laughter and witty speeches. Shani and Irving dancing the day away once they took to the dancefloor, but this was short lived as time managed to slip away from them, it was time to view the parade.

Later that day, both Shani and Irving were to walk part of

the way from the Capitol to The White House before climbing into a limo to be driven the rest of the way. The crowds on both sides of them were large, people were shouting his name, Irving had no idea the number of people he influenced—this making him cry. Waving back and forth, Shani, Irving, Robert, and Isabelle stepped slowly down the brick road. Shani and Isabelle draped in custom designer coats, while Irving and Robert wore a trench, their gloves leather considering the chilly winds.

That day before visiting their quarters, Shani and Irving took a look around upon entering The White House, their children with a nanny and another caregiver walking behind them. Approached by Secret Service Irving was advised that he would not be allowed to take anything from his home, this was his new home and new communication devices, clothing and any other personals he would need or that of his wife would come from members of his team. Shani stood overhearing them.

"I have things from the house that I need to get, for my kids too," she said concerned. Irving calmed her.

"Okay—okay, no problem, we can head to the house later right, pack some things?" he asked apprehensively. The strange man nodded.

"Yes Mr. President, but please note, we cannot take long," he confirmed. Irving nodding his head as he tapped his shoulder, thanking him. Shani stood from behind with her arms around his shoulders, reminded of the night before and the elegant ball, she saw the way Irving looked at her, although they were surrounded by people, press and media, she couldn't help but stare at Irving marveled by how far he had come.

"Can we talk privately?" she then muttered to him, reporters and security detail all surrounding them on the front steps of The White House. Irving grabbing her hand looking around.

"Yes, maybe down here," he said walking down the long corridor where he found an unlocked door, stepping inside the dimly lit closet. Irving, too, needed a break, feeling overwhelmed.

"This is a lot huh," Shani giggled.

"Oh, my goodness, yes."

"Irving, I just wanted to say thank you," she smiled. Irving quickly turning to face her.

"For?"

"For this. I would never have imagined in a million years that I would be the First Lady of The United States and it's all because of you and the hard work you do. I truly admire you and, I know my next statement may come as a shock, but I really believe we can make this work. The right way, us, as a family and maybe have another baby—the public would love that," she humbly stated while rubbing his chest as she slowly unbuttoned his suit jacket. Irving stopping her, grabbing her arms.

"What? Shani, no. I mean we've been over this a thousand times."

"Right, but last night the way you kissed me, today, the way you looked at me, I mean why are you denying how you feel?" she begged, "Please, just stop it," she continued.

Irving taking a deep breath before responding.

"I was told to do those things," he admitted, watching as the tears flowed from her eyes. "I think they're calling for us to do the Oval Office photo shoot." Irving, removing his hands from her wrists and stepping out into the hallway, reporters and cameras locating them began snapping pictures.

Robert called, "We're off to the west wing, man." Irving turning to face Shani, inside begging that she plaster a smile on her face before stepping outside, and she did. Taking Irving's hand, she walked out with confidence, her tears dried.

The tour of The White House was exhausting. Irving was shown his study, the private restroom he would use annexed to the Oval Office along with his own kitchen—all for his personal use. The master bedroom on the second floor makes up The White House master suite along with the adjacent sitting room and a smaller dressing room, all located in the southwest corner. Irving politely requested that he and Shani have separate sleeping quarters, he was told this would be an easy accommodation.

When the night came Shani and Irving prepared for their night in The White House. Newspapers, bloggers, media influencers were all at the gates reporting live that the President and First Lady were now alone and preparing for their first night. Irving unwrapped gifts and put away clothes they received from locals, designers, Senate and members of Congress—neither of them needing anything additional. Alone now, free from the press and the commotion, Irving walked around, finding himself back inside of the Oval Office where he dialed Christopher to give him a first-hand look. Jasper answered on the second ring.

"Hey man."

"Hey, where is Christopher?" he asked.

"Sleeping, but don't worry, he saw your oval pictures, never seen him so happy. I guess I should say thank you," Jasper whispered.

"Why?" asked Irving.

"For doing something for him that I couldn't do," he responded before hanging up. After hearing the dial tone Irving took one last look around, excited to begin his day tomorrow making his way back upstairs where Shani was in his room unpacking the items she begged security to retrieve from their home.

"We don't sleep in the same room," Irving said to her.

"I can't sleep alone in this big house. Irving, please don't make me beg, I am your wife. I want to sleep with my husband and I want us to be a family," she demanded but Irving was growing impatient.

"I don't want us to be together intimately," he emphasized.

"It's been years! Years and you won't touch me, I can't even date anyone outside of this relationship and now you're telling me you still won't satisfy me? I want to have sex, I want to sleep with my husband and I want us to cuddle. I get it, maybe you feel like it's impossible, but dammit at least try," she screamed.

"…and what if I can't get an erection?"

"You have in the past, so it isn't impossible."

Sitting in the airport Shawn waited to hear from Irving, but nothing. He called, text, left voicemails, but Irving remained unresponsive. Shawn felt left out, unloved and uninvolved. He wasn't even allowed to leave with Irving's parents and his sisters, he had to wait until they were gone. Shawn was growing tired, for years Irving promised that once he landed in The White House things were going to be different and yet, things were different, only not in a good way. Arriving at the yellow brownstone Shawn was greeted by three large bouquets of white roses—balloons and an oversized teddy bear once he entered into the foyer. Initially, Shawn did not believe the roses to be for him, but they were stationed in front of the staircase leading up to his apartment, just then Frances stepped outside.

"Wow, someone really loves you."

"Franny," Shawn laughed. "When—when did these come?" Shawn stuttered, his eyes gleaming.

"About two hours ago," she said. Frances and Shawn became very close, spending a great deal of time together, he was grateful for her. She was often times calm and level headed. Her roommate Noel was quite thoughtless, however, having one time caught Frances putting her things in the hallway as if to kick her out for missing a birthday dinner, Shawn found himself trying to convince Frances how much of a bad idea that was. But he respected her for how passionate she remained, caring and of course down to earth. This was what he needed in a friend.

"Why don't you and I have brunch tomorrow afternoon," she smiled. Shawn happily agreed.

The communication between Shawn and Irving was much better as the next morning Irving contacted Shawn from his office telling him about the night before and the fact that Shani requested that they have another child. Shawn found these types of advances to be amusing because he trusted Irving to make the right choice when it came to their relationship. It was so odd to him, how easily he was always able to forgive Irving for any of his wrongdoings. That was love he guessed, or perhaps he was feeling needy.

As the day pressed on Irving contacted Shawn during any

and all of his free time, in the morning alone as he dressed for brunch Irving was texting, calling—Shawn intermittently responding; finding him now to be quite annoying. Irving was missing Shawn, his companionship, as the leader of the free world his day was packed with meetings, forms requiring his signature and press conferences addressing the issues plaguing the communities—so much was expected of him in such little time. The media now crucially watching him as they counted down his first one-hundred days in office, any changes he would make. Similar to his duties as Mayor, the scrutiny was heavy.

Shani spent her morning attending conferences, book launches, community rallies and fittings with stylists for parties and engagements that were forthcoming. She was feeling overworked, told constantly that while Irving handled the paperwork, she had to manage the general public and so, she did as she was told. Both Shani and Irving spent little to no time with their children, which too caused her grief. Day one and while Shawn enjoyed mimosas and chicken with waffles accompanied by Frances; Shani and Irving were swamped with work.

Back at The White House, Irving moved with purpose, by day four he was introduced to new staff members, new members of press, Congress, and senators. A newly married Johnson his chief of staff stepped swiftly alongside him.

"How's marriage," Irving asked chuckling as they all made their way down the long corridor on the east wing.

"Ha! Why didn't you warn me? I'm fucking miserable man and it's only been a month!" he replied; Irving giving him an astonishing look before replying,

"I hope for your wife's sake, you're joking."

"Hope is one hell of a drug," remarked Johnson stepping into the meeting room, closing the door behind him once everyone piled inside. The house was filled with exhilaration, everyone constantly on the go, and while Irving was accustomed to this, he was finding himself in a position where thinking was not required, he was just merely there to listen, nod and smile, he did not feel challenged at all. As the meeting went underway, Irving whispered to Johnson, "Blow my brains out."

Members of Congress and state senators all explaining in detail the changes they need to be enforced or policies enacted for their states, but Irving wanted to focus on decreasing the unemployment rate, tax cuts, Veteran Affairs, and economy as a part of the Houston Administration.

"Healthcare?" one Senator asked.

"Obamacare is ironclad at this time, I think we will continue to let that play out," advised Irving.

"No, we have state officials and community leaders arguing daily about this unrealistic expectation that everyone is to have healthcare or pay a fine," another Senator said. Irving was in no mood to vindicate his position politely requesting additional detailed documentation to support their claims for further review.

Ninety days later Irving was ready to retreat, requesting a private flight to New York where he would spend time with Shawn now that he was nearing his hundred days in office and the media was slowing down—for this he was glad. Shawn was elated too, he had not seen Irving in months but continued to receive his generous gifts daily. Shawn was flattered, but running out of room to fit all of the roses and gifts he received—his apartment resembling a conservatory.

The more Irving traveled between New York and Washington, D.C. with no on growing suspicious is when he increased the time he would spend away; the hour-long flight now taking place twice a week—every Tuesday and Friday evenings. The security detail discreet and while no one knew of the yellow brownstone, Brandon was still his go-to for pick-ups and drop-offs. His businesses ran efficiently and even increased in revenue because his supporters often times patronized his franchises. This was great for Rose as she was able to increase her salary.

Private dinners and trips were all blissful moments that Shawn and Irving now shared, neither of them wanting or needing anything else. As Irving lie naked in the apartment he watched Shawn make his way around the kitchen, preparing him a home-cooked meal.

"You look so naturally beautiful," flirted Irving.

"You're always complimenting me," he laughed, pretending to be shy.

"That's just one of the many jobs I am tasked with as your companion my dear."

"Compliments?" laughed Shawn.

"Making you feel beautiful," Irving quickly replied. A knock came to the door. It was Frances.

"Shawn!" she called. Irving, now scurrying to get dressed was fumbling into the bathroom where he stood behind the curtains, hiding. Shawn opened the door to greet her.

"Good morning beautiful." Frances now pushing her way inside.

"Something smells really good," she laughed. "Shawn, I'm losing my mind. Maxwell is staying with us and Noel is miserable, I mean, totally miserable and I feel bad because he's just trying to finish school you know," she said as she sauntered around inside, removing bacon strips from the pot before taking a seat to chew.

"Franny, darling, can we talk about this later?" Begged Shawn, Frances took a look around.

"Oh crap, you're not alone?" she asked noticing the extra pair of shoes by his bed and the articles of clothing thrown around, chuckling, "You're hiding him from me?" she laughed.

"No, no, but I do need to be alone," voiced Shawn once more. "We can talk later though," he continued.

"Oh no, you've met all my lovers, where's yours?" she asked as she searched inside, "Come out, come out wherever you are," she sang. Irving shoved the curtain to the side, proceeding to brush his teeth in the bathroom, listening to the faucet run, Shawn was both angry and anxious, patting his head in frustration.

"Oh Jesus," he griped. Frances stepped to the front of the

bathroom laughing.

"Well hello there," gasping as she took a long look at Irving. A panicked Shawn beside her.

"Just why? A few more minutes she would have been gone," Shawn wailed to him.

"Well, from the sound of it, she's quite comfortable and so, no, in a few more minutes she wouldn't have been gone. Are you eating my bacon?" Irving asked her as he made his way into the kitchen wearing nothing but a pair of boxers. Frances continued watching him, her mouth open.

"Th—this-this is the—the President; he's um—the President Shawn. Shawn—Shawn, this is the—the—President," she stuttered.

"Listen, you have to be quiet about this Franny," Shawn begged.

"But—but, Shawn, you're like a mistres—"

"Don't say it," Shawn interrupted her.

"But, you're like—a like—guy, and, oh my God, what am I doing? I need my camera. Wait, but can I have your autograph?" she requested giddily, afterward racing to the door and then back into the kitchen where Irving sat reading the newspaper and having his breakfast. "You act like you're normal," she said enthusiastically. Shawn continued looking on.

"No photos and you have to be quiet about this." Shawn commented. "Franny, seriously, this could ruin him if it gets out, so you have to be quiet okay. Nothing to Noel or Maxwell, nothing to Africa or her loud ass sister Abigail, understand?" Frances nodded.

"Okay, but Shawn, you are so naughty. At least can I get one photo?" she begged. "Please!"

"Can it be a selfie, because I don't really feel like getting dressed right now?" joked Irving.

"Oh no, get a shirt," Shawn demanded "...and hurry it up Frances," he shouted to her placing his hands atop his hips. Filled with excitement Frances raced down to her apartment, grabbing her cellular phone.

5

"Hey newbie!" Walter called to Ivy as she stood in the center of the hall down by the offices and the media room; her press badge tangible. Lucky to begin her internship straight out of college, she and Walter began working closely together, slowly she was learning the benefits of being the sister of the President. Irving was visiting Russia for a meeting, eleven months later and he was looking to retain the peace between nations. Ivy and Walter began moving, Ivy struggling to remove her pen and pad to begin taking notes.

"Listen, I'm doing this as a favor to your brother. So, here are my rules: you show up before me, I get here at 8 a.m. every day, which means you should be here by 7:30 the latest, come prepared, coffee, most important, coffee," he emphasized. Ivy taking notes, "Coffee, got it," she said scribbling.

"By noon we have to have at least eight press releases drafted and not just any press release, we need news and we aren't going to get it by sitting around on our asses. We need to pound pavement, put our ears to the streets, try to bring as much pressing issues to Johnson as we possibly can—the more information he has for Irving to fix or combat, the more stories we can write about our beloved President and his diligence across our nation," Walter continued, handing Ivy a personal tape recorder.

"Get stories, report to Johnson, find solutions, and write about it?" she looked to confirm.

"Good. Also, you don't talk to the President and you don't talk to the First Lady. You've already received special privileges for being his family member, but this is a real job, you don't get to just take breaks and hang out with the leader of the free world at your own leisure, got that?" he said. "That recorder in your hand is going to become your best friend, in journalism when our memory fails us, machines pick up the slack."

"Yes," Ivy replied.

"You want a job in journalism; this is the best place to start. But if you disobey any of my rules Ivy, I will fire you, you stick with me and only me, after coffee of course, in which case I am in need of a cup. I take mine black." Ivy continued standing before him. "Ivy, move," he thundered.

"Oh—oh, yes, coffee, so sorry. I will get it," she hesitated, everyone walking quickly past her, Walter too stepping away. Ivy stood confused, it was her first day and she had no idea where the cafeteria was located. "*Shit*," she whispered to herself feeling hopeless.

As the day went on Ivy continued to shadow Walter, forgiving her for failing her first task of the day, Walter enlisted another member of the press to make coffee runs. Irving was to return that evening, knowing this Walter had no plans on working a graveyard shift and so, he assigned Ivy with the grueling tasks of contacting local newspapers fishing for stories and follow-ups. Working late on her first day was not fun, but once the sun went down and the offices emptied it wasn't half bad. Ivy loved being alone in the computer room, she could research with no one in her ear chewing gum, tossing papers, flying paper airplanes or distracting her from reading and listening to her recordings as she typed her stories.

Ivy, now twenty-four years old, her hair a fire red often tossed into a ponytail, standing 5'5 with a love for American Eagle clothing and loafers. Shani was wandering the halls when word came back that Irving was heading to The White House after landing on Air Force One. She was sad and thought a walk would do her good after putting the children to sleep. Stopping now as she watched Ivy in the media room typing away an article she had been working on from the morning,

"Ivy?" Ivy afraid to face her,

"Oh, Madam First Lady—I think," she stuttered reaching for her notepad as she stood abruptly.

"Please, there is no need to be so formal," Shani laughed, her long duster swaying behind her over the silk pajamas she wore. Shani walked inside taking a seat, instructing Ivy to do the same, "Why on earth are you so uptight?" she asked chuckling, "Relax, we're family."

"I'm technically not allowed to speak to you," Ivy said slowly taking a seat.

"What? Did Irving say that?"

"No, no, Walter did. He told me not to get too comfortable just because I'm family, you know to avoid any speculation of favoritism." Shani was appalled.

"That's nonsense. You come and find me anytime you want to, plus it's nice to have a familiar face to talk to."

Ivy felt relieved, "Yea, I can imagine," she laughed. Suddenly Shani's expression went from playful to dreary. "What's wrong?" asked Ivy placing a hand on her knee. Shani looking up at her,

"I just wonder, how did you mother deal when she learned about Irving?" she asked. "It's so weird, because of all the times I've met her, she seemed so genuine and I honestly kind of resented her for knowing about Irving and not telling me." Ivy remained clueless.

"Wait, my mother? Did you resent us? Why?"

"Because she let me marry her son, and have a child with him knowing he was gay Ivy, I mean, someone could have warned me," she said. Ivy's eyes widened.

"Gay?" she snickered. Shani shot her a loathsome look.

"This isn't funny Ivy, this is my life. I'm so emotional, I'm depressed. I wake up in the mornings, upset that I'm alive. He doesn't touch me—or—or show me any kind of affection," she continued, rambling, but Ivy could not believe her ears, thinking her sister-in-law must be going crazy.

"Shani, I am not one to pry, but if Irving is acting funny or not showing you affection, I think it's kind of extreme to rule that he's gay." Shani knit her brows,

"Ivy—what do you mean? Irving has a boyfriend, a boyfriend in New York," Shani said, her voice slightly elevated. Ivy could not listen any further as she locked her computer screen, standing up, preparing to leave,

"Look, I don't know what kind of sick game you're playing at here, but my brother is married, to you with two children. Your willingness to make such a lousy assumption is highly disappointing. You resenting my mother over something as far —fetched and ridiculous as this is also despicable," Ivy told her before leaving. Shani remained seated—perturbed.

In the Oval Office the next morning sat Irving, Ivy, Robert, Walter and two senators from Iowa discussing their state's reform. Walter removing his tape-recorder, tapping Ivy as to inquire about the location of hers.

"Where is your recorder?" he asked, whispering. Ivy arising frantically; everyone stopped speaking to stare at her.

"Ivy what's wrong?" asked Irving nonchalantly.

"Oh my God," she panicked, inadvertently knocking over papers as she raced out of the door.

"What's that about?" Robert asked. Walter bent down to clean up the mess she made.

"She's new, my apologies everyone, please carry on," he said.

Ivy ran to the media room, out of breath as she searches along her computer desk looking for the tape recorder. The room filled with her co-workers and outside journalists.

"Did anyone find a tape recorder on this desk?" she asked pointing to the empty space next to the desktop. But everyone remained silent, "Come on, please, if this is hazing it's really not funny, I'll get into a lot of trouble if I lose that," she pleaded, her voice trembling. Ivy had no idea what to do next, she felt dizzy—her entire conversation with Shani was on that tape. Racing back down the hall and up the stairs Ivy flew open the doors to the Oval Office, the receptionist standing as she called for Walter, interrupting their conversation.

"Walter, please!" Her face red. Walter looked to her, embarrassed as the men all turned to watch him; Irving sat quietly, motioning for Walter to assist her. He was irate.

"You're fired!" he said stepping into the hallway. Ivy could not process what she had just been told.

"Walter, okay, no problem, but listen to me," she pleaded grabbing a hold of his arm, speaking quickly as he turned to walk back into the office. "Last night while I stayed here to work on the Russian story, Shani came down to the media room and my recorder was on," Ivy cried.

"Okay, and?" Ivy stood on her toes to whisper in his ear.

"She said Irving was gay and has a boyfriend in New York." Her breathing heavy, Walter pushing her to the side as he raced down to the media room. The sounds of journalists typing along their keyboards resonated as Walter stepped inside, he and Ivy, slamming the door behind him and closing the shades.

"It's been brought to my attention that something that belongs to Ms. Ivy is missing. Whoever is in possession of this item, please return it," Ivy trembling. "Let me just make myself clear, surely whoever located this device is aware of its contents. If anything from this tape is leaked, or any article written or released through our public relations database I will see to it firsthand that its originator is punished to the full extent of the law—you will be handled as a terrorist and a threat to our nation's leader. Is it within your best interest to discard of this tape, or return it discreetly to its owner," Walter said bluntly before walking away. "Get upstairs, we need to have a meeting with Irving," speaking to Ivy. The room filled with chatter and gossip, everyone speaking amongst one another, questioning their peers.

Concluding his assembly Irving was asked to remain in his office as Walter and Ivy stepped inside, bidding the senators a farewell. Walter asking his receptionist to have Johnson join them. Waiting around for a few minutes Walter took a seat, crossing his legs, unbuttoning his suit jacket.

"You seem really relaxed for someone who needed an emergency meeting," Irving said to him. "Ivy, sit down, he instructed her, realizing she was frightened. Johnson entered wearing a three-piece suit, Walter turned to face him.

"Make sure that door is locked tight," he bellowed.

"Alright what is it?" asked Irving taking a seat at the edge of his desk.

"Ivy," Walter motioned.

"Irving, um, last night, Shani visited me in the media room and I had my tape recorder on because well, I was working and I was speaking my notes into it when she walked in. Um, she mentioned that you were gay and that you have a boyfriend in New York…" Irving knitting his brows, standing. Johnson was appalled.

"What the fuck!" he shouted.

"We don't have the tape recorder," Walter intervened. "Someone took it and no one is talking," he continued.

"The room is full of fucking interns; we can't be bested by a bunch of fucking children. Turn them upside down and beat the tape out of them," Johnson roared, his arms folded.

"Irving, we have to assume, whoever took the tape has listened to it and they've taken it to an outside outlet," Walter said. "Otherwise, why isn't anyone willing to give it back?" he continued.

Irving now stood, his back to them, "Have you told mom?" he asked. Ivy surprised.

"Oh my God, it's true?" she asked, her eyes welling.

"Walter, Johnson, can you give us a minute?" Irving asked, his face to the blue sky as he stood with his hands behind his back, listening patiently for his friends to leave. Once alone, Ivy began her interrogation.

"You've been lying to us?" she cried.

"Listen, this is my own personal affairs. Alright, we did what needed to be done to get to where we are now." His tone brazen.

"No, you don't get to do that! You've been lying to me and mom for years! Shani, oh my God, that poor woman, do you even love her?" Ivy screamed. Irving turned to face her.

"The depths of my marriage are not your business. My family has come to know Shani and of our children and that is all there is to it. You want to fact-check me?" he asked.

"Fuck you! This isn't a story I want to run, this is our family, and this is about the betrayal, you lied!" she shouted pointing to him. "If someone leaks that story to the public and mom finds out from some NBS news reporter she's going to die. How long were you planning to keep this from us?" Ivy panicked. "Jesus, we have to call her," falling to her knees as she searched her tote for her cellular phone.

"We're not calling mom?" Irving said sternly.

"You're so selfish," she cried, standing now as the tears fell from her eyes, grabbing her things, rushing through the doors. Irving stood watching her, emotionless as he dialed reception.

"Have Zoey, William and Kenneth in my office within the hour," he demanded.

"Yes sir."

Irving waited patiently for the clock to strike noon, sitting at his desk, he refused to contact Shawn, he was afraid of evoking dread. Kenneth making his way inside first—the leading man in public relations management, Kenneth greeted Irving with the utmost respect before taking a seat,

"Good afternoon Mr. President."

"Glad you could make it from the big apple, huh, Irving said as he was feeling truly grateful.

"When the President calls, you come running. It's that simple." Kenneth replied. Zoey and William entered as Walter happened to pass by, curious as to why he was not invited to the conference—he entered.

"Walt, have a seat," Irving instructed him. Walter was shocked but decided it best not to question him. Irving called to his receptionist, "I need Johnson," he shouted. Standing now as everyone sat around in the sofas surrounding the coffee table, Irving rubbed his smooth hands together.

"Kenneth, that fire we feared, I think it's just started," Irving began. Everyone fidgeted, both Zoey and William confused as they too took their seats.

"Fire?" William questioned.

"The story about Shawn, there's a possibility it might be leaked," Walter expressed to them, Johnson stepped inside, shutting the door firmly behind him.

"First things first, we need to move Shawn to a safe house," spoke Kenneth unbuttoning his suit jacket, crossing his legs.

"What, why?" asked Irving.

"Because you have to leak the story and when you do, people are going to go into a frenzy, they don't have access to you, but they'll have access to him and it can get pretty dangerous," Zoey said. Kenneth pointing to her,

"Bingo."

"We don't know for sure anyone is going to leak the story, I called you all here so we can figure out a precautionary measure, not me standing in front of hundreds of journalists outing myself." Irving beginning to pace.

"What makes you sure, someone, anyone is going to sit on this?" Walter asked. "Let's face facts here, this is the next Bill Clinton and Monica Lewinski scandal on steroids."

"There are no facts," Irving replied.

"Your wife is on that recording, that's all the facts they need. She's the closest to you, therefore the strongest source," Walter exclaimed.

"We all need to relax," interrupted Kenneth. "Irving believe it or not it's time for damage control. We set up a personal interview with someone well known; introduce the story as breaking news and have you come clean. But not in a way of outing yourself, but more like getting the LGBTQ community on your side, choosing to no longer hide your sexual preference; choosing to be who you are publicly. I'm telling you guys, it'll work, but we have to hit them before they hit us," Kenneth said.

"I'm with him." sided Zoey.

"….and what about Shawn?" Irving asked.

"We need to act fast, time to move him. I'll send Air Force One to do a pickup. He's out of state so it'll take them longer to track him," spoke William, standing to make a phone call. "Irving, have someone get him now!" he shouted facing him.

"Okay," Irving said. Everyone began moving quickly, hustling almost as their phones now sat in their palms, Irving fighting tears.

"Someone bring in Robert and Shani," Walter demanded. Seconds later in came reception.

"Mr. President sir, I've been told that The First Lady has gone for the day and is nowhere to be found. Also, your mother is on line two." Walter and Johnson exchanging a look before racing out of the Oval Office. Irving answering, the sound of a heartbroken woman on the other end.

"Irving," Rose whispered. Irving remained stationed as everyone around him was moving hastily. Ivy stood inside the room, listening to Zoey and William make arrangements while Kenneth scribbled notes.

"Mom, I'm very sorry," Irving remarked realizing as the words left his mouth just how remorseful he was. He didn't trust the one person in the world who would have killed for him, Rose.

"Irving, why sweetheart, just why not tell me?" she asked, Irving called to his sister, the phone to his ear as she too began crying upon entering The Oval Office; holding her now. He stood apologizing to them both, again, the receptionist making her way inside, slamming the door open, outside the sound of screams emanating through the halls.

"Sir, the conference room."

"Mom, I have to go," Irving hanging up the phone, he, Ivy, Kenneth, William, and Zoey all racing down the hall into the large conference room where the news blared. There it was, a photo of Shawn and across from him a photo of Irving. Listening as the anchorwoman outline the details of their relationship.

In the distance, a voice yelled, "Get Air Force One in the air now!" he screamed.

Ladies and gentlemen, we interrupt your regularly scheduled program to bring to you a breaking news announcement. Newly elected President, Irving Houston is, in fact, a Gay man; his lover and boyfriend photographed to my right; Mr. Shawn McDonald. According to sources the pair have been in a serious relationship spanning well over fifteen years! It has further been proven that his wife, born Shani Richardson was in fact in the know of this relationship but chose to remain silent in exchange for the opportunity to stand with our new leader of the free country. Ladies and Gentlemen this news is devastating, while members of the LGBTQ community have all taken to social media venting their frustrations, disappointed in our new President.

"This is not good," Kenneth shaking his head. Irving racing out of the room as his subordinates all turning to look at him.

"Why has no one been able to reach Shawn?" he screamed removing his trench coat and making his way downstairs to the limo. Secret Service racing behind him.

"Sir, we have called his cellular phone and house phone. At this rate Mr. President sir, it will take a little over three hours to get to New York," spoke Ryan, one of his Secret Service men. Irving stepping to him.

"Listen to me, I don't care how you do it, just get me in the air now!" he screamed. Both Ryan and Andrew shouting in unison, "Sir, yes sir!"

The White House came down under seize as reporters, press

and employees all began chattering about the events of that day, Walter moving swiftly by them, shouting, "Get back to work! This isn't a government shutdown," on his way to meet with reporters. The room filled, at least fifty guests, their pads, pens, and notebooks all in hand. William standing by his side as the plethora of questions began.

"Sir, my name is Steven from The Post: What can you tell us about Mr. President and the accusations of him being a gay man? Is it true?" he asked. Walter clearing his throat, turning to face Kenneth who now entered, nodding his head in approval.

"Yes, the accusations claimed today are true. Next question," Walter announced as the murmurs in the room increased, making it hard for him to hear the woman in the back of the room. Speaking quickly,

"Miley Mitchell from The Sun-Times: Why did the President keep this a secret from the nation? Was he ashamed to be gay? And where is the President now, why is he not here to address the press, these accusations have fallen on him? Please respond."

"As of right now our President is engaged in a mission and will return shortly to answer your questions and address any concerns you may have. Lastly, we must remember that our President is still our President and deserves our utmost respect—for the record, he was not ashamed, by far, no further questions at this time," Walter said walking away from the podium. Kenneth moving behind him.

"Social media?" Kenneth asked Walter.

"On fire, we're being tweeted left and right and now Shawn and Irving's lives are being threatened. Where's Johnson?" Walter asked looking around.

Boarding the aircraft, Irving and two members of Secret Service, both Ryan and Andrew stepping inside—their pilot nervous.

"Mr. President sir," the pilot stood saluting him.

"I need this aircraft in the air now in transit to New York. Listen, I don't have a lot of time to get there, can we make it quick?" he asked dialing Brandon who answered on the first ring. Putting the phone to his ear as he dismissed the pilot, Irving spoke quickly, "Brandon, listen to me I need you to go to the brownstone and pick up Shawn, right now! Understand, right now, bring him to his address. You have a pen and paper?" he asked awaiting confirmation.

"Yep go ahead," Brandon said, his monotone voice never changing.

"MacArthur Airport in one hour."

"Copy boss," Brandon hung up. Irving continued texting Shawn, calling and leaving countless messages, he was beginning to panic.

6

The morning of...

Shawn turned to find the time reading 8:49 a.m. although Irving had been gone, his scent still lingered. Frances banged on his door.

"Wake up!" she screamed. Shawn sometimes hating the fact they were so close, but loving her was all too easy. Crawling out of bed, Shawn reached for the silk robe he tossed at the foot of his bed, opening the door to greet her.

"Eww," he teased, "I'm the one who just woke up, but you look like road kill," he laughed. Frances stepped inside dressed in a pair of baggy sweat pants, snow boots, a jacket, hat, and gloves.

"Say what you want but I really think you should come with us."

"Absolutely not. I already hate hearing you and those hyena's downstairs on a regular basis, now you're asking me to be cooped up with all of you in a cabin for five days? Tuh! Shoot me now," he chuckled, grabbing a grape from the counter.

"You have no clue what you're going to be missing."

"Where's the brat?" he asked speaking of Noel.

"She spent the night with her boo, so, she'll be meeting us there," Frances said.

"I strongly believe her pussy burns; I mean she's only been here a year and some change and every time I ask you about her she's with another man!" he chuckled.

"That is none of my business," Frances teased. "However, she is my best friend so, I feel bad for even laughing."

"Yea yea, which cabin are you staying in?"

"Drumroll please!" she screamed. "The Brimson Estate. You know those people are worth millions!" she said with excitement.

"Well, well, well, let's forget about Noel, it seems you've been sucking the right dick too," Shawn giggled.

"Yes, I have, his name is Maxwell. I would never cheat on my prince. Remember I told you he gave up his apartment to stay with us, so, he's been saving and managed to afford us this trip. He's an accountant for one of the Brimson sons," she vocalized raising her eyebrows.

"Well Goddamn bitch," Shawn said eyes wide. "Well, congrats to you for sticking with bae through his struggles. I mean really, that is impressive—he's come so far, in such a short period of time." Outside the taxi cab horn now blaring.

"That's my taxi," Frances said pouting. "I really wish you'd come," she pleaded one last time.

"Go, have fun and I'll see you guys when you get home," he smiled walking Frances to the door where they exchanged air kisses to the cheeks before closing the door behind her. Frances felt strange reaching down to the foyer, she turned to look upstairs, shaking away the negative thoughts that made their way into her mind.

Shawn stepped into the shower where he shouted and danced to the stress-free sounds of Calypso music, another genre he favored, twisting his hips and moving his shoulders. Now overhearing the commotion of the kids playing outside as they made their way to school—the truant officer children. Getting out of the shower, Shawn dried his hair, continuing to sway his hips, sending Irving his infamous *Good morning baby* text message, but he didn't expect a reply right away, it was Monday morning so of course Irving was working, as always.

By 11 a.m. Shawn decided to invite Connor over to hang out, he was the jock of the group but never turned down the chance for a pow-wow. He had a daddy, so he was always free during the day. Conner, of course, obliged, promising his attendance in the next fifteen minutes—he would be leaving the gym. Shawn waited by preparing a big brunch: waffles, chopped strawberries, whipped yogurt, chicken fingers he made using the air fryer he recently purchased along with blueberry pancakes and freshly sizzled bacon. His morning delightful.

The doorbell buzzed, it was Connor wearing a racerback tank and shorts. Deciding to jog from the gym, refusing to spend cash on a taxi seeing as Shawn lived so close by.

"It's January, you're aware of this?" asked Shawn.

"Right, but when you're jogging, there's this thing called body heat bay-bee," rolling his tongue. "Ohh, it smells like porn in here," he continued.

"Porn?" questioned Shawn.

"Oh but of course, this is the meal fit for a porn king. What kind of sex are you having darling?" Connor said laughing hysterically.

"Well as of right now, none, but I just wanted to cook something nice," Shawn smiled. "Waffles?" he replied offering Connor a plate.

"Carbs? How dare you feed me carbs? Daddy likes my waist small. So, I need vodka and fruit."

"Well suit yourself flower, more for me," Shawn smiled, just then a brick came flying through the window nearest his bedroom,

"Whore!" a loud voice screamed from the back ally. Both Connor and Shawn exchanging a bewildered look.

"Oh, dear God," Connor scurried towards the shattered glass, Shawn dashing into the kitchen to retrieve a broom and dustpan.

"The nerve of these assholes!" he shouted. The morning was pressing on, now at half past eleven. Shawn and Connor furiously making their way downstairs, the door slamming behind Connor as Shawn looked outside to see no one. He was hoping to catch the little turd who was responsible for breaking his window—but nothing. The front door closing behind them once Connor too looked outside. Making their way around the perimeter both men came up ended handed. There was no one in sight. Only the regulars waiting by the bus stop and some storefront owners. Shawn and Connor exchanging brief dialogue before returning to the steps, freezing now, Connor prayed they would hurry inside—but the door was locked from the inside. Shawn pushed,

"Connor, you didn't put anything at the door?" Connor stood looking on,

"What—what, no, I mean, you don't have your keys?" he asked, rubbing his hands up and down his biceps quickly for warmth.

"Well, no and this door is a slam lock," said Shawn. "Oh dear God, my phone is upstairs too!" he shouted.

"Does your neighbor have a spare?" asked Connor. "We can't stand out here, we'll get sick, your pajamas are silk and I'm practically naked."

"Mrs. Biel has a spare, but she doesn't come home until four and the girls are gone for the week," quivering now.

At approximately 12:44 p.m. Air Force One landed, to greet Irving at the airport was Rose. The fifty-eight-year-old woman struggling to run up to him as he made his way down the stairs once it was safe to do so. Both agents moving quickly behind him, Rose now hugging him as tight as she could before stepping back to slap him across the face.

"How dare you lie to me?" she shouted. Irving could not

focus on her, although he hated that she hit him, he had to keep moving, as the news he was receiving by way of text message was completely unpleasant. Walter informed him of the nasty tweets that were being spewed by the public, news stations and broadcasters located Shawn and were now on their way to the brownstone, people threatening to kill him now—radicals and homophobes. Irving moved with purpose climbing in the back seat of the limo that awaited him, Rose as well.

"Mom, no!" he shouted attempting to have her removed.

"No! You will not face this alone. I swear to God! I want to be there, I have got to be there with you. You are not going to push me away!" She screamed, the two now tussling in the back seat, Irving careful not to use his strength on her.

"Mom, please!" he sat sobbing now, "If anything happens to you, I will die. Just please!" Irving cried. He was far too emotional to remain stoic. Rose grabbing his face as she pressed her palms against his cheeks.

"It is my job to protect you, now, please let me protect you!" Irving deciding to quarrel no more instructed the driver to move along, texting Brandon, but there was no reply—worrying him.

Outside the brownstone, Shawn and Connor stood shaking.

"Let's just go back to my place, we can warm up and come back at four when your neighbor gets here," Connor suggested.

"I can't leave. It's Monday and Irving always have a gift delivered to me and roses, if I miss the delivery someone may steal the gift. You go, I'll be fine." He told Connor.

"No, I'm not leaving you, Jesus, what time does the mailman come?"

"Well, it's after 12 now, so soon," Shawn said taking a seat on the cold concrete. Both Shawn and Conner waited, unaware of the news broadcast that sprung across televisions throughout the country. Seconds later Shawn felt something flick at his head, a child laughing to his left.

"Faggot!" he screamed, both Shawn and Conner looking at him disgusted with what they had just heard. The crowd was small as the vans and reporters came bending the corner. Shawn stood now, scared for his life, his jaw dropping. He wondered what was going on.

"Oh my God, what's happening? Are they coming here?"

"Yes, it appears so," Shawn said his voice just above a whisper. Without realizing a woman made her way to them dousing bleach onto the stairs.

"Homewrecking bitch!" she screamed. Suddenly Shawn was no longer feeling cold, he was frightened beyond his wildest imagination.

"What the fuck is wrong with you crazy ass people?" Connor shouted, "It's 2018, it's a new year, stop the hate!" he continued. A woman tossing a ball at his head, they were all careful not to come past the gate, Shawn wondered what was taking place and why.

"What the hell is happening," he cried. As a group of teenagers ran across the street, tossing water and eggs at them, reporters from all angles piling out of their vehicles.

"We have to get the police," Connor cried as the egg yolk stuck between his lips. Every man, woman, and child within a five-block radius made their way onto his street, shouting obscenities. Shawn could not help but cry. Reporters standing just by the edge of the sidewalk, encouraging the people to stand back, whilst they asked questions.

"Mr. McDonald, do you have anything to say for yourself?" a young woman asked shoving her microphone towards his face, the crowd grew larger, the media attracting them. Shawn could not believe his eyes.

"No, what is happening?" he asked innocently.

"Mr. McDonald, have you been having an affair with the President?" a man asked, another pedestrian tossing a book at him, the reporters turned to face the angry mob, it was catastrophic.

Shawn deciding not to answer as Connor turned to face him, "What?" he asked, his eyes wide. As if things could not get worse, the police sirens now blared, the people on the street beating their hoods with baseball bats, sticks and tossing bricks through the windows—complete anarchy as the officer made their way onto the street where hundreds now gathered, swarming to the brownstone, rallying.

"No gays in The White House!" they all chanted.

"We don't want a gay President," women screamed. The officers warning them to stay back, they were all divided but at least they stopped throwing things at Shawn, but that didn't stop the reporters from asking questions. Minutes later more people arrived, Shawn bawling as he prayed there was a way inside the brownstone. The air felt brisk, the mailman arriving jumping back into his truck to leave, the pedestrians tossing eggs, water bottles and anything else they could find to throw at just about everyone. Shawn stood sobbing, outraged that reporters were still trying to question him despite all of the ruckus that was taking place behind them.

The police officers were meticulously moving towards Shawn, hoping to block him from the angry mob as Conner and Shawn ducked behind them, a woman climbing over the gate punching Shawn profusely.

"You cheating bastard!" she cried, Shawn did not hit her back, he never hit women. Watching the woman step over the gate others now joining her—fifty, maybe sixty people, stepping inside as the mob began to trample them, officers fighting, letting off warning shots as Irving arrived in the black limo, removing his blazer and grabbing the gun from Ryan's gun holder before stepping out of the car. It was all happening so fast, the officers climbing over the gate; breaking it, but they were outnumbered. Shawn and Connor getting dragged, punched, kicked, and tasered accidentally—beaten with batons as the officers could not tell who needed to be apprehended. Secret Service firing two warning shots in the air—sidestepping, one foot in front of their other, Rose covered her ears as Irving ran outside the vehicle, two more gunshots heard in the distance.

"Faggot ass bitch," a man yelled standing, his face reading guilty as he took off running dropping his pistol in the grass.

But Brandon was just arriving as the perpetrator sprinted down the block, he chased behind him hitting him into bushes. When the fourth gunshot was heard everyone scattered, lying there now, a dead Shawn and Connor. Irving stepped past the gate, the officers begging him not to.

"Mr. President no," But Irving was strong, overpowering them as the tears fell from his eyes—falling to his knees, he wept. Grabbing a hold of Shawn's lifeless head, holding him in his arms as Rose stepped out of the vehicle sobbing hysterically. She could not believe her eyes, the blood dripping from Shawn's mouth, his eyes left open. The sight of him horrific, shot in the chest, Irving put his hand over the wound as Shawn continued to bleed out. Irving sat rocking him back and forth, closing his eyes as the tears continued to fall, his heavy breathing heard from afar. He thought of his smile, his laughter—his touch; all bringing Irving to a place of regret.

Thirty minutes later Irving sat Indian style holding onto Shawn's corpse. The New York City Examiners arriving to remove the bodies. But he would not budge, Rose begging him.

"Baby, they have to take him," she pleaded as she cried. She did not know Shawn, but watching her son, hurt, was painful for her to see. As word spread across the city, people began showing up, most from the housing development in Ubers, Starbucks employees and Church officials. As the helicopters whirled above him, Irving made primetime news—the world was watching him as he sat in mourning.

The officers on duty that afternoon watched as Brandon tossed the culprit into the back seat of his wagon. Ryan, flashing them his badge.

"Official Secret Service business, we'll take over from here," he said climbing into Brandon's car. Watching the car drive away, one officer commented,

"That man is about to erased from the face of the earth," unremorseful as he began clearing the city street.

January 8, 2018

On his 36th birthday there he stood at the military funeral of his beloved. Hensley, Rose, Walter, Johnson, Patrick, Zoey, William, Kenneth, Robert and Ivy all standing behind him; Asha and Amara off in the distance. The McDonald's were heard weeping from across the yard—their only son, taken from them so prematurely. The ceremony carried out with both dignity and respect. Shawn received what was known as the standard honor considering his Veteran status—his casket draped in the flag of the United States and as a pall. The casket team serving as honor guards—pallbearers, Irving dreading the fact that he could not join them. As an officer, Shawn had his casket transported using horse-drawn limbers and caissons—fighter jets performing an aerial flyover. This was the first half of the ceremony, the formation of a rifle party immediately followed, consisting of an odd number of service members, five to be exact firing three-volley salutes. Following was the playing of tapes a performance by an audio recorder at a distance, forty-five yards from the gravesite, while a final salute was given.

The American Flag was then meticulously folded thirteen times by a total of six honor guards, three on each side of the casket. Once the flag was completely folded, the stars pointed upwards, a reminder to Americans of our national motto, *In God We Trust.* The flag now completely folded takes the form of a tricorne hat, reminding Americans of the soldiers who served under President George Washington. Moments later once they concluded, the honor guard presented the flag to Shawn's parents by leaning forward, with the straight edge of the flag facing forward, he said, *"On behalf of the President of the United States, The United States Army, and a grateful nation, please accept this flag as a symbol of our appreciation for your loved one's honorable and faithful service,"* Irving no longer able to fight the tears sobbing like a child—the media and news outlets all standing by, upsetting him. Upon receipt, Mr. McDonald turned to face Irving, now, presenting him with the flag, his hands shaking from the Parkinson's disease.

"My son was happy because of you, he was different, in a good way. He was in love and I never seen him glow the way he did that day you put that ring on his finger. He said, "*Dad, that man is going to marry me one day,*" and I laughed and said, of course son, because you deserve it. Irving, I shouldn't have, but I watched that video of you holding my child in your arms and, there are no words, no words. This flag was presented to me, but I want you to have it. We're a lot older than we look, his mother and I and uh—I don't want this to end up in a storage box somewhere or in the hands of someone who won't appreciate it. So please, take it and let us remember him this way," his father said. Irving wore a pair of leather gloves, wrapping his hands around the flag, pulling Mr. McDonald in for a hug, patting his back—both men continued crying.

"Thank you," said Irving, his eyes red and puffy from weeping. It was a sad day, the ceremony concluding with an eleven-gun salute fire; a personal request from Irving himself.

7

I Irving disappeared from the funeral, tossing his trench over his shoulders as he and Hensley both walked away to the limo awaiting them—Zoey later joining.

"What are you doing in here?" Irving asking her.

"Don't ever ask me stupid questions, Mr. President," she replied fitting on her brass knuckles.

"Huh, right," Irving scoffed. Hensley was now the terrorist operations manager. Working from a bunker in the depths of The White House, he made sure to label their assailants active terrorists, both of them. Walking down into the basement, there were no reporters, no media, only the brown mundane walls. Irving removed his coat and his blazer, dousing hand sanitizer on his hands before walking into the empty basement. In the center there it was, a large iron cell, in it, a murderer.

Hensley handed Irving a folder, inside were details of his life: Steven Myers, 34, two kids, unmarried and unemployed. Three felonies reduced to misdemeanors and time spent in prison—8 months. Irving had seen all he needed to as he handed the folder back to Hensley. Zoey watched them. Loosening his tie, Irving stepped into the room, a malodorous smell hitting his nostrils. There he sat, Mr. Myers, a black bag over his head, six of his fingers chopped off, blood dripping, rotting in his own defecation and piss. Irving took a chair, setting it backward, spreading his legs as Hensley removed the black bag from his face. Steven trembling.

"Take off the duct tape," Irving instructed him. Hensley ripped the duct tape from his mouth, Steven let out a shrieking cry.

"Please—please, please, let me go. I'm sorry! I swear, I'm so sorry!" he begged, spit leaving his mouth. Irving took a deep breath.

"Do you know the man who you shot?" he asked him, calmly.

"No sir," Steven sobbed.

"Oh, so why shoot him?"

"I—I just wanted to be a part of something, but-but I know now, I've learned my lesson. I won't do that ever again—I swear! I swear to God," he continuing to spit as the words left his mouth.

"You don't look alight, Steven," Irving teased removing his cufflinks and rolling up his sleeve, Brandon entered the room. Steven's eyes darting back and forth.

"Jesus Christ, you're the fucking President, you can't do this shit! What about my rights huh? I'm a fucking citizen!" he screamed, tears leaving his eyes, "Look, please, look, I have kids, I have two sons," he wept.

"Oh, you're bi-polar too," Irving laughed facing Brandon.

"Must be bi-polar boss," Brandon agreed.

"Let me tell you something, at a young age, I was watching niggas get popped in front of me, you think because you're Black you know some shit. I know how to use a piece, but I also know how to use my words, because I had to learn how to use my intellect to get to a place of power. See fools like you wanna be dumb all day, play around in the streets, not learn anything, get revenge by capping niggas and then face a bid. Meanwhile, an intelligent motherfucker like me just wiped you off the face of the earth and yet, I'm a street nigga. But the difference is, I use my brain to get what I want, you used your bullets and unfortunately, you shot the wrong nigga—nigga," Irving said slowly as he arose.

"Please—please, we're brothers, we're—brothers, don't lemme go out like this, I haven't eaten, or even used to bathroom in days. I respect you, I understand. I can see you're about your business," Steven said whimpering.

"I look like a motherfucking judge to you, it's too late to repent, my man is the grave, but you'll understand soon," Irving announced, retrieving a pistol from Brandon.

"No, no, no—" Steven pleaded before Irving shot him in between the eyes; feeling numb—the sound of the blast from the pistol brings him temporary relief.

"Where's Shani?" he then asked Brandon.

"Interrogation."

"Hensley, clean this up," he told him exiting. Zoey filled with blood lust.

"Of course," Hensley laughed.

Irving and Zoey made their way down to interrogation, it was a different atmosphere. The halls were white rather than grey and the rooms padded, similar to that of an asylum. As Irving made his way inside to greet his wife, he wondered, why. But Shani was lucky, she was fed and allowed to use the bathroom, she was even allowed to be removed from her cuffs once a day—Irving was not inhumane, all compliments of William.

"I have human rights!" she screamed as he and Zoey entered, shutting the door behind them. Irving took a deep breath.

"I have no time for small-talk. Why did you do it Shani?"

"I did nothing," she said. her face bloody from being beaten—but she remained strong. Zoey walking to her now using the brass knuckles to punch her across the jaw-line. Shani let out a cry.

"Oh my God! Bitch!" she screamed, tears falling from her

eyes. "This is excessive, I didn't know they would kill him. I have children Irving. I have small babies, you can't take me from them," She pleaded. "I know you didn't love me and I resented you for that, I was jealous of him and I am sorry, but you have to believe me, I had no clue, no clue they would do that," she cried.

"Okay, okay, dry your eyes. My other question is, why Ivy?" he asked.

"She was new and I thought the blame would have easily fallen on one of the other journalists. I didn't think it through, I gave the tape to The Sun-Times." She stammered.

"Hmph, so you just spoke knowing the recorder was on?"

"Yes, I saw the red light and just assumed she had forgotten it was, and yes, I spoke. I did, but it's your birthday baby, let me make it up to you, please!" she said. Irving now arising.

"Zoey when you're done, come on upstairs," Irving advised, he could not bring himself to pull the trigger. Walking out now he could hear Zoey punching her face, her bones cracking. That was it.

Three weeks later after locking himself away in his quarters downing alcohol, mourning and sleeping as Richard overlooked his affairs, Irving was finally ready to face the public, ready to discuss the mistakes he made and ready to take accountability. The country was at a standstill in lieu of recent events, but with a statement written from his heart, he sat in the Oval Office where cameras were set up to capture this moment. He was finally ready to speak out against the injustices of the world. Walter standing behind the camera counting, three, two, one...

"Good evening, just three weeks ago America was rocked with news of a life that, I, President Irving Houston kept secret. Immediately following this a life was taken—my apologies, two innocent lives were taken. In the wake of this tragedy, I throw myself to the mercy of the American people, requesting forgiveness for my injudicious decision. First and foremost, American people, please understand I am by no means ashamed of who I am or my sexual preference. However, we cannot deny that we live in a nation where the LBGQT community and minorities still continue to fight for their rightful place in society. We are judged without question, racked with discrimination and belittled by our own races. As such, I was diffident and made an illogical decision to keep my sexual preference a secret—for this I apologize if ever, it was thought of as shame.

Ladies and Gentlemen, I am proud of who and what I am, I have come a very long way and not due to my sexual preference but due to my own intellect and intrinsic ambition. I never want anyone to be ashamed of who and what they are, we are not different, we are not a curse among mankind, we are not to be condemned. But unfortunately, we live in a Country where we are limited, as such, I was a coward for choosing not to deviate from what I knew to be wrong. But now, I sit here before you, humbly apologizing and saying now with confidence that I, President Irving Houston, am a gay man. I fell in love with a man many years ago by the name of Shawn McDonald, and due to my actions and cowardice, he is no longer with us," Irving fought back tears, taking a deep breath he continued, "To my fellow brothers and sisters, I erred in my judgment and I am asking for your forgiveness." Irving said.

"I vow from today onward to represent who and what I am to the absolute fullest while still representing my country with both honor and dignity. I ask you Americans to stand with me, believe in me and allow us to make history together. We will break down barriers for the new generations to come, and allow me to lead by example. Let us responsibly choose to unite, let us choose to deviate from the norm, let us be a nation, under God, for liberty and truly show justice for all," Irving concluded.

Walter shot him a thumbs up, yelling, "Cut!" Irving immediately broke down to cry, Walter cradling him. "Good freaking job," he whispered as everyone began moving around, checking their phone. Walter seeing Twitter, the people were elated. "Irving! They loved it! Brother, they freaking loved it!"

he smiled shouting as he ran behind the desk shouting. Everyone's phone buzzing loudly. It was a triumphant moment. Rushing into the office came Ivy, hugging her brother.

"I am so proud of you! You're such an inspiration!" she cried. Irving stood, taking a deep breath, he felt liberated.

Epilogue

Robert and Irving continued their reign as President and Vice President of the United States of America, raising his children with the help of Zoey who spent much time with Irving. He was a new leader, children from all walks of life aspiring to be him—one day President. By his fourth year Irving decided to pass the torch unable to let go of the pain and regret he felt for losing Shawn the way he did, he blamed himself daily and was losing sight of his true tasks.

Three days after the inauguration ceremony Irving relocated to Napa, California to the 4,000 square foot home left to him by Christopher in his Will. It was gorgeous—the wine region was especially large. Chugging along at a steady pace one morning at 5 a.m. Irving was slowly getting back into his workout routine. Now forty-years-old, his body felt great and he looked great as well.

His friends all remained in Washington, D.C. raising their families and training the new faces who were to come onboard. Still regarded as Mr. President wherever he went, Irving was now giving motivational speeches around the globe. He made himself proud, daily. It wasn't long before he began making new friends, his mother Rose visiting periodically. Jasper and Ivy were now in a relationship and Asha and Amara had the absolute best connection with Irving and his children, who were growing nicely—highly intelligent they were.

Although Zoey resided with Irving in the country-side she was still working remotely in other locations—city to city practicing political law. As he ran, he noticed for the first time his new neighbor. Walking over to him Irving decided to introduce himself.

"Well good morning sir," he said politely. The elderly man turning to face him, African-American, 5'8 with an athletic build, a head full of grey hair, there he stood, looking Irving up and down.

"Good morning," he replied.
Irving introduced himself.

"Great, you can just call me Mr. Signature," the old man suggested.

Made in the USA
Monee, IL
16 June 2021

71488571R00187